COLD COMFORT

Decker's War — Book 2

ERIC THOMSON

Cold Comfort
Copyright 2015 Eric Thomson
This paperback edition February 2019

Published in Canada
By Sanddiver Books
ISBN: 978-1-989314-09-8

— ONE —

"Bastards are learning how to aim. That was the last of the counter-measures." Frustrated beyond words, he slammed a calloused fist against his console and swore at the empty launcher, at their pursuers, and at the universe in general.

The small freighter shuddered as its failing shields barely blunted yet another anti-ship missile. Alarm sirens blared, warning them of impending system failures all over the ship while the damage control AI fought to stay ahead of the cascade.

"We're not going to make it, are we?" Her sad eyes nearly broke his heart.

He tried to put on a confident smile, but she wasn't fooled.

"Where there's life, there's hope, love. Those damned assholes don't have us yet."

She smiled weakly at his heartfelt use of profanity, fingertips reaching out to touch his cheek with such tenderness that he felt tears welling up.

They'd been waylaid by a pair of pirate sloops on the edge of an unremarkable and mostly uninhabited system in that gray area where neither the Commonwealth Navy nor the bad guys held ultimate sway. Arranging an attack like that, on a fast and nimble trader, was too much work for too little profit, which meant it wasn't a random piece of interstellar bad luck. Zack Decker's past had finally caught up with him.

Even though he'd killed the head of the wealthy Amali family, a thoroughly corrupt man who'd been trying to build his own cyborg or more precisely cy*bug* army, there were still plenty of people who wanted his head.

Walker Amali had also been the de facto leader of the Coalition that sought to bring the Outworlds and colonies back under the sway of the dominant central systems. The other members of that conspiracy remained powerful and, more importantly, still had a long reach. It had taken them a year to track down *Demetria*, as his ship was known, and now it was payback time.

"Shit." Decker roared in frustration as another warning light turned red. "The aft turret's done for."

"And the keel turret isn't doing much better."

He slumped back, staring at the tactical schematic. As a former master gunner and sometimes ship weapons specialist, he could read the situation all too well, and it showed him that there was no way out. At least he'd had a year of happiness after turning down the chance to be reinstated in his beloved Marine Corps. Perhaps he should have taken the offer and spared her what was about to come, but it was much too late for regrets.

"Listen," he locked eyes with the woman who'd become his entire life, "they want me. Those assholes back there are working for the Coalition, if not the Amalis directly. It's too much of a coincidence to be anything else. We won't hold on much longer, so I'm going to surrender myself to them. With any luck, they might agree that not having to expend any more ordnance is worth giving you a way out. I'll climb into the rescue pod and let them pick me up."

"No."

"It's your only chance."

"No." Her voice rose to a shout. "I'll not buy my escape with your life, Zack. I love you too much for that."

He sighed. The reaction wasn't unexpected. She might have been scared, but there was a granite core beneath that soft exterior.

"And anyways," she continued, "they won't let me go, no matter what. Pirates never leave witnesses behind, so it's beside the point. We'll fight it out. Maybe there's a frigate near enough that heard our distress signal and all we have to do is hold on a little longer."

Decker shook his head, feeling despair set in. The Navy wouldn't be sailing to the rescue, not this time. If the Coalition was behind the attack, they'd have made sure to specify an area where no naval patrol was scheduled for some time. Even the Fleet's operational secrets weren't safe from them.

He stabbed an angry finger at the communications console.

"Pirate vessels, this is Zack Decker. I know that it's me you want, and I'm prepared to save you some expensive missiles. If you let my ship go, I'll surrender."

"Zack, no!" The plaintive note in her voice was almost more than he could bear.

She needn't have worried: the only reply was another volley that finally overwhelmed the shields. A powerful energy surge coursed through the hull, tripping safeties and triggering more warning sirens. The light in the cockpit flickered and then went out as the AI redirected the remaining power to critical systems.

Moments later, the marauders' main guns opened fire and plasma arced through the void. The glowing rounds struck both nacelles hard, and the ship shuddered as they were torn off and sent spinning away.

"We've lost the hyperdrives."

"That means they're going to board us," Decker snarled through clenched teeth as he desperately fired back with his pitifully few remaining guns. "If they just wanted us dead, they'd have targeted the main reactor."

The freighter shook again as more plasma struck, this time destroying the sublight drive nozzles. One of the rounds ate through the metal far enough to activate the fusion reactor's fail-safe, designed to prevent a catastrophic explosion. With the main power cut, most of the cockpit control panels went dark.

"We're on battery power only." Though her voice quivered with fear, she still managed to work through the damage control problems like the seasoned starship captain she was. An unaccountably strange mixture of pride and tenderness turned his guts to water.

"They'll be launching a shuttle any moment now." He struggled to push the emotions aside and concentrate on survival. "It's a good bet they'll latch on to the main airlock rather than try to cut through the hull. We'll ambush them there and then fall back towards the hold. Maybe if we make it too expensive, they'll back off."

Even as he spoke, they both knew that the pirates would never back off. Not after they'd stalked them for days, waiting for the moment *Demetria* had to drop out of FTL and recalibrate her drives for the next jump. If they were under contract to the Coalition, they had to produce results or face their own deaths at the hands of professional killers, like those employed by the secretive and deadly Sécurité Spéciale. It was as powerful a motivator as any for the degenerate beings that crew those ships.

Decker stood up and worked his tense shoulders.

"Come on. There's nothing more we can do here. The AI can handle what little is left."

He jogged aft, down the passageway to the small armory and pulled out a pair of scatterguns. Though they both carried plasma pistols already, in Zack's case his beloved Imperial Armaments fifteen-millimetre blaster, taken off a Shrehari raider years before, dealing with the boarding party would require something more substantial.

"Here." Decker held out one of the stubby, shotgun-like weapons and a box of ammunition. She took it and worked the action, making sure it was ready to fire. He slung the other one over his shoulder and then took a pair of plasma rifles off their racks, along with power packs and ammunition clips.

"We'll use the scatter guns when they step out of the airlock. It's too tight for plasma down there. The rifles will come in handy when we draw them into the hold, where there's more space to fight."

A loud thud reverberated through the hull.

"They've latched on. It'll take them a few minutes to work their way through the hatch."

He wished he had some armor on hand, but they'd never gotten around to buying any, an oversight that might shorten what was already likely to be a short fight.

Once settled into position near the airlock, they could hear the pirates working their way through the latching mechanism. Decker had a brief moment of terror when it occurred to him that they might not have sealed their shuttle to the ship. It would mean catastrophic depressurization the instant they defeated the locks, and there was no time left to put on pressure suits. But, he quickly reasoned, there was no point in boarding the ship if they intended to kill them right away. Another brace of missiles would have done a thorough enough job.

The noise suddenly changed from a frenzied scraping to a more deliberate staccato.

"They're through," he whispered. "Get ready - it won't take them long to breach the inner hatch."

In the reddish glow of the emergency lights, the corridor looked like an antechamber of hell and Decker was determined to make it so for the pirates.

With a painful screech, the final barrier gave way. Several beams of bright, white light cut through the gloom, propelled forward by large, dark, humanoid figures. *Demetria* wasn't a big ship, and only four of the intruders could fit in the passageway at once. It would have to suffice for the first volley.

"Now!"

The confined space erupted in a frenzy of shots as they pumped round after round at the pirates, the force of the impacts making them stagger as they fought to get their bearings and return fire.

"Buggers are armored," Decker shouted. "Aim for the faceplates."

It quickly became apparent that they weren't expecting this much resistance and when one of them collapsed to the deck with a shattered visor, his face shredded, the other three took a few steps back into the airlock compartment.

"They're running." Hope, for the first time since the pirate ships descended on them, filled her voice.

"No." He grabbed her arm as he rose and pulled her back around the corner with such force that she almost bounced off the bulkhead. "They're about to toss something nasty at us."

"How do you know?"

His hard grin was almost demonic in the low light.

"I've done it often enough when I was boarding pirate ships during my time in the Corps."

A metallic thunk confirmed Zack's guess.

"Close your eyes and cover your ears."

The high-pitched whine of a flash-bang spooling up pierced through their skulls, then a light brighter than the sun washed out everything while the sound of an exploding fusion bomb resonated through the ship.

Fighting the pain and disorientation, Decker peered around the corner, just in time to see the pirates creeping through the hatch again, their lights aimed in his direction. He fired off three rounds in rapid succession, but the storm of ball bearings and tiny tungsten darts did nothing more than annoy the boarders. It would have to be plasma now, and that meant falling back until they had enough room to use the longer rifles.

He grabbed her by the arm again and pulled her aft towards the cargo hold. There was no point in speaking. Their ears still rang from the grenade's violent explosion.

Demetria was running half-empty, and there was ample room to move about between the neatly stacked containers. They took cover as far from the entrance as possible and dropped the useless scatter guns in favor of their rifles, waiting for the pirates to appear.

Zack put his lips against her ear, inhaling the clean scent of her soft blonde hair. Another pang of despair wrenched at his guts.

"Let them all in before shooting. I'll take the first, you the second. After that, it's potluck."

She nodded, her face showing determination mixed with sheer terror. It was all about to end. If only he'd taken up the offer to rejoin the Corps...

The first pirate cautiously entered the hold, rifle held high, ready to sweep them away. His helmeted head swiveled left and right as he sought them out among the cargo. A second one followed, then a third.

"Fire," Decker shouted.

Where their armor had held off the scatterguns' payload, it wasn't quite as capable of absorbing plasma hits, and the lead boarder fell, his chest stitched with several smoking holes. To their credit, the other two quickly returned fire, joined by a further pirate who'd remained in the corridor until now.

Cargo containers weren't meant to act as protection against concentrated plasma and the pirates' volleys quickly ate through the thin metal, sending clouds of vaporized aromatic oils into the air. Decker, seeing an unexpected opportunity, decided to take advantage of the improvised smoke screen and shifted his position to the right, to take them in the flank.

A sudden scream of pain brought him to a halt. He turned back to see her slump to the deck, bleeding profusely through an open hole in the abdomen. The pirates' plasma had punched through the container at last. Long years of experience had taught him a wound like that, without immediate medical treatment, was invariably fatal.

Rage surged through him, blind, berserker rage, pushing aside all rational thought and he stood to charge at the pirates, firing from the hip as fast as his finger could stroke the trigger, feeding copper disc after copper disc into the ignition chamber. Plasma splashed everywhere, and he was faintly conscious of another intruder falling down amid howls of agony.

He didn't realize that they had stopped shooting until the first rifle butt caught him on the side of the head. It was followed by a second one to the kidneys and then a third to the knees, the pirates battering him down to the deck with unrestrained savagery. He was quickly trampled into unconsciousness by armored feet, but they didn't stop until their leader, a brutal man wanted by the law on two dozen worlds, remembered his captain's orders, and put an end to it.

— TWO —

Pain. Deep, nasty, bone-breaking pain.

It was as if the universe had decided to disassemble Zack Decker atom by atom and reassemble him randomly and without order.

He opened his eyes and immediately wished he hadn't. The hot needles of light that pierced his cornea and seared his retina triggered a spasm of nausea that threatened to further throw his reconstituted body out of alignment. Though his stomach contracted and heaved, nothing by a thin trickle of bile escaped his bruised and cut lips. He screwed his eyelids shut again and waited until the convulsive shaking had passed.

As consciousness returned, he stretched out his thick, muscular body and forced his throbbing brain to take stock of the situation. First item: his wrists were manacled, which made him a prisoner. Second item: considering the pain he felt even though he was still in one piece, he'd been worked over by real artists. Third item: he had no idea where he was, except that he was on a starship traveling FTL if the subliminal vibrations were anything to go by. Fourth and final item: he was screwed.

A fresh wave of pain racked his body, but this time from sheer horror and anguish as his memory fully returned.

Zack slowly opened his eyes again, feeling tears flow freely as his mind's eye offered up the image of the pirates cutting through their airlock and boarding the ship, heedless of the damage they caused. He flinched at the recollection of her dying scream and a new wave of emotion overcame him, throwing his abused body through another cycle of pain and nausea.

Then the hatred came, sheer, raw and unadulterated hatred, drowning out the grief and the physical torment, threatening to overwhelm what few reserves he had left.

His eyes gradually got used to the harsh illumination, and he saw that he was lying on a bare metal floor, in an empty metal compartment only slightly bigger than a closet. He gently turned his head to either side, grimacing at the artillery barrage in his skull, and decided it would be foolish to try to sit up. They had tied his hands in front of him rather than in the small of his back, and he raised them to the tune of screaming muscles so that they were in line with his eyes.

His knuckles were bloody and swollen, and a few fingers felt like they'd been broken, courtesy of the sustained beating inflicted on him after he passed out. He was alive, although between the physical pain and the anguish at her death, he almost wished he wasn't. The fact that they'd taken him and were even now transporting him to an unknown destination meant his enemies had a worse fate in mind than mere death.

An uncomfortable sensation suddenly radiated through his lower abdomen and Zack cursed in a hoarse whisper. He needed either to stand up now and find a toilet or piss himself where he lay. With a force of will that surprised him in his current state, Decker rolled over and pulled his knees under his stomach, then levered his back upright. He paused for a few moments to let a wave of dizziness pass. Thankfully, the renewed bout of nausea stopped short of a further heave and he was able to haul himself up against the bulkhead.

He barely managed to stumble to the waste disposal funnel and open his pants before his bladder let go. Urinating had never felt so painful and looked so bloody. Even if they had meant to take him alive, his captors obviously hadn't shown much concern for internal injuries. Hopefully, he had nothing that would require a medic. He doubted there was one on board, and he really didn't want to risk a reiver's autodoc. On the other hand, if he was indeed taken at the orders of the Amalis or the Coalition, he was dead already.

Sitting unsteadily on the narrow steel bench that passed for a cot, he struggled to bring his breathing under control. Around him, the ship hummed patiently as it ate up the light-years and for all Zack knew, he could have been the only living soul on board, destined to fly across the galaxy until he encountered a gravity wave strong enough to collapse the FTL bubble and bring him back to normal space.

The hum had an underlying note of discordance, hinting at skipped maintenance and worn-out components, at poorly tuned reactors and general neglect. Exactly what he expected of a reiver, which meant he wasn't headed for the Commonwealth to be delivered to his enemies for an exquisite torture session crowned by a gory execution.

No. Whoever had put out a contract on his head had other ideas in mind, ideas that didn't involve anyone in the Coalition dirtying their hands. They knew naval intelligence had been keeping an eye on him after he'd led the raid that destroyed the bug factory. Although he'd refused the offer to rejoin the Corps, preferring to make his life with the one woman who'd genuinely cared for him, he had agreed to pass on anything interesting, thereby joining the loose group of veterans and inactive reservists who still kept one toe in the Fleet.

When the door opened with a tired squeal, he looked up right into the mouth of a large-bore blaster. A human face, female by all appearances and of indeterminate age beneath close-cropped hair, stared at him over the length of the barrel. Hard, black eyes set deeply in a seamed face turned almost leathery by decades of exposure to deep space radiation, examined him mercilessly. She could likely have passed for any number of humanoid aliens whose reptilian ancestry left them with a rough hide, but she was indisputably of his own species.

"Put your hands behind your head," she ordered in a gravelly voice, "and drop to your knees. Try anything else and I'll wing you. Painfully. My contract is to deliver you alive and functional. No one said anything about leaving you pretty, although nature already took care of most of that."

Wincing, Zack obeyed her without speaking a word. She didn't look like the chatty type, and she wasn't appealing enough for him to try the patented Decker charm. In fact, if it wasn't for the evidence of breasts and the absence of an adam's apple, the matter of her gender might have been in dispute.

"We were warned about you and after what you did to my men, I'll not be taking any chances." She wrinkled her pug nose in disgust. "You managed to stink up this place real quick."

"Getting the shit kicked out of you often does that," he replied, eyes locked with hers in a contest of wills. "I hope those assholes I damaged smell worse than I do, preferably like they were decomposing."

"Maybe I should let their buddies in here so you can check up on them real close," she cackled. "They're kind of mad at you, but like I said, I have to deliver you alive and functional, so I can't let my boys indulge themselves."

"You come here to ogle me, or you have something intelligent to say?" Decker tried to sneer, though he suspected the expression was indistinguishable on his battered face.

"Feisty, aren't you? Too bad I can't keep pets. I might enjoy your company in my quarters after you get cleaned up and suitably disciplined."

"Wouldn't work out. I only fuck women." His attempted sneer turned into a nasty grin.

"Joke all you want, Decker. Where you're going, the laughs are going to be pretty scarce."

"And where's that?"

"Why should I spoil the surprise? You'll find out soon enough." She smirked back at him, and it turned her face into something from a child's nightmare. "I'm to give you a message: Harmon Amali sends his best and hopes you live long enough to suffer an eternity's worth of torment for what you did."

"Fancy bugger," she commented when Zack didn't reply. "An eternity's worth of torment. I'll try and use that in casual conversation someday."

"What happened to my ship and my wife?" He asked even though he didn't want to hear the answer.

The reiver shrugged.

"Contract said we were to take you and make sure the wreck will never be found. I didn't want to waste ammo on a ship with no engines, no power, and no radio, so she's just a piece of drifting junk now, lost in interstellar space. As for your woman, the boys reported she was bleeding out on the deck, gut shot. She's probably dead by now, but who knows. Maybe she'll hang on for a while, wondering where you've gone to."

The pirate cackled again.

Decker felt a surge of fury overtake him. He had no doubt he'd be able to launch himself at her from his kneeling position before she had the time to adjust her aim and pull the trigger. But then what? He forced himself to remain still, but his eyes betrayed his inner fire.

"Don't," she said, shaking her head. "Even if you're quick enough to take me, my man in the passageway will end any funny business. Since the contract didn't define functional, I figure my crew might decide to geld you if something happened to me."

"Got it." Decker nodded. He had no problems believing they'd carry out the threat and wasn't about to risk castration for what would be an empty gesture.

"Good." She tilted her head to a side, like an ugly little bird. "Now listen up, big boy. We have to feed you and let you clean yourself up, so here's how it'll go. I'm going to remove the handcuffs while you stay right like you are. Then, I'll let you get up and walk you to the showers down the passageway, and you're going to get clean while we hose down your cell. Do anything other than obey orders and you'll spend some quality time as a punching bag. If you're a good lad, you'll get some food."

"Got it," Zack repeated. His eyes promised violence, but not in the near future, and she seemed satisfied with that. "What am I supposed to call you?"

"You can call me captain, or boss. My name isn't something that'll be of much use to you. I'm going to remove the cuffs now, so stay nice and quiet."

She handed her weapon to the Kardati tribesman who had appeared behind her and entered the cell. The gray, leathery-skinned humanoid kept the blaster aimed steadily at Zack's gut. He'd been in the boarding party, and his hateful stare promised further artistry with a club if he so much as moved a muscle without permission.

"Okay, Decker," she said after removing the manacles, and tossing them at the Kardati, who snatched them out of the air with his clawed left hand, "stand up, but keep your hands on the back of your head."

When he'd obeyed, her rough shove propelled him past the tribesman and into the corridor. He might have been weak from his beating, but she still had a strong arm for someone that wiry.

"Get in," she pointed at an open door, "strip and drop your crap on the floor. Wash. Then put on the clothes you'll find on the bench. You can keep your boots. Everything else gets tossed into the disposal."

Decker briefly glanced down at himself. He'd been wearing his usual shipboard outfit when they were attacked, and it was now thoroughly soaked in blood, sweat, and vomit. There was no point in keeping anything.

Ten minutes later, he was standing in the corridor again, this time, dressed in what he'd decided was reiver casual: worn black coveralls that stretched over his solid frame like a second skin, the pant legs tucked into his calf-length boots. The captain gave him an appreciative once over, and Decker couldn't resist a wink and a smile, but she responded with a scowl and pointed back at his cell.

"There's a ration pack waiting for you. If you keep quiet and clean, you'll get one every eight standard hours."

"Any chance of getting something to read?"

"Cute," she replied with a snort. "Half of my boys can't read Anglic to save their lives and the other half prefer to watch holoporn. What in the galaxy makes you think I have any reading material on board?"

"Doesn't hurt to ask." He shrugged and shuffled off to where the Kardati was waiting with the blaster.

"Be happy that I don't let my crew use you for entertainment. The last time we had prisoners, they kept us amused for days before they died."

— THREE —

A screeching siren blared three times, pulling Zack from his endless contemplation of the universe's unfairness. It beat re-playing the final moments aboard *Demetria* over and over again. The searing pain he felt whenever his mind's eye saw his wife was almost enough to drive him over the bounds of sanity. Only his need for vengeance kept him grounded in an increasingly bleak reality.

The one redeeming feature of his descent into a private hell was to find the food on offer wasn't the nasty, if nourishing Fleet-issue ration bar, but commercial grade packs containing edible, if not exactly varied meals. There had been enough times in the past when ratbars were all he had, and he thanked the sarcastic gods watching over him that this trip to whatever hell Harmon Amali had consigned him wasn't as rotten as the last journey to a purported doom. On the other hand, that hadn't worked out so well for the man's predecessor.

Along with food, they'd given him a bedroll to provide some comfort on the cold metal. The cot, welded to the bulkhead, was too narrow for his wide body and he'd elected to sleep on the floor. For some reason, this seemed to amuse the Kardati, who was his chief watchdog.

He still ached all over but had stopped pissing blood, to his great relief, which probably meant he had no major internal injuries. The few times he caught sight of his face however, he had to laugh at the purplish, yellow, and green mottling from the fading bruises. They made him look more like an Itrulan than a human. All he needed was a forked tongue and eyes with a long, vertical pupil.

Zack stretched out on the bedroll and relaxed. Ten seconds after the last screech, he felt the disorienting nausea of emergence from hyperspace. Had they arrived at their destination or were they simply tacking? In the time since his capture, they could have covered many parsecs, but if they were going well and deep into the Coalsack, where human law and order hadn't the glimmer of a chance to rescue him, this might just be a waypoint check.

Nothing happened for the next two hours, and he went back to his bleak contemplation of life's unfairness. Then, without warning, the door to his cell opened, and the Kardati poked his head in.

"You come now," he growled, his words barely understandable, as he pointed a blaster at Zack's midriff. Decker shrugged, got up, and stepped past him into the corridor.

"What's up, leather-face?"

"You are leaving now." A rumble escaped from deep within his chest. Decker had learned to identify the sound as the alien's version of laughter and concluded that the unexpected amusement didn't bode well. He was about to ask another question when the Kardati poked him roughly in the back with his weapon.

"Go."

When he got to the portside airlock, the ship's bosun was waiting for him with a being that looked even more villainous than the reiver's crew did.

"He is as described," the newcomer said after examining Zack intently. "I trust he's fully functional."

"If you're asking whether we gelded him, no we didn't," the bosun replied with an evil chuckle. "Mister Decker here was wise enough to cooperate."

"Most excellent." The man handed a case to the reiver. "The agreed upon price."

After checking the contents, he nodded and passed the case to the Kardati.

"Put the cuffs on him."

When Zack was manacled, hands in front, the bosun said, "He's all yours, but before he goes, I'd like to say farewell."

Without warning, a fist lashed out and caught Zack just below the sternum, sending a blast of pain through his chest and abdomen.

"That's for the men you killed, you ugly sonofabitch. I hope your girlfriend died in agony."

Decker bent over with the force of the punch, gathered his fury and, hands joined in a double fist, straightened up as fast and hard as he could manage. He struck the bosun under the jaw with the force of a pile driver and had the satisfaction of hearing his teeth shatter before the man screamed out in pain.

Zack looked at the newcomer.

"Time to go, before they change their minds and cut my balls off."

The man stared at him for a few heartbeats, as if wondering about the wisdom of his purchase.

"Follow me," he finally said.

Under the bemused stare of the Kardati, who seemed to be paralyzed by Zack's sudden outburst of violence, they scuttled through the airlock and into a waiting shuttle. Another one of the newcomer's species sat at the controls and quickly shut the hatch before undocking. Zack expected the radio to come alive with outraged messages from the reiver but they sped away in silence towards a blocky ship of a type he'd never seen before. The markings on its flared nacelles resembled nothing so much as runes and were indecipherable to his human eyes.

When he looked back at the being who'd fetched him, he saw curious black eyes staring out from under thick eyebrow ridges, and what was unmistakably a weapon aimed at his chest.

"You'll want to cooperate fully with me," he said in a guttural, heavily accented Anglic. "You may be able to pull one over those oafs, but in my business, we're used to dealing with all sorts of disobedient merchandise."

Decker snorted.

"Sure you are. Does that mean you're running a circus?"

"No, my friend. We're running a slave brokerage."

His smile was so predatory Zack wouldn't have been surprised if he'd suddenly sprouted fur and claws.

"We know how to keep our products in good condition for the auction block, so a shot from this pistol will not kill you but you won't want another dose for as long as you live. Imagine the worst nausea you've ever had, and then multiply it by a hundred."

As he watched his new captor, it dawned on Zack that his seat was designed so that he wouldn't have a chance of moving fast enough to avoid being shot. They did indeed know how to manage their wares. This, then, was the Coalition's revenge: spending what remained of his life in slavery on an alien world half a galaxy away from home.

He might as well have shot himself with his last round instead of letting the reivers take him prisoner. At least she wouldn't have to face this fate. A surge of grief and despair welled up at the thought of her and at the idea that he would never be able to avenge her death. Few humans sold into slavery ever made it back.

Shortly after arriving on board the unknown ship, they confined Decker to a pen which was even smaller and less comfortable than his cell aboard the reiver. He was but one of hundreds of beings, mostly non-human, confined in this manner in the slaver's hold. Though he expected an almighty stench when he passed through the doors, it smelled remarkably antiseptic. The spray nozzles on the deckhead over each pen probably had something to do with it.

None of the captives paid Decker any attention and he figured that they were probably sedated in some manner, which was smart. No riots, no self-mutilation, just compliant chattel ready for the market. He would soon be in their zombie-like state, of that he had no doubt. He could already feel his senses getting dull and his limbs heavy. The neural inducer they'd slapped on the back of his neck was doing its work. He hadn't even bothered to try removing it. The cold sensation of the glue was enough to tell him that short of using a scalpel, it would remain there until a counter-agent was applied.

To amuse himself, he started to count backward from one hundred. Before he reached seventy, his mind had begun to wander, and he found himself incredibly fascinated by the metal deck. Then, all conscious thought vanished, and he became nothing more than a living automaton, eating, voiding himself, and sleeping in his little pen.

He'd had no sense of elapsed time when he felt himself awaken from what seemed like a long, strange dream, but fragments of memory told of several bouts of jump and emergence nausea. He was still dressed in the coveralls given to him by the reivers, but now wore wrist and ankle restraints that forced him into an uncomfortable shuffle.

His pen opened, and non-human guards shoved Zack into a long, winding line of slaves inching their way towards the rear of the hold, where a shallow ramp opened onto a hard, dark surface. A gust of damp, thick air hit his nostrils, and he grimaced at the underlying smell of putrefaction that drove away the last of the sedation.

As he walked off the incline into the gray, diffuse daylight, he saw that the landing strip was on the edge of a beach strewn with decomposing organic matter, not all of which came from the sea.

The procession snaked across a tarmac and into a windowless building, watched over by two loose rows of guards equipped with shock sticks. As he walked through the high door into the brightly lit hangar, a pair of rough hands yanked him aside and shoved him down a narrow corridor between wire fences humming with electricity. To either side of him, other slaves shuffled down other chutes, though it wasn't immediately obvious what sorting criteria the slavers used. He got to the end of his passage and stopped at a closed door. It opened inwards with a snick and a bored voice called out in Anglic.

"Next."

Decker stepped in and found himself facing an obese human female sitting behind an old console.

"Stand on the green spot."

He obeyed, and a glow played over his body as she scanned him. When it was done, she stared at her screen and grunted a few times.

"Healthy, physically fit, age around forty standard years; signs of recent injuries but all superficial. I'm going to ask you some questions. It's in your interest to answer them honestly. Life as a slave can suck but if you provide value to your owner, you might not have such a bad go of it, so make sure the skills you claim to have are for real. If they aren't, you'll pay for it." Her chuckle wasn't entirely devoid of humor. "You'll pay for it. Name?"

"Decker, Zachary Thomas."

"Profession?"

"Commercial starship gunner and security officer."

"Huh." She grunted again and stared at her console. "I don't doubt you're a guns and sticks guy, Decker, but if you've been in the military, you'd better say so."

"Why?"

"Humans who've served in the Fleet are worth more at auction and get better conditions than regular security dicks or second-rate soldiers, once they've given proof of their abilities. You've got some of the usual telltales, so you'd best tell me about your career before you became a commercial trooper."

Decker hesitated, and then decided that whatever slaves who were ex-military ended up doing, it had to give him a better chance of escape.

"Commonwealth Marine Corps, twenty years."

"Knew it." The fat woman sounded pleased with herself. "Rank and specialty?"

"Command-sergeant, pathfinders."

Her eyes widened.

"Oh my! You'll fetch a pretty penny. We seldom get career Marines through here, and I've never seen pathfinders in all my years. Any interesting qualifications that could influence your price?"

"Marine Master Gunner, which pretty much covers all the lesser qualifications, and I'm rated as a merchant warrant officer by the Shipping Guild. How about you? Been here long?"

"Since I was sold the first time. They needed decent personnel specialists, and that's what I did back home." There was a perverse hint of pride in her tone.

"You're a slave?" Decker knew he shouldn't have been surprised. Why pay someone when your business is buying and selling unpaid laborers?

"Going on fifteen standard years now. It's not so bad once you get used to it."

"No worse than being a corporate drone, eh?" Zack chuckled.

"It beats working the xantun fields or the gemstone mines, or even worse, the whorehouses." She shuddered.

Decker smiled at her but bit his tongue instead of remarking that the last option wasn't likely in her case. She had some petty power here if only the authority to classify him in preparation for sale, and could certainly do her best to screw him over if he indulged in his usual wit.

"Okay, Decker." Her console extruded a small plastic square. "Come stand beside me."

He did as he was bidden and she reached up to slap the square behind his ear.

"This has all your vitals and your suggested product categories. Go through that door and follow instructions. Welcome to lifelong servitude."

Zack shuffled through the opening where a large holographic arrow led him down another maze of wire-enclosed chutes until he reached a room filled with small individual pens. There, a dour-faced humanoid with enough body hair to knit a decent area rug, waved a sensor near his left ear and glanced at the readout.

His eyes widened at what he saw, and he raised his wrist to his lipless mouth, emitting a string of sounds that were obviously some sort of language, but one Zack couldn't begin to understand. No sooner had he finished than another humanoid of the same species came striding across the room, fixing his emotionless gaze on the ex-Marine.

"You will go with me," he said in broken but understandable Anglic, before turning back the way he came. The alien led him to a small room that seemed, after weeks in reiver cells and slaver pens, the height of luxury, even though it only held a cot, a chair, and a waste disposal unit.

"Did I win the slave lottery or something?" He asked as the being tossed a food pack at him.

"You valuable merchandise. We take care of valuable merchandise."

Then he closed the door and left Decker to his privacy.

"Zack, old boy," he murmured. "Things are looking up if the old soldiering skills can buy better treatment. Heck, I might just make it. The Amalis better start writing their last wills and testaments, because this time, I'll be taking out the entire clan, just to make sure it doesn't happen again."

**

The door opened again a few hours later and tall woman, clad in an unusually cut suit made to resemble raw leather, filled the frame as she stared at Decker. Never one to let an interesting sight go unseen, he rose from the cot and returned the favor.

She was bald, except for a long ponytail growing out the back of her skull. The pale flesh of her scalp was covered in elaborate tattoos. Piercings studded her elongated earlobes and flared nostrils, while her lips were tinted in the same black as her nails.

The military style outfit was a dark shade of crimson, like that of old blood, and bore metallic devices that could be decorative or, for all he knew, could have more common functions. She was not visibly armed, but based on her size and the way she carried herself, Decker was sure that the woman could give him a good challenge in any hand-to-hand fight.

"You are Zachary Decker, former command sergeant in the pathfinders, yes?" Her accent was strange though she appeared human, albeit a tad exotic.

"That's the name my mammy gave me and that's the rank my pappy the Corps said I could wear. And I was stupid enough to jump out of perfectly good shuttles from low orbit."

Her black eyebrows shot up at his sardonic tone while a small, speculative smile played on her full lips.

"A comedian. It shows spirit. I like that in a silahdar."

"What the hell is a silahdar?" He looked at her quizzically. "And who the hell are you?"

Her laugh was deep, throaty and Zack felt a tingle run down his spine.

"A slave soldier, of course. You were if you told the truth, one of the elite warriors in your Commonwealth and now you are a slave, offered up for sale. I train silahdars for my master, and he sells them for a price. By the look of you, master gunner, pathfinder and command sergeant all rolled into one, you'll make the Atabek a fortune."

Her hard eyes danced with amusement at his defiant stance and his evident interest in her, not all of which was professional.

"And what if I don't want to become a silahdar?"

"That would be unwise. Your value is based on what you can do. If you cannot do anything, you have no value. I'm sure you can follow the logic and how that relates to enlightened self-interest."

Decker nodded once but held her eyes.

"A lot of people have tried to kill me, and they're the ones sucking tree sap by the roots."

"When you are a silahdar, a lot of people will try to kill you as well, but your employer will allow you to kill those people in turn, and that is preferable to an early death, is it not?"

Her smile was half-seductive, half-predatory, and all enticing. Decker figured a recruiting sergeant like her would do wonders to swell the ranks of the Corps.

"I'm Mala Daran." She nodded politely, as one warrior to another. "I too am a silahdar, and my employer bought you the moment your name and pedigree appeared on the net. You now belong to the Atabek, our master."

Decker cocked an eyebrow and gave Daran his best 'aw shucks' grin.

"If you're a sample of what I'll find in the ranks of your organization, all I can say is: Lead on, McDuff."

She looked puzzled at the unfamiliar reference but then shrugged and pulled a thin collar from her tunic pocket.

"This is the mark of a slave of the Atabek. You will have it around your neck at all times. Failure to wear it will result in severe punishment."

Without waiting for a reply, she stepped close enough to Zack that he could inhale her musky scent, and put the slave collar on him. He felt a faint tingling as the metal touched his skin and smiled at Daran, whose face was so near to his that had he wanted to kiss her, he could have done so before she reacted. Of course, he would sport a few additional bruises, if not broken bones almost instantly since he was still manacled.

Daran stuck her head out the door and barked an order in an alien tongue. The same guard who'd escorted him to the room appeared and quickly removed his restraints.

"Come, slave," she said, turning on her heels.

"Slave? Why not silahdar?" Decker asked, more to amuse himself than for any other reason, since he already knew the answer.

"Because we've yet to determine whether you truly are the warrior you claim to be. Until then, you are nothing but an animated piece of meat whose value remains to be tested."

"And you'll do the testing?"

"Perhaps."

She led him to a skimmer that bore little resemblance to anything he'd seen in the Commonwealth. The proportions were just off enough to make him uncomfortable as he dropped into the passenger seat.

"You're not afraid that I'll try to overpower you while you're flying this crate?" He asked, smirking enough to let her know he wasn't serious.

"You're a smart man, Decker. Otherwise, you wouldn't have made it as far as you did in your Marine Corps."

"I was dumb enough to get captured and shipped to the ass-end of the Orion arm."

"Perhaps, but bad luck and worse enemies will eventually wear down the best of us. No doubt your story will be one that combines both in the least pleasant way possible. But to get back to your question, you might be able to fly this skimmer if you manage to overpower me, but where would you go?"

"Head for the hills, hide until I could stow away on an outbound freighter."

She laughed delightedly.

"I do admire your spirit, Decker, but you're not getting off this planet without permission, believe me. The collar around your neck is a tracking device, all ports are carefully guarded against escaped slaves, and you'll find no one among the population to help you. The penalties for harboring fugitives are too high. No, your best chance of ever seeing the stars again is to become a silahdar and serve."

"Until I die a slave?"

"You will die a slave, no matter what. As will I. You may think it unkind of the universe, but this is what we are and will always be."

"Permit me to disagree," Zack countered. "I have a debt to collect back home, and I'll do it before I meet whatever deity set up this sorry excuse of creation and give it a piece of my mind."

"I like you," she turned her head sideways and smiled at him as the skimmer stabilized a few meters above the dark water and headed towards the purple hills on the distant continent, well away from the island spaceport.

"Most of our new additions have little fight left by the time I collect them, and then it'll be weeks of training under our Swordmaster before they regain it. You'll be a pleasant change."

"Swordmaster? Seriously?" He sounded incredulous.

"We call him that, but he is adept at all forms of fighting and is the final authority on the instruction of silahdars. He'll be looking forward to your entering the arena. Be warned that he has a particular dislike for humans who think they're the best fighters in the known galaxy."

Decker snorted derisively.

"I don't think I'm the best fighter in the galaxy, but your precious Swordmaster might still get a few bumps and bruises."

"We'll see." Her throaty laughter sent a renewed tingle down his spine. "I love your self-confidence, but hope it's backed up with actual competence. If you've lied about what you are, you'll be lucky to escape the arena alive."

"Yeah, yeah," he shrugged. "Less talking, more speeding. I need to up my status and get a contract off planet. The folks who owe me aren't going to live forever."

Daran skillfully piloted the skimmer over the narrow seas and through a long mountain pass leading to the interior. As the vegetation-encrusted ridges finally parted to reveal a broad valley, Zack saw the outline of a massive compound in the late afternoon mist.

"That is our garrison and training camp," the silahdar said pointing down. "It will be your only home until you are sold to a new owner or sent off-planet on a contract."

"What if no one wants to buy me?"

"Then one of two things will happen, depending on the reason. If no one wants to purchase you because your price is too high, then your value is such that you will become a trainer of silahdars. If no one wants to purchase you because you're not worth the expense the Atabek put into you, you'll likely be sold off as a general laborer or killed."

"You're just a bucketful of cheer, aren't you," Decker replied sarcastically. With the idea of being owned gnawing more and more at his spirit, he found himself becoming increasingly irritable. Soon, he knew, he'd be looking for someone on whom to work off his bad temper, and that might bring trouble he didn't need.

He shouldn't have worried.

— FOUR —

She landed the skimmer at the edge of an earthen parade ground in the middle of the garrison and, climbing out, told him to follow her. Where she had been relaxed and friendly during the flight, she was now abrupt and cold, a transformation that made Zack edgy.

He examined the wood-clad buildings, their outlines blurred by tendrils of fog and a sheen of moisture, as she led him down a well-tended path, and tried to act as the pathfinder he once was by collecting as much data as he could about his surroundings. It didn't do him a great deal of good. Windows were either shuttered or opaque to his eyes, none of the structures betrayed their function and signs were non-existent. In the muffled silence, it was as if Daran and he were the only living beings around.

She took him up a short flight of steps and through a simple door into the eerie silence of a building that smelled of incense and waxed wood. Daran stopped in the antechamber and held up her hand.

"Remove your boots."

"Why?" Zack asked, more out of annoyance than anything else. He already had a good idea of what was about to happen. No matter where and on what planet, dojos always smelled of incense and waxed wood.

With a speed that surprised him, the silahdar whirled around and punched him in the stomach. He just had time to tense his abdominal muscles and turn what would have been a painful, if not disabling strike into something that elicited a brief grunt.

His instinct was to hit back harder, but he managed to remain still, understanding that retaliation would have been seen as mutiny. On a planet where slavery was a vibrant commercial undertaking, any move against authority likely meant death or something that might make him wish for a quick end.

"A slave does not question orders," she said, anger and contempt dripping from every syllable.

Decker obeyed, all the while watching Daran from the corner of his eyes. He figured he'd be tested and tested hard, but hadn't known when and how it would begin. Now he knew. When he'd bared his feet, she pointed at the open inner door, through which he could see a large, gray exercise mat.

"You will stand on the triangular marking, as if you were in a military ceremony, and wait for your next order. You will not move other than to breathe and blink your eyes."

"Yes, sir!" Decker barked in his best Marine command voice.

"You will also not speak. Unless you are permitted to do so by your betters, such as myself or the Swordmaster, you will signal acknowledgment of your orders by bowing to the one who gave them."

He wanted to ask how he would indicate that he didn't understand an order but realized that she expected the strictures she was laying on him to come into effect the moment the words left her mouth. It was up to him to figure it out. No doubt he would soon receive a command he couldn't execute without further clarification and then they would see how he handled it.

Decker bowed to Daran, bending his torso at the waist until he was roughly thirty degrees from the vertical; deep enough to acknowledge what he judged was her status among the silahdar. It was obviously sufficient.

"You may go, slave."

He entered the training room and stopped at attention on the red marking, eyes looking straight ahead at the intricate carving of what he assumed was a mythical creature on the far wall. Without appearing to move, he let his muscles relax and started breathing in a slow, deep rhythm. The next test might come in many forms, and he could do nothing more to prepare than center his spirit and calm his body.

A faint noise sounded somewhere to his left, like that of a blade drawn from its sheath. He should have guessed that this would be how it started: the title Swordmaster was descriptive enough.

Bare feet moved quickly on the mat, and he felt a presence behind him just as the air above his head was parted by something swinging at the speed of a turbofan. It came close enough to his scalp that his already short, sandy hair had probably been shortened by another millimeter. Decker remained stock-still, eyes fixed on the carving as if trying to bore a peephole through the wood.

A being, clad in black, danced across his line of sight and a sword blade swung past the tip of his nose, leaving behind the scent of oiled metal. The swordsman suddenly stopped and drove the point of his weapon straight at Zack's right eye, stopping it a hair's breadth from the surface of the cornea.

The ex-Marine didn't flinch, and the blade disappeared downwards until he felt its pressure against his groin, as if it was about to slice him from crotch to navel. The pressure increased, and Decker began to fear they would geld him after all, but then blade and swordsman spun out of sight.

He forced his tense muscles to relax again and blinked a few times to lubricate dried-out eyes he'd been holding wide open while he was being used as a fencing post. The dojo had fallen back into absolute stillness, with not even the hint of another being breathing somewhere out of his view. The minutes passed as they often do, at the rate of sixty standard seconds to one and if anything, the silence deepened to the point where he felt his irritation grow even further. Yet he had no choice but to endure with all the patience he could muster. On this nameless planet, he was nothing more than a slab of meat until he'd proven he was worth more than his weight in dog food.

The blow to his left kidney, when it came, was utterly unexpected. His assailant had moved with such stealth and speed that he'd had no time to prepare. Decker bit back an agonized grunt, struggling to remain still. All of his instincts screamed that he needed to defend himself, if not retaliate, but he managed to keep his eyes on the far wall and his arms hanging loose. A succession of blows followed the first one, each carefully applied to a different part of his body, each measured to cause pain without permanent damage, and each designed to break through his stoicism.

One hit on a particularly sore spot, thanks to the tender loving he'd gotten from the reivers weeks ago, made him stagger, but he regained his original posture quickly, hoping that he wouldn't get additional punishment for having moved without orders. The hope was in vain. A calloused hand struck his face hard enough to split the skin on his right cheekbone, leaving behind a sting that spread up to his forehead and down his neck.

It was sufficient to force his head to the left, and that unauthorized movement earned him a similar slap on the other cheek. He forced his eyes back on the carving and waited for the next strike, but nothing else came. The same stillness descended on the dojo again, broken only by Decker's increasingly labored breathing.

"You will assume a fighting stance of your choice," a raspy voice commanded in thick, guttural Anglic from somewhere to his right, "and you may look around."

Decker shook his shoulders as he spread his feet and flexed his knees. His body was throbbing from a dozen spots, not least his head, thanks to the beating inflicted by the unknown fighter. He had no doubt that it had been a master, if not *the* Master. It took real skill to cause that kind of pain yet leave a man virtually undamaged.

A humanoid slowly walked around him, keeping at a distance that was clearly out of Decker's reach, and stopped when he was standing between the ex-Marine and the carving that had served as his focus.

The being was tall, but where Decker was thick with muscle, it was thin to the point of emaciation, yet the corded tendons and muscles under its dull green skin were clearly outlined. Two large black eyes considered him expressionlessly, or at least without any expression the human could identify.

It was hairless and had large angular ears on either side of a blocky skull covered in elaborate tattoos, ears that twitched minutely as they adjusted to capture every last sound. The black clothing Decker had seen was a close-fitting singlet that bared the lower arms and legs, and the large, calloused hands and feet.

"I am Ktek, Swordmaster. You will now be allowed to defend yourself using whatever techniques you please."

With those words, he turned into a whirl of controlled limbs and Decker found himself flat on his back without really understanding how he got there. Ktek stepped back to let him rise but drove at him again the moment Zack was up. This time, he was ready and managed a few defensive moves before the Swordmaster had him flying back again with a new bruise in the middle of his chest.

Zack felt his irritation give way to fury as he rose once more and prepared to charge at Ktek with all the murderous intent he could summon. Then, as if blinded by the revelation, he understood that this was precisely the Swordmaster's objective. A cold hand extinguished his fury and for the first time since he entered the dojo, he felt calm.

Decker adopted a low stance designed to both stop Ktek's next attack and then turn the power of it against him. His intent must have shown in his eyes for the alien took a step back and clapped his hands twice. A low rumble came from his lipless mouth, and he bowed his head briefly.

"You may go now, slave. Mala Daran is waiting for you by the shomen."

Remembering the silahdar's instructions, Zack bowed at the waist, this time deepening it to a forty-five-degree angle. When he straightened his back, Ktek was gone. Trying not to wince, he walked out into the antechamber where Daran, a sardonic smile on her face, was leaning against a roughly hewn wooden post.

"Put on your footwear."

Decker nodded, expecting punishment for failing to bow, but she passed it in silence. Bending over to fasten his boots was an interesting experiment in anatomical design, as all the muscle groups involved in the movement bore evidence of Ktek's tender mercies. He grimaced to himself, but when he got up from his crouch, his face was as bland as he could make it.

"You may just live after all," she commented as they left the dojo. "Ktek was impressed with your self-control. He saw that he wouldn't to break you anytime soon and ended the session earlier than he usually does. You may speak, by the way. I shall let you know when that permission is suspended again. Or perhaps you'll figure it out by yourself."

"How did you know Ktek was impressed?"

"He rarely laughs and claps at the same time. A clap signifies satisfaction, but the laughter modifies that to what he says his people call being impressed."

Decker remembered the rumbling sound that seemed to originate deep in the Swordmaster's chest and nodded.

"What is his species? I've never seen or heard of his like before."

"We're not quite sure. He says he comes from another part of the galaxy. Like most, he was taken and sold as a slave, though in his case, this happened well before my birth."

"I think he kind of looks like an orc."

"Is that a species known to humans?" Daran sounded genuinely curious.

"Only to those who indulge in fiction. Orcs don't really exist." He chuckled. "Or I suppose they do, but they're not exactly the orcs humans have imagined – more like a cultural subset of our species than another one altogether. You said 'like most.' What do you mean?"

"Many are born into slavery."

"Grow your own, eh? How about you? You're human, but you don't sound like you came from a human world."

Daran shook her head.

"I was born into the silahdar, as were my progenitors but I was told my people do not come from your Commonwealth."

"Lost colony, maybe?" He shrugged. "You speak Anglic well enough to understand, even if your accent is strange."

"And many other languages besides that. Humans are preferred as slaves on many worlds, so our tongue has become somewhat standard."

They walked out among the silent buildings as the light faded and, for the first time, Decker saw signs of life. Individuals and formed groups moved about with hushed purpose, readily identifiable as silahdar by uniforms resembling that of Daran in all but richness of texture. They also resembled her in the tattooing they wore on their bald heads.

"These are the trained soldiers," she said, noticing his interest. "Recruits are confined to the far end of the garrison. They do not wear the Atabek's uniform and are not permitted outside their barracks individually."

"Is that where I'm going?"

"Our owner has not yet decided. He wished to hear from Ktek and after that from me."

They came to a large building constructed of sturdy materials. Its window shutters and doors were unmistakably made of steel and Zack figured this was an armory of sorts. He was about to face the next round of testing. His stomach growled just loud enough for Daran to hear and she chuckled.

"Food is not served for another hour, so you might as well tell your body to keep its silence."

They entered the building and were met by a lean, hatchet-faced human female with expressionless eyes. She also had a bald skull decorated with tattoos and wore old but clean coveralls with the strange runes he'd seen before stamped on what had to be a nametape.

"This is our chief armorer, Lora Cyone," Daran said by way of introduction. "Lora, you are to examine claims that this slave is well versed in weaponry."

The armorer examined Decker from head to toe with an unnerving intensity before turning to Daran.

"I'll let you know when I'm done. If he's shamming, it'll be clear pretty quickly. If he isn't, I'll see how good his skills are, and that can take a while."

The silahdar nodded and with an ironic smile at Decker, walked away.

"Okay, you," she pointed at an open inner doorway, "in there, and you'd better not be wasting my time."

With that, she led him to an open weapons' locker and selected what looked like a carbine. She tossed it at him, and when he caught it, she crossed her arms and waited.

Zack went through the prescribed motions to ensure the weapon was safe, after spending a few moments identifying its various mechanisms, but when he was done and looked up at Cyone, he saw she expected something more than routine safety procedures.

He stepped over to a nearby table whose top had been thoughtfully cleared and methodically stripped the weapon down. When he had all the components he could take apart without specialized tools laid out in orderly rows, he began to examine them one by one, searching for whatever Cyone wanted him to find.

It was a subtle flaw, one that wouldn't incapacitate the carbine for a bit longer, but it was something that a good armorer would deal with now rather than risk having it jam in the middle of a firefight. He held the receiver up to the light and nodded with satisfaction. That was it.

"The connectors are worn," he told Cyone. "Maybe another five hundred rounds and they're toast."

She nodded but didn't otherwise move, or change her expression.

Decker put the receiver back on the table and continued his inspection of the parts. He was too experienced to stop after finding one defect. If this thing was all original parts, there would be more. Someone pretending to have a master gunner's qualification might well have ended it there and then, but not Zack. He found three more parts close to needing replacement. After he had shown her the final one, she uncrossed her arms.

"Leave it dismantled. One my techs will take care of the repairs. Let's see how well you know chemically propelled projectile weapons."

Zack looked at her in surprise.

"You mean gunpowder?"

She snorted derisively.

"You thought I meant methane gas? Did your training not cover primitive weapons?"

"Sure," he replied, "I just never encountered any outside the School."

"It may not be gunpowder in the way you think, but out here, chemical propellants are pretty standard. It's easier to cast solid shot and mix up a good compound than it is to build power packs and mint pure copper disks, let alone machine a bore that will take plasma instead of a bullet." Cyone sounded contemptuous.

"I guess I get that," he replied shaking his head. "And I suppose I'm far from home, aren't I?"

"You have no idea." She opened another cabinet and hauled out a long-barreled weapon. This time, instead of tossing it at him, she motioned Zack over and showed him how the action worked. When he nodded his understanding, she handed him the rifle and stepped back.

Decker examined it carefully, turning the weapon over in his hands and running his fingers over its surface. It looked exotic, but there were only so many ways to design chemical propellant arms and most variations stemmed from physiological differences between the species using them.

"By the way, I'm Zack Decker. What do I call you?" He asked conversationally. "I don't know anything about rank in this outfit."

"Rank is a relative term in a slave army," she replied, her eyes fixed on Zack's hands as he began to disassemble the rifle. "Since we're property, we have functions, not military ranks as such. For example, Mala Daran is called a sanjaqui, which means standard-bearer in our owner's language and her primary function is to be something like an adjutant. We call our owner 'Atabek,' which translates roughly as lord-father. Other slaves are called by other names, depending on their function. I am simply the armorer, and you may refer to me as such in Anglic, or use bekar, which is the proper term."

"Cute," Decker said, as he looked around for a tool to knock some sense into a balky part. "So I guess platoon leaders are called platoon leaders and not lieutenants. Sounds very egalitarian."

"It is," she replied dryly. "We're all equally slaves and will be until the day we die. The equal sharing of miseries, you might say."

"Been here long?"

"Long enough. We have a rule in this outfit, Decker. Slaves don't ask each other about their past before they became chattel. If someone wants to tell you, they will. For some, remembering we have families hundreds of light years away that we'll never see again is pretty depressing."

He nodded as he examined the rifle's breech bolt.

"Here's your problem. The firing pin's stuck. Either it's seized up because it hasn't been cleaned in twenty years or the spring is worn. It may even be broken."

"With a Holkan weapon that's seen a lot of use, you can generally bet on a worn-out spring. Leave it. My tech will take care of that one as well."

She led him deeper into the armory and through a set of heavy steel doors. There, he saw racks loaded with large, crew-served weapons and fancier ordnance like missile launchers, automatic mortars and the like.

"I'm not going to ask you to troubleshoot any of these. They're all in good condition, but I will describe the weapon. You can tell me how it's best used and what characteristics you expect it to have on the battlefield."

Recognizing one of the standard tests given to Marine master gunner candidates, Decker looked at the older woman with renewed interest. She saw the question in his eyes but instead of giving him a reply, she pointed at a large-bore piece.

"Let's start, shall we."

Half an hour later, Decker figured he'd disgorged every bit of gunnery data he'd ever accumulated. His stomach felt hollower by the minute, and he hoped the tests were over for the day.

Cyone, aside from identifying the item, said nothing. She didn't nod, smile or otherwise give any sign that he was right, wrong or just plain useless. Tempted as he was to probe her about her past, he decided that it was best to follow the rules and kept strictly to the answers she was expecting. Daran had returned and observed the last few minutes of his test, her face equally expressionless as she leaned against the wall, arms crossed. When Zack fell silent, she looked at Cyone.

"And what is your verdict?"

"He has the knowledge one would expect of a human master gunner."

"Very well." She pointed at Zack. "Your permission to speak freely has ended. You will follow me."

He bowed in acknowledgment, wondering what would happen now. Daran led him out of the armory and across the parade ground to a long building whose walls were pierced with numerous windows.

"This is the food hall," she said. "We will enter by the cooks' door. Once inside, you will sit at the table I designate. You will be given a meal that you will eat quickly and in silence."

He nodded, relieved to finally get some nourishment. With any luck, it'd be better than the tasteless paste he was fed on the slaver ship.

The kitchen staff, a motley collection of humanoids, stared at him curiously as they walked in. One of them, perhaps the head cook, nodded politely to Daran and asked a question in the same alien language he'd heard before. Upon her reply, he turned to one of his helpers and issued instructions. Meanwhile, she pointed to a scarred steel table.

"Sit."

Moments later, the helper deposited a tray with several lumps of both hot and cold organic matter on it, handing Decker a utensil closely resembling a spoon. He murmured something that Zack couldn't understand and left.

The food didn't smell particularly appetizing, nor did it look very edible, but he took a chunk from the brownish substance and popped it in his mouth. It tasted awful, indescribably so, and he realized this was yet another test.

He suppressed a retch with great difficulty and swallowed. The piece from the next lump was heavily spiced and burned his mouth, yet he swallowed that too. In the end, Decker mixed up all four piles into one multicolored mash and shoveled the resulting mess into his mouth, swallowing convulsively so it spent as little time as possible in contact with his taste buds.

Throughout the meal, Daran had watched him with expressionless eyes, but didn't speak, nor did she eat anything herself. If this was the chow hall's usual standard, he couldn't blame her, although he suspected that he'd just been given food that appealed to someone like the orc Swordmaster.

As long as it didn't give him the runs or make him puke, he'd be okay. They'd have made sure not to feed him anything that could harm a human, otherwise what had been the point of testing their newest merchandise all afternoon.

When he was done, Daran nodded her head towards the door.

"Come."

This time, she led him to a two-story building made of cut stone sitting at the other edge of the parade ground. A pair of sentries guarded the glass door at the top of a short flight of stairs, and they acknowledged her with a polite nod as she took Decker inside. Once in the atrium, she pointed at a hard chair pushed up against the wall.

"Sit. Remain there until you receive new orders." Then she disappeared up a curving stairway, and he was alone.

After a ten minute wait, she re-appeared and motioned him to follow her.

"You will be brought into the presence of your owner, the Atabek. He may ask you questions, and you are to answer those as precisely and concisely as possible. Otherwise you are not to speak. You will stand at attention and keep your eyes to your front, even when answering the Atabek."

She preceded him into a lavishly decorated office and held out her arm to stop him a few paces in front of a large desk. Zack's fixed his gaze on a faded banner hanging from the wall, but it was a hard-won battle against his curiosity at examining the being who considered him his personal property.

The quick glimpse he'd had as he marched through the door had been of a non-human with indistinct features and a pale hide. The Atabek also had what seemed like a shock of reddish fur on his head, the only one he'd seen so far who wasn't bald.

"My advisers tell me you are very likely what you claim to be, Decker," a sibilant voice said from somewhere below his line of vision. The Anglic was distorted but perfectly understandable.

"They tell me the price I paid for you was not too much, even if you did not, in fact, serve in your Marine Corps. But whether or not you will make a useful silahdar remains questionable. A human of your skills will not have the right disposition to be a slave until he has been carefully trained and therefore you will not be admitted to the Kashdushiya until my training masters are satisfied you will obey all orders. I can see in your stance, your eyes and the way you breathe that your will must be broken. Only when you have fully accepted that your life belongs to me, and your destiny is to die as a silahdar, will you become a soldier. Until then, you are as dangerous as a caged predator and not much more useful."

He paused, to let the words sink in before continuing.

"All who come here from the slave market dream of escape but there is none. We are surrounded by a dense jungle that no one can cross. If by some miracle, the jungle doesn't get you, the Rekar tribesmen who live on its far edge will, and if the Rekar don't get you, we will. Be assured that if we get you, you'll wish you had been flayed alive by the Rekar."

He switched to his own language and spoke to Daran, but Zack understood that she was to take him to the training barracks and his heart sank. All day long he'd been hoping he could pretend to be reconciled to his situation, and had apparently failed. He wouldn't be placed with the fighting units and thus in a position to escape anytime soon. Now, it would be recruit training all over again, but without the restraints placed on sadistic sergeants by the naval code of discipline.

"You will execute an about turn," Daran ordered, "and then follow me."

"Try not to fight it, Decker," the Atabek said as they were about to walk out. "You are a warrior, and I am giving you a warrior's life. The alternatives for a slave on this planet are much, much worse."

— FIVE —

Daran led him to the far end of the garrison, where a high palisade split the installation into two separate areas. Signs in a runic alphabet hung on either side of the barred door. For all Zack knew, they could be telling him to abandon all hope as he entered here.

The thought made him smile briefly. He'd endured basic training, he'd survived Pathfinder School, and he'd been through combat many times. What could they do to him without ruining his value to the Atabek? He wasn't running his slave soldier operation for shits and giggles. He was running it for profit. Every sentient species known to humanity understood that concept and practiced it, some with far more abandon than others.

Daran rapped on the door twice. When it opened to a bald human with the same type of tattoos on his scalp, she issued orders in the Atabek's language and then turned to Decker.

"This is where our ways part. Whether or not they will rejoin is up to you. While the Atabek does not wish you to die in training or be deemed suitable only for the mines, he cannot afford to let a feral ex-Marine join the ranks of the Kashdushiya."

The guard barked an order at him in an alien tongue and then smiled cruelly.

"That was in Danjori. You will learn to speak it. What I just said was follow me. I will give you one translation of each order, and one only. If you fail to memorize it on the spot, you will be punished. Now, what did I say to you?"

Without missing a beat, Decker repeated the order in Danjori, right down to the guard's accent. He knew how this game was played.

"Funny," the guard grumbled, "real funny."

He shut the gate behind Zack and prodded him with his stick.

"It's too late to begin your training today, slave. You'll be confined to barracks until tomorrow. Take it as a chance to make some new friends."

When Zack didn't reply, the guard looked disappointed. It was a clear indication that the preferred training method was a variation of writing the test before getting the lesson; in this case, a misstep would earn him a beating before he got an explanation of what he'd done wrong. Though it was an effective way to instill utter subordination in people who hadn't stared death in the face as often as he had, the method wouldn't do much for Decker. While the guard led him across the compound, Zack took the occasion to examine his newest surroundings.

The recruit school, well lit now that night had fallen, was a more modest version of the main base, but was as spotlessly clean and well maintained. Wooden barracks, classrooms, and a large chow hall flanked a smaller parade ground, while shooting ranges and an obstacle course edged the fence separating it from thick jungle vegetation. It looked like every other low-tech boot camp Zack had seen and his spirits lifted. He definitely knew how this game was played.

They stopped at the entrance to one of the long barrack blocks and the guard unlocked the door by placing his palm on a keypad. It clicked, and he opened it with his stick.

"Inside with you. Take one of the spare bunks and try to get some sleep. Tomorrow's going to be a day like you've never experienced."

Decker stepped over the threshold, and the door swung shut behind him. He stepped out of the small, airlock-like lobby into the barracks proper where the smell of several dozen unwashed bodies assailed his nostrils.

A furry Darsivian jumped up from a cot next to the entrance and growled something in his tongue. It didn't sound complimentary.

"He says we have fresh meat," a raspy voice informed Zack from the other side. He glanced briefly at the speaker, a gray-skinned Kardati tribesman who was leering at him.

"Thanks, but I've already eaten," he replied.

"No, human, he means you."

"How about you tell your friend that I'm too tired to turn him into a rug, and we'll call it a night."

"He hates humans. Humans captured him and sold him to the slavers."

"Big fucking deal," Decker said resignedly. He was going to have to do this the hard way. "I'm human, and I got sold into slavery by other humans, yet you don't see me beating myself up."

The Kardati seemed genuinely puzzled by Zack's statement, and he took the opportunity to slip between the two humanoids, to give himself room to move rather than be pinned between them and the locked entrance. They were slow to react, and he had time to look around for other threats, but the beings he saw were either watching with interest or moving away from what they expected to be a bloody battle. Darsivians and Kardati were fierce fighters, but they weren't known for being disciplined. The trainers were going to have fun with those two, Decker figured.

If they really wanted to take their anger out on him, they should have attacked the moment he walked in, not wasted precious seconds with dumb posturing. They'd lost their advantage but were too stupid to realize it.

"Seriously, guys," he said, adopting a relaxed fighting stance, "if you're that desperate to take a beating, you should have sassed the guards when they brought you here. Those sticks they carry aren't just so they can poke at anthills."

The Darsivian shook himself and advanced on Decker with the lumbering gait of his species. His interpreter was climbing over a few bunks to take Zack from the side, forcing him to make a quick decision.

He pivoted on his left heel and charged at the Kardati, aiming the top of his head at the tribesman's nose slit, where he knew it would hurt the most without causing permanent damage. Breaking the Atabek's possessions wasn't likely to be a good survival strategy, and there was no doubt in his mind that they were being watched by the staff via hidden cameras. Slaves whaling on each other was all right as long as they could still train effectively the next day, but sometimes that meant the guards had to wade in with their batons.

The impact momentarily stunned Zack, and he overbalanced, pushing the Kardati against the wall. His opponent roared at the blinding pain, hands reflexively going up to his face. Zack took advantage of the opening to land a couple of punches in the midriff, and the tribesman dropped to the floor like a sack of rocks.

Unfortunately, that had given the Darsivian enough time to close the distance, and Decker felt a pair of powerful paws take hold of him from behind. He dropped into a crouch, grabbing his opponent's thick wrists and pulled him over his shoulder, using the alien's own bulk against him. The Darsivian rolled on top of his companion with a surprised roar that was abruptly cut off when Decker's right foot lashed out, catching the side of his shaggy head and knocking him out.

Zack cautiously approached the pair and looked into the open eyes of the Kardati, wondering whether the Darsivian had squashed the life out of him, but his nictitating membranes flicked as the tribesman focused on him.

"See what you've made me do?" Decker's voice was a low growl. "The next time, it won't just be some love taps. I'll be breaking bones and then what use do you think you'll be to our owner? He'll probably turn you into pet food. I hear he has a herd of vorpal bunnies at home that eats a hundred kilos of kibble each day."

He saw the Darsivian stir and gave him another sharp rap on the head with the tip of his boot, sending the ursine slave back into unconsciousness. Leaving the duo sprawled on the floor, Decker found an empty cot at the far end of the barracks among half-dozen humans who looked at him with fearful respect.

"Buggers make a lot of noise," he told them, grinning, "but the only thing that's dangerous about them is the stink when they haven't been hosed down for long time."

When none of them reacted to his attempt at humor, the grin vanished, and he frowned.

"You guys understand Anglic?"

A few of the young men nodded.

"We do understand you," the brawniest among them, who was almost Decker's size, replied, "but we do not see why this is funny."

His accent was a thicker version of Mala Daran's as if he came from a place where the language had evolved separately from the human mainstream.

"I'm going to guess you folks aren't from the Commonwealth."

The young man nodded.

"You are correct. Are you from this Commonwealth, sir?"

"Yep, and I'm not a sir. Decker's the name. Born and bred on Mykonos Colony."

"We are from Nelva, but our legends tell that our ancestors came from a place called Earth. My name is Krath."

"That's where all of our ancestors are from, Krath. This Nelva must be a lost colony. How long have your people been there?"

"We do not know. Several thousand years, it is said."

"Bull!" Decker laughed. "The first sublight colony ships left Earth no more than five hundred years ago, so even if your ancestors got sucked into a wormhole and spat out in these parts, you're not talking thousands of years."

"Perhaps, Decker," Krath replied, "but I have seen the ruins of the first settlement, and it is much older than five hundred years."

"Huh, interesting." He shrugged. "But since we're not getting out of here, it's kind of academic. Tell me something, those idiots I just played with, have they been pulling the fresh meat thing on all newbies?"

"They have, but you're the first to best them in the time since we arrived."

"Well, I wouldn't worry much about the buggers for now. Bullies slink back into their holes when you give them a good whacking."

He settled back on the cot and closed his eyes.

"If you guys wouldn't mind warning me of any trouble you might see coming my way, I'd sure appreciate it."

Decker fell asleep within seconds, his battered and bruised body screaming for rest and regeneration. He woke hours later to the muffled sounds of a scuffle a few meters from his cot and was instantly alert. The Nelvans, having taken heart from his example the previous evening, were facing off with the Darsivian and his Kardati comrade. But before it could erupt into a full-scale melee, the door burst open and half a dozen silahdars entered the barracks in a single file, their discipline batons at the ready.

The first one, a green armband prominent on his biceps, shouted an order in Danjori and even though Decker didn't understand the words, he knew what the senior instructor wanted. He jumped up and stood at attention at the foot of his cot, mentally repeating the phrase to memorize it.

Batons flew as the others proved too slow in reacting until there was complete silence once everyone had imitated Zack. He could play the boot camp bullshit all day long if that's what they wanted.

It wasn't.

The head silahdar walked up to him and stopped so close he could feel the man's breath on his cheek.

"Decker."

Zack nodded, keeping his eyes staring straight ahead.

"You will follow me." He repeated the order in Danjori, then spun on his heels and walked towards the door.

As Zack stepped out of the barracks into the early morning mist that hovered over the garrison, he noted another silahdar standing to one side of the door. Before he could process the thought any further, the man punched him hard in the right kidney.

Though his knees buckled at the unexpected violence and pain, he remained upright and kept his eyes on the one with the green armband. If they hoped to provoke retaliation, they were going to be disappointed. In this too, Decker knew how to play the game. They must have watched him take down the two non-humans the previous evening and knew he could lash out hard and fast.

The leader kept walking without turning back, and Zack followed, conscious of the other silahdar on his heels. As they cleared the cluster of huts and neared the fence, the leader broke into a trot, then a run. Decker followed suit, and as they curved off to jog along the edge of the fence, he began to feel every bruise left by Ktek as his booted feet pounded the hard earth.

The training camp was surprisingly large, and it took almost fifteen minutes to complete the first circuit. As they ran, he watched other slave recruits form up for morning exercise and noted that humans seemed to predominate. Whether they were from the Commonwealth or those strange lost colonists who claimed to have lived on a planet called Nelva for several millennia, he couldn't tell.

Of the other species, he recognized many and was amused to note they were all from societies considered by the Fleet to be techno-barbarian: primitive, aggressive and tough, yet having acquired the means for FTL space travel from unscrupulous traders.

At the end of the fourth circuit, his stomach was protesting noisily, and he was getting thirsty, but since he had not been given permission to speak, he couldn't ask the silahdar for water without risking what he suspected would be a very imaginative beating with a baton. The only good thing was that they too would need to drink at some point and if they hadn't already done so, eat as well.

By the sixth circuit, Decker was beginning to falter, and he stumbled over a piece of uneven ground, barely avoiding a crash that would have taken the squad leader down with him. The one behind, who'd witnessed it, said nothing though he cracked his stick across Zack's shoulders.

Slave recruit formations were now headed for the largest building from which the aroma of food wafted. His stomach rumbled much more painfully this time.

At the end of the seventh circuit, they led him to the back door of the chow hall and Zack was given a few minutes to scarf down a mushy pile of food whose taste made last night's supper seem like heaven.

The day wore on with silahdars relaying each other to keep Zack in constant motion. As he became more and more tired, they began using their batons on him with increasing frequency. By the time the sun vanished behind the purplish mountains, he was sore, exhausted, and surprisingly angry.

He was equally astonished when they shoved him into a small box-like structure after he'd swallowed his supper, again in isolation from the rest of the slave recruits. Throughout the day, they'd only barked short orders at him, first in Anglic, then in Danjori, but with his growing fatigue, memorizing the words was becoming harder, and he was made to pay for his mistakes.

The box, barely big enough for him to lie down in, was bare, and he understood that this would be his own private quarters for the night. Settling on the floor, he removed his muddy boots to use as a pillow and stretched out, feeling more worn than he'd been in a very long time. Zack nonetheless fell into a troubled sleep, where dreams of pirates, slavers, and Mala Daran mixed in a toxic stew.

At sunrise the next morning, the same routine began all over again, but as he got progressively weaker, his mistakes multiplied, as did the beatings. That evening he fell asleep almost immediately once they slammed the door to his box shut. This continued for two more days, and he felt light-headed when they shoved him back into his cell the fourth evening. His body had worn a gentle groove into the bare ground, and he was out almost before he'd made himself comfortable.

A brutal kick woke him to a moonless night. His internal clock had failed him since arriving on this planet, and he had no idea of the time, except that it felt like the latter part of the night, in the hours before dawn. He felt painfully stiff as he pulled on his boots and crawled out of the box.

The two silahdars who'd rousted him weren't shy about using their batons and Zack felt his anger flare up again, this time with the acid of a fiercely burning hatred rising in his gorge. Boot camp bullshit was one thing, but this smacked of field interrogation techniques, except they weren't asking him any questions.

A savage blow in the small of the back sent him to his knees on the edge of a puddle, and as he lowered his head to avoid looking at the silahdars, fearful of losing control of his rage, he saw his battered face reflected in the dark water. An underhand whack with a baton split his cheek open again, and droplets of blood-tinted the puddle a deep crimson. A second blow to the other cheek likely meant they wanted him to look up, and he humored them, as he had since his private tutoring in the brutalities of slave life had begun.

Seeing the dangerous glint in the squad leader's eyes, the whole purpose of this treatment became evident. Since Mala Daran had brought him here, everything they'd made him do was designed to test and ultimately destroy his self-control. She'd called him a feral ex-Marine and he was annoyed at himself for not understanding. They were trying to break him, just as one breaks an animal before training it to do a task and that meant the punishing pace of physical exertion, as well as the beatings, would continue until he lost his grip on his temper, and struck back at the silahdar.

What would follow was sure to be painful to a degree he'd never experienced, but he couldn't go on much longer with this charade. He needed to remain the Zack Decker he was, the one who had to get away from here and hunt down the people who'd killed his wife and sold him into slavery. If he let them wear him down any further, he might lose part of that man and turn into what they wanted him to become — a slave in his mind and not just his body.

He looked down at his reflection again and tensed his muscles. When the baton came swinging down, his right hand snapped up and snatched it, pulling the silahdar off balance. Decker lurched to his feet twisting the hard wooden cane out of the man's hand and swung it at the squad leader, catching him on the side of the head before turning it on its former owner with equally devastating results.

They had wanted him to break and come at them. They just hadn't been prepared for it, and Zack smiled as he systematically rained blows on each silahdar in turn. He ignored the sound of running feet because he had no intention of fighting them all; he just wanted to enjoy his brief and ultimately futile revenge on his tormentors.

It took six of them to subdue him, and he eventually lost consciousness under the onslaught.

His eyes opened to the milky glow of full daylight, and he discovered that he was lying on the ground, spread-eagle, unable to move. The soft morning breeze on his exposed skin quickly confirmed that he'd been stripped naked. His head was caught in a block of some kind, rendering him unable to move anything but his eyeballs and they weren't seeing anything but low, gray clouds.

The shape of a silahdar in a more elaborate uniform than his tormentors had worn came into view as the man stepped over Decker with one leg to straddle him. He held a small, writhing object between his thumb and finger.

"Decker," he said, his voice loud enough to carry, "you are about to undergo the punishment reserved for one of the worst crimes a slave can do: assault a silahdar. You've compounded your crime by using the badge of office as your weapon."

"This," he continued, bending over to show Zack the centipede-like thing he held, "is a juluk, a local insect that likes to swarm its prey and bring it down with venom before consuming it. We humans are not compatible with the juluk's digestive system, and they cannot actually eat us, but while they figure that out, the pain they can inflict is indescribable. We don't get many chances to use the juluk punishment and yours will be witnessed by the entire recruit contingent, as well as our Atabek and his staff."

He tossed the insect to the side and disappeared from Decker's sight. This then was how they intended to break him. The brutality had merely been a way to push him into earning his punishment. Insect bites — how bad could they be?

A horrible sensation of tiny hairs brushing against his skin suddenly came from the inside of his right thigh and ran up his leg. Another brushed the crack of his buttocks and Zack couldn't suppress the urge to move, anywhere and in any direction, but his restraints were too strong.

Then, a mass of them began to scuttle along his legs, over his groin area, and up his torso. The feeling of thousands of tiny feet was one to induce horror in even the most stoic of men, but if that were all, he figured he could probably handle the punishment. Then the first bite came in the soft area by his crotch.

It was as if a very narrow laser beam had burned through his flesh right down to the bone. He gasped at the unexpected pain. All of a sudden, dozens upon dozens of laser beams pierced him from his face down to his feet as the juluk struck en masse. Decker's gasp turned into a scream that echoed across the nearby mountainside, tearing at his vocal cords. His body shuddered under the assault, and he felt his right arm leave its socket as he tried to escape the agony.

He had no idea how long the ordeal lasted because his spirit, under the relentless assault, had shut its connection with reality and hidden in the darkest corner of his brain, gibbering in fear. Slowly, however, he became aware that the searing burns had stopped, leaving his body throbbing as it fought off a venom that couldn't quite kill it.

His breathing was ragged, agonized even, but when he opened his lids, no juluk tried to bite his eyeballs. In fact, he quickly realized that he couldn't feel the masses of tiny insect feet crawl over him. Then the pain of his dislocated shoulder hit and he sobbed.

Unseen hands removed his shackles, and his head was freed from the restraining block as silahdar medics brushed off the last juluk corpses and tended to the hundreds of bleeding punctures the insects had inflicted.

"It is fortunate," one of the medics said as he tended the wounds in his face, "that a taste of our blood is more fatal to the juluk than their venom is to us. Otherwise this punishment would mean certain death."

The words registered dimly in Decker's consciousness, but before he could croak out a question, another medic wrenched his shoulder back into place, and he blacked out again.

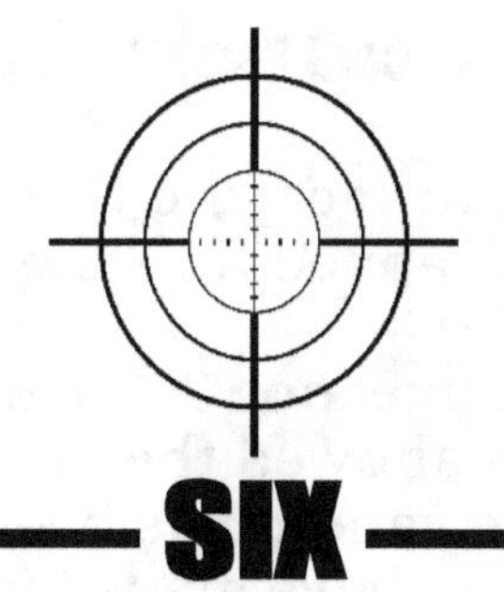

— SIX —

When he woke, he was on a hard cot, his bare body covered by a thin sheet of silky material. The air around him had the universal smell of antisepsis that could only mean he'd been taken to the infirmary. He could feel each puncture throbbing, and when he tried to turn, his ruined shoulder forcefully reminded him of its presence.

"Ah, you're awake." A wizened human face appeared in his line of sight. She had what he'd begun to call the Nelvan accent. "I suggest you try to move as little as possible. It takes two or three days to shake off a juluk attack." She shook her head. "Barbaric, but since we're property and not autonomous beings, it's considered as nothing more than an attitude adjustment. I'm Tika Bron, by the way."

Decker grunted in reply, not trusting his vocal chords to cooperate. Bron nodded her approval.

"The way you screamed out there, you'll not want to be talking for a while. The Atabek had the juluk count increased since it took you such a long time to lose consciousness. You've probably impressed him if he's ever impressed by his possessions. If you think you can sit up, I have some nourishing soup for you. It's none of the swill they give to the hard cases."

At the mention of food, his stomach reliably grumbled, and he gingerly pushed himself up against the wall.

Bron took a small, cylindrical container from the sideboard and removed its lid. Immediately, a strange, but appealing aroma filled his nostrils. She grabbed a spoon and settled on the edge of the cot, facing Zack.

"I'll be feeding you, for now, so just open wide." She dipped the spoon in the thick liquid and placed it in Zack's mouth. The taste was as good as the smell, to his great relief. It was, in fact, the tastiest food he'd eaten since the reivers kidnapped him these many long weeks ago.

"What happens to me now?" He asked in a hoarse whisper after he'd swallowed the last of it.

"When I'm sure the venom has been flushed from your system, the Atabek will have made his decision. For now, you're in my charge."

"How long?"

"It's different for each person. You appear to have an efficient metabolism, so maybe twelve to eighteen hours. Try to sleep some more. It helps speed up the process."

Decker lay back and closed his eyes, intent on probing deep within himself to find out whether he was still the same man or whether he was on his way to becoming a tamed slave soldier. That he'd shatter if they ever subjected him to the juluk punishment again was beyond question, but that led to the risk of destroying the part of him that was valuable to the Atabek. A thoroughly ruined man was useless as a warrior.

The terror he felt at remembering the first brush of juluk feet on his skin made it clear that the lesson had sunk in, and they would always have that lever to control him. But as he probed deeper, the part of him that had vowed to collect the debt he was owed remained intact. They'd failed to break him completely. He still had enough of his strength when they staked him out. If he hadn't understood their purpose so quickly, he couldn't imagine what his mental state would be right now. He doubted that he'd still be Zack Decker — at least not fully.

He let a small smile play on his swollen lips before drifting off into a deep sleep.

**

"You're being discharged this morning," Bron announced with a smile as she returned from analyzing the latest blood sample a few days later. "There's no more venom in your system and the bite wounds are healing nicely. The shoulder will take a little longer, but you shouldn't be asked to do any acrobatics for a while."

"Oh? Why's that?"

"I've received instructions to remove your head hair and give you the tattoo. You've been declared a silahdar."

"That was quick." Decker sounded dubious as if he were about to face another test.

"Hardly," Bron chuckled. "Trained warriors don't need to spend the full ten weeks in the school, and the Atabek has decided that you've passed the required tests."

"Yeah," he replied sourly. "That was quite the initiation, wasn't it?"

**

Decker examined his shiny bald head in the washroom mirror with a sinking heart. He hadn't realized that he actually valued the bit of individuality his hair represented. Now he looked just like the others, right down to the black and red marking on the left side of his skull, a representation of the same mythical creature whose carving he'd stared at for so long in the dojo.

Bron had applied a thick paste to his head and then, after a ten-minute wait, she had hustled him into a shower stall to rinse it off. His hair wouldn't re-grow for months, she said, and for some, it never came back at all. The tattoo took slightly longer to apply, but it was permanent. He was going to scare little children looking like that when he got back to the Commonwealth.

Realizing that he was convinced it was just a matter of time before he was on his way home, Zack smiled at his reflection. With any luck, he could return the juluk punishment favor to the Atabek before leaving. Decker liked to settle his debts.

They'd left him a new uniform, of the same reddish brown as the full-fledged members of the Kashdushiya, the slave regiment, rather than the dull gray of a trainee. It fit loosely enough to be comfortable, even if the material was a bit coarse. There were no identifying marks on the tunic so he couldn't guess at what they might have in mind for him, but that was of no concern. He could do virtually any job in an infantry battalion and then some.

Mala Daran came to collect him just as the sun was nearing its zenith. She inspected him carefully, paying attention to his visible injuries and to the fresh tattoo.

"Well met, silahdar," she finally said, smiling. "You may speak at your leisure, Decker. The enforced silence is for mere slaves, not soldiers."

"Nice to see you too, sanjaqui." If she noticed the sarcastic edge to his tone, she didn't show it.

"You may call me by my name if you like. We only use function titles in formal settings."

"Very egalitarian." He gave her a sardonic smile.

"We're all equally slaves." She nodded as if to emphasize the point. "It's almost time for the midday meal, and I thought that I would eat with you. Afterward, we can discuss your assignment."

As they joined the throng of silahdars lining up in a chow hall decorated with barbarous banners and trophies, Decker had a very eerie sense of belonging. He wore the same uniform, had the same identifying marks as these soldiers and that made him feel more at home than he had in a long time. Never mind that he found Daran to be fascinating, now that she'd lost the formality she'd shown when he was still a recent purchase.

That unsettling thought seemed put into question the strength of his will to get home. Perhaps the horrifying juluk treatment had succeeded to a greater degree than he thought. Could there have been something in the venom to change him? He scarcely thought it possible.

"You look lost, Zack," Daran murmured as she prodded him to move and close the gap in the line.

"I just had a ghost walk over my grave, that's all."

"I don't understand."

"Do you ever get a strange, unnatural feeling that's gone almost the moment you notice it?"

"I have, a few times in my life."

"That's what we call it back home." Decker shrugged.

"And what caused the feeling?" She sounded genuinely interested.

"I recognized this place as belonging to soldiers, and as I'm one of you now, it belongs to me as well."

"It's a good feeling isn't it?" She said, a gentle smile transforming her face.

"Yeah. I just hope the food is better than the slop you had them serve me my first night."

Now she laughed openly, a throaty, rich sound that he found curiously alluring.

"It is, have no fear. You'll see the choices clearly indicated by species. Though we can eat each other's food, tastes vary too much to serve single meals."

And she was indeed right. He took generous helpings of unidentifiable dishes marked for his race after Daran had taught him the runic symbols for 'human' and they were delicious if spicier than he expected.

"I'm surprised that I've been turned into a silahdar so quickly," he said settling back in the hard wooden chair after finishing off the last bite.

"You made it to the juluk punishment a lot faster than anyone expected. The few times we've had to tame feral former soldiers, the process was quite lengthy. The Atabek expects a contract soon where your skills would make a difference and ordered that you be pushed to the limits of endurance. He was impressed by the amount it took to make you break."

Decker smiled. They had no idea that he'd figured out their game early enough and that he hadn't quite reached his limits at that point. So much the better. Yet his earlier reaction, when he felt part of a military unit again, had disturbed him. It wouldn't do to develop loyalties that might stay his hand at the wrong time, or even anchor him here.

He had no one to return to, so the temptation could be great, especially if he made some close friends, he thought, admiring Daran's muscular shape across the table from him. He could get used to bald women with body art on their scalps. They had a certain barbaric something that stirred feelings he'd thought dead since the fateful pirate attack.

Zack was amused to find Daran examining him with a knowing look in her eyes as if she could read his mind. Considering his eyes probably betrayed his interest, that wouldn't be too far from the truth.

"So now what?" He asked.

"Now you learn Danjori quickly. Trainees usually absorb it while in the school, but since you'll not have that luxury," he smiled at her use of the word, "we're to help you along, and you're to study every evening after your day's work is done."

"I'm realizing just now that I don't know a lot of the basics. I guess Danjori is native to this planet, but no one's ever told me its name."

"Keeping new slaves in ignorance is normal, Zack. It helps create the disorientation needed to bring them under effective control. This planet is called Danjor by its natives and Danjori is the primary language spoken by Danjorans like the Atabek. Don't ask me about its galactic coordinates. I have no idea where this system lies in relation to any other."

She clapped her hands once and stood with a graceful fluidity Decker found fascinating.

"Enough lounging about."

They took their trays to the cleaning station and left the dining hall with the last of the stragglers.

The day had grown hot and humid while the sun still valiantly tried to pierce the ever-present veil of clouds, yet the garrison looked more cheerful than the last time he'd walked its paths. Or it could just be that his future was that much clearer.

"You still haven't told me what my day's work will be."

"Patience. The commander of the Fifth Orta, the battalion now forming here, wishes to evaluate your suitability as a member of the staff."

Decker snorted loudly.

"You put me through hell, beat the living crap out of me, test me on just about every weapon you have in your armory, and you're going to make me a staff officer? You people are insane."

"It is the Atabek's wish that we use all of your skills to the utmost. He paid a good price for you and intends to make an even better profit."

"You're in the boss' confidence?" He glanced at her skeptically.

"But of course. I was chosen to serve the Atabek personally. You'll see that this is a better life than many. Our 'boss' as you call him – never do that to his face, by the way – is a decent being who takes good care of his slave soldiers. We're more than just an investment for him. He considers us almost like his children."
Zack shook his head.
"I've got to get myself a cup of whatever you're drinking, lady. Parents don't let their kids get overrun by fat caterpillars with an attitude problem and the venom to prove it."
"Do parents not punish their children?" She asked mischievously. "Perhaps this way is normal for the people of Danjor. You look at things through your own cultural prejudices."
"Bull." He shook his head with amused resignation. "Wrong is wrong, no matter where you are. But that's beside the point, right? If the boss tells me to put on a tutu and dance the rumba while reciting Sanjay Peters' Ode to the Void, I have no choice but to do it."
"Though I don't understand your words, I think I get your meaning. Know that the Atabek will never issue an order that isn't for the greater good of the Kashdushiya and its missions."
"That I can relate to," he replied, thinking back at past commanding officers who'd been in the habit of issuing dumb orders that didn't do squat for the outfit. Like the captain who got him pensioned off early even though Decker had been right all along. On the other hand, he had to admit to himself that clocking him in front of the squadron had probably been the final straw in a long career of arguing with incompetent officers.
"Let me reframe," she said, stopping. When Decker turned to face her, she touched his arm with a hard, calloused hand that had seen a lot of harsh training. "How do you feel, I mean physically?"
He considered her question and was surprised by the answer.
"I feel pretty good, actually."
"Then reflect on the skill of the medical staff that treated you and the efforts they took to heal you so

quickly. Does this not indicate that the Atabek is genuinely concerned about the welfare of his soldiers?"

Decker laughed bitterly.

"He bought a new toy, almost broke it, and then fixed it. All I see is someone taking care of his investment."

"Fine," she scowled at him, though he got the feeling it was more in jest than meant seriously. "There's no convincing you right now. You'll learn in time."

"Still," he shook his head, "a damned staff officer."

"The Atabek bought you for your mind, Zack. He has leaders of scout units, weapons specialists, even pilots, but he has few who combine many talents, especially from the human Marine Corps."

"I combine squat," Decker replied. "I'm just a washed-up airborne grunt who knows his guns."

"You are clean, I'll grant you," she replied, laughing softly, "but you underestimate how valuable your experience and learning is to an army that fills its ranks with slaves."

"Then it should try an all-volunteer system. That's what we do, and we tend to attract a better sort of recruit."

She had no answer to his bitter retort, and they resumed walking in silence, the tenuous bond momentarily broken.

"So when do I get to meet the great commanding officer of the Fifth Orta?"

"You've already met her." She stopped again and smiled wanly. "I've asked the Atabek for permission to evaluate your tactical skills. If you show that you can help me train and fight the orta skillfully, I'll be able to keep you as my orta sanjaqui."

"Battalion standard-bearer?" Zack translated the Danjori words. "Sounds suspiciously like an adjutant's job to me. Does that mean I get a captain's pay?"

She laughed at his mock-greedy leer.

"I've told you, we are slaves and have no rank, only responsibilities. You would be equal to the balukbashis, the company commanders, and receive the same stipend."

Decker grunted.

"I'm not going to ask what the stipend is. I suspect that it doesn't matter. Property cannot own property, right?"

"Wait before you pass judgment, Zack. Our lives aren't all that bad, and we get to kill people," she added with a wicked grin.

"You take pleasure in killing?" He asked skeptically. The Marines he'd known who enjoyed it were all nuts to some degree or other, just not crazy enough to be discharged on psychiatric grounds.

"It's the only freedom a slave can exercise," Daran replied, shrugging. "And we in the Kashdushiya are superb fighters. That's why our Atabek sells many excellent soldiers and gets many contracts for our services."

"Like the one that'll see you take a battalion, with me along as adjutant."

"Precisely."

"And you guys trust me to be a battalion adjutant so quickly after buying me off the slavers?"

"No one who's been through the juluk punishment has ever failed to serve with the utmost of their being," she replied as if it were the most natural thing in her world.

The ugly thought that the venom had some ability to condition his brain came back to haunt Zack as she guided him to the headquarters building.

They entered a sparsely furnished office on the ground floor, and though he couldn't yet read the alphabet, he had no doubt the sign on the door probably said something resembling 'Fifth Orta – Commanding Slave.' Pleased with his own wit, he smiled as he took one of the hard chairs set around a small table.

"I'm going to take a wild guess that we're not here to play whizzbang," he said.

"Since I don't know what this whizzbang is, your guess is correct." Daran settled down across from him. "What I would like to do is discuss tactics with you, to get a sense of your experience and knowledge. Feel free to elaborate as you wish. I've had a fair amount of experience in combat myself; else the Atabek would not be charging me with the command of this unit and the ensuing mission."

"How does that work anyways?" Decker asked. "You form a battalion, sell it off, and bang, you're gone?"

"Not always. Some units are sold to new owners, sometimes with a contract to provide replacements, but often, the Atabek contracts to provide military forces for a given mission or a specified period of time or both."

"You're going to have to enlighten me as to why slave soldiers instead of outright mercenaries. It can't just be lowering the cost of your input."

She smiled.

"Mercenaries have been known to abandon their contracts when their lives are at risk. Either slaves fight on as ordered or they're executed. That makes us more valuable to potential clients and thus the Atabek can command a higher price."

"You've never had a whole unit sit down and say 'enough'? I find that hard to believe."

"I'm surprised that you cannot accept as true that we train dependable soldiers. If one-fifth of the battalion is ready to complete the mission because they know it's the closest thing to a guarantee for survival, the other four-fifths will go along or suffer the consequences at the hands of their comrades."

"Peer pressure." Zack grimaced. "I suppose there are enough historical examples that could apply. Juluk pressure works as well, I'll bet."

"Some of our most loyal silahdars have undergone the juluk punishment, and many consider it a mark of courage."

"You're all demented." He shook his head. But he did understand. Good military training conditioned humans to be loyal to their comrades, to show courage and resilience in the ranks and to value unit cohesion and honor. All he had to do was think back at that feeling of belonging he got when he entered the mess hall, with its banners, while wearing the silahdar uniform for the first time.

"As I may have mentioned before: you'll see in due course." Her smile was all the more dazzling for the genuine feeling it expressed, and Decker noticed that even with a hairless head and the intricate scalp tattooing, she was a rather attractive woman, in a muscular, warrior-queen sort of way. He forcefully quashed that line of thinking before it could go any further; having impure intentions for your commanding officer never ended well, though he was happy that the juluk venom hadn't affected that part of him.

"Tell me about your last command," she said, leaning forward. "Something must have gone wrong, since you're here instead of with your Corps, even though you're no older than I am."

"Do you know what pathfinders are?"

"Elite shock troops that are sent into action first so they may find and hold the enemy until the main body arrives."

"Pretty close. We have something called Fleet Pathfinders and their primary job isn't reconnaissance. They're a rapid-reaction strike force, and the squadrons are permanently stationed aboard patrol frigates. For instance, intelligence gets word of a pirate nest on a given planet or asteroid and HQ will send the nearest Pathfinder squadron to wipe it out in a shock and awe kind of raid."

She nodded.

"We've heard about them but only at several removes, and that likely from victims of your squadrons, so it's been difficult to form a clear picture."

"On my last mission in the Corps, my CO had been temporarily replaced by another from outside the squadron while he was in medical treatment. This officer was looking for a tour with my unit to polish his performance evaluation for the next promotion board. Serving with pathfinders looks good on an infantry officer's record. The problem was, he didn't know how to command something like a fleet squadron, but since we weren't expected to see hard combat, the commander of my regiment was persuaded to let him try. We were alerted for a raid on a suspected reiver base shortly after his arrival, and that's when he and I butted heads on just about everything."

Decker shook his head, grimacing.

"The idiot's plan showed his ignorance of reiver tricks, his ignorance of how to deploy pathfinders from high-flying assault boats and a lot more besides. We argued about his plan, and when he refused to listen to experience, I simply took my troop down where I thought it made the most sense. Turned out the drop zone he'd assigned me was an ambush. Heck, the whole reiver base was an ambush. We were lucky that the casualties were light, but those we got were pretty much all my folks. When we got back to the ship, I disagreed with his after action report and used my fists to make my point. Of course, I was arrested. They gave me the option between early retirement and a trial. If I'd chosen the trial and the judge had found me guilty, I'd be in a similar situation to what I'm in now, except we call it a penal battalion and eventually I'd have been released."

"You struck your commanding officer?"

Decker nodded.

"I should have let the regimental commander sort him out when we got back to our home station. No way would the colonel have let his file go in front of a promotion board after that, but I have a bit of an anger problem, and that bastard's pig-headed ignorance got to me."

"Do keep in mind that striking me or any other silahdar set above you means a return visit to the juluk pit."

"I get that." Decker's wince was only partly exaggerated.

"Your Corps' loss is our gain, then. Or at least I hope it will be our gain." She pointed at the smooth white wall behind her. "Please draw and explain the operation to me."

For the next three hours, Decker went through half a dozen Pathfinder missions under Daran's detailed interrogation. She had a sharp tactical mind and plenty of combat experience, judging by her probing questions. When Zack finally fell silent, she rose and stretched.

"You know what you're doing, Decker. I can see that. Since it's the latter part of the afternoon, we shall go for a run around the perimeter, and I'll be asking you more questions. After the evening meal, we'll come back here, and I shall have you work out some tactical problems involving a silahdar orta.”

Decker snorted softly.

“You do understand that I’ve never commanded anything bigger than a Pathfinder troop, so battalion tactics are a bit over my pay grade — or would be if I had a pay grade. By the way, if we’re to go running, do I get a change of clothes or am I expected to live in this snazzy uniform until it rots off my body?”

“I shall bring you to the barracks. You’ll find your basic issue waiting for you.” As he followed her out and down one of the well-tended paths, he couldn’t help but notice again the way she moved. The juluk definitely hadn’t broken that part of him.

— SEVEN —

Decker's first glimpse of the silahdar quarters surprised him. He had imagined something less austere than the trainee barracks, but there wasn't much difference between them. They'd assigned him a cot in an open room big enough to house around thirty soldiers, which, as Daran indicated, was where her HQ platoon would lodge. She pointed out her own cot in the corner.

"As I said, slaves have no rank and those with command responsibilities live just as ordinary silahdars would. You will find all you need in the box under your cot."

With that, she went over to hers and stripped out of her uniform in favor of a singlet and light shoes. Decker tried not to admire her hard, if scarred body but failed. The tattoos weren't confined to her skull. Neither was the hairlessness.

As they finished changing and headed for the door, others began to drift in, nodding politely at Daran but looking curiously at Decker. He saw no hostility in their eyes. In fact, he thought he might have glimpsed a sliver of respect from some. Perhaps his new commanding officer wasn't blowing smoke when she called surviving the juluk pit a mark of courage.

The run nearly killed him. After the first two kilometers, it became apparent that the last few weeks had sapped his energy and stamina. Daran was forced to relax her pace so he could keep up. Meanwhile, conversation was reduced to a bare minimum, and when they'd completed one loop, she stopped and looked him over critically.

"We shall have to place you on a special training regimen. I can't say I'm surprised that you're not in as good a shape as you initially appeared to be, but it won't do for a silahdar preparing to deploy. I think a good cool down period is advised."

She took him through a series of extended stretching exercises, some of them bringing the two in close contact, and he remembered that strenuous exercise had a tendency to release his endorphins. Hopefully, the showers wouldn't be co-ed.

They were.

Daran's examination of his equally scarred but as of yet unadorned body under the cascade of warm water caused him momentary embarrassment, but her amused smile soon set him at ease. He'd simply have to get used to a life where privacy was non-existent and where his battalion commander shared the barracks room and showers with her staff. As they got dressed again, he wondered how the slaves worked out that messy sex thing humans liked to practice regularly, but he wasn't about to ask Daran. She might take the question the wrong way.

At the evening meal, she introduced him formally to the others who would form the Fifth Orta's command and staff team. They seemed like a hard, experienced bunch, dominated by people with the strange Nelvan accent though there were a few Commonwealth humans who'd likely been taken by slavers a long time ago.

"Do we get any non-humans in the unit?" He asked Daran around a mouthful of bread.

"No." She shook her head. "The Atabek prefers single species units for combat contracts. It enhances cohesion and simplifies logistics, and clients prefer human silahdars because our species, for some reason, is considered to be the most disciplined and martial in these parts."

"Which is why slavers are willing to go as far as the Commonwealth for merchandise," he replied knowingly. "Humans get a good price at market."

"Just so."

He noticed the others at the table didn't rise above small talk and unit gossip, not even the ones who spoke Anglic with the accent of home, even though they had to be curious about Decker's sudden appearance in their midst.

When they left the mess hall to return to their tactics discussion, he noticed that most of the silahdars had stayed in the large building, sipping drinks, playing games or talking.

"What do you guys do for fun around here?" He asked.

"The eating hall is the social center for this installation," she replied. "There are various diversions. We also have an extensive library of books in many languages. You'll find a reader among your issued kit. Our lifestyle is really quite simple."

"Any place a human can have something alcoholic?"

Her delighted laughter pealed in the evening air.

"The Atabek is very desirous of keeping his silahdars in prime condition, so no. Mind-altering substances or alcohol are not permitted, and as you'll have noticed today, the food is nourishing."

"Damn." Decker sighed. He'd just found the first big downside of this new life, after the whole matter of him being an alien's property, of course. It was going to be a long wait until his next taste of Shrehari ale. He was beginning to think sex was off the list of permitted recreational activities as well when he saw Daran's speculative gaze out of the corner of his eyes, and that lifted his spirits just a bit.

Later that evening, when he slipped into bed, he felt physically and mentally drained, but in a good way for once. The hours they'd spent wargaming had been a lot of fun. He'd forgotten how much he had enjoyed the intellectual part of leading troops: the planning, the debating, and the what-ifs. Sleep came quickly and for the first time since the fateful day of the reiver attack, it came without nightmares. When the morning chimes woke him, he felt refreshed and at greater peace with himself than he had ever since the reivers had taken his ship.

Over the next few weeks, his days alternated between physical training to rebuild his strength and working with Daran's staff to build the battalion. The Atabek wanted the Fifth Orta to be closely modeled on a

Commonwealth Marine light infantry unit, a key selling point as Daran noted, and Decker was the walking encyclopedia who'd make it happen. He began to spend more time with Lora Cyone as well. She'd been appointed battalion armorer with responsibility for all its ordnance. Though he was ordered to speak Danjori at all times so that he could learn faster, when the two of them were alone, they used Anglic.

"I know I'm not supposed to ask, but you've got the markings of someone who went to the same schools as I did," he said one day after they revised the scale of issue for the heavy weapons platoons. "You got the distribution of automatic guns and mortars laid out as per doctrine for a light battalion in a standard line regiment."

She sat back and examined him with her hard eyes. Zack met her gaze with a small, encouraging smile. He knew that under the tough shell, there was another, harder core, but he got the distinct impression she was warming to his sardonic charm.

"If I did, it would have been before your time, so there's no point in singing auld lang syne. Let's just say, for the sake of the Corps, that I was retired when the slavers nabbed me, on a private military company contract that went wrong."

"So you were a filthy corporate merc before you became a slave merc," he joked. "See much difference between the two?"

"Screw you, Decker," she replied in mock disgust.

"Anytime you want, buddy." He grinned. "Just not in the barracks. I'm not the kind to give a show."

She shook her head, but he could see the hint of a smile on her thin lips.

"Trust a Marine to think with his personal weapon when he should be thinking of setting the basic combat load for a composite weapons platoon."

Jase Resson, the battalion second-in-command, stuck his head into the small office, forestalling a retort that was sure to drag the conversation well away from small arms. A short, stocky, middle-aged man, he was another enigma in an outfit teeming with them. By his accent, he was clearly a Commonwealther but Decker hadn't been able to figure out his background like he had Cyone's. Resson had the well-worn look of a long service veteran, but in whose army?

"Time to wrap it up, folks. The Boss Lady wants all the staff to join her on the afternoon run around the perimeter."

In the time it took Decker to shake off his idle thoughts, he realized Resson had spoken in Danjori, and he'd understood it without having to mentally translate. He couldn't remember any other time he'd learned a new language that fast, let alone an alien one.

There was plenty of strange around the slave regiment, the Kashdushiya, starting with the fact he'd been so caught up in the work of designing a battalion along Marine lines that he'd been thinking less and less of his past and the debt he'd vowed to collect.

**

"The Atabek is stripping First and Second Ortas of their most experienced cadres," Daran told the assembled staff, "seeing as how First is taking up the guard contract at the Ytrell mines on the southern continent and Second is going to regenerate after their latest off-world mission. That means we'll be getting the cream of the leadership. The ordinary silahdars will be coming mostly from the current crop of trainees finishing basic, with a leavening from other units."

At the pained look on some of the faces, she smiled.

"It'll be difficult enough to get our folks thinking in terms of the new organization, so be happy that over half the troops won't need re-training. We get fresh minds that we can mold as we wish."

She glanced at Decker, who gave her his usual sardonic smile. He'd been invaluable in designing a light infantry battalion on more professional lines and developing tactics, techniques, and procedures modeled on those of the human Marine Corps. That he'd been doing it enthusiastically, considering his brethren's stance on slavery, didn't even register with her, nor did Zack see anything wrong with it.

"It is the Atabek's desire that we create the most fearsome fighting unit within a hundred light years so that we have a wealth of contracts to choose from. If we need to rid ourselves of some of the old ways, then so be it."

A few of the others looked surreptitiously at Decker, knowing full well from whence came the drive to shed methods and ideas that had served them for decades. His quick elevation to battalion adjutant had not pleased everyone. The silahdars may not have had rank, but they had a keen sense of status among themselves.

Cyone nudged him in the ribs and whispered, "You'll be having us pounding the square with close order drill next, you sad bugger."

He chuckled.

"Give it time. I'll be having these sad sacks jumping out of perfectly good shuttles too."

She shivered.

"Might be fun for some, boyo. Just leave me out of it, though you might want to mind young Norik." She nodded towards the senior company commander. "He's not a big fan of these innovations, and he has a lot of the Nelvans listening to him."

"If he's as smart as he thinks he is, the bugger will go along quietly."

"Anything you'd like to share, Decker?" Mala Daran looked at him curiously.

"No commander. Just commenting to my colleague here that these are fun times."

Daran narrowed her eyes, aware on some level that he was amusing himself at her expense, but she let it pass. Decker had proven invaluable in carrying out the Atabek's will and had become in fact, if not on the roster, the third in line in the Fifth Orta's chain of command, outstripping even Norik, who was first among the balukbashis and quite aware of his station.

The look of pure loathing the latter gave Zack as he replied to Daran's question was educational, to say the least.

"You've all seen the proposed table of organization and equipment I've submitted to the Atabek," she continued, "and I'm pleased to announce that he's approved it. In fact, he's quite satisfied with our work and is looking forward to his first inspection of the new model battalion. The initial drafts from the First and Second Ortas will arrive over the next four days, and the first graduating class from basic training will be turned over to us in a week."

She paused and let her eyes roam over the assembled senior silahdars. Decker's expression still held that mildly amused glint and she was pained to discover it infuriated her.

"I expect excellence from all of you and will accept nothing less. Dismissed."

Zack walked out into the night air with Cyone, ignoring Norik and his clique chattering in low voices behind them.

"Hey, Decker," the senior company commander called out in his thick Anglic accent before they'd had the chance to take more than a dozen steps, "you got some Commonwealth hand-to-hand magic to teach us too? Something that'll beat old Ktek?"

Cyone put her hand on Zack's arm as if to restrain him, but he ignored her.

"The Swordmaster stands in a class by himself," he replied as he stopped and turned around. "I doubt anyone here is going to beat him anytime soon."

"Are you afraid of the green-skinned bastard? I thought you Marines feared nothing." Norik laughed.

"I've met the Swordmaster on the mats. Have you?"

When the other didn't reply, Decker smiled cruelly.

"I guess not. Have a good evening."

He was about to leave when Norik stopped him.

"You and me, Decker. On the mats. Show me how good you are without armor and heavy weapons."

Zack glanced at Cyone. She scowled at him but didn't otherwise comment.

"Now?" He asked.

"Now would be okay. Let's change into appropriate clothing." He muttered a few sentences in Danjori to his cronies and stalked off to First Company's barracks. Decker shrugged and, Cyone in tow, headed in the other direction.

"You know what will happen if either of you damages the other?" She sounded worried, and that brought Zack up short.

"If you're going to say juluk pit, then I might just decide to kill the arrogant little snot and really deserve the punishment."

"Depending on the amount of damage, the penalty could be death, Zack." For the first time, he saw something more than mere concern in her eyes.

"Norik's aware of that, isn't he?"

"No doubt. He was taken as a child and reared as a silahdar from a young age. He's also very skilled at inflicting pain and humiliation without causing permanent harm. You, on the other hand, are trained to kill. I'm afraid Norik is going to goad you into doing something irreparable, perhaps even at the cost of injury to himself just so he can see you gone."

Zack smiled tightly.

"If I didn't know you were a dried-up, heartless old bitch, I'd think you cared about me."

Her punch, when it came, left an impression on his right biceps.

"I may be many things, Zack, but I'm not always heartless. Not with some people. Losing the bout to Norik may not do wonders for your ego, but it might be the best course of action. No one will fault you for being bested, and you get to keep your position as adjutant, where you're needed."

"Are you coming?" He asked when he'd changed into his fighting singlet.

She shook her head.

"Challenges are fought privately."

"No public loss of face for whoever gets the short end of the stick," Decker replied approvingly. "Sensible rule. I've seen too many unscheduled grudge matches when someone gets his ass handed to him in front of his buddies."

Cyone snorted.

"If you beat him, he'll not forgive or forget."

"Then I'd better lose the fight on a technicality if I want him off my back. See you later."

**

The building was empty when Zack let himself through the doors and into the training room. He inhaled the pervasive smell of incense and polish with a strange feeling of nostalgia. The sound of bare feet on wood made him turn around.

"I was afraid you might have decided to forfeit the challenge," malice glinted in Norik's eyes, "but here you are, big as life and ugly as ever."

"Freestyle?" Decker asked, ignoring the jibe.

"By all means, though where an oaf like you is going to find style, free or other, baffles me." The man smiled at his own wit.

Zack shrugged dismissively and turned to take his place at the far edge of the mats. He was unprepared for Norik's sudden rush, having expected the bout to start with the usual courtesies.

The Nelvan struck him hard. Decker went flying backward with the impact and just had time to tuck into a roll, to avoid getting rug burn on his face. A brief flare of rage lit in his gut, but he suppressed it, realizing that was what the other wanted: an angry opponent who'd make mistakes.

Norik was smaller than Zack but just as muscular, and he quickly established that he was faster. He kept the ex-Marine on the defensive through a flurry of leg and elbow attacks Decker immediately recognized as a form of capoeira. Each strike would leave a bruise, but so far Norik had been careful to avoid areas where even a bit too much force could do permanent harm. He seemed so well practiced that Zack had no doubt the man used martial arts training as a way to punish those who crossed him.

The Corps taught several fighting techniques, but as Cyone had reminded him, they were all geared to kill as quickly and with as much violence as possible. He saw the growing look of triumph in Norik's eyes after the next blow made Zack stagger to the side, and that was what he'd been waiting for. Norik danced around to build momentum for what he clearly hoped would be the kick that would send Zack to the mats and end the bout, heedless of telegraphing his next move.

The silahdar's foot lashed out, and Decker dropped into a crouch, hands shooting forward. He grabbed Norik's ankle just as his heel was about to connect with Zack's throat and pushed up, rising at the same time. It was enough to divert the man's momentum onto a vector that threw him completely off balance.

Norik tumbled into a backward roll, rising fluidly to take up his fighting stance again. Surprise and anger had replaced the triumph, and Zack could see him gather his strength for what would be an even more forceful attack.

A loud smack of wood on wood broke the two opponents' concentration, and their heads snapped around to look at the far end of the room, where Ktek had appeared, wearing a black robe, and carrying a long staff.

"Enough," he growled. "The challenge is complete."

"We have no victor," Norik objected.

"And if I allow this bout to continue, you still would have no victor, but the Atabek would have two valuable silahdar damaging each other. I rule that the contest is a draw."

Decker bowed respectfully, accepting the Swordmaster's decision. It was the best outcome he could hope for. Norik wasn't quite as ready to let it go but eventually, under Ktek's cold, black stare, he bowed as well.

"If you would spar with each other in future, you would do so under my supervision. Two men as evenly matched and skilled in dealing out death will eventually forget restraint, and nothing good can ensue."

They both bowed again, to signify acceptance of Ktek's strictures.

When the Swordmaster had gone, Decker walked up to his opponent and stuck out his hand.

"No hard feelings, Norik. You're a damned good fighter, and you might have taken me down, given time."

The silahdar ignored the proffered hand.

"There is no 'might,' Decker. I would have taken you down, and you would have remembered it for a long time."

His face was hard, and his eyes were burning with a mixture of hatred and contempt.

"Take care that you don't give me cause to forget the Swordmaster's instructions and keep in mind that once our Mala Daran has squeezed every last bit of information from your memory, your usefulness won't be much greater than that of any other ordinary soldier."

"While you, on the other hand, are a proven leader with a lot of combat experience and well regarded by the Atabek," Decker nodded, conceding the point, "got it. I'd offer to buy you a beer, but there's none to be had within a few thousand kilometers if not a few hundred light years."

"Just make sure you remember who I am," the man sneered as he turned and left Zack standing alone on the mats, lost in thought.

He hadn't considered that his advisory role might have a best before date, but it would make sense. Once he'd helped them create an effective light infantry battalion patterned on what the Corps fielded, he'd be of more use carrying a machine gun in one of the heavy platoons he'd designed.

"Norik is an excellent fighter," Ktek's raspy voice startled him. Decker turned and nodded politely at the Swordmaster. "But he has not yet learned what you already know instinctively: the only blow that counts is the final one. You did well to restrain yourself. I knew you showed promise when we first met."

Since he had no idea what to respond, Decker bowed again. When he raised his head, the orc was gone.

With the Swordmaster's words still ringing in his ears, he left the building and returned to his barracks. The camp lay silent under a thick cloud blanket that threatened more rain before the night was out. Even the mess hall was dark, where on a typical Marine base it would have been hopping until late in the evening.

Most of the headquarters staff was already sleeping but a few, Daran and Cyone included, were reading. They looked up briefly as Zack entered, then returned to their pads. He smiled tightly at Cyone's quizzical look; the bruises on his body would speak for themselves.

Though Daran seemed uninterested, she must have known about the challenge and by tomorrow she'd know the Swordmaster had declared it a tie, leaving the matter unresolved as far as Norik was concerned.

Decker mentally shrugged. As long as the motherless bastard adopted the TTPs as laid out, he couldn't care less about the commander of First Company. Everything else was Daran's problem.

— EIGHT —

He woke the next morning feeling melancholic for the first time since arriving and remembered the debt he'd vowed to collect. The searching gaze he got from Cyone during breakfast added to his inner misery, and he wondered what had triggered this change in his mood.

Norik nodded curtly as he sat down at the next table. "Decker."

"And a good morning to you as well," Zack forced himself to smile.

"He looks a lot less bruised than you do," Cyone whispered. "I thought you said it ended in a tie."

"So the Swordmaster decreed. He also said the only blow that counts is the final one." He cocked an eyebrow at her.

"Seen." A small smile appeared on her bloodless lips. "If you're quite done emptying out the food stores, we might get to work."

"We might as well." He pushed himself up with a sigh. "I still want to review the translation of the field logistics manual. Considering the mistakes they made with the infantry TTPs, I'd rather not have the Danjori version specify something utterly bizarre. How is it that the Atabek never bothered to hire a military specialist to help him upgrade his organization and methods?"

Cyone shrugged.

"no one around here could do what you did and hiring an advisor from the Commonwealth is an obvious non-starter. I think there's even a law against it back home. A lot of the surrounding systems are like the technobarb kingdoms we all love to hate."

"Even Nelva?"

"Especially them. You'd think a human colony wouldn't regress so much in a few hundred years, but they seemed to have managed it quite well."

"Kid in the training barracks told me they'd been there for a couple of thousand years."

"Bull."

"That's what I said. It has to be tough for them, though. A lost colony, too far from the rest of us for regular contact and obviously prime culling grounds for silahdar force generation."

"Maybe living as a slave soldier for the Atabek beats whatever life they might have had at home." Cyone shrugged dismissively. "They certainly produce interesting specimens. It wouldn't surprise me if it were a high gravity place. A lot of them are almost your size, and you're kind of big for an average human."

"Ain't that the truth?" Decker chuckled.

She elbowed him in the ribs.

"Head out of the gutter, buddy."

"Only if yours gets out of it first." He winked at her.

**

The barracks in their corner of the camp began to fill up as the first drafts of silahdar from other units arrived over the following days. Decker and Cyone were kept busy on the logistics end of things, the former finally equipped with a pair of competent clerks of his own to run the battalion office.

His descent into melancholy hadn't reoccurred amidst the bustle of activity, and he'd put the incident out of his mind. He still got the occasional dirty look from Norik, but the company commander was too busy integrating new arrivals to pursue his vendetta.

The night before the arrival of the new silahdars from basic training, Decker was in the armory, helping Cyone wrap up some paperwork. The Atabek might have been running a slave army, but the bureaucratic nonsense wasn't all that different from what he'd seen in the Corps.

"The records show we're short one carbine, chemical propellant, ten millimeters." He pointed at the screen.

"Let me see." Cyone leaned over the seated ex-Marine, pressing against his back.

The sudden contact and tickling of her earthy scent in his nostrils caused a reaction that shouldn't have been unexpected, but it was. He'd been working side by side with Lora Cyone for weeks and had grown comfortable in her presence. They might have exchanged sexually charged banter from time to time, but he'd not seriously considered anything intimate.

She wasn't his usual type, but he felt an unexpectedly strong attraction he couldn't fight. Turning his head towards her, he brushed against her cheek and reveled in a sensation he hadn't enjoyed for a long time.

Rather than withdraw, Lora leaned in. Their lips met and then, as Zack stood to gather her in his arms, so did their tongues. He might have felt hungry for her, but she seemed to be thoroughly famished. They shed their uniforms and cleared off the metal desk as the urgency overwhelmed them. As far as comfort went, it wasn't much, but at that moment, neither cared.

**

"So what do people who don't have access to a nice private room like the armory do when they want to screw?" Decker asked as they lay together afterward, Lora running her hand over his scarred chest.

"There are a few places around the base where you can catch a few minutes of privacy."

"A few minutes?" Decker chuckled. "I pity them."

She playfully slapped him.

"Bragging again, Zack? I'll agree that you're a bigger boy than most, though."

"So now what?"

"Now? We get dressed, go back to the barracks, shower, and get in bed - our separate beds."

"No. I mean are we still just friends, or are we headed for something more?"

A frown creased her forehead.

"Does it matter? Neither of us is going anywhere until we're posted to separate units and when that happens, it won't matter what we were doing beforehand because it won't occur afterward. Enjoy it, Zack. This place is no different from the Corps in many respects. Shit will happen when it happens."

But Decker was thinking about the women he'd fallen for over the years. Three were dead now, one in his arms from a Sécurité Spéciale assassin, the assassin herself, and the third left to die on a wrecked freighter by the reivers who seized him. He didn't want to get close to another if he was going to see her die as well.

"Let me guess," she said, correctly interpreting the emotions chasing each other across his face, even though Zack tried to conceal his thoughts. "You don't want to get too close. Casual sex is fine, but anything more will mean loss, and you've had enough of that."

"Got it in one," he grunted. After a few moments of contemplation, he told her his story, letting it all out as she listened, enthralled.

"You've led a tough life, Mister Decker," Cyone said when he fell silent. "I can see where you want to stay buddies with me and no more. Can't say I blame you. Can't promise I won't fall for you either, but if that happens, I'll keep it to myself. In the meantime, we have what fun we can. Deal?"

"Deal."

She reached down to grab him, a quiet chuckle in her voice.

"I guess we should shake on it."

Zack reached over to cup her buttock and gave it a squeeze.

"There. All done."

When she didn't let go, he said, "Don't start something you're not going to finish."

"I don't intend to."

Mala Daran gave them strange looks when they got back to the barracks. She was the only one still awake and reading. They trooped off to the showers silently and afterward, slipped into bed separately. Daran's reading light clicked off soon after Decker had turned on his side, eyes closed as he let himself drift off, a contented smile on his face. His last thought was about the annoyance of having his commanding officer bunk with the rest of the staff. It made keeping things quiet a little more difficult.

A few days later, as Zack was by his office window, watching a platoon of silahdar jog by in full fighting order, the battalion's deputy commander walked in, closed the door and went to stand beside him.

"How's it going, Decker?"

"One still hanging lower than the other." He looked suspiciously at Resson. "Busy man like you doesn't take a time-out with the adjutant for no reason."

"I've come to bring a word to the wise. You and Cyone playing hide the salami out of sight, no problem. In fact, I might be just a bit envious, even if she isn't my cup of tea. But you have to be more discreet. The Boss Lady's noticed, and she's none too happy."

Before Zack could open his mouth and say something foolish, Resson raised his hand.

"Nelvans can be pretty uptight about sex compared to us Commonwealthers, some more so than others. What I'm saying is don't advertise by the two of you coming into the barracks together, late in the evening, smelling of *Eau de Rut*. That way you're not waving it in Daran's face. Stagger your arrival out a little, maybe wait until you two don't have that freshly fucked look on your faces. You know — give everyone the pretense that you've actually been working late, not screwing each other's brains out."

"Got it, XO."

Resson clapped him on the shoulder.

"You're a good man, Decker. It would be a shame if you pissed her off enough to be sent down. Seeing as how we're going to fight someone else's war soon enough, I'd rather have a *bona fide* Marine on my team, you know, to increase our chances of beating the other side."

He turned on his heels and headed for the door. Stopping, hand on the latch, he said, "You'll be letting Lora know?"

"For sure. Right after we play a game of you know what."

The deputy commander laughed, made an obscene gesture, and then he left Decker to his thoughts.

**

"Truth for truth," Cyone said, half draped over Zack's body as they lay on a tarpaulin at the back of the weapons shop. "I was in the Corps, did twenty-five years and yeah, I did the master gunner's course when you were probably still a lance-corporal. Cavalry was my basic branch, in the 12th Regiment. They gave me my warrant after I finished the gunner's school. I had one disagreement too many with my superiors and requested a transfer. When the Corps turned it down, I cashed out and applied to the Avalon Military Corporation. They jumped at the chance to get a qualified master gunner."

"Unfortunately," she continued after a slight pause, "they weren't as good when it came to vetting contract offers. My company group was sent deep into the Coalsack and didn't come out again. Those of us who survived the massacre were captured and sold off. I ended up here when the slavers advertised my credentials. Going on fifteen years now."

"No escape, eh?"

"Not a chance. The Nelvans seem to like the lifestyle, and they'll make sure a body doesn't go AWOL from the Kashdushiya – they actually like putting people in the juluk pit, the sadistic bastards. But you get used to it. Running an armory here or in the Corps isn't much different. I have no one back home waiting for me, and I doubt Avalon would take me back. That mission was such a fuck-up I'm sure they'd rather it remained buried forever so the shareholders don't find out what idiots they appointed to the executive suite."

"Sounds familiar," Zack snorted derisively. "Good non-coms get screwed over and end up fighting for no money."

"By the way," he pushed himself up on his elbows and looked down at her, "the XO gave me his best Uncle Jase speech. It seems the Boss Lady's not too happy about us showing up in barracks smelling of each other and looking happier than the rest."

Cyone grunted.

"Jealous, more like. I've seen the way she sometimes looks at you. I'll bet the only reason she's not eaten you up yet is that she figures she can't afford to be seen playing with a subordinate, which is common sense. But I get the message. Resson's good people and he wouldn't have warned you if it wasn't for real. A quick sponge bath in the armory washroom is probably a good idea from now on, and if my inner clock is right, we should shove off. I get first dibs."

When Zack got to the barracks, both Cyone and Daran were tucked in and ostensibly sleeping. The wipe down hadn't done much to remove Lora's scent, but he slipped into bed anyways, smiling to himself. After the morning run, he'd smell only like good, honest Zack Decker, erstwhile command-sergeant, 902nd Pathfinder Squadron.

******

"Sanjaqui."

Mala Daran nodded pleasantly at Zack as she joined him on the low hill overlooking the training ground. Both were in full silahdar fighting order, and Decker felt more like a historical re-enactor than a twenty-sixth-century soldier. It was probably good enough for the technobarb kingdoms who bought the services of slave soldiers, but he'd rather be wearing solid Pathfinder scout armor.

"Commander."

He displayed his most charming Decker grin, mainly to acknowledge the thawing in her manner since he and Cyone had become more discreet.

"How's Second Company doing?"

"They still look like a herd of *veerats* humping ant hills, but at least they're not scoring own goals every few seconds." The Danjori vernacular had come to him more quickly than he expected and his comment drew a brief smile.

"We have a few weeks left before the Atabek wishes to see a full-fledged battalion demonstration. I hope

Second Company's tendencies will have morphed into something more useful."

"If you think they're bad, you haven't seen Third Company yet." He grimaced. "They haven't graduated to humping ant hills yet. I think their cadre can't wrap their heads around the new TTPs."

"Perhaps they need some encouragement," she mused. Zack felt a chill run down his spine at her tone. A brief vision of the company commander, a pleasant Nelvan, staked down and overrun by bugs flashed in front of his eyes. He wouldn't ever wish that on her or on anyone else. Not after what he'd been through.

"They're the most recently formed," he replied. "Give them another two weeks or so and they'll be as good as that lot below."

"And them?" She nodded at the skirmishers crossing the training field.

"They'll be up to First Company's standard. Krait's no dummy."

"Some disagree with your assessment of Second Company's balukbashi." She raised a skeptical eyebrow.

"Norik thinks he's the only one who knows how to maneuver his unit. We have a saying back where your ancestors came from, 'pride goes before the fall.' I'd keep my eye on the lad once we're in operations. He might be your biggest liability."

Daran scoffed at the idea.

"Just because he almost beat you in the challenge doesn't make him a bad commander."

"No," Decker agreed, "only an overconfident one. The Swordmaster stopped the fight because I was about to break his neck."

"That's not what Norik said."

"Then with all due respect, commander, you've made my point."

"How would that be?"

"Norik boasted to you."

Daran seemed at a loss for words and averted her eyes. He could see her jaw working as she processed the thought and after a while she looked up at him again.

"Some days I wonder whether you're still a feral ex-Marine, my sanjaqui."

He shrugged as if it didn't matter.

"My work here speaks for itself. That bunch down there couldn't find its collective ass with both hands two weeks ago. Now, they're capable of giving most armies a deadly dose of silahdar love."

She nodded thoughtfully.

"Point well taken. I shall keep an eye on Norik."

"Then pay particular attention to his company's martial arts sessions. There's a reason his troops have twice as many training injuries as the rest of the Fifth Orta. You'll no doubt have observed that fact after reading my daily reports."

When she didn't respond, he knew that she had noticed and had so far failed to make the connection. It was a small thing, but lump it in with the other little things Decker had been tracking and it all added up to Daran's lack of experience at commanding such a large unit.

He could produce the best training plans, organizational designs, and tables of equipment, but if the battalion commander wasn't up to the job, she could get them in trouble pretty quickly when the plasma began to fly. Not for the first time, he wondered how she'd gotten the assignment to form the first unit based on Marine light infantry lines.

Her reaction to his and Lora's relationship wasn't exactly designed to inspire confidence either, cultural differences notwithstanding. Jealousy in a senior officer was a dangerous thing for everyone under her command.

"Keep me apprised of progress," she finally said before turning to leave.

"As you wish."

Decker quickly bowed at the neck to acknowledge the order. He watched her climb aboard her skimmer, take off, and vanish behind the tree line.

Turning back to the mock battle below him, he made a few notations on his pad. The after action review was going to be rough for Krait, but the bugger would learn from it, which was more than he could say for Norik. The commander of First Company was good, but he reminded Zack of the man who'd cost him his career: too eager for promotion, even at the expense of his troops. Nelvans or Commonwealthers, ambition remained an all too human trait, and it all too often meant that ordinary soldiers paid the price.

— NINE —

"My evaluation is ready." Zack stood at attention inside the doorway, filling the frame with his solid bulk. Daran and Resson looked up from the map spread over the table in the battalion commander's office.

"Come in," Daran nodded, "and close the door. I think your comments are not for everyone's ears."

"Very much not," he replied with a grimace while he did as she ordered.

"We were planning the battalion demonstration for the Atabek's benefit."

"You may want to hold off on that a little longer, commander. There's still a problem to iron out before this unit can fight as more than a couple of disjointed companies."

"Norik?" Resson asked.

"Yeah."

Daran sighed and waved Zack to a chair.

"What is it now?"

"He's operating under the belief that his shit doesn't stink," Decker replied. "He refuses to adapt to the new TTPs. Oh, he'll make a great show of it when one of us is around, but I've watched him when he thought no one outside First Company was in the area. As far as he's concerned, this realignment on Marine light infantry lines is just bullshit, and that means his troops don't know which way to turn."

"Is it that bad?"

"It's worse, XO. He hasn't wrapped his head around the use of his heavy platoon. The other company commanders have, but not Mister Norik. He keeps using it as his reserve instead of pushing the weapons teams forward to support the rifle platoons. Last after action report I gave him on the subject almost ended badly for him. I've got a real aversion to assholes yelling at me where the troops can hear every word."

"Norik is one of our best," Daran said, looking worried. "He was given First Company at the Atabek's command."

"And someone is going to get sent to a rifle platoon as blank file filler when the Atabek sees the clusterfuck that I guarantee will occur when you have two rifle and one Support Company following a single set of TTPs and the other doing whatever it likes."

"We should run First Company through all its paces again," Resson suggested, "and make sure we're there to watch."

"As I said, he'll put on a good show. To really get a sense of it, I suggest all three rifle companies be pushed to the next level. Second and Third Companies will be able to handle it, even if they won't look slick. Norik's not so much."

"You have an idea?" Daran looked at him quizzically.

"Always," Zack grinned. He went on to explain what he had in mind. When he was done, the two senior silahdars nodded, thinking about his proposal.

"You do realize that if Norik humiliates himself in front of his troops, things will get seriously ugly."

"No question, XO," Decker shrugged. "But I'd rather it get ugly here while we're not shooting live ammo than on a mission twenty light years into the back of beyond where the games are for real."

"You don't yet understand how the Nelvans think, Decker. They're a lot touchier than we are, and a mortal offense can turn, well, mortal."

"I'm starting to get the picture, Jase. While we're on that subject, did either of you notice that First Company is all Nelvan, unlike the others?"

Both Daran and Resson nodded.

"Company commanders have some latitude in choosing their silahdars," she replied.

"And there's some prejudice against Commonwealthers?"

"We're considered softer, less adaptable by some Nelvans," Resson said, "Norik being the most obvious example of that kind of thinking."

"Yeah," Decker snorted, "I have no problems believing guys like him are harder. A skull filled with rocks is pretty tough. As for adaptability, looking at the training results, the less said, the better."

Daran seemed pained at his contemptuous tone.

"You have to understand that those of us born to the silahdar or taken at a young age have a hard time finding respect for captured slaves who don't adapt well. It may not be fair, but it is human. Many Nelvans taken into captivity have as much difficulty adjusting as Commonwealthers do. This is why the Atabek encourages the breeding of silahdars."

"I'll bet," Decker replied, a sour note in his voice. "If you want my opinion, you'd do better to reshuffle the troops around so you don't have one company filled only with people like Norik. A wise man once said that if everyone's thinking the same, then someone's not thinking."

"Understood," Daran nodded. "But it's too late for any significant changes. The companies have been training together for weeks, and we don't have enough time left before we have to be ready for use."

"Ready for use." Zack chuckled. "Just like we're tools, eh? I don't think I'll ever understand you people."

"You will in time, buddy," Resson gave him a friendly punch on the arm. "We all do."

"Heh." Decker shook his head, unsure of his feelings. Not for the first time, he got the strange sensation that life among the silahdar might not be so bad after all.

But you have a debt to collect, he reminded himself. Once that's done, you can spend the rest of your life screwing around with slave soldiers, in both the figurative and literal sense.

"So are we agreed on the combat readiness test?" He asked, pushing his inner conflict aside.

"We are," Daran said.

"It'll only work if you take personal charge, commander. I'll do the staff work, like a good sanjaqui, but I've got to stay in the background."

"Indeed, commander." Resson agreed. "When it comes time to sort Norik out, it'll be better coming from you than through an after action review from Decker."

"So be it then," Daran rose from her chair. "I wish to see the plan by the end of day tomorrow."

"You will." Zack nodded formally.

**

They watched First Company vanish into the misty forest on the opening leg of their test. Mala Daran was shadowing Norik to evaluate his every move. If the Nelvan silahdar resented her presence, he kept it well hidden.

"That's me then." Zack thumped Resson on the shoulder. "It's time to get Third Company out to their positions. It'll be interesting to see Norik's clusterfuck from the other side."

"You think he'll bugger it up?"

"Guaranteed. The way the battle run is set up, if he doesn't use his heavy weapons properly and doesn't deploy in accordance with Marine TTPs, he'll get creamed."

"Yeah and he won't be too happy that it's a Commonwealther who does it to him."

Resson's smile was almost beatific.

Decker climbed into his skimmer and lifted off, heading for the first of three combat problems strewn along Norik's path.

It was almost dark by the time he set down behind the well-hidden ambush site. First Company wouldn't pass by until just before sunrise and most of the troops, other than security elements, were in a hide, eating and resting. The platoon leader, Tran Kidder, was a middle-aged human who'd been taken from a colony ship that had strayed well out of the Commonwealth thanks to a faulty navigation computer. He'd been with the

Kashdushiya for almost two decades, having risen through the ranks by sheer pig-headed determination.

"Hey sanjaqui," he whispered after the sentries had let him pass, "how're they hanging?"

"Still the same, Tran. Glad to see your folks are awake and doing it right."

Kidder smiled.

"Doing it right is my motto, as friend Norik is going to find out in a few hours. Kahvass?" He nodded at a trooper busy around a flameless stove.

"Sure," Decker replied, settling on a fallen tree trunk beside the other man. Kahvass, the local stimulant drink, wasn't exactly as good as real coffee, but it had to do. He pulled a battered canteen cup from his fighting rig and held it out to the silahdar.

"How are your kids feeling?" Decker asked once he'd taken a sip of the bitter liquid.

"Nervous," Kidder admitted. "This is the first time we've gone force on force within the battalion, and everyone knows that Norik does things whichever way he wants."

"Not that you're gossiping," Zack grinned, his teeth unnaturally white in the growing darkness. "It's okay to be nervous, just as long as they do their jobs right. If Norik does his job right, he'll likely get the best of you. If he doesn't, then your ambush could be a success."

"The Boss Lady's with him, right?"

"Yep. It's company evaluation time. When you guys go through your battle run, she'll be tailing your commander the same way."

"And you're not here to evaluate me at all." Kidder sounded skeptical.

"Everyone's always being evaluated, but my primary job here is to look at First Company's actions from the enemy side. Mind you, if you fuck it up, I will be holding a formal after-action review on this platoon."

"Then I better make sure we get Norik good. My boss may not be as touchy as your average Nelvan, but she's still got a lot of pride, and she doesn't like her platoon leaders to get jacked up by a damned Marine."

"No company commander does." Zack drained his kahvass and shook the last drops from the mug before stowing it. "At what time are you calling the stand-to?"

"Four. Intel has the target due to come through around five thirty."

"Word to the wise, Tran," Zack patted him on the shoulder as he rose, "make it three. In the dark it takes twice as long to get into position and betting on the enemy to arrive on time rather than forty minutes early is always going to give you grief."

"Got it." Kidder nodded. "You can curl up at the base of the tree here. You'll get woken with the rest."

**

A gloved hand gave Zack a gentle shake, and he rolled onto his back, eyes snapping open. He saw a dark shadow that waited until he sat up before going on to the next sleeping trooper.

The Atabek's armory didn't go to sophisticated battle suits, but the face shield attached to the silahdar helmet did adequate double duty as a night vision device and primitive battle computer readout. He slipped his on and activated it. Two-fifty.

Someone had been thinking. Wake the leadership up first and then the rest, making sure the last trooper was up by three.

He could see the silahdars packing their gear and forming into squads, ready for the signal to move out. They were under radio silence so everything was done by hand signal or in a low voice. It wouldn't do to have Norik's folks pick up stray emissions.

Kidder tapped his arm.

"We're moving into position now. Where do you want to be?"

Decker had given it some thought. Sitting with the platoon leader in the middle of the ambush zone might give him a general idea of the action, but he would learn more about Norik's readiness by joining the rear cut-off team. If the commander of First Company had done his usual planning, the heavy platoon would be tail-end charlie and outside the ambush zone, where it wouldn't do a damn bit of good during the opening moves. Of course, it was always possible that Norik might think it out properly once the fight was on and swing them around to drive through Kidder's flank.

"Rear cut-off."

"Follow me."

He led Decker to the squad leader charged with securing the entrance of the ambush zone.

"Have fun, sanjaqui."

"Isn't that what we're all here for?"

"Not even close." Kidder shook his head. "We're all here because we're not all there."

Decker laughed at the wry expression.

"Good luck. Try to learn something from the enemy's experience. It beats learning by getting your ass kicked."

With an assurance born from long training, the four silahdars and Decker slipped between the trees, steps muffled by the rotting vegetation and headed for the spot where the valley narrowed sharply enough to force Norik right into Kidder's ambush.

If the Nelvan had been thinking, he'd have figured out this was the riskiest part of his approach and planned accordingly, like put some heavy weapons up front, where they could tear up the enemy. But Norik had proven over and over that he preferred to plow his way through problems with brawn rather than brains. If he was considered one of the best, it said something about the quality of military leadership in this part of the galaxy.

Thankfully, the commander of Third Company wasn't that single-minded. She'd given Kidder a heavy weapons detachment and the platoon leader, in turn, had split them evenly between the two cut-off teams and the main body.

The silahdars settled in, machine guns sited behind bushes, ready to push out when they received the order to open fire. The squad leader had done a proper reconnaissance during the daylight hours, and there was little chance that Norik's scouts would stumble over them. They just didn't have enough time to thoroughly clear the forest on either side of the small stream that provided the only open path.

Part of Zack's plan had been to force the company commanders into situations where they had to make hard choices so Daran could see how they handled themselves. The inflexibility of getting to the assigned target on time was going to drive them into making mistakes, and the only question was how bad and how they'd recover. It wouldn't quite be a no-win scenario, but it wouldn't be pretty.

Decker lay down between the silahdars and made himself comfortable enough so he'd not be stiff when it was time to pull out, but not so much that he'd fall asleep. He passed the time trying to identify, from memory, the nocturnal creatures around him by sound. For all that Danjor was alien, its wildlife wasn't terribly exotic. Decker could easily link Earth equivalents to the various avians, reptilians, and what passed for mammals.

He was so lost in thought he almost missed the faint sound of boots carefully walking among the stones on the stream's far side. His time readout showed it was just shy of five o'clock. Norik was pushing the pace.

The indistinct shapes of scouts materialized in the darkness. Zack noted with approval that they moved cautiously, one leap-frogging the other to pause, listen, and watch before his partner took the next bound.

A second set of footsteps sounded on the near side of the stream. Norik had set out two scout teams. Perhaps there was hope for the bastard after all.

Funny, Decker thought, the critter noises had stopped. He smiled to himself. If Kidder was paying attention, he'd have his platoon on full alert by now.

None of the scouts left the narrow open space between the stream and the forest's edge, even though the vegetation was relatively sparse compared to deeper in among the trees. If Zack had been in charge, he'd have figured that the tight slash through the hills would be prime ambush country. He'd have told his scouts to spread out and check the first couple of meters into the woods, even if it slowed them down. The sensors issued to the silahdars were primitive compared to what

Marines used and couldn't detect human bodies wearing Kashdushiya-issued battledress.   Not if they were keeping tight emcon.

Norik's men vanished into the darkness and not a minute later, the sounds of many feet arose from the still night as the first of four platoons passed the cut-off team.

They moved well, kept proper spacing and seemed alert.   But he didn't see heavy weapons detachments interspersed with the rifle platoons, let alone the heavy platoon as a single formation in the middle of the column.

Daran's shape was easy to distinguish as she passed by along with the small cluster that was the company headquarters team.   Decker mentally calculated time and distance, and just as he was about to urge Kidder on, the radio came to life with a single word.

"Fire."

Immediately the machine guns to either side began hammering realistically as they shot training rounds that were designed merely to trigger the war games sensor each silahdar wore.   To his right, the remainder of Kidder's platoon opened up and the night was torn apart by the gunfire.   Norik had his company shooting back within seconds, but it didn't sound organized.

Decker shifted his position to get a better glimpse of the soldiers that hadn't entered the kill zone, and there it was, big, bold, and clear as day: the heavy weapons platoon.   Considering how little use Norik had made of them in previous training exercises, it was little wonder that its leader was unable to take the initiative and force his way into Kidder's flank.

Training grenades exploded, sending puffs of white powder into the air and triggering the sensor of anyone who'd have been within the danger radius.   First Company's radio net was alive with shouts, barely decipherable orders, and general confusion. Kidder, on the other hand, remained silent as his platoon kept shooting.

The volume of fire from First Company began to decrease and then dwindle away as the sensors registered hits and disabled the wearers' weapons. The heavy platoon, stuck on the other side of the cut-off, failed to move.

They returned fire, to be sure, and managed to force the cut-off squad deeper into the woods, but Norik had either forgotten its existence or he'd been hit, and his radio disabled. The Nelvan wasn't one to foster a take-charge attitude among his subordinates, lest his methods are challenged. Now, his ego had bitten him in the behind.

"Withdraw."

The single word cracked in Decker's ears, and he saw the cut-off squad scramble behind a thicket of trees before rising to jog back to the collection point from which the platoon would get out of range before Norik, or whoever was now in command, could call down notional artillery support.

Since his skimmer was also there, he followed them. Daran would give him the run-down on her side of the operation when they met to compare notes in two or three days.

By the time the platoon reunited on the far slope of the ridge, Daran had reset the war games by reviving everyone's sensor and getting Norik back on track. Zack did a quick headcount of Kidder's people who were showing as wounded or dead and was impressed to see how few casualties they'd suffered. Kidder been paying attention during the work-up training and had pulled out at the right moment.

The tendency to withdraw early could be insidious. An ambush was complete chaos at the best of times, and if the victim wasn't quite out of the fight by the time the ambushers left, it could get ugly. Shot in the back kind of ugly.

"You did well, Tran." He clapped the man on the shoulder.

"Buggers just stood there, sensors blinking on as we got them. It was breathtaking. For us, I mean, not for the poor idiots of First Company."

"No reaction at all?"

"Oh, they got themselves sorted out right quick and dove into the woods on the far side of the stream. But short of climbing the cliff in full view of my position, they weren't getting out anywhere other than through my folks. By the time it occurred to them that they needed to charge at us, they didn't have much left that was still walking."

Kidder shook his head.

"For all their crowing about being the best in the Fifth Orta, they sure as shit didn't show it."

"That's what happens when you don't evolve while others do."

"Wiser words were never spoken on this night," Kidder sonorously replied. "I'm guessing the Boss Lady will be ripping friend Norik a new and improved orifice."

"No doubt. Make sure you don't revert back to the old ways when it's your turn to go through the battle run."

"Fat chance of that." Kidder snorted.

Decker grinned at him in the darkness.

"Glad to hear it. Now off with you. The thopters won't wait forever."

"Enjoy the next one, Decker." He waved his troops into line. "Or rather, don't enjoy it *too* much."

"No promises."

Once they'd vanished, Zack climbed aboard his skimmer and shot up through the narrow opening between the trees. Glancing at his navigation readout, he pointed the tiny craft at a ridge ten kilometers away.

— TEN —

Daran must have given Norik a right reaming out, because his approach to the next target, later that day, was better than he'd expected.

Too bad it didn't last.

Decker and Daran had to physically pound on a couple of troopers who got at it hand-to-hand when the assaulting platoon took exactly the wrong way to the objective and stumbled onto one of Third Company's defensive positions. This time, Norik had placed his heavy platoon in the right position to support the attack, but regrettably, it wasn't quite good enough to help the unfortunates sent through a narrow gully.

The silahdars of First Company weren't used to getting their heads handed to them like that. Norik had spent so much time talking up Nelvan superiority that they believed they could do anything, even if it was backed by poor planning and even more careless recon.

The battalion commander called a reset to the operation and forced Norik to go through all the steps again, by the book, before letting him launch his attack. Decker had stayed carefully out of sight after separating the brawlers, and he was sure Norik was cursing him to whatever gods the Nelvans believed in. It was no secret that the ex-Marine had designed the combat course and that he was lurking somewhere on the mock battlefield.

By the time Norik finally swept over the defenders after a more satisfactory performance, Decker was already perched the next ridge to watch the action from a distance. Though the battle run was as much a test of character as it was of combat skills, sticking around would only serve to goad the Nelvan and it wasn't time for that yet. Not long after the thopters pulled out the defenders, he saw Daran take Norik aside for the after action review. With nothing more to see, Zack left for the site of the third and final tactical problem, where Norik would face the entire strength of Third Company.

**

"It hardly seems fair," Jan Latour, the company commander, said as she handed Zack, a hot ration pack. "Even if Norik's the tactical god he thinks he is, there's no way he manages this one."

"You've never heard of a no-win situation, I take it?" Decker cocked an ironic eyebrow at the short, brawny woman. "War isn't fair, and some tactical problems are more designed to reveal how a leader reacts under pressure than to test his battle skills."

"So you're going to do this to me as well next week?"

"We'll do something to you for sure, but you'll have no idea going in what that is. Combat's full of surprises, some fun, some not so enjoyable. All I can tell you is that each of you gets something that pokes at your weaknesses."

"You're a strange one, Decker," she shook her head. "I've never seen a newly captured Commonwealther take to this slave soldier life as quickly and with as much enthusiasm as you have."

"Adapt and overcome, Jan." He took a bite of the protein slab. "I'm good at fighting, and if I'm stuck here until they spread my ashes over the manure pile, I might as well do what I've done all my adult life. Or most of my adult life."

"True," she nodded, eyes staring over Zack's shoulder at a point in the distance.

Sensing that the conversation had roused something long suppressed, he contented himself with his meal and another in a long string of hot kahvass servings.

Supper taken care of, Decker walked around the company perimeter in the growing twilight, chatting briefly with the silahdars to gauge their morale and confidence. The ones who belonged to Tran Kidder's platoon were, understandably, a bit cocky after their successful ambush the previous night, but Kidder seemed to have no overconfidence issues.

He was more worried about the platoons that had defended against Norik's raid during the afternoon. There were still some lingering bad feelings, and he had a quick private talk with the platoon leaders to make sure things didn't get out of hand tomorrow. Satisfied that all was ready for the next morning, he settled down on a pile of leaves and did like every good infantryman when he had a bit of quiet time: he fell asleep.

**

Zack woke with a start. The jungle was smothered in a thick blanket of mist and in the darkness, all sounds were muffled. He tried to figure out what had jerked him out of his slumber. His internal clock still hadn't adapted to Danjor's rotational cycle and the hour remained a mystery until he pulled on his helmet and called up the display: another two hours until sunrise. Norik's company wasn't due to arrive for an hour after that, even moving at best speed, yet the jungle critters had fallen silent. He felt a body stir near him.

"You too?" Latour whispered, rolling over and onto her knees.

"Something's out there."

"The sentries haven't alerted," she replied dubiously.

"If I were Norik, I'd have sent out a platoon's worth of recon patrols. Maybe they're here." He breathed in deeply as if to catch a human spoor on the Danjoran air.

"Any advice?"

"I'm just here as an observer. You're on your own."

He slowly stood up, senses alert, and let his ears scan the perimeter. If Norik pulled off a surprise against Third Company, he might just save his bacon along with his pride, but there was no way he could have moved his entire unit this far, this quickly. At best, there couldn't be more than a handful of patrols just beyond sensor range, staking out the position.

Latour scurried away to find the company pickets while all around Decker, troopers stirred silently as their squad leaders nudged them awake.

If Norik's recon was the reason for Third Company standing to before time, the game was over before it had started. Of course, he reminded himself, in a no-win situation, there was never a fair game to begin with.

Decker joined Latour and her platoon leaders when he saw them coalesce in the middle of the hide. Instinctively, they made room for him in the tight circle, even though he wasn't part of their team.

"The sentries have picked up four separate instances of movement to our front," Latour said in a tone so low it didn't carry more than a meter. "Scans are, as expected, inconclusive since whoever's out there is on tight emcon. We're going to begin withdrawing as per plan when I'm done talking and suck them into the kill zone. They're a bit earlier than we expected and the trap might not work if their recon finds this place abandoned, but they'll still come looking for us. Any questions?"

When no one replied, she nudged one of the platoon leaders.

"Off you go, Harry."

Ten minutes later, Third Company left the hide silently, hoping that Norik's recon patrols would believe they were still there. A few flameless cookers had been left behind, merrily boiling kahvass pouches, just to confuse their sensors.

"Shame, though," Latour muttered as they trudged up a narrow path that would have challenged the best Earth-born mountain goat.

"What is?" Decker's breath was becoming as labored as that of the other silahdars.

"Leaving all that kahvass to those arrogant bastards."

"They can have it for all I care. It's an evil brew."

"Sure, but you have to admit it has a good kick."

"That's because it tastes so vile." He grimaced in the darkness. "I hope your folks didn't spike the stuff with anything amusing on the off chance that someone would be thirsty. I'd rather not see a company's worth of soldiers puking, getting the runs or start humping trees."

"Seriously, Decker?" She snorted softly. "You noticed yet that this outfit is kind of short on practical humor?"

"Yeah. I guess I have," he replied, remembering the juluk pit.

When they reached the summit of the ridge, Latour made sure her company was deployed in proper order while Decker headed for a promontory to the left of the path. It would give him a good enough perch to watch the action without being in the way.

He settled down to wait for the curtain to open on the third and final problem of this battle run, wondering what would happen to Norik if he seriously screwed the pooch again in front of his battalion commander. Surely a blowhard who failed because he couldn't be bothered to apply the new TTPs wouldn't amuse Daran.

An hour passed, then two, and a band of molten lead began to paint the far horizon as the sun rose behind the clouds, yet Decker sensed no movement below. Norik was taking his time, which would be nice if his recon patrols had done their job and he didn't waste what they brought back. But if they hadn't spotted Third Company pulling out, he could be preparing a deliberate attack on an empty hide, which would put him right under the guns on the ridge.

Although Decker thoroughly disliked the conceited Nelvan, he hoped there would be a marked improvement in his performance for the final act if only to avoid throwing the battalion in turmoil when the Atabek expressed his displeasure. He wasn't even sure that any of Norik's screw-ups would rebound on him personally. Their owner might just take it out on Daran for having failed to school one of her subordinates.

Without warning, the vale below him erupted in heavy gunfire. From either flank, heavy machine guns hammered the humid dawn air, underscored by dozens of grenade launchers peppering the shallow bowl at the center of the depression. It sounded like Norik was expending his ammunition at a high enough rate to run out before realizing he'd been suckered.

When there was no return fire, First Company slacked off until silence returned to the forested crags. The critters, stunned by the noise, remained carefully hidden and quiet, leaving nothing but the sound of the wind sighing through the purplish, fern-like trees.

Shouted orders rang out and soldiers in silahdar battledress cautiously advanced up the vale and to the tree line where brush gave way to a rock-strewn rise at the base of the cliff.

First Company's radio frequency came to life.

"Nothing more than heaters and kahvass bulbs," a rough voice reported.

"They're here, somewhere." Norik sounded agitated. "You don't set a trap and then leave it without covering fire."

"I'm telling you. Whatever recon reported a few hours ago is gone." The rough and now increasingly testy voice belonged to one of the platoon leaders, Ker Terkis. "They were here, but they're not anymore."

"There's no way an entire company could have vanished into thin air. Recon would have seen them pass if they tried to exit the valley."

"Then maybe they levitated." The undisguised sarcasm was a sure sign that his patience with the egotistic company commander had just about run out.

Decker smiled. Terkis was, from what he'd seen, the better of the platoon leaders and apparently not shy about laying out the truth. The fact that this discussion was occurring at all and over the company net, showed the beginnings of a breakdown in the command relationship.

Without rank to impose on subordinates, all a commander had was the Atabek's appointment and his or her own leadership ability. If the last tactical problem was to be as much a test of character as of skill, then Norik's chances of failing looked pretty good.

"Search the cliff face. Maybe they've found a cave or a passage."

Third Company had masked the path after the last trooper had passed, but it wouldn't take much to poke through the camouflage and realize that there was indeed another way out, even if it seemed more suited to mountain beasts.

"Will do." Truculence replaced sarcasm. "Though it may have occurred to you that our mission coordinates were wrong all along, and that Third Company only left us some tidbits to attract our attention. For all we know, they could be preparing to take us from the rear."

Norik swore in Nelvan Anglic, his strange accent making the scatological expressions sound weirdly colorful to Zack's ears.

Latour had been given wide latitude in deciding when and how to open fire. If Norik chose to turn around and leave the vale, she might let him go. Her mission was to stop his advance, not destroy his company. The Nelvan on the other hand, had to find and pin down Third Company so that a notional battalion attack could be mounted.

With frantic orders, Norik turned his other platoons, including the heavy platoon, back towards the far end of the valley, by all appearances sure that his worst fears were about to materialize.

For the next hour, Decker watched First Company spin around in circles, wondering what was going through Daran's mind as she watched the company commander lose his grip on the situation. It was almost enough to make him wish she'd call an end to the battle run and put Norik out of his misery. He was three for three when it came to missing the mark.

When Terkis found the steep, rocky path at the far end of the crevasse, Norik seemed uninterested and gave the platoon leader leave to reconnoiter.

Latour let them climb up and through her masked fighting positions before springing the trap. Terkis' men didn't even get off a shot. They were tired, frustrated and getting more demoralized by the minute. Surrendering under the barrels of the heavy platoon's machine guns seemed like the best thing to do. Those who wanted to play hero thought better of it when they saw Decker shake his head.

Third Company quickly collected the helmets as they disarmed them, to make sure no signal made it back to Norik. As far as he'd know, the platoon had vanished just as mysteriously as his quarry.

Decker flicked his radio over to the encrypted command channel.

"Latour took Terkis' platoon without a shot. I suggest you end the battle run before Norik humiliates himself any further. He probably doesn't have much credibility left with his silahdars. It would be kinder that way."

"Agreed," Daran replied after a few moments. "Stand Third Company down and have them, along with Terkis' troops, start for the landing area. I'll call the thopters."

"Acknowledged."

Decker headed towards the hollow between two large boulders on the ridge's reverse slope where Latour had established her headquarters. The silahdars from First Company were sitting disconsolately nearby, though Terkis was chatting quietly with his captors.

At his approach, Latour looked up expectantly.

"I gather you have news."

"The battle run is over. Have your troops secure weapons and unload all ammunition." He pulled off his helmet and ran a gloved hand over his bald skull. "You're to head for the LZ and take the thopters back to the forward operating base. Terkis, you go with Third Company, seeing as how it makes little sense to send you all the way down the cliff and across the valley to rejoin your commander. They'll be flying out to the FOB in due course."

Both Latour and Terkis nodded formally to acknowledge the order, knowing that things had ended on a sour note. The next few hours might get rather interesting, but neither thought it prudent to question Decker.

With a resigned sigh, Zack made sure he had all of his gear and then headed downhill towards the small glade where he'd parked his skimmer. It was time to lay low in the command tent. A storm was coming, and he didn't want to be in its path, even though he was responsible for its genesis.

**

Jase Resson, alone in the headquarters bunker at the heart of the FOB, looked up from his field desk when Decker shoved the door flap aside and walked in with a face like thunder.

"Bad?"

"You have no idea, XO." Decker dropped into a folding chair and unfastened his combat harness. "On the bright side, the boys and girls from Second and Support Company have this place buttoned up tight. Couldn't find fault with any of the defensive arrangements or the way they made sure I wasn't some asshole trying to infiltrate."

"Holding this place is easy." Resson made a face. "Running that cruel gauntlet you call a battle test isn't. By the look on your ugly mug, I'm guessing the Boss Lady isn't going to enjoy giving her after action report to the Atabek."

"Nope." Decker shook his head. "If I'm right that the Atabek was figuring Norik as his golden boy, destined for great things as slave soldiering goes, he'll have to think again. The idiot didn't take the battle run seriously, even though he knew better. Latour was fully switched on, and her platoon leaders had his ass for breakfast, twice. The third time, he got spooked and shot up an empty position, after which he panicked and turned one-eighty on Latour. He even lost Terkis' platoon without realizing it. At that point, I suggested we call it a day."

Resson whistled.

"Oh, that's going to hurt. This is one of those times I'm glad that the Atabek prefers Nelvans for battalion command."

"You think he's going to relieve Daran?"

"Doubtful. He has to have a lot invested in offering a light infantry battalion trained on Commonwealth Marine lines. Daran was always the first and only choice. She's the smartest among the senior silahdar and if anything, a bigger favorite with our owner than Norik."

"So Norik's done."

"Like a carbonized steer. The Atabek has little patience for failure, notwithstanding the boy's previous stardom among us peasants. He'll be relieved of command pretty much the moment Daran lands with the rest of First Company. Speaking of which, I hope you told Terkis to make himself scarce."

"Yeah. I can figure out what Norik might do once he realizes he's got nothing left to lose."

"Good. Terkis is the smartest of the Nelvan meatheads in First Company. It'd be a shame if anything happened to him. Norik's successor is going to need all the help he can get to repair the damage and have the troops ready for the grand unveiling."

When Resson's significant stare finally registered, Decker shook his head.

"No. No, how, no way, just no. There's any number of smart platoon leaders ready for a step up in this battalion."

"But there's none that can sort out the mess Norik made of First Company quickly enough."

"Forget about it." Decker shook his head again.

Resson laughed softly.

"It's kind of cute that you think you've got any say. This isn't the Corps, where you can refuse a promotion. This is slavery, where you do as the boss says, or you end up making mine owners really happy to get a big buck like you for a few creds."

"Let's just see how things unfold," he replied angrily. That small part of him still planning to escape and repay those who'd taken his life away knew it would be easier for him to run if he wasn't responsible for over a hundred soldiers. It wasn't just that he'd have more eyes on him; it was also because he'd be unable to abandon troops who looked to him for leadership.

The wait wasn't destined to be long. As he'd parked his skimmer in the vehicle enclosure, he had watched Latour and Terkis unload their commands at the double, after which the thopters had pulled away for the second load. That second load was landing now, judging by the thumping of wings.

Shortly afterward, Mala Daran stalked into the command tent, eyes shining with a mixture of fear and anger.

"Resson, get me a call to the Atabek. When we have a connection, I want everyone out."

"As you command." He nodded and then glanced at Decker, his expression giving Zack the unmistakable order to vanish.

Expelled from battalion headquarters and anxious to avoid an enraged Norik, he did the only sensible thing he could: he ordered himself on a one-man patrol outside the FOB's defensive berm, preferably beyond weapons range.

— ELEVEN —

"Decker."

Zack jumped as Resson's voice blared in his ears.

"Yeah?"

"Commander wants to see you. Where the heck did you go off to?"

"Keeping my ass out of the line of fire, XO. You know how it is. I'm down by the river looking at footprints the size of blower fans."

"Tell me you're kidding."

"Nope. Beautiful fresh tracks. Mud's still shiny, and the edges haven't collapsed. Must be some big critter. Looks like it headed for the water."

"Get. Out. Of. There."

The vehemence in Resson's tone caught his attention, and he rose from a crouch, looking around with alarm.

"You do not want to meet a strilak. At least tell me you're armed."

"What do you think, XO? Of course, I'm not armed. Lora's sitting on what live ammo we brought. What's a strilak, by the way?"

"Ever heard of an Earth critter called a crocodile?"

"Vaguely," Decker replied as he cautiously retraced his steps uphill to the FOB.

"The strilak's sort of like that and even though it can't digest humans, especially those wearing battledress, it'll try. Every time. It's a lot faster than you are, buddy, and a lot bigger."

"Why wasn't I told?"

"There hasn't been a strilak spotted on the entire peninsula in years. I guess one made it upriver and found itself some happy hunting grounds."

A hoarse cry that reminded him of nothing so much as an out of tune bugle made Zack look over his shoulder.

"I guess it found me."

He broke into a run, legs pumping as he pushed his way through the brush dotting the hillside.

"Watch for covering fire. I'm getting the sentries to load up," Resson replied. "The boss would be really annoyed if you turned into lunch for the beast."

"Not that I'd care," Zack grumbled, conserving his breath. Running in full fighting order wasn't particularly difficult, not when he wasn't loaded down with weapons and ammo, but the hillside was steep, and he had to watch his step at all times. Stumbling over an exposed rock or stepping into a hidden pothole could spell the end to a promising slave career.

The strilak bugled again and this time, it was close enough for Decker to grimace at the carrion stench on its breath.

"Now would be a good time, XO," he shouted into the radio.

He felt jaws snap by his heels and redoubled his efforts to push up the slope. His leg muscles were feeling the burn, and it was just a matter of time before he lost speed.

"Decker, when I say drop, make yourself one with the ground."

"Aw, crap. You're going to do it, aren't you?"

"No choice, buddy. The shot has to go down its throat if we want to kill it instantly. The thing's better armored than your skimmer and its brain case even more so."

Zack cursed at his own stupidity. The strilak's call, close enough to make the air vibrate, had woken an atavistic fear in him, and he struggled to contain the growing sense of panic at what seemed an inevitable end as critter snack.

"DROP."

With one last shove uphill, he threw himself down and prayed.

Plasma cracked over his head, and the strilak's triumphant cry became a scream that turned Zack's muscles to jelly.

A gush of gore splashed over him but thankfully the dying beast's jaws snapped shut a few centimeters short of his outstretched legs.

"Clear." Resson's voice had never been so welcome. "You owe Breen, from Second Company, a big one, Decker."

Zack weakly raised his arm to acknowledge his gratitude but remained prone, letting the adrenaline surge bleed off. When the stench of the dead strilak hit his nostrils, he found enough motivation to push himself up and slowly trudge back to the FOB. Unfortunately, the smell followed him, and he understood why when he looked down at his legs: they were covered in greenish blood and flecks of unidentifiable flesh and bone.

"Got anything to hose me down?" He asked wearily over the radio. "I doubt the commander will want me anywhere near her the way I am."

"The field shower's ready. No need to strip, and yeah, we can smell it from here."

**

Decker lifted the command tent's door flap and poked his head inside.

"You wanted to see me?"

Daran jerked her chin towards the empty field chair by the folding table. Resson and Cyone already there, the latter examining him critically. Decker had shed the combat harness, but his battledress still dripped water from the impromptu hosing down.

"First off," Daran said, after he took his seat, "I have accepted full responsibility for not taking your warnings about Norik more seriously. That failing has cost the Fifth Orta and the Kashdushiya as a whole a capable, if overconfident company commander."

Zack managed to keep a straight face at her characterization of Norik. Overrated was probably a better word.

"The Atabek has chastised me, as was proper, and has set me the task of fixing the problem before the new model battalion is unveiled. Should I fail to do so, I will suffer Norik's fate."

At Decker's questioning look, she glanced down at the table, clearly embarrassed.

"He has been reassigned as a simple silahdar in the First Orta. The thopter that just departed is carrying him back to the base for onwards transport to the Ytrell mines. If the Fifth isn't up to the required standard on the appointed date, I will join him."

"The big boss doesn't screw around, does he?" Decker asked no one in particular.

"I've been given complete freedom to do as I like," she continued, ignoring his comment. "These then are my orders: Decker, you will take command of First Company. Cyone, you are now the Fifth Orta's sanjaqui. You may appoint the best of your technicians as armorer in your stead."

"As you command," Cyone nodded.

When Decker didn't follow suit, Daran gave him a curious look.

"You have problems with my orders?"

"Seeing as how I don't have much choice in the matter, may I offer suggestions to speed remediation up a bit?"

Her hard eyes met his for a few moments.

"You may."

"First Company, as it stands, cannot be brought up to the new standards in the time available. Not by me, not by anyone. The silahdars will resent me and drag their feet enough to make sure I fail and join Norik in the mines."

"He's got a point," Resson said, nodding. "I hope you've also got an answer, buddy."

"I do." Decker's smile was grim. "You're going to love this. The other company commanders are going to love this even more."

"Why do I suddenly feel like I'd rather not hear your proposal?" Resson made a sour face.

Daran held up her hand to forestall any more banter.

"Go on."

"Spread the misery and the work needed to get First Company up to snuff. I keep two platoons, Terkis' and the heavies, and swap out one platoon each with Second and Third Company. I'll take Tran Kidder and his troops from the latter, and the pick of the Second Company litter. I know it'll bring down Second and Third's standards for a while, but it'll give me a fighting chance to bring up First Company's."

And a better chance of not ending up with a juluk shoved into my ear by disgruntled Nelvan soldiers, he thought.

Daran looked at her second-in-command who chuckled, if not at Zack's words, then at the somewhat exaggerated pleading expression on his face.

"Makes sense," Resson said. "I can't see any other way to go. Just a question, Zack: why keep the heavies? Wouldn't it be better to swap them out at the section level?"

"I think I can work them through it, XO. They have to be frustrated at Norik never having used them correctly. Just for that, I figure they'll listen to me."

"Cyone?" Daran glanced at her new adjutant.

"I don't see what else we can do, commander."

**

If the sign of a good compromise was no one leaving the table happy, then Decker's platoon swap had to be the best idea since the invention of slave soldiering. No doubt the same lack of enthusiasm would permeate down through the platoon leaders to the last of the silahdars since they would see it as forcing them to re-do the last few weeks' worth of training.

But, as Decker was beginning to appreciate, slave soldiers were easier to handle under these circumstances. They didn't dare openly object or slack off in a way that was too obvious, for fear of punishment up to, and including the juluk pit. That meant they paid attention when he spoke.

The two platoon leaders he'd kept, Terkis and Sal Aran, who had the heavies, seemed relieved to have Decker take over. The fiasco of the battle run had drained away any confidence they had in Norik and demoralized their troops.

Kidder and Nik Vulin, the other platoon leader transferred in, weren't impressed, but they were smart enough to understand why it had to happen. At least now he had an even balance between Nelvan and Commonwealth platoon leaders, even if First Company was still slanted towards the former in the lower ranks.

"So?" Resson asked as he walked up to where Decker was watching his company pack up their part of the FOB, three weeks after Norik's ignominious departure.

"They're about up to average colonial rifles standard, which isn't bad when you consider they started at mid-wit Nelvan levels. Given another month, I could've had them run circles around the rest of the battalion, but that would have been beside the point."

Resson slapped him on the shoulder.

"At least we now have three infantry companies that are better trained than any others in the Kashdushiya, and probably better than most of what's available this side of the Coalsack."

"I sure as hell hope so. Daran's a good sort when she finally opens her eyes, and it would have been a shame to lose her."

"Not to mention the possibility of you seeing your old buddy Norik again in the barracks of the First Orta," Resson grinned. "That would have been the grudge match to end all grudge matches."

"Followed by a screaming duet in the juluk pit," Zack replied dryly. "No thanks."

"Scuttlebutt has it that Norik demanded a session with the damned critters to expiate his failings."

"And not coincidentally raise his profile again," Decker grunted. "I hope the Atabek refused."

"Resoundingly, I hear."

"Good."

"It'll be nice to get food from the mess hall again," Resson looked around at the rapidly vanishing encampment, "and a hot shower."

Decker snorted.

"Too bad there's no cold beer waiting for us."

"The Danjorans have an analog, from what I've heard, but apparently the only effect it has on humans is a case of the screaming runs."

"Then it's not an analog, just some alien drink that sucks."

"What sucks?" Daran asked, joining the two men.

"That which passes for booze among our owner's species, apparently," Decker replied. "I was telling Jase how much I want to make love to a cold beer when we get back to base."

"Some days I worry that you're losing touch with reality, Zack." She shook her head in mock despair. "You'll be pleased to hear that the Atabek was satisfied with my last after action report. We've been given two days of full rest before we start working on the demonstration battle drills. The date has been announced to prospective clients. And with some of them traveling from a great distance, there will be no change.

She touched Decker's arm.

"I don't believe I've thanked you yet."

"I hate seeing good troops wasted by arrogant commanders, Mala." His voice was soft, but his tone was hard. "Although I didn't want to become a company commander, I did a damn better job at it than Norik ever would have. His head was never going to come out of his ass. You may want to think about how breeding slave soldiers might limit their ability to think. Having your every minute owned by someone else doesn't exactly make for intellectual flexibility."

"I was born to the silahdar," she countered with asperity.

"And you gave Norik a pass until I forced you to look at him clearly."

Stung by the accusation, she turned her back on Decker and took several deep breaths.

"Once again, you are correct."

"Give it a couple of generations," Zack continued, "and you'll have bred out the qualities that separate cannon fodder from soldiers who can think their way out of the worst crap. I have a couple of third generation silahdars in my company, and they're by far the most arrogant and least capable of showing initiative. Food for thought, commander."

"Perhaps we should breed you." She gave him an appraising stare. "And collect some of those genes that make you so infuriatingly correct."

"It's got nothing to do with my genes. I was the most useless, ungrateful little bastard when I grew up. The moment I turned eighteen, I joined the Corps just to spite my parents who were anti-military to the bone. Damn near didn't make it through basic training because of my smart mouth and my adolescent belief that I knew better than anyone else. But the instructors figured out a way to get through the dumbass shell and turn my stupidity into Marine smarts."

"And yet you climbed to the highest levels of your profession if I understand your Corps correctly."

"Guys like Zack are pretty rare," Resson said, "and no breeding program is going to give you a litter of them. You'd have to invent your own version of all the schools he's been through and all the battles he's fought. As he told you, the raw material wasn't promising."

"Then perhaps the Atabek needs to encourage slavers to find him more Marines," she replied with a mischievous smile, knowing what the men's reaction would be.

"Good luck." Decker snorted. "I think I may have said this before, but setting up a mercenary outfit made up of free men and women, well paid and well treated, will get you better raw material than the slave market."

Her retort died when the sound of thopter wings reached their ears.

"Our transport's here. Make sure everyone is ready. I'd like to be able to dismiss the battalion before the evening meal is served."

"As you command."

**

"Since you're no longer the armorer, where are we going to go for some after-hours fun?" Zack asked Lora

Cyone as they walked out of the mess hall, replete and happy to be back on base after more than two months in the field.

"The new armorer's not going to complain if I kick him out. I taught him everything he knows, including when to give his seniors some space."

He wrapped his arm around her shoulders and squeezed.

"Well done, my dear. Since I can't make love to a cold beer, how about I make love to a warm battalion adjutant?"

"As long as you let me make love to a company commander, I'm good."

Decker's grin turned into an enthusiastic leer. Weeks without intimacy had brought its own share of frustrations on top of everything else.

When they finally got back to the barracks, well after the rest of the Kashdushiya had gone to bed, they found it dark. Even Daran had succumbed to the lure of a soft cot after so long on a hard mat. They didn't bother with another shower, and Zack fell asleep with Lora's scent still strong in his nostrils.

The next two days were surreal for the ex-Marine. He'd not had a day off in so long that he didn't know what to do with himself. The limited recreational facilities didn't particularly appeal to him, sex had its limits, and of course, there was no leave to be granted, never mind taken.

Instead, he spent a lot of time shooting the breeze with the silahdars of First Company. The Nelvans, once you got through the almost xenophobic mindset, were pretty much like any other humans, although he had a hard time getting their strange humor and he suspected that they gently laughed at his apparent cluelessness.

He was almost relieved when the regular garrison duty cycle resumed on the third day. At times, it was getting hard to remember that he was a slave, far from home. The fire within that demanded vengeance was still alive, but it wasn't quite as hot anymore, or as bright.

Like Lora Cyone, he didn't have anyone or anything back home, but here on Danjor, he had her, he had his company, and even a decent if somewhat inexperienced commander. Overall, an improvement over the last time he'd worn a uniform if you forgot the fact that he was owned by a non-human intent on profiting from his property.

**

The demonstration, when it finally occurred, was not quite anti-climactic, but it didn't give Decker the same feeling of accomplishment as when he'd taken First Company through a successful battle run. They'd worked so hard and so long to satisfy the Atabek's exacting demands that it had seemed almost too easy to put the Fifth Orta through its paces before several dozen sets of eyes, not all of them grouped in symmetrical pairs.

That night, a special meal greeted them in the mess hall, a token of their owner's satisfaction. Decker would have preferred a wee dram of single malt, but he kept his ungrateful thoughts to himself.

Training returned to the regular routine the next day, and they waited, but weren't quite sure for what. An air of expectation hovered over the base, and it wasn't until three days had passed that Daran called the command group to her office.

"The Atabek has been offered a contract for our services." She seemed flushed with pride. "The bidding has pleased our master, and it will be profitable indeed. Shipping is being arranged, and we should be ready to move in two weeks' time."

"Any details about the contract?" Decker asked.

"The Gwangar of Chuluk, from a world called Garada, has an infestation problem his household troops can't manage."

"Bug hunt?" Zack groaned inwardly. His last one had been enough for a lifetime.

"I don't know what that means," Daran replied, and he realized that the term didn't translate well into Danjori.

"What's the nature of the infestation?"

"A species calling themselves the Shrehari have decided to establish a colony on Garada and they refuse to recognize the Gwangar's sovereignty."

The Commonwealthers around the table looked at each other in astonishment. It was a long way to the Empire.

"Is it wrong," Decker finally said, "that my first thought was about capturing as much Shrehari Ale as I could?"

— TWELVE —

"Charming." Zack wrinkled his nose at the stench as he led his company down the transport ship's ramp and onto a cracked, undulating tarmac.

"What is?" Tran Kidder looked around at the dismal sight of a crumbling spaceport. "All I see is a place that seems to have gone from barbarism to decadence without the intervening stage of civilization."

"Everything."

He shrugged, something that wasn't exactly easy since he, like all of the silahdars, was lugging everything he owned on his person. The battalion's vehicles, small in number to begin with, carried the second and third line supplies.

Native Garadans observed the disembarking troops from a distance, many of them armed and twitchy. If they didn't look like something that reminded the humans of mutated frogs, then he had no idea how to describe them adequately.

Mala Daran and Jase Resson had met with the Gwangar and his advisors earlier that morning, returning with instructions, intelligence, and not much in the way of help.

A fifteen-minute march over the edge of the landing strip, through a bare field and across a broken roadway brought them to an enclosure surrounded by a high earth berm.

"It's an old Chuluk army camp." Resson trudged beside Decker, as heavily laden as the rest of them. "That's about the extent of what they're willing to share. We're on our own for nearly everything else."

"Why am I getting the feeling our dear Atabek was a little too quick in accepting this contract?"

"Pessimist," Resson smirked at his friend. "Just because the place smells like a sewer, looks like a dump and the locals are about as friendly as crocodiles with a toothache doesn't mean things aren't hunky-dory."

"So says you." They walked through the single opening in the berm and Decker's disgust went into overdrive. "I think I'll bivouac my company on the outside of this cesspit, thank you very much, XO."

"Nothing doing. First order of business is fatigue parties to clean the place up. We need a base camp near the spaceport, and this is it."

"I think I'm going to have a talk with my recruiting sergeant to see how I can get out of this chickenshit unit."

Resson laughed aloud, drawing strange looks from silahdars just as disgusted as Zack.

**

"Let me see if I have this straight: after they got their scaly asses whipped by these Shrehari, the Chulukians just buggered across the mountains and haven't been back?" Decker stared at the map projection. "It means their intel is months old. I'd say we need some serious recon before we go for a nature hike."

"We can't afford to take too much time before engaging the enemy." Daran's lack of enthusiasm wasn't lost on any of them.

"Why is that?"

"The Atabek gets a bonus based on how fast we do the job and, of course, the longer we stay in the field, the more supplies we consume, meaning the costlier the mission."

Decker snorted derisively.

"That's what I love about private sector soldiering: profits trump common sense. According to the locals, the Shrehari haven't been spotted anywhere south of this place." He put his finger on a spot that supposedly marked the presence of a ruined fortress. "I suggest we move up a forward element to here, and if the fort's still usable, we make it our FOB. Then we send out the drones and maybe some patrols. After we know what the

Shrehari are up to, we bring the rest of the battalion north of the Gandabeg Mountains. I just wish we had thopters. They would have saved us a lot of time."

"Too expensive to ship."

"Profits again, eh, Jase? Let me take First Company and set up. Offload the trucks and transport us there. It'll take maybe eight hours. If we do it on foot, it's more like three days. Since time is of the essence, I'd say it's the only sensible thing to do."

The other company commanders nodded their agreement, in terms of both sending Decker and his men first and using the few vehicles they had. Zack didn't know whether it was because they trusted him to do a better job of recon than anyone else or because they were glad their own companies wouldn't be taking point.

"Very well." Daran nodded reluctantly. "It shall be done as you say, but I will bring up the rest of the battalion, company by company, while you reconnoiter. We don't have time to wait for results. Resson will remain here with the personnel we don't need in the main body. Everyone else will move north within the next thirty-six hours. Decker, you will leave as soon as possible."

"I'd like to take Cyone and some of her folks with me to prepare a forward headquarters for you."

"Very well. If there's nothing else, you have your duties." Daran clapped her hands once, dismissing them.

**

The fortress was a dismal place, looming over the surrounding countryside like a malevolent pustule. Hewn from granite, its stones still stood guard over the mountain pass centuries after the natives had forgotten how to build such massive structures.

The trucks, after a long trek across the Gandabeg range and over a raging river, had deposited First Company and the advanced headquarters crew at the base of the hillock, leaving the silahdars to trudge up the last bit.

"As FOBs go, this isn't actually so bad." Cyone looked around the cobblestone parade ground fronting the keep. "We don't have much to do other than site the heavy weapons and put out the observation posts."

"I'd best be about it then." Decker walked through an opening that may have once held a door and into the base of a semi-ruined tower.

He looked around at dank walls streaked with fungus and dissolved minerals. For all he knew, the locals probably found the wretched atmosphere congenial. Decker most emphatically didn't.

"We'll set up headquarters here."

"Not in the keep?"

"I don't want to run across a wide open space to get to the walls if ever we're under fire. Strike that. When we're under fire."

"Makes sense. I guess that's why you're the company commander, big boy. Not sure our Boss Lady would approve, though."

"She won't stick around long enough to care." Decker walked back out into the watery light of day. "I'll bet you two things: one, she'll be on the next convoy up the pass and two, the moment everyone's here, she'll head for the field to hunt herself some Shrehari."

"Shouldn't we try to find them first?"

"You'd think so, wouldn't you?" He shook his head. "But now that we're here and nothing's shown up on those sorry excuses for sensors we got, I think I'm not going to use the drones just yet, in case the buggers spot them and decide something's up at this old pile of rocks. I'll have Tran send a recon patrol to the top of that cliff over there. They should be able to see twenty, maybe thirty kilometers without being spotted."

"Daran might not like that."

"She'll take what she gets." He waved at his platoon leaders, calling them together. "If she decides it's time for the drones when she arrives, at least we'll have two companies defending this place, which will make me feel a whole lot better."

Cyone looked at him curiously, worry lines creasing her forehead.

"You really don't like this, do you?"

"Ever had the feeling you're on an operation that's about to go down a black hole?"

"Sure. It happens to all of us over the years."

"The feeling I've got is worse than that, and it's not just because this planet is a depressing hunk of crap populated by the most useless sentients I've ever seen."

"Aren't you the cheerful one?" She patted his arm. "Do you need a hug?"

"What I need right now is way more than a hug. A heavy Marine battalion group with assault shuttles would do nicely, thank you."

Cyone laughed softly.

"And here I thought you'd say you needed a good session with Mama Lora."

"Later. Business first."

The platoon leaders clustered around them, waiting for his orders, Tran smiling because he'd overheard her last few words.

**

"This place is easily defendable, commander." Decker walked Daran around the walls, showing her what he'd set up. "We have a good field of fire all around, and the walls are so thick and dense that they'll hold off anything short of heavy artillery."

"What about the recon?"

"I've got an observation post on top of the cliff there." He pointed into the distance. "They can see up to fifty kilometers across the savanna, past the next big river. So far, nothing in sight, not even large animals."

"No drones?"

"Too easy to spot with the right gear. They'll know something's come across the Gandabegs looking for them."

"The last sighting the Chulukians reported was on the far side of that big river, wasn't it?"

"Sure." Zack nodded. "On the map, it shows some nice open fields backed by hilly woodlands, just the kind of place to establish an agricultural colony."

"These Shrehari, they farm?"

"Every species that moves beyond the hunter-gatherer stage does, commander. It's a universal constant, just like the notion of profit and its corollary, living off someone else's profit."

"Then we must head for that area and inform them they owe tribute to the Gwangar. As soon as everyone is here, I intend to head out."

He'd given up trying to explain the Shrehari mindset to her well before they landed on Garada. The Nelvan mentality just couldn't grasp that some species were inherently tougher and more violent than they were.

"Are you leaving anyone at the FOB?"

"I thought I'd have your company stay behind. You're already settled in and establishing a reserve is one of the principles of war, no?"

Decker nodded, an unexpected sensation of relief burning away his worst fears.

"Agreed. Having a decent force holding this place is a good idea so that you can fall back on something defensible if the enemy's too powerful."

Daran scoffed at the notion.

"I think we're strong enough to handle a bunch of colonists. You've seen the native troops. We could probably topple the Gwangar and take over his kingdom with a single platoon."

"Perhaps, commander, but I urge caution. As I've told you before, I've fought Shrehari outlaws in the past, and they're superb fighters as well as being sneaky bastards. Don't underestimate what you might find."

"Noted." Her dismissive tone hinted at irritation that he'd reopened the subject.

Ever since the Norik incident, their relationship had become less friendly, more formal. It was as if, deep down, she figured the ex-Marine would have been a better choice as commander of the Fifth Orta. Perhaps she felt threatened by that notion to the point of giving his advice less than her full attention.

At dawn, two days later, she led the main column out of the old fortress with a pair of drones flying ahead to scout out the terrain. Decker and Cyone stood on the massive ramparts and watched the battalion recede in the distance.

"You still have a bad feeling about this, Zack?"

"Daran's not taking it seriously enough. You know how nasty the Shrehari can be, and yet she seems to think she's going after Rekar tribesmen back on Danjor. It's that damned Nelvan arrogance and the way they think the Kashdushiya is the be all and end all of soldiering."

"Come on. I'll buy you a mug of khavass." She elbowed him in the ribs. "We'll watch the feed from the drones for as long as it lasts."

Which turned out to be only a few hours; after that, the regular radio check became their only link with Daran and the remainder of the battalion.

When nothing happened for the first forty-eight hours or so, Decker began to relax, wondering whether he'd been looking for trouble where none existed. Then his observation post spotted figures moving in the distance, along the mountain range, before vanishing out of sight. But, as it turned out, not out of range. The first mortar rounds came whistling in shortly after that.

— THIRTEEN —

"Bugger the Gwangar of Chuluk and his entire race."

Decker dropped to the ground by the wall as another mortar barrage came whistling in.

"A small infestation of Shrehari, they said."

"Small if you're a frigging division," Cyone replied, hugging the hard ground beside him. "I wonder if Daran and the rest of the battalion are doing any better than we are."

Gouts of earth and rock erupted further down the slope as penetrator rounds searched for silahdar bunkers. Fortunately, the Shrehari gunners' aim had been less than precise, and the shells mostly missed the FOB. Without satellites, in the pea soup of Garada's atmosphere, they had to work by sound ranging. Decker's troops had shot down their drones the moment they'd appeared. The battalion's own drones were long gone.

Three days had now passed since Daran had taken most of the Fifth Orta up into Shrehari-held territory to root them out. Decker, with his company and some of the battalion headquarters elements left behind in the abandoned Chulukian fortress, guarded the only available route south through the Gandabeg Mountains, and it was becoming apparent that the Shrehari hadn't been idle from the moment the silahdars had shown up.

"Still no radio contact with the commander?" Cyone asked when the barrage stopped as abruptly as it had started. The Shrehari likely had the same supply problems as Decker and needed to husband their ammunition.

"Nothing since dawn. Nothing from the other elements of the battalion either. It could just be the lousy atmospherics. Our radios aren't exactly up to Marine Corps standards."

"Or they could have met an overwhelming Shrehari force," Cyone replied somberly.

"I sure as hell hope not," Decker rose, brushing the dirt off his battledress, "because if that's the case, our sweet asses are next."

"We're about as well sited as possible." She looked around at the thickly walled ruins. "The only way in is uphill."

"And the only way out is downhill." His sour tone betrayed the anxiety he was trying hard to conceal. "If everything's gone to crap, the evil buggers will have no problems keeping us bottled in until we surrender once we've run out of ammo and food."

Decker shook his head angrily.

"The damned Atabek was way too anxious about showing off his newest toy. Getting some more intel about the opposition before signing a contract wouldn't have hurt the profit margin a bit."

The silahdar next to them was startled at Zack's casual insult to their owner, something that could have earned him a turn in the juluk pit back at the Kashdushiya base on Danjor. Decker, seeing his expression, winked.

"I'm going to send a couple of patrols northwards, to see if something's brewing."

"Probably a good idea." Cyone nodded.

"I'm glad to see our esteem adjutant agrees with me."

When they were out of earshot of the nearest troopers, she laid a hand on his arm.

"This isn't Fort Wagner, Zack, and we're not the 3rd Regiment."

"But we could be buggered just the same," he replied, not bothering to hide his growing sense of doom. The complete and utter destruction of the 3rd Marines on Farhaven three hundred years earlier was still seared into the Corps' collective memory.

"Look at us and tell me we're not stuck in a fort just like they were, cut off from help and holding the shitty end of the stick."

"You don't know that Daran and the rest of the battalion have encountered misfortune. They could just as well be in a dead zone when it comes to radio transmissions."

"Anything?" He asked the silahdar on radio watch when he entered the command post.

"Nothing. It's like I've got the only receiver on the planet and everyone else is using semaphore flags."

"Huh," Decker grunted, "if it's the local atmospherics, then going back down the tech ladder might not be a bad idea."

He nudged the duty runner who was happily snoring in the corner. The placid Nelvan had probably slept through the last barrage without a twitch.

"Get me the platoon leaders," he said when the man looked up, instantly alert. "Ten minutes."

**

"What's up, boss?" Kidder sounded cheerful enough as he walked into the bare room.

"When everyone's here, Tran. I don't want to repeat myself four times." Decker's tone of voice was so devoid of humor that the platoon leader closed his mouth and went to lean against the wall by the radio operator. A quick glance at the log gave him the answer. Before he could make up his mind whether or not to speak quietly with the silahdar, the others showed up.

"Gather by the map, guys," Decker waved them over. "We haven't had radio contact with the rest of the battalion since before dawn. All night, the radio checks were on time, then about an hour before the sun came up somewhere on the other side of this pea soup the locals call a sky, it was 'nothing heard, out.' If the commander went according to plan, they'd have dug in, so there's no reason to have missed the morning check unless the atmospherics are so screwed up around here that a five by five signal goes to zero when daylight comes around."

"You think it might be something else." Kidder nodded. "Nine hours without contact, even with the short days around here, isn't a sign that all's well."

"Aye. And if the Shrehari are bold enough to mortar us, then they could just as easily have run over the battalion and not circled around."

"Doom and gloom, boss." But Sal Aran, who had the heavy platoon, didn't contradict Decker. "You're thinking of sending a few patrols out into the wild."

"One patrol per platoon, to even out the task, except for yours, Sal. If the Shrehari have pulled off our worst case scenario, I'll need all your firepower here."

Decker ran his finger over the map projection.

"Tran, you'll send your patrol down the center, following the route taken by the battalion, though I suggest they don't actually walk on the track itself."

When Kidder nodded, he turned to Ker Terkis.

"Head northwest on a thirty-degree angle to the left of Tran's patrol route. If the enemy's circling around the battalion to get at the pass, we'll find out. Nik," he nodded at Vulin, the fourth of the platoon leaders, "you'll do the same but on the right, heading north-east."

"Will do, boss."

"The patrols turn around either at first contact or after ten kilometers. It'll be radio silence except to report an enemy sighting."

"Does that mean all patrols turn if one makes contact or is it only the patrol that finds the enemy who turns back?"

"All patrols, Ker. And they're to high tail it. No sense in letting the Shrehari catch up by playing king of the jungle scouts. Any other questions?"

When the four platoon leaders shook their heads one after the other, Decker clapped his hands.

"Departure in one hour. I'd like them back before full darkness."

"Daylight patrol?" Cyone asked once they were alone with the radio watch.

"No choice, I'm afraid. I don't want to wait much longer without hearing from Daran. She's been in a hurry since we got here and you know what that can do to a commander's ability to make the right decisions."

She knew him well enough to understand that he was fighting off any number of misgivings. Decker had good instincts, and he'd learned to trust his gut. If he was this uneasy about the situation, there had to be something very unpleasant coming at them. History had proven often enough why the old tale of a company alone and cut off, sitting in a hilltop fort, had become such a Marine Corps staple.

Unable to do more for the moment, the two senior silahdars walked the perimeter of the FOB, trying to look unworried, though Decker's eyes missed very little and he was already mentally preparing to hold off against a much larger force.

The troops, attuned to their leaders, knew something was off, and although Decker tried, he couldn't stop the speculation. Like soldiers everywhere, his silahdars were prone to exaggeration, and all he could do was keep the story to what they knew, which was precisely nothing, hence the recon patrols.

They'd just finished their evening meal when the sentry called the command post.

"The patrol from first platoon is back, and they have a survivor from the commander's column."

"Shit." Decker tossed his pouch aside and rose from the stone he'd been sitting on. "Radio, call the other patrols back."

"Survivor?" Cyone's eyebrows had shot up in surprise at the word used by the sentry.

"We'll see. Lora, do me a favor and go around the platoons. Tell them to very quietly stand-to. If the enemy has us under observation, I don't want to give them the impression that we found out something they'd rather we didn't."

As she turned to leave, the squad leader who'd taken out the patrol from first platoon stepped in, leading a bloodied woman in dirty battledress, missing her helmet and weapon.

"This is Mariko, from Third Company. We came across her about seven kilometers out. She was headed our way."

Decker waved his hand toward a granite block by the wall.

"Sit."

"We've given her what first aid we could and fed her on the way back."

"Thanks, Harris. You can go back to your platoon now. We'll take care of Silahdar Mariko."

The radio operator handed her a canteen cup filled with hot kahvass and Decker waited until she'd had a few tentative sips before speaking.

"What happened?"

She stared at him for a few moments, as if unable to understand the question at first.

"Near as I can tell," she started in a quavering voice, "the enemy infiltrated the camp in the hours before dawn without anyone raising the alarm. Must have been the better part of a company. When their main body attacked in force from two sides, just before sunrise, we found ourselves caught between people shooting us in the back as we shot to the front. They got over the berm within minutes and then, it was a massacre."

Mariko shuddered at the memory, her smeared face contorting with fear.

"I got knocked out by a shot glancing off my helmet, and when I woke up, I was under a pile of bodies." She stopped, shaking her head. "It was panic more than anything else that got me out from under them. By the time I was free, everyone was dead, and the Shrehari had gone. I didn't know what else to do so I ran back the way we came until I met Harris."

"Any idea where the Shrehari went?"

"No."

"Their strength, weapons, anything?"

"Sorry, no. It was all so confusing. There seemed to be a whole lot more of them than there was of us, but in the dark, who can tell?"

Decker got up and walked over to the map projection. He didn't think the Shrehari wanted to invade the Gwangar's heartland. At least not yet. Maybe when they figured out how useless the local troops were, they might change their minds. But they didn't want anyone in the territory they'd claimed as their own.

How a bunch of Imperials had ended up on Garada remained a mystery, but Zack suspected it was another case of a colony ship gone off course, like the one that created the Nelvans. The Survey Service had witnessed a few wormholes appearing and disappearing over the centuries, and many a ship's disappearance had been blamed on the poorly understood phenomena. There was even that story about a frigate finding a weird human colony hundreds of light years into the black during the last war.

Perhaps these were Shrehari who'd left on a long-range expedition and were sucked halfway across the Orion Arm. Who knew when they'd left the Empire? If they had traveled in stasis, their departure could easily predate first contact with the Commonwealth.

If that was the case, there could be thousands of them, perhaps even tens of thousands. The Garadans had been pretty vague about the how and when of an 'infestation' that was beginning to seem more and more like colonization.

"I'm getting the feeling that his contract's quickly becoming the biggest mistake the Atabek's ever made," he muttered to himself. "I hope he got a healthy advance payment."

"You hope what?" Cyone asked as she joined him by the far wall.

"I hope the Atabek got his money's worth out of his new model light infantry battalion because it's gone. We and whatever Resson has back in Chuluk City are all that's left."

She nodded with resignation.

"Word's already made it round the FOB. Don't you just hate it sometimes when you're right about something awful? What are we going to do now?"

"Get the hell out of here. Save what we can. This mission is over. If the Atabek expects us to fight to the last silahdar, to prove a point about our bravery and keeping to the letter of a contract, he can think again. This isn't the 3rd Regiment, and I'm not going to die for the glory of the colors. Heck," he chuckled grimly, "we don't even have colors."

He was about to send the runner out to gather the platoon leaders when they appeared on their own. Decker quickly relayed Mariko's story.

"As soon as full darkness has fallen, we're exfiltrating to the south," he announced. "There's no point in staying here. No one's going to come to our relief, and there are no friendly forces to our north."

"We were ordered to hold here," Aran pointed out. "In the Kashdushiya, the last order is the one we follow to the end. We are slaves."

"What we are," Decker countered angrily, "is humans held against our will and made to fight someone else's wars. I've had just about enough of the bullshit mentality and the damned mystique with which you all seem to surround the honor of the Kashdushiya. We're marching out of here tonight, south across the Gandabegs to rejoin what's left of the battalion, then we get the hell off this rotting planet. The Shrehari can have it for all I care. It's not as if we owe the Gwangar of Chuluk and his people any favors. Damn froggies can fight their own wars."

The platoon leaders were taken aback by the vehemence in Decker's tone, but none dared contradict him. Even Aran simply bowed his head, acknowledging Zack's authority. Cyone, who was watching from the edge of the circle, caught an expression of relief in the man's eyes before he looked down.

"We're going to have to assume the enemy is watching us closely, so everything we do out in the open has to be done with that in mind. Make sure the troops understand. Since their attack on the main column was so successful, they'll try a repeat, which means we have about eight hours to prepare the FOB so it looks like we're still here before we slip out the back door without being seen. I want us at least five kilometers away by the time they make their move."

"They'll know where we're headed," Kidder pointed out, "and five klicks isn't much of a buffer."

"That's why we'll move in two columns, Tran." Decker's smile was almost frighteningly vulpine. "You'll take your platoon down the obvious route, to give them a trail to follow. I dare say you can move a lot faster on your own and that'll be enough of a buffer against any Shrehari pursuit. I'll take the rest of the company over the western ridge through this narrow pass."

He pointed at the map.

"From there, we'll head towards the other side of the Gandabegs cross-country. If you get to Chuluk City before us, tell the XO what happened. He can decide whether to send some transport or wait until we show up on our own."

Kidder looked dubious but bowed his head briefly.

"As you command."

"Nik, you'll take the lead of the main column. Send your best squad leader ahead of time to reconnoiter the way through what is likely no more than a crack in the rock."

Vulin nodded.

"As you command."

"Now here's how we're going to make the bastards believe we're still holding this place like good, obedient slaves..."

**

"Have you given thought to what will happen once we're back at the capital? The Gwangar won't be happy to see his investment wiped out, and I'm pretty sure the Atabek won't be chartering a ship to haul us back to Danjor."

Cyone handed the canteen cup back to Decker, who took a sip and grimaced.

"So we charter our own ship, at gunpoint if necessary."

"And then what?"

He grinned, his teeth preternaturally white in the glow of the radio set.

"Then we head for home."

"Just like that."

"Yeah, just like that. Playing slave soldier was fun for a while, but I have some unfinished business."

"You're a real piece of work, Zack Decker. Here we are, for all we know, surrounded by a regiment's worth of Shrehari who wiped out the rest of our battalion, and you're already planning on hijacking a starship to leg it for the Commonwealth."

"A man's got to have a dream, sweetheart. Killing the trash that sent me into slavery is my dream."

"You seemed happier with your lot before we left Danjor."

"That was before the situation went FUBAR on us. As far as the Atabek's concerned, we're bad publicity now, never mind no one bothered to see if the Shrehari were actually weak enough to be whacked by a single battalion. He'll want to sweep us under the rug as quietly as he can."

"You're pretty cold."

"No, I'm a realist and not very pretty either, but there you have it."

"Some of the Nelvans might not want to travel to the Commonwealth."

"Yeah, I thought of that, though I figure we might be surprised. If there are any, they can stay here, or we can drop them off along the way, but there will be a starship hijacking, and there will be a long trip, and no Shrehari assholes are going to stop me, let alone anyone in what remains of this battalion."

Before Cyone could reply, Harris stuck his head inside the command post which was now totally bare save for the radio.

"Vulin says to tell you the recon patrol has left the lines."

"Is anything moving outside?" Decker dumped the contents of the canteen cup on the ground and shook the last drops from it.

"Quiet as the grave, balukbashi."

"Screw that, Harris. I've decided that we're not slave soldiers anymore, so dump the stupid Danjori titles."

The silahdar smiled and snapped to attention.

"It's about time we sounded like a proper military organization, Captain Decker."

"It is, isn't it, sergeant." Zack slapped the man on the shoulder. "Tell the lieutenants to get ready."

"Aye, aye, sir!"

He saluted enthusiastically before making a perfect about-turn.

Decker grinned at Lora.

"What do you say, Captain Cyone. Shall we herd our lost sheep back to the Fleet?"

Nonplussed, she stared at Decker for a few seconds, and then burst out laughing.

"You can take the Marine out of the Corps, but you can't take the bloody Corps out of the Marine. I used to be a warrant officer. That's good enough for me."

"And I was a command sergeant, but I seem to be responsible for a company now, and I need a good battle captain. Shall we get on with it? We still have to slip out from under the bony noses of a bunch of nasty Shrehari."

"Well," she said, dusting off her legs as she stood, "you won't find the headquarters staff dragging you down, sir. I'll meet you by the back entrance in thirty minutes."

"Carry on, captain."

Decker grinned at her and she felt a warmth that she had never thought to feel again. They still wore the uniforms of slave soldiers, but somehow, he made her believe they were back in the Service, as free men and women.

"I'm going to check the perimeter," Decker said as he pulled on his helmet and grabbed his rucksack. "You can go on ahead with Januz and wait by the breach."

"Got it – sir." Cyone picked up her gear and nodded at the silahdar with the long-range radio set. "Come on, son."

— FOURTEEN —

Zack took one last look around the bare room and grimaced. If the Shrehari figured out they were running before he could get the company far enough into the mountains, things might get gruesome. On the other hand, making a final stand in an ancient Chulukian ruin would be suicidal and not in the least noble.

Screw the Atabek. He could figure out how to recover from this public relations disaster. Probably by pretending the Fifth Orta never existed. A surge of unrestrained rage momentarily flared up, but he quickly suppressed it, knowing that he couldn't afford emotions if they were to make it through this alive.

Sal Aran met him by the ramparts.

"All of the booby-traps we could build are in place, as are the decoys."

"Since I didn't hear any screaming, I guess your boys were able to set them without blowing off any extra fingers."

Aran chuckled.

"I got a couple of scares, but I'll recover. If you're good with checking only the odd few, we can stay behind the walls. Less chance of a Shrehari wondering why we're climbing all over the place again."

"Lead the way."

"My guys have mixed feelings," he said as they edged around the improvised explosive devices carefully sited at spots mostly likely to be used by Shrehari infiltrators.

"How so?"

"We gave up a good bit of our heavy ammo for the traps, which leaves us only a few rounds for each tube, but on the positive side, we won't have to hump all that weight back to the other side of the Gandabegs."

"They can count themselves lucky I decided to keep all of the big guns. I seriously considered abandoning most of your ordnance so the column could travel faster, but Lora talked me out of it."

"Trust her to keep an eye on the toys." Aran grinned behind his visor.

Decker knelt by a cleverly concealed mortar round with an exposed fuse tied into a trip-wire.

"Fiendishly simple." He nodded. "Even if they have night vision gear, the wires are so fine they'll be missed."

"We used most of the mortar rounds like that."

Zack stood up, careful to keep his head below the top of the wall.

"If that's an example of your platoon's work, you did well."

They quickly inspected a few more of the improvised explosive devices and decoys, then Decker checked the time readout in his helmet's visor. If the enemy was going to do a repeat of the previous night's performance, then according to what Mariko had told him, they had four hours at best to get away.

"Okay. I think you've done what you could. Time to pull out." He clapped Aran on the shoulder. "I'll send Kidder on his way as soon as I get to the breach."

Decker scampered down to the lowest part of the fort, where the curtain wall had crumbled and left a rough opening that was well hidden by the surrounding vegetation. A narrow path, carved out by running water, went to the base of the hill, from where they could go left towards the overgrown road running through the pass, or right and into the mountains.

He found Kidder waiting just inside the opening, his platoon already strung out along the path beyond.

"You're good to go, Tran," Zack whispered. "We'll meet you at home base in three days unless we catch up along the way."

He nodded.

"Three days it is. Good luck, sir."

"You too, lieutenant."

Soundlessly, Kidder slipped through the breach and vanished. When Zack went to look, no more than a minute later, the entire platoon was gone. Five minutes after that, the remainder of First Company melted into the night.

**

Progress beneath the thick, leafy canopy was surprisingly fast, even though the ground was spongy. Little daylight reached through the foliage, and the undergrowth was stunted. By the time they crossed the tree line at the foot of the cliff, only three hours had passed. Vulin's recon patrol waited for them at the appointed spot.

"The pass is doable, barely," the squad leader reported. "We'll be in a single file for about a kilometer. Anyone gets above us, and it'll be a shooting gallery, but they'd have to be flown in, so we're probably safe."

A dull thump echoed over the forest and then two more.

"I think the Shrehari have found our little presents." A cruel smile creased Decker's face. "They're a bit early, but it'll do. Let's move out. The less time we spend in the open, the better."

Three more thumps went off.

"Looks like they're not fast learners," Aran said, grinning. "I'd figure it would be wise to stop and regroup after the first one blew."

"The fog of war will do that to you. Multiple entries, not particularly well coordinated, and not expecting IEDs."

"We'll ask them for an after-action report," Zack said. "Once we're across the mountains, so let's get there."

They had heard two more explosions in the distance before the narrow pass swallowed them, but no one had the time to crack wise at Shrehari ineptitude. The recon patrol had been generous when they called it barely doable.

Anyone with less physical conditioning than the silahdars wouldn't have made it to the other end. It was just as well that the heavy platoon had left most of their ammo behind. The bottom of the pass, which was at times not much wider than Zack's shoulders, was a jumble of broken rocks just waiting to snap a careless ankle.

Adding to the misery, it rose at a sharp angle before flattening out a few hundred meters above the valley floor. That first kilometer took almost an hour, and daylight was smearing the horizon with a band of dirty gray by the time they crossed a broader saddle between two peaks and descended into the next valley.

The column marched on, stopping for five minutes every hour and for two half hour breaks to eat. There were no signs of pursuit, nor was there any radio traffic. It was as if Decker and his company were alone on the surface of the planet. He said so to Lora Cyone as they chewed on cold rations.

"I've been on worse low-tech missions than this," she remarked between bites. "The kind where you got a couple of animal-drawn supply carts every few weeks, but of course those weren't the absolute clusterfuck this one has become."

"Talking to you always cheers me up." He shook his head. "It would have been nice, though, if the Atabek's budget went to communications satellites. Then we could have called the XO and gotten the battalion skimmers to extract us once we were clear of any pursuit. As it is, we'll all be a few kilos lighter by the time we can hitch a ride."

Cyone snorted derisively.

"Our former owner is in it for the profits, not for our survival. I'm pretty sure the Gwangar of Chuluk, crap be upon him, paid enough money for our services so that even if we're a total loss, it'll have been worthwhile. High tech? That would eat into his margin."

"I was going to make a smart-ass comment about officers caring for their troops," he responded after swallowing a hard chunk of protein. "But then I remembered that I was the nearest thing to an officer right now and that the Atabek isn't an officer; he's just another piece-of-shit slaver."

"You think the Shrehari are on our tail?" She asked, changing the subject.

Decker shrugged.

"No way of knowing. They might have figured that there was no good reason to pursue, now that we're out of what they probably consider their territory. That would be the smart thing to do, especially if they think there might be backup coming through the mountains."

He carefully rolled up the empty ration pouch and tucked it into his rucksack.

"Pass the word to police the area before leaving," he told Cyone. "If they are following us, we might as well not make it too easy."

A sudden shout stopped him in his tracks.

"Drone!"

One of the sentries pointed at a small dot above the mountainside they'd crossed earlier that day.

"I guess they fixed one," Cyone said as she ducked under a bluish aspen-like tree. All along the trail, the silahdars had hidden as best they could the moment they heard the warning shout.

"And they had a brain flash that we might have decided to do a side-trip on our way out."

"No one ever said the Shrehari were dumb."

"It's turned back without coming near." Decker stepped back out onto the narrow path. "Looks like the buggers need line-of-sight to control it, which means the AI's buggered."

"And it means they're still in the valley next door. I suggest we get moving, just in case."

"Agreed." Decker made the 'mount up' signal, ordering the long column into motion again.

By late afternoon, they slowly trudged up and over the next steep crest, Decker anxious to put more distance between them and the Shrehari, and to avoid spending the night on the valley floor. The local wildlife might not find humans digestible, but that didn't mean it was a good idea to tempt them. Better to spend the night high up, where it was cooler and less infested.

Just as the last of the company vanished down the reverse slope, the same sharp-eyed soldier called out a drone warning again. This time, the craft came much closer.

"The controller's climbed up the path we took and is sitting high on the other side of the valley." Zack looked at his company strung out over the bare rocks.

"Or they could have fixed the AI," Cyone suggested once they were clear of the ridgeline.

"Maybe, but I'll bet they've seen us this time for sure. The fact that they're still interested in us isn't a good sign." Decker scanned the narrow gorge below them. "I don't like that we're going to be walking eastwards for a while before we can find a slope that's safe. If the buggers are on Kidder's trail, we might stumble across them in the dark."

"We're not stopping?" She sounded more resigned than surprised.

"Not yet. We need to keep going for a few more hours."

Night fell with the surprising abruptness they'd learned was the norm on Garada, and soon even the usually stoic silahdars felt the strain as they made their way across the broken terrain, caught between a steep slope on one side and a deep canyon on the other. Though their helmet visors gave them night vision, it was never the same as seeing dangerous ground with one's own eyes.

Decker called a two-hour halt around midnight, the company strung out on a narrow shelf running above a chasm filled with rushing water. Though bone-weary himself, he declined Cyone's offer to keep watch while he got an hour's sleep.

"I'm too twitchy, Lora. You might as well take two hours."

"A tired commander makes mistakes."

"True, that's why I have you as my better rested XO."

Alas, it was not to be. A sound like tearing cloth filled the night air. Though distant, it brought everyone back to full alertness.

He quickly made his way to the sentry at the rear of the column, stepping over the prone bodies of his tired troopers.

"Where away?"

"Down in the valley behind us, I'd say," the man replied. "A dozen or so klicks."

"Did that sound Shrehari to you?"

"Not a clue, sir. I can't say that I've heard what their automatic guns sound like before this."

His reply brought Zack up short. He'd forgotten that almost none of his soldiers had ever met a Shrehari, let alone fought one. The closest they'd come was the harassing mortar fire the previous day. He patted the man on the shoulder and turned back.

"How far are we from the main pass?" Cyone asked when he rejoined her.

"Just under ten kilometers." He called up a map projection inside his visor. "We'll be able to get off the side of this mountain in about two, but the closest usable ford isn't for another three klicks after that — if this map is accurate."

"So much for the Shrehari being happy with us just leaving."

"Sometimes, they want to make a point, like for instance, don't bother us or we'll wipe you out to the last hairless ape." He shrugged. "Mind you, when we went after Shrehari marauders, we did pretty much the same thing. Wiping them out to the last bony skull ridge, that is."

"I wonder what caused the shooting."

"Some idiot tripped over a root with his finger on the trigger, or they ran into something bigger and meaner than they are? Who knows? At least we got an early wake-up out of it."

"True." She stood and stretched. "It occurs to me that we owe Norik a solid for having been such an ass."

"Why?"

"If he still had First Company, we'd be dead by now, him trying to defend a useless pile of stone because it was the last order he got, and you and I with the main body."

Decker grunted.

"I'll buy him a beer if I ever see him again, which is probably never."

With that, he hoisted his rucksack and made his way to the head of the column. It wasn't where a company commander was supposed to be, but if they were getting close to the main pass, he had a decision to make no later than when they passed the next ford and for that, he needed to be at the very front.

Accompanied only by the sound of running water, they eventually made their way out of the narrow gully, walking downhill until they reached relatively flat riverbanks at the bottom of a broad vale. If the Shrehari were still closing the gap, they were more circumspect after warning them by accident.

Decker called a fifteen-minute halt and allowed the troops to replenish their water containers. The built-in bug zappers would take care of any microorganisms that could give a human the runs or worse.

"You know what I miss?" Cyone asked between bites of a ration bar.

"Booze, sex and old-time religion?"

"Seeing stars in the night sky. It's been a long time since I've been on a planet that wasn't covered in perma-clouds."

Decker looked up.

"Sure, but it might be brighter. This mud ball does have a moon or three and that would help the Shrehari more than us."

"Trust you to be unromantic and practical." She chuckled throatily.

"Someone has to, sweetheart, and I was voted in as the designated adult, whether I wanted to or not."

"Yeah, but if it hadn't been you, we might not have made it this far."

He considered her statement and then, without any sense of false modesty, he agreed.

"I suppose I am the best qualified for a company-sized game of escape and evasion. Buggering slave soldier bull pucky. The last thing I wanted in life was to be a damned officer."

She laid a hand on his arm.

"You're doing fine, Marine."

Distant gunfire shattered the still night air, and everyone in the column froze.

"That wasn't behind us," Cyone said, eyes narrowed.

"No. That was probably close to the bridge on the main road."

"So the buggering Shrehari did like us and split up their pursuit."

"Yeah," Decker nodded as he climbed to his feet, leg muscles screaming in protest. "It's time to fix that mistake. Four or five klicks on even ground, say one hour. That's all Kidder has to hold out for."

"What if they're setting a trap?"

Cyone slung her rucksack over her shoulders and picked up her carbine.

"This whole planet's a damn trap, Lora. We might as well concentrate our firepower. What was it the wise man said: if we don't hang together..."

"We'll surely hang separately. When we get close, let Vulin take point. We need you to get us out. No one else in the unit has enough gall to hijack a starship."

He sketched a mock salute and lumbered off into the night.

The column moved as fast as it could, propelled by legs that had given their best hours earlier. Slave soldiers might not have colors or regimental badges, or even a flag to fight for, but they understood strength in numbers. Kidder's platoon needed them, and they needed that platoon.

Decker's estimate was optimistic, but the sporadic shooting continued, giving him hope that Kidder was still in the fight.

He didn't dare use his radio until the last minute. If the Shrehari were to listen in, they'd know he was barreling up their flank. It would be a delicate balance between keeping them in the dark and letting Kidder know the cavalry was on its way.

He needn't have worried. Less than five minutes after he fell back behind Vulin's platoon, they made contact. The volume of firepower that erupted from the head of the column was more than enough to tell the beleaguered silahdars that help had arrived.

Help, unfortunately, had no idea what it was running into, nor did it know what was on its tail. All Decker knew was that he'd thrown the company into a firefight where the only way out was through the enemy screen and over the bridge. He had no other choice left after passing up the ford in favor of the most direct route.

The Fifth Orta's dead bore witness that these Shrehari had no compunction about massacring humans. What they didn't know yet was that Decker had no compunction about returning the favor.

— FIFTEEN —

Zack joined Vulin and his automatic weapons squad in a thicket on the water's edge.

"Where?"

"The tree line on the other side of that bend in the river. I make a dozen shooters, say half a platoon. Probably the flank guard. I've got a section probing around the bight, but I think that's the extent of it."

"Who fired first?"

"They did. Could have mowed my point down, but their fire went right over our heads."

Decker's eyes narrowed.

"Inexperienced? That's hard to swallow if they managed to infiltrate and massacre the better part of a battalion. Experienced troops would have let you walk right into them, and they wouldn't have shot too high."

"Their second string, then?"

"That would mean we have the first string behind us. Cheerful thought, lieutenant."

"It's been a pleasant mission so far, sir."

A rustle of leaves announced the arrival of the heavy platoon. Cyone hadn't been idle while Zack went up to see the situation for himself.

"Sal," he grabbed the platoon leader by the arm. "Set up here. Nik's people can show you the best positions. I'll take the company around once recon comes back. Make sure you're spotting IR signals. Three shorts, one long means open up hard, two long means stop. I don't completely trust the IFF in these helmets, so pay attention. I want to punch through their flank and roll them up until we meet Kidder's platoon. The moment you see us clear the far side of the bight, pack up and move as if you got the devil on your tail. The bogeys behind us will want to close the distance as fast as they can now that they've heard shooting. And Sal, machine-guns only. Something tells me we'll need what little we have left of mortar and rocket ammo soon enough."

"Got it, captain." Aran nodded.

"Good man." Decker slapped his shoulder and rose from behind the fallen tree trunk. "Come on, Nik. Time to get us some Shrehari."

Terkis, the remaining platoon leader, was waiting for them just inside the tree line, crouched beside Cyone.

"It'll be quick and dirty, folks," Decker whispered. "They know we're here, we know they're there, but I'm pretty sure what's sitting on the other side of the bend is a small screen, half a platoon at best, and none too experienced. There's not much room to deploy so we're going in column. Nik, since your folks have seen the enemy position, you're in the lead. Ker, your platoon's in support, ready to either pass through Nik or do a flanking on the left if Nik is pinned down. Sal will provide cover on order. Once we're through the screen, we don't stop until we meet up with Kidder and his folks. Lora, you move the HQ folks up one tactical bound behind the rest. You're my only reserve. I'll be up with the lead platoon. Questions?"

The officers shook their heads, knowing that time was no longer on their side. They had to hit fast, hit hard, and do it now.

"Off you go, Nik."

**

The jungle was eerily green in their night vision visors, parts dull and parts glowing, and somewhere among the trees, the foe waited for them to walk into their cross hairs. Contact, when it happened, was as unexpected as it was violent.

Closed terrain made this a platoon leader's battle, and Zack kept out of Vulin's way as the latter leap-frogged his sections forward to push the Shrehari back. As he did so, the heavy machine guns on the far side of the river bend began chewing through the vegetation, forcing their enemy to keep his head down.

Decker didn't want a hand-to-hand battle their adversaries were sure to win by dint of their larger size and greater strength, but it would have to be a melee nonetheless. Between the soupy darkness of the forest and the starless, moonless night, soldiers would be almost on top of each other before they figured out they were in contact.

The volume of return fire told Decker that the Shrehari weren't going to make this easy so he quickly found Ker Terkis and grabbed him by the arm.

"Take your platoon twenty meters to the left and pivot ninety degrees to roll them up from the side. Make damn sure your IFF beacons are on because you'll need Nik's fire support until the last minute. I can't have the heavies continue. As soon as you're away, I'll be shifting their fire right and the moment you're on the attack, I'll be moving them up to join us."

"Got it, captain."

"Once you're through, which you'll know when you've reached the river, pivot left and head downstream towards the bridge."

With a final, nod, Terkis jogged off through the thick ferns to where his section leaders were waiting for orders. Shortly after that, they were off, gliding through the undergrowth noiselessly and hopefully unseen by the Shrehari. Decker had joined Vulin up front and briefed him on the change in plans while the troops in contact kept exchanging fire with the enemy to keep them occupied. Suddenly, shots rang out behind him, and the radio came to life for the first time in many hours.

"Decker, this is Cyone. We're about to be squeezed in a vice. My people just took out four Shrehari scouts, and we can hear their main body pushing through the forest. They're getting really close now."

"Understood. Aran, this is Decker, time to pull out. Cyone will cover your withdrawal and then follow."

"Aran here, understood.'

"Cyone, understood."

It meant lifting the covering fire early, but he needed the heavy platoon too much to risk having it cut off. Terkis would just have to move faster, and to Decker's everlasting joy, he did.

"Terkis here, boss. Situation understood. Stand by. We're pushing through now."

A barrage erupted to Decker's left, streams of plasma cutting through the night. Terkis' flanking wasn't a perfect ninety degrees, but it would do. Caught between two fires, the Shrehari screen collapsed with surprising quickness.

Within minutes, the company's front was clear of enemy soldiers and Decker, all too cognizant that he was about to be caught between the main body behind him and whatever enemy was facing Kidder at the bridge, pushed through the last of the triple canopy jungle and into the low brush fronting it.

They stayed down, to avoid giving the enemy too good a target, and took stock of the situation. Gunfire flashed over the vast open space around the old stone bridge, between Kidder's platoon, already on the far side of the river and the Shrehari hidden among the trees by the overgrown road.

"Decker, Kidder here," the radio came to life again, "about time you showed up. We were starting to get bored trading pot-shots with guys whose aim isn't much better than the Gwangar's slugs."

"We had a little argument with a flank guard, and we're about to have a bigger discussion with the main body coming up our behinds. Any suggestions?"

"Yeah. Suppress the enemy on either side of the road and send the heavies across. Have Aran deploy them on the right side of the bridge to cover the remainder of the company. I'll keep an eye on whatever might pop up behind you."

"Works for me."

He turned to his other platoon leaders, waiting patiently behind him.

"You heard Tran. When the heavies are in position to suppress, Lora, you take HQ platoon over. Once you're across the bridge, keep going until you're at the next ridge. Cover us from there. Sal, you can use a couple of mortar rounds to suppress the Shrehari, but don't expend all of them. As soon as the heavies open fire, Nik, you lead your platoon across and take a position to the left of the bridge. Ker, you're last. Once you're across, join Lora on the ridge directly. We do this on the run, folks. I aim to break contact cleanly this time. With any luck, the Shrehari will see the river as the natural boundary to their claim and leave us alone."

"What about the casualties?" Terkis asked.

Decker swore under his breath. He'd forgotten to account for any injured after they punched through the screen. Being a company commander wasn't without its drawbacks.

"What's the butcher's bill?"

"Larkat's dead. We left him there after taking his weapons and ammo," the platoon leader replied emotionlessly. "I have two walking wounded and one barely walking."

Zack looked at the others in turn.

"No dead," Vulin said, "one non-walking wounded and three walking."

"No casualties." Aran shook his head.

"Okay. Ker and Nik, hand your casualties over to HQ. They're going straight up the ridge with them."

The platoon leaders nodded and, at Zack's signal, melted back into the night.

"Ready," Aran transmitted after a minute or two, during which Kidder and the Shrehari traded desultory shots.

No sooner had the heavy platoon leader spoken that the gunfire increased to a fevered pitch and Decker saw three dozen shadows jog out of the brush in extended line, headed for the bridge.

For a few tense moments, he expected a previously hidden enemy unit to spring into action, but Aran and his men made it across unscathed.

They had the mortars set up and firing within moments and, as the first round hit the wood line to the left of the road, Lora Cyone, and the HQ folks sped across the open ground, over the bridge. They quickly disappeared up the road leading to civilization and their way off the planet.

Vulin's silahdars sprang up the moment the last of Cyone's troops were across and ran like the devil was on their heels, which, as it turned out, he was — in the form of an infuriated Shrehari company stomping through the jungle behind them.

"We'd better move now," Terkis' alarmed voice broke through the crescendo of gunfire as Vulin's platoon joined Kidder and began to shoot into the brush at Decker's back.

With that, Zack got to his feet up and ran towards the bridge, suddenly conscious that as company commander, he should have crossed with Aran's platoon so he could direct the covering fire.

A sharp cry rang out behind him just as his feet touched the granite of the roadway and a stray shot grazed his helmet: the pursuing Shrehari had arrived. He made it across and joined Kidder.

"How many?"

"Hard to say. Two platoons' worth at least."

"Aran, this is Decker. Put some rockets on the wood line we just left. Fire when ready, two canister rounds."

"Roger."

Just as Terkis and his troops were at their most vulnerable, crossing the bridge, the heavies opened fire. Both rounds passed close enough to the platoon's tail-end charlie to singe his battledress, but the devastation they caused when the warheads exploded over the shrubs, sending thousands of sharp steel slivers into the night, was worth it.

Inhuman screams of pain drowned out the continuous machine gun chatter as a swath of forest, and the Shrehari it hid were transformed into a cloud of shredded organic matter.

"Decker, this is Cyone. We're in position and can cover the whole area."

He tapped Kidder's arm.

"Off you go. I'll keep Nik and Sal to hold them until you and Ker are over the ridge."

Zack had the other two platoons shooting continuously to prevent the enemy guessing about his dispositions, but the moment Cyone confirmed that both Terkis and Kidder had joined her, he gave the order to pull out.

"Aran, this is Decker. Break contact."

He turned to Vulin.

"When his last trooper's past the bend in the road, pull out. Cyone has the bridge and the wood line beyond ranged in. Anything moves, she's got your back."

After the platoon leader had nodded his understanding, Decker slithered backward and out of his firing position before running towards the side of the road, bent over at the waist to make himself as small a target as a man of his bulk could. He joined the heavy platoon's ranks as they jogged uphill, panting at the exertion after a long night of marching and fighting.

Gunfire erupted from the crest and Decker swirled back, going down on one knee, as he tried to see what Cyone was shooting at.

The enemy seemed to have figured out he wanted to break contact and were trying to rush the bridge the moment Vulin's platoon stopped firing in preparation for their withdrawal. A few smoking bodies later, an unnatural silence fell over the valley, punctuated here and there by the sobs and gasps of wounded Shrehari.

At the top of the ridge, he dropped to the ground beside Cyone, his head buzzing with adrenaline and the exertion from his hard run uphill.

"Any more movement down there?"

"None. I have Sal ready with another canister round just in case, but I think we gave them enough of a bloody nose that they'll likely count their blessings and leave us alone."

He called the platoon leaders together in a quick huddle.

"Casualties?"

"Ulian bought it as we were rushing the bridge. We didn't have time to recover his gear."

"You're sure he was dead?"

"If anyone can live with a fist-sized hole in the chest, it's news to me," Terkis replied dryly. "A few nicks here and there. Nothing that'll keep 'em from moving."

"Same here," Vulin added. "Rudy caught one in the arm, but the way he's cursing, it's not a big deal."

Decker nodded. Two dead and a dozen wounded meant he got away cheaply, especially compared to the rest of the battalion.

"I know we all desperately need rest," he said. "But we can't afford to hang around too long, in case our friends decide that chasing us south of the river wasn't enough to heal their wounded pride, and believe me, a Shrehari battalion has enough pride to equip a whole human division."

"Sal," he tapped the heavy platoon leader's arm, "set up your rocket launchers and mortars to cover the bridge and its approaches. The rest of you, have your folks eat, take care of the injuries and grab a few minutes of shut-eye. We're leaving in two hours. By then, it'll start getting light, and we'll be able to move faster. Once we're out of the Gandabegs, we'll stop for a longer rest. With any luck, we'll be able to raise the XO on the radio and get the battalion skimmers to start ferrying us back."

"And then what?" Kidder asked the question they'd all held back during their frantic escape from the Shrehari trap.

Cyone glanced at Decker, intrigued by how he'd handle the situation. She was the only one who knew his intentions, and since Aran and Vulin were both Nelvans, his goal to head for the Commonwealth might not go over too well.

"Then we find ourselves a nice ride and get the hell out of this part of space."

"Home?" Kidder asked, hope barely masked in his voice.

"The Commonwealth. It's not necessarily home to everyone in the company."

Aran stared at him wordlessly for a few heartbeats.

"Nelva isn't really home for most of us so-called Nelvans either. We show up there as escapees, we'll just get handed over to the Atabek or someone like him and then beware the juluk pits."

Zack started in surprise.

"Your own people would do that?"

"It's either deliver the strongest children to become slave soldiers or suffer a worse fate," Vulin replied, anger hardening his eyes. "It's not just the Danjorans. Plenty of predatory societies around here. I figure if we put it to a vote, nearly all of the Nelvans would rather follow you to Earth than return to our supposed home."

"Not to rain on your parade," Terkis sounded unconvinced, "but how do you propose to seize a starship and force the crew to sail us hundreds of light-years through the Coalsack and beyond. As far as I know, we don't have anyone in this outfit that can do astrogation worth a crap."

"One thing at a time." Decker squeezed the other man's shoulder. "First, we rejoin the XO and the rear echelon. Can't leave 'em here. They're just as much junk for the Atabek to hide as the rest of the new model battalion."

"And what if we just go back to the Kashdushiya?" Terkis asked. "No harm, no foul."

"Do you really think the Atabek will welcome us with open arms?" Cyone's voice was soft, but no one could miss her contempt for the suggestion. "He made his profit with our lives. That we failed to deliver is the Gwangar's problem, not his. He might raise another new model battalion, or he might just forget about the whole idea. Us showing up will just annoy him. I say the CO's right. We try for the Commonwealth."

"Or die trying," Terkis sighed. "I guess you're right. What a mess."

"One man's mess is another man's opportunity." A hopeful smile creased Decker's tired face. "But the only way we're going to make this opportunity work for us is if we stick together just like a good Marine company, discipline and all."

"Are you going to rustle up colors and a band too?" Terkis didn't quite sneer, but he still seemed to be wavering. Zack examined the man's face in the growing light of dawn. His platoon had taken the most casualties and perhaps he was merely experiencing the shock that sometimes overtook men once the shooting stopped.

"If I had a way to do it, I would," he replied. "In the meantime, I'm counting on all of you to keep this outfit together and operating at maximum military efficiency. Otherwise, we might not make it at all."

He caught each officer's eyes in turn, and they nodded, even Terkis after a brief moment of defiance.

"Talk to your folks, make sure they understand what I intend. Anyone not wanting to come along can either stay here or leave us anywhere along the way. But they have to be clear that as long as they're in this company of fools, they're subject to all orders. I may not have a portable juluk pit, but I know a couple of field punishments that'll do just as well. We leave in two hours."

**

Decker had barely fallen asleep when he felt a firm hand grasp his shoulder.

"They're stirring down by the river," Cyone whispered.

"You'd have thought the dumb buggers would know when to quit," he grumbled, stretching his tired limbs as he rose to his feet.

He quickly made his way up to the observation post and peered over the ridge. About two dozen Shrehari, easily recognizable by their bony, ridged skulls, were cautiously crossing the bridge. They wore dun-colored uniforms of a type Decker had never seen before and carried plasma rifles that looked strangely archaic to his master gunner-trained eyes.

"Another bunch of lost colonists for sure."

"Sir?" The sentry sounded surprised.

"Shrehari colony ship that went off course, got sucked up by a wild wormhole and spat out near this system. A bit like your Nelvan forebears, son."

"But we've been on Nelva for thousands of years, and we've been told you Earthers didn't make it into space until a few centuries ago."

"Mysteries of the universe." Decker shrugged, eyes fixed on the advancing enemy. "Now why is it that they're sending a platoon's worth across when they know damn well we're a full company?"

"They're dumb?" The silahdar ventured.

Zack's chuckle sounded cold and harsh to the young man's ears.

"Shrehari are a lot of things, but never dumb. Not when it comes to fighting. The only reason our last war with them ended was that they had a rather forceful change of government, not because we beat them. I guess that the bunch down there is a recon patrol sent to make sure we actually buggered off. I think we should oblige them."

He flicked on his radio.

"Decker to all, rise and shine. We've got visitors coming, and I'd like to be gone when they get here."

Within moments, the soldiers were up and ready to move. Zack took one last look over the ridge, to gauge how much time they'd have before the Shrehari reached the top, then jogged off to join the already moving column, trailed only by the two men from the observation post. Getting out last because he wanted eyes on the enemy was becoming a bad habit.

They made it around a sharp bend in the road by the time the Shrehari patrol crested the ridge, but Decker didn't stop. He'd managed to break clear in the hours before dawn and sure as heck didn't want to renew his acquaintance with their pursuers. This wasn't his war anymore.

The company kept moving until they reached the point where the mountains petered out among the rounded hills marking the southern edge of the Gandabeg range.

Decker ordered them off the road and under the triple canopy jungle to set up a bivouac. The exhausted troopers needed a full night's rest before tackling the last leg to the camp where they hoped the battalion's rear party still waited. If nothing else, they needed to replenish their ammunition and rations before they could even consider hijacking a starship.

With sentries set and most of the company fast asleep, Kidder joined Zack on a fallen log, a cup of weak kahvass in his hand.

"The troops are pretty excited at the idea that we're no longer slaves," he said, "even the Nelvans. Seems they can't get enough of using proper military rank. It's kind of cute actually, just like over-eager puppies."

Decker nodded, smiling.

"It's a rare soldier who won't obsess over military trivia. Next thing you know, they'll want me to sew them a company pennant."

"Close," Kidder replied, grinning. "They've been talking all day long about a proper name for us. If we're no longer owned by anyone, we can't be called the First Company of the Fifth Orta."

"How about Decker's Demons," Cyone suggested as she sat down next to the two men. "It has a certain mercenary ring to it."

"Not even in your nightmares, Lora," Zack growled, shaking his head like an angry bear. "I'd rather we remain First Company before we take on some funny moniker."

"Sir," the radioman suddenly called out. "I've got battalion rear on the blower."

"Finally!" Decker dumped out the last of his kahvass and stowed his canteen cup before taking the proffered handset.

— SIXTEEN —

There was a lengthy silence after Decker finished relating the events of the previous forty-eight hours to Jase Resson, now the senior surviving leader of the Fifth Orta's remnants.

"What do we do, Zack?" He finally asked, sounding shaky to Decker's ears.

"We grab a ship and go home, and by home I mean the Commonwealth, not that shit hole called Danjor."

"Just like that?"

"Yep. I can't see anything else for us to do. I've decided that we're no longer slaves but free soldiers who just happen to be between employers. With the bunch you have, we're a respectable little company group. How'd you like to be a major?"

Again, there was silence from the other end of the connection.

"I've got a better idea," Resson finally replied. "I can't think of anyone who stands a chance of pulling this off other than you, my friend. I used to be a logistics puke in the Colonials before I ended up as one of the Atabek's little toy soldiers. I'll be glad to act as your XO. I'm pretty good at that job, but I'd make a lousy CO. Consider yourself elected to the rank of major in our private army, Zack. Being a captain again is just fine for me."

"Buddy, I was a command sergeant. I'm not competent to run a company, let alone a company group."

"You're more experienced than any of us so stop trying to hide from your responsibilities, Marine. Tempting me with a promotion so you could duck the work won't cut it." The chuckle in Resson's tone took the sting out of his words and from of the corner of his eyes, Decker saw both Cyone and Kidder grin like naughty school kids.

"What are your orders, sir?" Resson was all business again.

"Hang tight where you are. First Company needs at least eight hours of rest and we're likely as secure here as we would be anywhere, so we'll be spending the night. Tomorrow morning, after first light, I'll give you the coordinates of a pickup point, and you can send every vehicle that still works to fetch us. We'll use the camp as our operating base while we figure out how to shop for a ship. That being said, make sure we can pull out of there in a matter of hours. At some point, the Gwangar will figure out he's pissed away his money on the Fifth Orta and might be looking for a bit of compensation out of our hides. I'd rather be gone with everything we can carry by the time his rotting brain synapses spark with anything more than hunger for a flying lizard."

"Roger that, sir. We'll maintain regular radio watch, now that you're back on the net, with the proper hourly checks. By the way, I think we need a better name than 'Survivors of the Fifth Orta' or something similarly Danjoran."

Decker groaned.

"Not you too. What is it with soldiers and their fascination with buttons and bows?"

"I still think Decker's Demons has a nice ring to it." Cyone made a face at him.

"If it'll keep you all happy so you stop bugging me and I can get some sleep, okay," he grumbled. "We can be Decker's Demons. Now if there's nothing else, your beloved commander really needs his rest if he's to lead you reprobates back to civilization before we all keel over from old age. Talk to you tomorrow, Jase. Decker, out."

**

Zack jumped off the back of an overloaded skimmer and landed in front of Jase Resson who was smiling broadly.

"Welcome back, sir. I trust you enjoyed the ride."

"What? No honor guard? No band? No salutes?"

"I thought you Marines didn't salute when you're wearing helmets."

"Getting all technical on me now, Jase? I guess it's the sure sign that we're degenerating into a regular unit. God help us all."

The second-in-command of the newly named Decker's Demons led his superior into the HQ tent and offered him a cup of kahvass while the latter stripped off his combat gear with a sigh of relief.

"Anything stirring around the Gwangar?" Decker took a big gulp of the bitter liquid.

"No. The liaison came by the other day, and he seemed just as bored and indifferent as ever. I doubt the Gwangar's army will be overly saddened by our demise."

"They'll find sadness when the Shrehari decide to expand south of the Gandabeg range, though it'll take a few generations, I think."

"Any idea how they got this far from the Empire?"

"Nothing concrete, though the little I saw of their gear makes me think they came on a ship that was launched quite some years ago."

"Having a Shrehari colony in the area isn't going to make the Fleet planners euphoric, you know," Resson said.

"Bah." Decker shrugged. "We're so far away, it'll take centuries before these buggers become something to worry about, not to mention what'll happen to them living on a planet that wasn't designed for their physiology. They might die out in a few generations. It's not our problem no matter what way you look at it."

"The Gwangar might have a differing opinion."

"Bugger the Gwangar."

"No thanks." Resson's face twisted in mock distaste. "Interspecies sex isn't my cup of tea."

Lora Cyone stuck her head in the tent.

"Everyone's inside the wire and accounted for, major. The troops are on equipment maintenance duties, after which I've told the platoon leaders to stand them down for additional rest."

"Thanks, Lora. Don't forget to take a little downtime yourself. Jase can handle the routine while we both catch some zees."

"Will do." She sketched a salute before disappearing.

Resson shook his head.

"It all seems so damn unreal, Zack. I've been a silahdar for so long that I can't quite wrap my head around being a free man again, and a free mercenary at that."

"When we get home you can re-enlist. That'll take away the feeling of freedom and the joy of soldiering for profit." Decker grinned.

"Is that what you're going to do?"

"No." He laughed bitterly. "The Corps offered me early retirement as an alternative to a court-martial. Considering that the chances of my serving time in a penal battalion would have been better than even, I handed in my papers."

"Clocked an officer?" Resson looked at him speculatively.

"Yeah. The asshole needed it desperately." Zack told him the story, as much to pass the time as to make sure his second-in-command knew exactly who he was.

"We had that type in the Colonials as well." The XO nodded knowingly. "It's not fair, but if you can't take a joke, don't join up, as they say."

"I had a good thing going in the private sector, as first mate on a trader. Maybe I'll go back to something like that."

A sudden stab of anguish lanced through him as the memories flooded back, no longer held in check thanks to his exhaustion. It must have shown on his face.

"Are you all right, Zack?"

"Yeah." He stood and tried to shake off the feeling. "Just got a reminder that I have some avenging to do when we get home. There are a few critters who owe me for killing my wife and destroying my ship."

"That's how you ended up with us?"

"Yeah, eventually, though I doubt they figured I'd be sold as a soldier-slave. They were probably hoping I'd end up in something with a shorter life expectancy and more physical abuse."

"You must have really pissed those folks off."

Zack grimaced.

"Massively. Now they owe me even more than the last time so I have plenty to do when I get home, stuff I can't do if I re-enlist."

"You know what they say about vengeance," Jase softly replied.

"Sure: first dig two graves. In this case, it'll be a few more than two. I'll be cleaning out the Amali clan so thoroughly they'll remember for a long time that it's a dangerous thing to mess with me."

"Care to talk about it?"

"Maybe some other time. I need a shower and some food that doesn't come in slabs. Then we need to figure out how we can rent a starship."

**

"What the heck is that?" Decker asked, pointing at Vulin's upper arm. The platoon leader had joined him in the chow tent, a tray of hot food in his hands.

"Our crest, sir." The Nelvan grinned.

Zack examined the patch carefully and snorted.

"Is that what I think it is?"

"If you think it's the Atabek's dragon design impaled on a bloody sword, then yes."

"A bit heavy-handed on the irony front, no?"

"It does express the troops' feelings." Vulin chewed thoughtfully on a chunk of unidentified vegetable matter. "Amazing how quickly years of conditioning can vanish, given the right circumstances."

"Good soldiers don't make good slaves, Nik. If they did, they wouldn't be much good as soldiers," Decker pointed out. "Historically, they tend to take over and become the rulers. If you ever get near a library terminal when we get home, look up the Mamelukes or the Janissaries. I've no doubt that our dear Atabek has already thought about using his silahdars to make himself king of Danjor, or whatever they call their despots on that bloody planet."

"No doubt," Vulin agreed.

"What are we talking about?" Cyone asked as she sat down beside Decker.

"The wisdom of using slave soldiers."

"Didn't do the Gwangar much good."

"It'll do him even less good if he decides that we're his to keep and doesn't want let us leave Garada." Kidder dropped his own tray on what was fast becoming the command group's table. "Frog hunt, anyone?"

"Feeling frisky, Tran?" Cyone lifted an ironic eyebrow as she spoke.

"It's amazing what a few hours' sleep and a lukewarm shower will do to a man's outlook on life, captain," he replied.

"True."

Before she could say anything further, a low rumbling began somewhere above their heads, its intensity increasing at a rather alarming rate.

"Starship coming down," Resson called out from the tent's opening.

"Let's hope it fits our requirements," Kidder said. "I can't get off this dank, smelly planet soon enough for my taste. Any idea on how you want to take it, sir?" He added looking at Decker.

"Very quietly and very quickly." Decker drained his mug. "Lora, find out who in this outfit has ever done so much as a day's familiarization training in boarding party procedures, no matter whose Navy they were in. If I don't have to teach them from scratch, it'll save time."

"Will do. Count me as being one of them."

"Figured as much. Jase," he called out to the XO who was still staring up at the gray sky as if willing the incoming ship to land faster, "when that thing's on the ground, rustle me up a section of troops under a good sergeant and a pair of skimmers with machine gun mounts. I think I'll go eyeball it myself and see if it fits the bill. I'm with young Tran here: the sooner we're off this mud ball, the better."

**

Decker stood on cracked tarmac shot through with purplish green vegetation and observed the freighter through his helmet visor. To either side of him, armed soldiers scanned the surrounding area, ready to make any interfering natives run for their lives. Those who might have noticed the humans were probably smart enough to stay well away anyhow.

The vessel itself was relatively large and probably near the upper limit of tonnage able to land on a planet's surface. Though no expert on starship construction, he figured its lines were familiar enough that it likely came from a yard that employed humans, if not from the Commonwealth itself. It could also be of Nelvan origin, which was almost the same thing, give or take a few centuries or millennia, depending on who you believed.

What he could see of the crew favored his own species, and that was all to the good: it meant food and other facilities would be useable by his troops. It certainly was big enough to take the entire company group and all the gear they could haul to the spaceport, though close to two hundred passengers might strain the environmental systems. But there was no way around that. The next ship might be smaller or non-human, or not for another two months. It had to be this one.

The best time to seize it would be after it unloaded its incoming cargo and before it took on the outbound consignment. If the local stevedores were as useless as the Chulukian soldiery, they probably had a chance, but they'd have to move fast.

"Sergeant," he turned to the Nelvan non-com in charge of the escort, "I'm going back to the base with your corporal's skimmer. You stay here and watch the ship. I need to know when you see them start unloading, and I need you to track the crew by individual so we can estimate its size. I especially need to know if crew members wander off into town."

"Got it, sir. And anything else unusual, of course."

"Of course. Take crew pictures with your scanner. It'll help break down the numbers."

******

"Funny," Jase Resson said, after Zack finished relating his findings to the assembled officers, "now that it's no longer just a concept but an actual operation, I'm feeling a bit — strange, I suppose. It's as if seizing a ship for ourselves marks the exact moment we break our slave chains. Up to now, it could have been nothing more than another day in the service of the Atabek."

"I get that as well," Cyone said, "but in my case, it's excitement more than anything else. I just want to get going and lift off."

"How do you intend to do this, sir?" Sal Aran asked.

"Like I said earlier, quietly and quickly. Sergeant Gesh has the target under observation, and when he reports the inbound cargo off-loaded, that'll be the time to offer ourselves as the outbound load. We'll leave the canvas here but take all of the other gear, ammo, and rations. I'm guessing that if they do offload today, they won't be taking on cargo tonight. There are not enough hours of daylight left, and what we've seen of the locals, they don't like to work in the dark. Jase, have the skimmers loaded up now, ready to move. Troops carry everything they can. It's only a few kilometers to the spaceport so we can cover that easily on foot in less than an hour. I'd like to be ready to move at thirty minutes notice after last light."

He looked at Lora.

"Did you have a chance to ferret out boarding party veterans?"

"Other than you and me, there were fifteen in the entire group, all of us ex-Marines or Navy. I've had them formed in an ad hoc platoon under Sergeant Nunez, late of the 10th Regiment. He says he spent a couple of years in a cruiser's Marine detachment."

"You verified that?"

"He knows the procedure well enough he didn't come by it through book learning only."

"Okay. I'll be leading the boarding party personally." Decker held up his hand to forestall the inevitable protest from his second-in-command. "I know, Jase, but I've got to be the one who sticks his blaster in the captain's face and offers him a deal he doesn't dare refuse. You're not ugly enough to scare him, and Lora isn't big enough. Plus, I have a few ideas to sweeten the pot and maybe buy ourselves some willing cooperation. I spent a fair amount of time working in merchant starships after I retired from the Corps and I know how the buggers think."

"Sir," the radio operator called out from the other side of the tent, "message from Sergeant Gesh: they've started unloading."

Decker glanced at the time on the computer screen and nodded.

"Only two hours left until last light. That ship is destined to spend the night empty. Or so its crew believes. With any luck, half of them will go out on shore leave, and if my time in the merchant service is anything to go by, they won't have more than twenty or thirty crew altogether, maybe even less, if they've automated."

"You intend to abandon part of the crew on this pustule?" Cyone sounded disapproving. "Those spacers didn't do anything to annoy us."

"Peace, captain, I take your point willingly." He raised his hands, palms outwards. "We'll wait for the entire crew to be on board before we lift."

"You sound very optimistic about our chances, sir," Terkis remarked. "What happens if we fail to take the ship, or if its crew refuses to lift off?"

"Taking a civilian ship on the ground is pretty easy, Ker, when you've got a fully armed company group to play with. The crew won't want their vessel damaged. Otherwise, they're stuck here for a long time, and they'll sooner surrender to us than fight. As for not wanting to lift off, a blaster shoved in the ear can be mighty convincing.

He shook his head. "No, getting off Garada and away from our dear Gwangar of Chuluk is going to be the easy part. The hardest is going to be sailing in that tin can for weeks on end before we get anywhere we can call for help from the Commonwealth Navy, not to mention crossing some dangerous badlands in between."

Terkis nodded but seemed unconvinced.

"If there's nothing else, go forth and get your people ready."

The command group snapped to attention and as one, saluted.

"You buggers are enjoying this regular military crap way too much," Decker grumbled as he returned the compliment, privately pleased by the display of discipline.

— SEVENTEEN —

Decker drove around the terminal in the first of two skimmers carrying the boarding party. Thanks to the anemic, poorly maintained lighting, he was unable to make out the almost two hundred soldiers and dozen carriers hidden in the shadows beyond the ship they were about to hijack. If he couldn't see them, knowing where they waited, the ship's crew didn't have a hope.

A few late workers had watched them speed by with those emotionless reptilian stares, but none dared question their right to be at the spaceport, let alone be heavily armed in the process. Of course, it was doubtful any of the Gwangar's lowborn subjects spoke either Anglic or Danjori, and none of the former slaves could master the sibilant sounds of the Garadan tongue.

Night had fallen hours earlier, and Sergeant Gesh had reported that all activity around the ship had ceased. A few crewmembers had wandered off towards town, but other than a bored guard at the top of the ramp, nothing was stirring as far as the eye could see. This close to what passed for civilization, nocturnal creatures kept quiet, and the only sound, apart from Decker's skimmer detachment, came from a desultory breeze.

They approached the ship from the side, out of sight of the sentry, banking over at the last minute to send the skimmers up the ramp. Before the startled guard had time to react, Decker jumped off the top of his vehicle, blaster drawn and ready.

"Open the hatch son, and no one gets hurt," he growled, knowing that he made a terrifying sight for a man whose only concern seconds before was reaching the end of his watch without falling asleep.

"W-what is this?" He managed to stammer out as he instinctively raised his hands above his head.

"We're your outbound cargo, and we're ready to load." Zack poked the man with the barrel of his gun. "Open the hatch."

"That'll trigger a warning on the bridge," the spacer replied, still not moving.

Decker reached out and grabbed him by the front of his coveralls.

"I'm not going to ask again."

With fumbling gestures, the man traced a pattern on a screen set into the wall at the top of the ramp. Almost immediately, the massive door split in two, each half sliding to one side, revealing the cavernous main hold beyond.

"Ramp, this is the bridge," a bored voice rang out from seemingly within the screen, "why did you open the main hatch?"

Zack shook his head at the sentry, warning him not to answer as two of his soldiers quickly tied him up. When the door leaves had fully retracted, the skimmers sped into the hold and disgorged the boarding party.

With methodical precision, the platoon split into squads, each dedicated to the seizure of a particular area of the ship: engineering, crew quarters, environmental systems and most importantly, the bridge, Zack's own objective.

A very confused human female looked up at Decker from the depths of an old, worn-out command chair as he burst into the compartment. At the sight of his weapon, she raised her hands, frightened eyes open wide.

"Where's your captain?"

She considered the question for a few seconds and then nodded towards a door at the back of the bridge. Moments later, a half-awake grey-haired man stumbled out of the cabin, prodded by Lora Cyone's gun. Unlike the woman who'd been sitting the harbor watch, his eyes did not shine with fear once he'd taken in the strange sight of armed, battledress-clad soldiers on his ship.

"What do you pirates want?" He asked angrily. "I've got nothing on board worth stealing, and you'll never get away with it anyhow. The Chuluk military will mow you down."

Decker chuckled, raising his visor to show his face.

"As far as the Gwangar of Chuluk and his army are concerned, we're still working for them. But we're not pirates, captain. We're escaped slave soldiers looking for a way home. Like I told your man at the ramp, we're your outbound cargo, and we're ready to load."

The spacer stared at Zack with amazed disbelief.

"Escaped slave soldiers, human ones at that? It's truly a wondrous universe. And where's home?"

"Anywhere that's under the protection of the Commonwealth Fleet. My name is Zachary T. Decker, late of the Commonwealth Marine Corps, and for my sins, the commanding officer of what my troops have chosen to call Decker's Demons."

"You're very far from home, Mister Decker. What makes you think I'll take you there? I doubt you can sail this ship yourselves. Otherwise, my crew and I would likely be bleeding our last out on the deck right now."

Zack raised his blaster to eye level.

"This, for starters. I've got almost two hundred more of them, and each comes with its own highly trained soldier, eager to get as far away as possible from the Atabek of Danjor, our former owner."

The captain snorted derisively.

"Guns won't buy you a passage that long. You do understand that you're looking at weeks of travel on a ship that isn't rigged for so many passengers."

"Perhaps, captain." Decker nodded agreeably. "But here's an offer you might want to consider. My unit is fully equipped, including heavy weapons, and we have over a dozen solid combat skimmers. Once we reach the Commonwealth, we won't need our gear anymore. It'll be all yours, and you know as well as I do that you can make a healthy profit with it in the badlands."

The man considered Decker in silence, his eyes betraying nascent interest as he calculated the benefits of the offer against the cost of transporting escapees across so many light years. The sight gave the ex-Marine renewed hope. Deep space traders understood profit and this one was no exception. It was time to sweeten the pot and seal the deal.

"There's another inducement," Zack said when the spacer didn't reply. "The Fleet offers a bounty for each human returned from slavery. I don't know that they'll apply it to Nelvans, but I have a good hundred or so Commonwealthers in my ranks. If you negotiate it right, you might even be able to get your fuel costs repaid."

"And what if I refuse to carry you?"

"Then I'll make the same proposal to your first officer."

A flare of anger briefly crossed the captain's eyes as he digested the implied threat.

"I suppose you would do that," he replied grudgingly.

"We're armed, and we're desperate. It's not a good combination from your point of view. I'll just throw this out for good measure, in case you're thinking of a double-cross. I spent a fair amount of time working an armed civilian freighter as gunner and security officer. In fact, I'm probably still on the Merchant Guild rolls as an esteemed member. I also have two dozen ex-Navy and Marine types in my outfit. We might not be savvy enough to sail your ship through the Coalsack, but we can figure out if we're being hoodwinked."

"I guess you leave me no choice, Mister Decker." The merchant held out his hand reluctantly. "You have yourself a deal: all of your equipment, plus the Fleet bounty the moment I transfer you and your unit to Commonwealth authorities. Though how we're going to manage with so many people on board is something I'll have to discuss with my officers."

"Glad that you've seen reason, captain..."

"Berand, Dirk Berand. Welcome aboard *Dragonfly*, I suppose."

Zack flicked on his radio.

"Decker to all call signs. It's boarding time."

With a sigh of resignation, Berand turned to the woman still sitting in the command chair, a look of pure astonishment on her face.

"Jenny, rouse the bosun. He'll have to show these fine soldiers how to secure their skimmers so they don't go bouncing all over the hold when we lift. Then, recall the liberty parties and have the purser figure out where we'll be bunking up to two hundred passengers."

"We come with our own bedrolls, captain," Decker interjected. "We can turn any cargo hold into useable barracks."

"Sure," he nodded, "but you'll need facilities, and we're not exactly over-endowed in that respect. I suppose you'll be sticking to me like a bad odor, speaking of facilities?"

Zack grinned.

"Of course I will, captain. You know how it is: trust but verify."

Berand nodded again.

"Sure, though I wonder which gods I pissed off to deserve this. As if being forced to trade on the far side of the nebula wasn't enough punishment."

"So you are from what I call home."

"Yup, though we're based out of the Yotai system on a route that connects the Commonwealth frontiers with the trans-Coalsack sector."

"Dangerous space."

"We have our guns and our engines to keep us out of trouble."

"And now you have a two-hundred strong security force as well." Decker's grin turned into a fierce smile.

"If it gets to the point where you're needed, we're probably well up the creek, and I don't aim to let things go that far."

**

By the time a misty dawn unfolded over Chuluk, Decker's Demons were stowed away, secured and beginning to grumble at the delay in lifting off. Though Zack had spent the rest of the night shadowing Berand while Jase Resson worked with the ship's purser and Lora Cyone made a nuisance of herself with the bosun, the crew of *Dragonfly* had accepted the change in cargo and destination with the calm stoicism of deep space traders. They were twenty-five in all, and when Decker remarked on the small size, Berand had shrugged philosophically.

“Finding honest crew ready to sail in these parts costs a premium over the standard pay rates. It’s cheaper to automate what you can.”

He handed Decker a mug of real coffee, its aroma instantly triggering an orgy of anticipation in his salivary glands. It was ambrosia to taste buds long since inured to the bitterness of kahvass and he said as much.

“We get ours at Yotai, shipped in from Earth. Costs a pretty penny. I tried to find some demand for it in these parts, but even the Nelvans, who are apparently as human as you or me, didn’t cotton to the taste, so now I carry enough for the crew. If you have inveterate coffee drinkers in your unit, Mister Decker, we’ll run out very quickly, and I’ll become very cranky.”

“Most of my folks who drank the stuff before they were taken have been cut off for so long, they’ve probably developed tastes more akin to the Nelvans, so no fear. Now if you have Shrehari Ale on board, that could become a problem.”

Berand snorted.

“Sorry, my friend. *Dragonfly* is a dry ship. I’ve had too many bad runs with drunken crew in the early days. If we get a reiver on our tail, one soused bosun’s mate could spell the difference between escape and disaster.”

Decker made a small grimace but nodded approvingly.

“Probably just as well. After years of abstinence, I figure a mere whiff of booze would set my troops on a massive bender.”

“Captain,” Jenny Marsh’s high-pitched voice cut through the thrum of a starship waiting for permission to lift off. “Chuluk control has given us their blessing, though they express polite puzzlement at our not taking on the planned cargo.”

“Tell them we got new orders,” he replied. “Anyone living under a piece of work like the Gwangar should know about capricious superiors. We’re going to have to continue this conversation later, Mister Decker. Finish your coffee. I'd rather not chance hot liquid sloshing around the bridge if we catch some bad turbulence in the upper atmosphere."

The ex-Marine nodded once and drained his cup.

"Tell you what, captain. This is going to be a long trip, and I can only stand being called Mister Decker so often. Reminds me too much of my old man and he didn't like me enlisting in the first place. Zack'll do fine between us."

"I was about to reply that you can keep calling me 'captain', but that would have been churlish. Dirk will do for me, but don't take it that we're friends. I'm still thoroughly pissed at being hijacked, even if the trip will make us a good enough profit, now that I've seen the quality of your gear."

"Understood, Dirk." Zack smiled. "And thanks for allowing me on the bridge whenever I want."

"It's not like I had much choice, boyo," Berand nodded at the blaster strapped to Decker's hip, "but you're welcome nonetheless."

"Just out of curiosity," he said taking the command chair from the first officer, "what was it you were doing for the Gwangar of Chuluk?"

"Getting rid of an infestation. Unfortunately, the infestation got rid of most of my unit. Decker's Demons are all that's left."

"An infestation of what exactly?"

"Shrehari."

While a stunned Berand digested the revelation, Zack strapped himself into the gunnery seat, feeling eerily at home even though it didn't look much like the one on *Shokoten*. He ran his fingers over the console, instinctively activating the pre-launch check of *Dragonfly*'s weaponry and sensors. What he saw made him smile with appreciation. It was indeed well armed.

A siren reverberated through the freighter, followed by the first officer's voice ordering all crew to secure for launch and all passengers to lie down on their bedrolls. A low, nerve-grating rumble began in the bowels of the ship, followed soon after by an alarming lurch and a feeling akin to a heavy weight bearing down on the humans as thrusters pushed them free of the tarmac and straight up into the gray clouds. Within moments, Chuluk vanished from sight and then sunshine, the first Zack had seen since arriving on Garada, bathed the hull.

Soon, the sky turned purple and then black while the pressure eased as artificial gravity replaced the pull of the planet. A brief exchange with the primitive orbital control station and *Dragonfly* broke away, leaving the Gwangar to deal with the Shrehari invaders himself, and good luck to him as far as Zack was concerned.

Though he felt a stab of regret when he remembered the hundreds of dead slowly rotting north of the Gandabeg Mountains, they were alive and headed for home where he could collect the debt he was owed. The debt for a life extinguished so brutally, and another life sold into slavery. No refuge was secure enough to protect Harmon Amali from his vengeance.

— EIGHTEEN —

"I don't know how you Marines do it." Jase Resson wiped the sweat from his brow with an already damp cloth. "Living for weeks on end in a tin can, using the strangest nooks and crannies to keep in shape."

"Nothing to it," Decker replied with a pleased smirk. "You just have to imagine you're training to take over the red light district in Niew-Amsterdam."

The XO snorted, eyes following the troopers of Decker's Demons as they raced through the hold along a parkour that Decker had laid out among the packed vehicles. Boredom was the worst enemy in deep space, but lack of exercise came a close second.

"That's the other thing with jarheads. Sex seems to be the first and only thing on your mind."

"Like a wise man once said," Zack replied with mock solemnity, "a man who won't fuck won't fight."

"In that case, you should be a one man army, the way you've been going at it with Lora since we lifted off." He jerked his chin towards Cyone, who was starting her run through the parkour.

"Jealous?"

"Nah, but well done, Zack, going where few men have gone before."

"She's not that scary."

"Frightens the pants off me, if you want the truth. You know that none of the troops dare bring back broken ordnance. Our Captain Cyone's basilisk stare is more than they want to face."

"She does love her weaponry," Zack nodded agreeably.

"And yours too," Resson added, laughing.

"Excellent parkour," a gruff voice boomed behind them. "No doubt the laggards will complain about all the sprains and bruises, but it's the best idea I've seen for keeping fit during a long crossing."

The two officers turned around as a sweating Lieutenant Kidder skipped off the top of a logistics skimmer, rivulets of perspiration running down his face.

"I had an even better idea," Zack said struggling to keep a straight face, "but it involved convincing the crew to open the airlocks during FTL travel."

"You may safely keep that one to yourself, sir," Kidder replied, leaning over to place his hands on his knees while he fought to recover his breath. "Some of us aren't getting any younger, and that includes you."

"Any idea how much longer on this leg?" Resson asked.

"A few hours at best," Zack replied, straightening his back with a quick grimace. Kidder hadn't been wrong with his quip about age. "We should emerge to fix our leg through the nebula before the end of the watch, if not earlier, and then it'll be a clear run to the Peralka system. Captain Berand said we'll need to stop there and buy new parts for the environmental recyclers. *Dragonfly* wasn't built to carry this many eating, breathing and crapping humans. Plus we need food. Lora says we're within a few days of going down to ratpacks."

"Ugh." Kidder made a face. "We go there, the environmentals are going to die an ugly death while we're still in deep space."

As if on cue, the emergence klaxon sounded three times and Zack quickly scanned the hold to make sure all the troops still on the parkour course froze in place. Smashing one's face against the armored glacis of a skimmer, on top of the usual nausea, wouldn't do much for morale.

Thankfully, everyone in sight had the brains to stop and hang on to the nearest solid surface, though Decker suspected they'd find the odd dumbass among the riflemen kissing the deck at something closer to terminal velocity than was healthy for a human.

Emergence queasiness gripped them without warning and Zack felt a fiery spear thrust through his guts. But before he could even acknowledge the awful feeling, it was gone. *Dragonfly* was back in normal space and at its most vulnerable. He hoped the ship's gunner was alert to any lurking asshole who thought bagging a nice fat freighter would be a good idea, such as the fine folks who sold him into slavery.

The intercom chimed twice, and a voice called out urgently.

"Major Decker, please report to the bridge at once."

"Uh oh," Jase Resson grimaced. "That doesn't sound like Berand wants to serve you a cup of coffee."

"No, it doesn't. Wrap up the parkour exercise and get the troops ready for action. I want Nunez's detachment at their stations stat. If we have a bad guy on our tail, we just might get to test the theory that bored ex-Marines make good starship gunners. I doubt we'll have to repel boarders but what the heck, never waste the opportunity for a good battle drill."

**

"What's up?" Decker, sweat-soaked towel still wrapped around his neck, stepped into a bridge seething with fevered activity.

"Two ships showing high power readings are accelerating our way. In these parts, they can't be honest. You claim you've got more experience with this kind of stuff than the rest of us, so do your best warship Marine act, Zack."

"Any identification on the bogeys?"

"None, sir," the rating at the gunnery console replied without looking back at him. "Just fast and powerful."

"Most ships transiting the nebula drop out of hyperspace to take a sighting, so I'm not surprised that bad guys would be lurking. It's just that this time, our number came up." Berand sounded worried.

"Sir, we're being hailed."

Decker looked at the first officer in surprise.

"It's coming from those two, Jenny?"

"Yes, sir. It's in a language I can't understand. I'm running it through the translator, but so far, it's drawing a blank."

"Put it on." Zack grimaced at *Dragonfly*'s captain. "It's never good news when pirates want to talk to you."

As soon as the first words rang out from the speakers, his grimace became pained. Decker not only recognized the language. He understood it all too well.

"That," he said, "is Danjori, spoken exclusively on Danjor and taught to all who become slave soldiers of the Atabek."

"What do they want?" Berand blanched at Decker's words.

"Us. When we disappeared from Chuluk, his royal grossness the Gwangar must have sent a pungently worded complaint via subspace to my former owner. As we're likely the first Danjoran silahdars to ever escape, it looks bad for business. I can't imagine how expensive it must have been for the Atabek to charter a pair of ships. That is if he didn't charter more than just those two to retrieve us, but there has to be considerable pride involved. I'd say that the end goal is to bring all of us back to Danjor for a lengthy stay in the juluk pits, until we die in agony, as a warning to others."

Berand shuddered at the thought, having been treated to a lengthy and detailed description of the ordeal over a cup of coffee one night watch when both were feeling restless.

"Basically," Decker continued, "you're being ordered to heave to and surrender us to the Atabek's men – in this case, men being figurative since, by the accent, the crews of those ships are likely all Danjoran. If you cooperate, you may keep the equipment as compensation, and you'll be allowed to continue on your travels. If you don't..." he made a cutting gesture across his throat.

"Do you think they'd really let us go if I surrender you?" Zack laughed humorlessly.

"Considering that I'd not allow us to be handed over, the question is moot, but for what it's worth, your crew would end up taking our places in the ranks of the slave soldier regiment. I can't see the Atabek letting prime human flesh go. I certainly can't believe that he'd let anyone keep the gear. The bugger likes his profit."

"That's what I thought." Berand nodded. "What do you propose?"

"First, we don't answer them. If they can't come up with a transmission in Anglic, they don't deserve a reply. How long until we're ready to jump?"

"At least thirty minutes, but ideally forty-five. Crossing the Coalsack shouldn't be taken lightly and if the engines aren't properly tuned or the course accurately calculated, we might have some problems coming out on the other side. Some weird navigational hazards are lurking inside all that dust, and they reach into hyperspace for reasons no one has ever been able to figure."

Zack leaned over the gunner's mate and studied the sensor readout.

"They'll overtake us in twenty-five minutes at the earliest, but if they have missiles and are willing to risk using them, we'll likely be in range in fifteen. It all depends on whether the Atabek gave them leeway to take us alive or dead. I suppose a few symbolic offerings for the juluk pits would be enough to restore face."

"How confident are you in the troops you assigned to man my weapons?"

"With all due respect to your lads," he clapped the gunner's mate on the shoulder, "they'll be better at it than your crew — no shame on them by the way. The Fleet simply trains folks better than the merchant service, at least when it comes to ordnance."

He turned back to Berand.

"I suggest you sound battle stations. Jase is already getting the troops ready, but there's nothing like a siren to get the lead out. And Dirk, it would be best if you let me manage the fight. I've done it before in an armed freighter. You'll have to be ready to maneuver the ship at my orders, though."

Zack saw reluctance in the captain's eyes. Relinquishing control of one's own bridge was a tough pill to swallow for a ship's master, but he could see the sense in letting a warrior take over. Berand stepped away from the command chair and nodded.

"Not necessary." Decker shook his head. "I'll be fighting from the gunnery console." He tapped the gunner's mate again. "Off you go, lad. Take the spare seat at the back of the bridge and follow what I'm doing. I might need an extra pair of eyes, hands and whatever."

Once the siren had died down, the intercom chimed.

"Bridge, this is Resson. Gunnery detachment is at its station, and the remainder of the Demons are ready to repel boarders. I'm guessing we have bad guys on our butts. Any idea who?"

"Three guesses, Jase. And they all end in the juluk pits."

He could almost see his second-in-command blanch.

"The Atabek sent ships after us."

"Got it in one. They want Captain Berand to surrender us on the promise of safe passage and our gear as compensation."

A female voice laughed bitterly at the other end of the intercom.

"I do hope the good captain understands that it's an empty promise," Lora Cyone said. "That Danjoran sonofabitch isn't going to let anyone connected with the failure of his new model battalion live to tell the tale."

"I do understand, Lora," *Dragonfly*'s master replied soberly. "Not that I would have considered handing you over in any case."

"Glad to hear it, captain," Jase said. "By the look in Lora's eyes right now, you might not have liked what she obviously had in mind if you'd decided to negotiate with the bastards."

"Jase, Lora — we have..." he glanced at the sensor readout, "twenty-one minutes before they overtake us. We'll need at least five more than that to finish spooling up for the next jump, and I suspect that the Atabek will be just as happy with a few survivors as he would for the entire company."

"Understood. We'll do what we can."

"Bridge, out."

**

"They've begun decelerating," the gunner's mate said from the spare console ten minutes later.

"Just about on time, if they want to match our velocity for a little ship-to-ship action. Boarding action that is."

"Sirs," Jenny Marsh piped up from the first officer's station. "They're transmitting in Anglic now."

"Aha. Someone in the Danjoran brain trust has begun to wonder whether we Danjori speakers are actually on board, which explains why they're decelerating instead of launching a few birds."

"Put it on speakers," Berand ordered.

"Unidentified ship, this the Danjoran vessel *Xeriak* on a mission for the Atabek of the Great Kashdushiya." The voice was gravelly, the words were slurred, but the speaker definitely came from of the same species as the Demons' former owner. "You are believed to carry something that belongs to the Atabek, namely a portion of the Fifth Orta that was tasked to fight for the Gwangar of Chuluk."

Berand raised his eyebrows in question when his eyes met Decker's.

"Go ahead. The longer we can keep them talking the better. They'll be less inclined to start shooting. Just play stupid. The lizards are probably better at it than you, but if you try hard enough..." He winked.

"Danjoran vessel *Xeriak,* this is Captain Dirk Berand, master of the Commonwealth-flagged freighter *Dragonfly.* You'll have to excuse me, but I don't understand what you're after. I must confess I've never heard of this Atabek person for whom you work, and you'll have to explain what an orta is, and why you think I might carry part of it. We did make a delivery to Chuluk recently, but took on no cargo there."

A human might have been irritated by Berand's whiny, plaintive tone, but the Danjoran seemed unmoved.

"Then you'll allow us to board and inspect your vessel. If you do not carry that which we seek, you shall be allowed to go on your way unharmed. If you do not permit us to inspect your vessel, we shall assume you do carry the Atabek's property, and we will seize it by force."

Decker made a cutting motion, and Jenny Marsh muted the transmission.

"Agree to an inspection, Dirk. It'll buy us time. Those jokers over there probably aren't particularly good at matching velocities in a hurry. If we do a little jigging of our own – blame it on bad engines – we can drag it out until we're ready to jump."

Berand nodded, but he swallowed a few times before speaking again.

"Put them back on, Jenny." When the first officer nodded, he squared his shoulders and spoke.

"Danjoran vessel, an inspection is agreeable to us, even though I do not recognize your authority to board me. I just want to get back to my homeport for fresh cargo, so in the interests of time, I'm willing to comply. Every day I spend in space with my holds empty eats away at my profits. I shall strive to maintain my current course and speed, but be advised that my engines are jumpy."

"Acknowledged," the alien replied. "Keep in mind that we will respond to any hostile act with maximum force. We shall speak again momentarily. Stand by."

When the radio link was broken, Berand wiped a bead of sweat from his forehead and looked anxiously at his second officer.

"How much longer before we can jump, Markus?"

"Fifteen minutes at the earliest, captain. The engines are on the up cycle now, but we still have to run the full readiness test. I've got the course plotted and laid in, but if our so-called jumpy engines slew us around too much, I'll have to adjust on the fly."

"Understood."

**

"Why don't we just go back to the Kashdushiya?" Ker Terkis asked angrily, pacing back and forth in the starboard cargo hold that doubled as barracks for half of Decker's Demons. "It wasn't such a bad life. I'd rather that than being blown up by anti-ship missiles."

"Because the moment we fall back into the Atabek's hands, you idiot, we're dead. Not just easy dead like with a bullet through the skull, but tortured dead. No thanks. I'd rather be on the wrong end of a missile."

Nik Vulin was quickly tiring of his fellow platoon leader's constant complaints.

Lora Cyone, sensing the potential for an unseemly display in front of the soldiers, stepped between the two lieutenants and grabbed each by the upper arm.

"That'll be enough out of the both of you," she hissed. "Terkis, defeatism is an ugly thing. Any more of it out of you and it's a turn in the brig as a private. Vulin, a bit more forbearance goes a long way. Major Decker expects the both of you to do your duty to the best of your abilities and so do the soldiers under your care. Capisce?"

Terkis nodded angrily, shook Cyone's hand loose, and stalked off to the other end of the compartment.

"Nik," she held the other officer's gaze intently, "keep an eye on Ker. If he looks like he's about to do something stupid, you have my blessing to take him out – with a round between the eyes if necessary. I don't know what the major has planned, but I do know that he's a sneaky bastard, and we can't afford Ker or anyone else messing up whatever scheme he's running to get this ship away from the Atabek's hounds."

"Will do, captain."

**

"We're only going to get one stab at this, folks," Decker said between clenched teeth as he tried to picture the relative positions of the ships in his mind. The computer was better at it than he was, but it had no gut instinct, and their escape would have to be based on a judgment call, not some fancy algorithm if it were going to work.

"Sergeant Nunez reports everything ready, sir," the gunner's mate said, sounding scared enough to prove he actually understood their precarious situation.

"How long until the jump drives have finished cycling?"

"Three more minutes, if you don't want to analyze the report," Berand replied. "Twice that if you want to make sure we didn't miss a minor flaw."

"We'll have to skip the review, Dirk. They're abeam of us and getting impatient. The moment I fire off a volley, we need to feel like we want to puke. I don't think we'll be able to shrug off anything they throw at us in return."

The radio came to life with barely understandable instructions and threats from the Danjorans, and Berand did his best to win the game of stupid without being too obvious. Zack's gunnery console had lit up with hostile targeting emissions, and he knew they could be seconds away from a volley that could slice their hyperdrive nacelles off.

If he allowed that to happen, they might as well self-destruct. He had briefly considered turning the tables on the enemy and forcing an armed boarding onto their ships, but it was so dicey as to be irresponsible in light of the countdown to their next jump.

"All drives green, course confirmed — we're ready to go," the second officer shouted.

"Wait for it," Decker's voice cut through the sudden surge of hope. "Targeting on — firing now."

Dragonfly's sides erupted in a massive bloom of plasma bolts.

"Jump!"

— NINETEEN —

"Congratulations, Zack, you came the closest to giving me a heart attack since the day I found my wife in bed with my former first officer," Berand said, slumping in the command chair once the bout of nausea had passed.

"Yeah, but unlike that unfortunate episode, the other guy got screwed this time. Oh, wait a minute," the ex-Marine laughed, "I think I got that backward."

"You're a right bastard, Decker," Berand grinned, "but not enough of one to send you back into slavery. If you ever need a berth on a merchant ship once we get home, I'll be glad to sign you on."

"I might take you up on that, but you sail through a part of the galaxy where my picture is likely to adorn the most wanted list for a while. I've done the Atabek's juluk pits once. I don't intend to volunteer for a return visit."

Berand waved his objections away wearily.

"Never mind then. Jenny, sound the all-clear and put the ship at hyperspace cruising stations."

"Why shoot at them if we were jumping out?" The second officer asked, sounding genuinely curious.

Zack shrugged.

"There's a chance I might have caused enough damage to make them abandon the chase and even if I didn't, they'll not be mistaking us for an easy target the next time if there is one. Plus," he smiled, "it felt good to fire at the buggers."

"Do you think they'll pursue?"

"Hard to say, Dirk." Decker frowned. "If they do, we'll have to be ready for them when we next drop back to sub-light. They didn't look big enough to carry anything that could force us out of FTL. I figure they'll be tracking us by our wake and waiting for it to vanish, which means the

191

next time we see them, they'll be five hundred thousand to a million kilometers ahead of us, and that'll make escape more difficult."

"You're a real bucket of cheer, you know that?"

"Hey don't blame me, buddy. I'm a victim in all this. One moment I was minding my business hauling ropi oil from Yotai to Dordogne. The next, I was conscripted into some bizarre slave army. I just want to go back to my old, money-grubbing ways."

"I have a hard time seeing you hustling for cargo, Decker. You're a soldier and nothing else. You have no idea how alive you looked just now when you were scheming to outfox the Danjorans."

"And on that note," Zack said, faintly embarrassed, "I'll go see how my little flock is doing. May I assume that we'll be sailing the dark channels of hyperspace for a very long time this leg?"

"Longest leg of the trip, sir," the second officer said. "This is where boredom meets insanity. They say the nebula has a way of driving men crazy."

"Only men?" Decker smiled knowingly. "Just as long as we get to Peralka before we're down to eating ratpacks, we'll be okay."

"Yeah." Berand looked pained. "Here's hoping the recyclers hold out until then."

"If you need someone to clear off vat sludge, I'm sure I can find you defaulters who need to work off their sins."

"I'll keep it in mind. Chess game tonight?"

"Sure."

Decker sketched a salute and left the enervated merchant spacers to ponder over their narrow escape.

**

"I'm getting worried about Terkis," Cyone said, dropping into the folding seat she'd just pulled out of the bulkhead. Decker, as senior officer, had taken a broom closet-sized cabin in *Dragonfly*'s tiny passenger section, forward of the cargo holds, and while the privacy suited him, command group meetings tended to be crowded.

By the time Resson joined them, it felt more like the inside of an escape capsule.

"Why? Other than the lad is about as twitchy as I've ever seen him, he does the job okay."

Cyone shook her head.

"Remember how he was always the first to doubt whatever action you were planning? He's taken a step further down the slippery slope of defeatism. I had to break up what was about to become a fistfight between him and Nik Vulin. Ker was indulging in a long monologue about the merits of surrendering and returning to the Kashdushiya."

"Huh." Decker ran a hand over his bald skull, suddenly finding the absence of hair more than a little disturbing. "There's this psychological syndrome called capture-bonding. I think Terkis is getting a full dose of it as we get further and further away from Danjor and the Atabek. Do either of you know whether he had a session or two in the juluk pit?"

"I seem to recall that he might have been a repeat customer," Resson nodded. "Why?"

"I have this theory that the juluk venom has a sort of mind-altering effect on some people. The way I thought and felt after I got out of the infirmary was off-kilter for someone who'd just gone through the worst torture of his life. In any case, we'd better have someone keep an eye on Terkis. If he does something really dumb that could make us drop out of FTL in the middle of the nebula, we could be in big trouble, especially if those buggers are still chasing us."

"What could he do?" Resson asked, puzzled.

"Get into engineering and start pushing buttons at random," Cyone offered. "That usually doesn't end well. I've asked his sergeants to relay each other in keeping a discreet eye on him."

"Thanks, Lora." Decker shook his head ruefully. "At times like these, I wonder whether we'll get home without losing what's left of our sanity. I'm pretty sure the inside of this tub is starting to reek from overloaded scrubbers, and we're just not noticing it on a conscious level."

⁎⁎

As the days dragged on, Captain Berand found he had an ever-growing list of 'volunteers' to carry out some of the smelly maintenance tasks. Although the parkour had become more elaborate and thus more risky, and the various battle drills more intense, disciplinary problems stemming from sheer boredom at being stuck in the bowels of a ship without recreational facilities were increasing. Some of the troops reacted by looking for fights, others, like Ker Terkis, withdrew into themselves.

"Courage, Zack," Dirk Berand smiled sadly at the ex-Marine after the latter had unloaded his latest barrage of complaints about troops getting into trouble. "We're almost through the nebula. Another thirty-six hours and we'll drop out of FTL for a navigation check."

"Let's pray the Danjoran bastards stayed on their side or if they didn't, that they lost us during the transit." He thought for a few moments, mechanically stirring creamer into his coffee. "Do you always emerge at the same spot after crossing the Coalsack?"

"Within a tenth of a parsec or so, like most ships returning from the other side; anything more regular, and the pirates could get wise to our habits. Why do you ask?"

"Just wondering whether our Danjoran friends, if they're still following us, would be expecting *Dragonfly* to go sub-light the moment we're out of the nebula."

"Depends on whether they've done the crossing before." Berand shrugged. "Any sane navigator would want to take a clean fix after such a long jump through such a nasty part of space, so it's not exactly a trade secret."

"Can you keep going on this leg for a little longer before emerging?"

Berand scratched his chin thoughtfully.

"I suppose a little further won't hurt, but not too much. The tack for Peralka gets trickier the longer we remain on this course. Speaking of which, have you thought about what you'd like to do when we get there? I need to dock at the station, in any case, to take on replacement parts, but I can't buy enough food for your troops with my funds."

"Do they have an armaments broker? Pretty much the only thing I can sell is my guns."

"Don't you mean my guns?" The spacer's eyes twinkled with mischief. "I seem to recall that all of your gear is payment for your passage."

"Fine. The only thing I can sell is some of your guns," Decker grumbled.

"I'll make inquiries when we get there. It'd be a miserable place if there were nowhere to trade ordnance. There are still plenty of techno-barbarian kingdoms in the area that prefer to buy rather than make their own."

"What..." Zack's next words died on his tongue as an insistent buzz came through the open door to the bridge.

"Captain," Jenny Marsh called out, "the starboard drive just went amber. We might be forced out of FTL if it doesn't stop flickering. For some reason, I can't connect to the controllers – it's like the bridge has been locked out."

The two men looked at each other, and then Decker reached over to the intercom.

"Decker to Cyone, get someone down to the engine room now. Make sure they're armed."

"I'll go myself," she replied, voice tense.

"Is your little man with the head problems capable of buggering up my drives?" Berand asked.

"Maybe, but let's not jump to conclusions just yet."

"Cyone to Decker: we found Sergeant Nairn, who was supposed to keep an eye on Terkis, half-dead in the passage outside the reactor compartment. The door's locked, so I'd say it's a given that Terkis is inside."

Zack turned to Berand.

"Please tell me you've got cameras in the engine room."

"On screen," the first officer said.

"What in God's name..." Berand exclaimed at the sight that appeared before them.

Lieutenant Ker Terkis, a manic look on his face, had opened the hyperdrive maintenance console and was merrily entering every command string he could think of.

"I'm going to guess he's trying to trip us back into normal space in the hopes that our Danjoran hounds catch up."

At Jenny Marsh's incredulous look, Zack made an apologetic grimace.

"Yes, I guess he is insane, and we didn't notice when he went full on crazy. Can you override the lock on the engine room door?"

Marsh shook herself and nodded.

"Done."

"Lora, go get him."

Terkis fought like a mad crocodile, but the burly soldiers who'd followed Cyone managed to take him down, though not without drawing blood.

"Markus," *Dragonfly's* captain pointed a trembling finger at the second officer, "go down there and undo whatever that madman did to lock out the bridge and then get the engines stabilized."

"Could he actually have sabotaged us?" Decker sounded dubious.

"Damaged? No. But by de-tuning the starboard nacelle, he could have caused the hyperspace bubble to collapse. I'll be making sure that no unauthorized folks get past the engine room bulkhead from now on."

"I'll assign a guard rotation if you like."

"Sure. Just keep any other head cases out of it."

**

"Where did you put him?"

"In my cabin," Cyone replied. *"Dragonfly* doesn't have a brig. He's sedated, but I've put him in restraints nonetheless. He gave Klem a bloody nose and damn near broke Farkas' jaw."

"One last victim of the Atabek's slave factory."

"Let's hope he's the last, Zack. We're not exactly equipped to run a full-sized detention unit."

He shrugged irritably. Commanding a company in combat was something he could handle. Dealing with the annoyances of garrison life, particularly aboard a starship with few amenities, was something he could gleefully leave to others. But since he'd been elected CO of Decker's Demons, he was stuck with it, warts and all, until he could hand it over to someone wearing the right uniform and rank badges.

"Have you thought about what might happen once we let them loose on the Peralka station?" Jase Resson asked. "Especially if they touch alcohol for the first time in years, or ever."

"We've got to let them off, even if it's just for a few hours. There's no telling how long we'll be cooped up in here again for the next leg. Weeks, likely."

"We'll see when we get there," Decker replied in a tone that signaled the end of the conversation.

The intercom chimed.

"Bridge to Major Decker."

"What fresh hell is it now?" He angrily asked, pushing past his officers and down the passageway to the front of the ship. When he got there, the gunner's mate waved him over to the sensor console.

"Is that what I think it is, sir?"

Zack leaned over the spacer's shoulder and examined the readout.

"It is." He straightened his back and turned to an expectant Berand. "The universe is immense, starships are tiny, and yet we still managed to stumble over the wake of another ship ahead of us and somewhere to port."

"The Danjorans?"

"Possibly. If they've been playing catch-up without actually tracking our wake, they could be overtaking us in an attempt to get to the other side of the nebula and wait until we appear for our navigation fix. If that's the case, their sensor gear isn't quite as good as ours, which doesn't surprise me at all."

Berand joined Decker and stared at the readout.

"If we stick to that ship's tail until it drops out of FTL, then keep going for a good long count of minutes, do you think we can stay out of their clutches?" He asked.

"Provided your helmsman is good enough to stay right at the edge of detection, sure. It's probably the best thing to do."

"There's another alternative." Berand bit his lower lip, looking unhappy at the thought. "Not one I like, but we need to stop for food and parts soon, and if those are indeed your bounty-hunting friends, we may not have a choice."

"What's that?"

"Ever heard of Tortuga Station?"

Behind him, Jenny gasped audibly.

"Nope."

"It's the most villainous hive of treachery and deceit for a hundred light years in all directions, a station carved out of an asteroid orbiting a small star within the nebula. There's nothing else of use in that system, other than some profitable mining operations. And because it's far from any government authorities, let alone your Navy, it's become a crossroads for smugglers, a place of exile to beings wanted for unimaginable crimes and a port of call for pirates seeking shore leave and a ready market for their loot."

"Charming." Decker's voice dripped with irony. "I'll bet the moment we appear, half of the inmates will be salivating at our fat, prosperous-looking hull while the other half will be busy sharpening their knives."

"Pretty much," Berand replied dubiously, "though the criminal consortium that runs Tortuga frowns on any independent piracy within the system. If there's ship taking to be done, they'd rather make the seizure, which happens when docking fees aren't paid in full, or crews get too rowdy."

"It sounds like you know the place."

"I've had to dock there a few times. Not in *Dragonfly*, mind you, but in faster, better-armed ships."

"Well, if someone's foolish enough to try boarding us, he'll get a very nasty surprise. There's not a pirate alive able to take on two hundred trained infantrymen."

"Perhaps," Berand sounded unconvinced, "but they might damage us enough to make escape impossible."

"I'd rather take my chances with the scum of the galaxy than with my former employer's bloodhounds. It's a given that they'll shoot your drives off the next time we see them. What are the chances they'd know to look for us at Tortuga Station when we don't emerge on the other side of the nebula?"

The merchantman pursed his lips in thought.

"If you've never been there before, you wouldn't have an inkling it existed. Going to Tortuga is by invitation only the first time, and after that, you'd better be prepared to spend money."

"Captain," Jenny called out, "the starboard scrubbers just went amber."

"That settles it." Berand looked unhappy as he went over to the navigation console and entered some numbers. "Markus, drop us out of FTL and calculate a course to those coordinates. A single jump, mind you."

**

Decker whistled softly as he studied the image of the station on the main screen some twelve hours later.

"A hollowed out asteroid, eh. I'd hate to see the size of the guns they've got on that mountain. It'll take a lot more weight than any regular orbital could and if they've kept the skin thick enough, it'll take a lot more punishment too."

"Pray that we don't see the size of the guns, Zack," the captain replied sourly, "because that would mean we're cooked. Although, if your Atabek's hounds show up uninvited, we might get a glimpse."

"That, I wouldn't mind seeing."

"The station authorities have accepted our codes and directed us to dock." Markus sounded nervous, more so than usual.

"Then by all means, let's get on with it. Those scrubbers are just about done for." Berand didn't sound terribly sanguine himself.

"Anything you want my guys to do?"

"Standing guard at the gangway, looking like death incarnate, is going to be just fine, though when I see the station's management to negotiate for the parts we need, I'd like you and Lora to come with me."

"Some muscle?" Zack grinned.

"That and the both of you are pretty good when it comes to technical stuff, so if they try to pass us some crap, there'll be three of us to call bullshit."

"And we'll get a better price for our gear than a pure civilian could."

"Sure, though they've got some tough hagglers on Tortuga, so don't expect to get top cred."

"We'll see."

"If you'll excuse me, the docking procedure is pretty hairy, the way that thing spins, and I'll need all my concentration."

Understanding that he was being asked to vacate the bridge, Zack sketched a salute and headed aft to the barracks. Sal Aran's heavies would be pulling guard duty, and he might as well make sure they memorized the rules of engagement properly. He didn't want to fight his way through a mob of pissed-off pirates just to get back into space.

"We almost there?" Lora asked the moment he entered the corridor to the officers' cabins.

"Pretty much. Dirk kicked me out so he could dock without hecklers."

"A wise decision," Cyone smirked.

"He wants the two of us to come with him when he goes to dicker for parts. Something about being more technically minded, if you can believe that."

"I think he may have conflated master gunners with ship's engineers, though if we're going to trade some of our ordnance away, it is best we be there."

"That's what I said, the part about us being there to get a good price I mean."

"See, I knew I could allow you out in public with no adult supervision." Her grin was positively evil, so evil in fact that he felt a rush of arousal warm his body, but sadly there would be no time for a little fun and he grunted in reply.

—TWENTY—

The first thing that struck Zack as they stepped through the station-side airlock was the smell. It wasn't a bad stench, but it was different and faintly unpleasant, and he said so.

"They're not as punctilious about their scrubbers as we are," Berand said by way of explanation, "and we're not talking about the cleanest and neatest beings in the galaxy either."

"I'll say." Lora Cyone wrinkled her nose in disgust. "I'm going to guess that they don't have sonic showers and water is strictly rationed."

"Probably," Berand agreed, "and they use some plants in their hydroponics that exhale more than pure oxygen."

"Plants that emit sulfur?" Decker grimaced at the notion.

The captain shrugged.

"It's a big galaxy. Not everyone breathes the same mixture we do."

A tough-looking duo, humans of some sort, waited for them in the hangar. Dressed in worn leather, festooned with knives, and carrying scatterguns, they bore a gold insignia on their left breasts. The male, almost as big as Zack, gave the ex-Marine a thorough once-over, scowling throughout.

Decker winked at him and then examined his companion, a muscular woman who'd likely taken too many testosterone supplements in her younger days. He gave her his best leer out of pure habit.

Oblivious to the byplay, the captain nodded politely.

"I'm Dirk Berand, master of *Dragonfly*. We've got an appointment with Ser Flawent."

"So he says," the male security officer replied. "We're here to take you to his office." He nodded at the two soldiers. "You can bring your guns, but you'll need to show me that you don't have a round up the spout. We don't like negligent discharges on Tortuga."

"Sure."

Zack lazily pulled his blaster out and worked the action, showing that he'd cleared it.

"I don't like them either. When I discharge anything, it's always on purpose and well-aimed."

"I can vouch for that," Lora added, eyes dancing with merriment, but the double-entendre passed well over the Tortugans' heads.

They were led through a warren of passageways to an immense cylindrical cavern at the heart of the asteroid. The main habitat area, it seemingly spun around a central shaft that provided illumination to open bazaars, closed buildings, and parks dense with vegetation from a dozen worlds.

The rotation of the station provided all the gravity they needed, though looking straight up at the other side of the cylinder, half a kilometer away and thereby looking down on the opposite surface, made Zack feel dizzy.

"Quite the set-up," he commented. "It must have taken a lot of time and money to excavate."

"Apparently the original owners found the asteroid already mostly hollowed out," Berand replied. "They simply made sure it was sealed and gave it a bit more spin. It's been around for a couple of centuries so they've had time to improve, though I suppose they could invest in a few cleaning droids. It seems some of the visitors don't exactly share our definition of hygiene."

"Must be expensive to maintain."

"When you've got a monopoly on lucrative business lines in the Coalsack, it kind of pays for itself I suppose."

"I think I'm going to dislike the price tag on the parts we need," Zack said.

"Likely." Berand shrugged. "We don't have many alternatives. It's still a long way to the nearest Commonwealth outpost."

Tortuga wasn't nearly as crowded as Decker had expected it to be, though he saw beings of many species, most of which ignored them. He thought their exotic head tattoos would attract attention, but perhaps the station was one of those places where anything went.

Not even their distinctly military uniforms and side arms drew curious eyes. They passed a large number of businesses designed to cater to the baser desires of sentients who ply the star lanes. Judging by the sounds, odors, and garish sights, his troops could get into real trouble on the station if he let them off the ship. Glancing at Lora, he saw that she had come to the same conclusion.

"We'd better get what we need fast and do the repairs under way," she muttered for Zack's ears only, "otherwise we might not get away at all."

"If only we had a juluk pit on board," he joked, "as an incentive for the lads and lasses to keep their collective noses clean."

"Not funny." She elbowed him in the ribs, her arm almost bouncing off the hard muscle beneath his battledress. "If we have to, we can make it small parties, with the platoon leaders and sergeants liable for any trouble; no splitting up and instant demotions for defaulters, not to mention sludge vat cleaning duties as a bonus."

"It might work."

They walked up a short flight of steps and into a broad building with little to distinguish it from the others on that street. Inside, it seemed like any busy corporate office Zack had ever seen, which, if truth be told, wasn't something he'd come across much in his life.

The guards led them down a quiet corridor to a small waiting room with a few bare chairs and a battered drinks dispenser.

"Wait here until you're called." The male half of the duo pointed at uncomfortable-looking seats. "Don't wander off, or you'll have security on your ass in seconds."

Then they were gone.

"Delightful," Lora commented as she scrutinized the labels on the old machine. "I wouldn't try anything that comes out of this. By my guess, it hasn't been cleaned or maintained for so long that the fungus you'd find inside could probably cure just about anything, including a too deep attachment to life."

Luckily, the wait wasn't long enough for her to contemplate taking it apart, just on general principles. A rather exquisite looking human male appeared as if by magic and made small 'follow me' gestures with his long, slender fingers. He took them through a sliding door and into a rather opulent office that reeked of old tobacco if Zack's nostrils weren't leading him astray. A fat, pouty, middle-aged man with a thick mop of hair sat behind a desk big enough for a five-some, glowering at them as they walked in. He waved a pudgy hand at a trio of chairs.

"Please sit, Captain Berand and company. I am Kon Tragg, business manager for the Tortuga Corporation. Ser Flawent is occupied at the moment and has asked me to take over this deal."

The breathless quality of his hoarse voice spoke of a man unused to physical activity.

Berand nodded politely.

"May I present Major Decker, commanding officer of Decker's Demons and Captain Cyone, his adjutant?"

"Decker's Demons?" Tragg sounded surprised. "A strange name for soldiers bearing the mark of the silahdar."

"You're familiar with the silahdar?" Zack didn't bother hiding his surprise.

Tragg nodded.

"The Atabek's slave soldiers are known even on this side of the Coalsack, if only by a few cognoscenti of the trade. I do find it difficult to believe that you've escaped and set up your own mercenary business."

"And yet here we are," the ex-Marine replied with an evil grin. "We're fresh off a contract on the other side, headed for our next one."

The man rubbed the side of his jowls, contemplating them silently.

"What you do is, of course, none of my business, provided you stick to Tortugas' rules and pay what you owe. One of the rules is that you don't bring trouble to this station, so I have to ask, is someone on your trail? The Atabek of Danjor is not known for letting anyone escape, ever. Once a slave belongs to him, he dies in his service."

"We came across two ships lurking on the far side of the nebula, looking for us," Decker replied. "I gave them a little taste of plasma before we went FTL, but we picked up some hyperspace wakes too close to our course for coincidence. When they emerge beyond the Coalsack and realize we're nowhere in sight, they might wonder."

"Thank you for your honesty, major. Slavers aren't welcome on Tortuga, so they'd have no way of finding us quickly, if at all, and they won't be allowed to dock."

At Decker's surprised look, Tragg smiled.

"The one thing that gives legitimate governments with big warships heartburn is slave taking and getting them annoyed at us wouldn't be good for business. Enough money flows through Tortuga that we don't need the flesh trade."

"Makes sense." Zack nodded.

"Now then, enough small talk. You've transmitted a list of parts you wish to purchase. We can provide those, but I'm afraid the price is in line with their importance to a starship's continuing operations." He pushed a pad towards Berand. "Take a look and then tell me what you have that can meet the price."

The merchantman blanched as he scanned the readout, and then passed it over to Decker, who tilted it sideways so Cyone could see.

"I'd call it highway robbery," he said, shaking his head, "but then I'd have to forget I'm in the biggest den of thieves in the Orion arm."

"We do pride ourselves on being the best, major," Tragg replied smoothly, taking the insult as a compliment. "If you're unable to pay, I can suggest alternate arrangements."

"Oh? And what might they be?"

"The Atabek has a reputation for producing superb soldiers, and we're always in need of good security here."

"I thought you said you didn't condone slavery," Zack glowered at him.

"You misunderstand. Some good troops staying here under contract at a preferential rate might significantly reduce the outlay for the spare parts."

Something about the way he said it triggered Decker's bullshit detectors. Lora seemed to have sensed the same thing, judging by the look she gave him.

"Do you perchance have an infestation of some sort, Mister Tragg, one that your security folks can only contain, not eradicate?"

"What makes you say that?" The man lost nothing of his oily smoothness.

"You have perfectly serviceable guards, judging by the muscle-bound duo you sent to greet us. Granted, they don't seem to be much in the brains department, but that shouldn't be a problem in a confined space like this."

Tragg's small, dark eyes hardened.

"You're very perceptive, Major Decker. One of my underlings made the unfortunate mistake of renting out a section of the galleries to a syndicate from – well, it's not important where they're from – suffice to say these folks decided they didn't need to abide by the letter of the contract and are refusing to pay rent or to leave. That underling, of course, no longer works for us in any capacity."

"Doesn't sound like a job for soldiers."

"If you'll just let me finish."

"Sorry." Zack didn't sound at all contrite.

"This syndicate, they call themselves the Kalin Partnership, have damaged several of my security guards and while they don't cause trouble unless provoked, they don't allow anyone to enter the section of the galleries they've taken over."

"So it's like they've set themselves up as independents." Decker nodded. "I presume they have the firepower to keep your guys away and managed to configure those galleries so that you can't just cut off their air, water or whatever."

"It gets worse," Tragg sighed. "They also have access to a docking array, through which they get their supplies and ship their wares. Indeed, they've taken a part of Tortuga and seceded from it, along with almost a third of our guns."

"What are these galleries?"

"An area where mining operations drilled out a maze of passages and chambers. We took the metals present in the asteroid as raw materials for the station."

"Do you have a schematic?"

"Of course." Tragg waved away the question, showing some irritation for the first time. "Might you be contemplating a proposal to take care of the Kalin Partnership in return for the parts?"

"I'll have to see how costly this is going to be first, hence the schematic. Rat-hole fighting can get bad real fast if you don't have powered armor and I don't. My combat skimmers aren't going to be of much use, and neither is my artillery. Getting those Kalin critters out of their tunnels is pure infantry work, and if they know their ass from a fusion reactor, they're going to make it really hard for anyone to get at them. Like you said, the Atabek produces top shelf soldiers, and I'd rather not waste them on your problem if it means I'll lose a bunch in the process. I've got another contract to get to."

"But without the scrubber parts, for one," Tragg smiled, "you'll not make it, so this debate is purely academic. I know from looking at Captain Berand that he doesn't have the money. What he has is cargo to trade, and you seem to be that cargo, major. Please turn your attention to the screen on your left."

Zack got up and went over to the three-dimensional image of a rabbit warren of galleries that had materialized by the far wall. Cyone quickly joined him and the two ex-Marines studied the schematic in silence, nodding when Tragg, without being prompted, displayed all of what was known about the Kalin.

"What do you think?" Lora murmured.

"I'd rather sell the gear, but I think our Mister Tragg knows he has us over the barrel and will offer bottom cred for it. We're the best solution that's come by ever since his problem started. But," he shrugged, "it's doable. The heavies have decent armor and can do the breaching work. We'll have to make sure that none of the tunnels are close enough to the surface that a stray round could compromise the asteroid's integrity. There's nothing worse than hearing air whoosh out into space when you don't have a suit."

"So?"

Decker turned around and faced Tragg.

"We clean out the Kalin, and we get everything on Captain Berand's list, plus a bonus of fresh food and drink, including ale, for two hundred humans for several weeks. I presume you're not fussy about our methods and don't need any of them alive by the end of it?"

Tragg's jaw worked for a few moments while he considered the offer. It clearly wasn't all to his liking, that much Zack could read on his face, but he also knew the ex-Marine had made him the best offer he was likely to get. Trained soldiers didn't exactly cross the Coalsack every other day.

"You have yourself a deal, major."

**

In twos and threes, soldiers straggled off *Dragonfly* ostensibly to take some shore leave, though an observer with a suspicious mind would have wondered why they were all carrying small packs, or in the case of the heavy platoon, somewhat larger bags. None seemed to stop at any of the more or less enticing amusement spots, no matter how hard the various shills tried to pull them off the streets and into dingy bars or cathouses.

It had taken Decker and his officers less than six hours to come up with a plan that would survive at least until the first contact with the enemy. After that, even Zack would have little control of the battle. Rat-hole fighting was a squad leader's war. A lot of the opening round would depend on how alert the Kalin were. If they figured out the soldiers with the head tattoos weren't out for a good time, the element of surprise would be lost, and that could mean additional casualties.

There were four possible entrances to the galleries, one of which was used by the Kalin as their primary access to the interior. The other three were blocked on both sides, two of them since well before the syndicate had taken over that end of the station.

Decker stared through the polarized window of an empty office suite sitting at the top of a commandeered warehouse, studying the main entrance, as if he could magically divine what the enemy was up to. Hand-held sensors weren't great shakes at penetrating rock, especially if it had a high percentage of metal, but what they could pick up was a concentration of bodies, weapons, and presumably detection gear where they expected them.

A quick reconnaissance of the other entry points hadn't revealed much beyond the fact that the Kalin didn't seem to be wasting any effort guarding them. It didn't mean, however, that there were no booby traps and the breaching squads would have to be careful.

"The temptation to storm through that big hole is pretty high," Lora remarked, her eyes on a small tactical display that showed where each trooper was. "I've always liked shock and awe."

"Sure. Satisfying too," he replied absently, still examining the target, "but I prefer surprise to shock and awe. One of them just stuck his head out and looked around. Do you think they got wind that something's up?"

"Scummy critters like that often have a sixth sense, just like the scurrying little animals they resemble."

Tran Kidder, whose platoon was waiting in reserve downstairs, came up to join them in the improvised command post.

"The boys in place yet?"

Decker turned his head and nodded.

"Sal's got the secondary entrances rigged. With any luck, the explosives will shake those hatches loose and set off any booby traps."

"Let's hope there aren't any. If the heavies and Nik's platoon can do the work by themselves, I'll be just as happy. I never liked this kind of fighting, if you want to know the truth."

Lora smiled thinly.

"That just shows you're a sensible man." Three little icons flashed on her display. "They've set off the breaching charges."

Zack turned up the magnification in his visor and scanned the main entrance.

"Nothing's moving."

"That you can see," Lora corrected him.

"You know, for an adjutant, you're kind of lippy with your commanding officer."

"Funny, you've never complained about my lips before," she retorted.

Tran shook his head, amused that they could toss innuendo around even though the operation had started.

"I guess I'd better leave you to it." He turned and ambled down the stairs, footsteps ringing loudly in the cavernous building.

"All three teams are in; no booby traps, no resistance." Cyone stared at the data feed from the squad leaders' battle computers.

"Okay, something's set the Kalin off — they're stirring by the main entrance like they've been kicked in the nuts." Decker rose from his crouch, carbine in hand. "They've left one man at the checkpoint."

"Where do you think you're going?"

"I've just had a very good idea."

"Changing the plan in mid-stream is never a very good idea."

"Why do you think we've got a reserve right here, where we can use it at any time, like when I see the enemy make a mistake we can exploit?"

"Just be careful, Zack. I'll have Jase send up third platoon to reconstitute our reserve, as per good old doctrine."

He waved at her as he clattered down the steps, bellowing at Tran to get his troops moving.

"What's up, boss?" The platoon leader jogged towards him as soldiers formed up in ranks.

"The Kalin have left the main entrance with only one man. Big mistake. We're going to give him the shock and awe treatment. Take your platoon there as fast as you can and seize the bloody thing. What happens after that we'll figure out on the fly, and that's why I'm right behind you, in case you were wondering."

"Got it. Squad leaders – on me," he shouted, waving over his non-coms. After quick orders, treating it like a routine hasty attack, the platoon ran out of the warehouse, in small fire teams, keeping to the shadows as much as possible. After seeing the platoon sergeant out with the support weapons, Decker fell in with the back of the column, at once elated to be running into the thick of things and embarrassed at having given into the desire.

The lone Kalin didn't stand a chance. One round from Kidder's platoon sharpshooter laid him down for good. They were cautiously crossing the security barrier, alert for any remote weapon stations when gunfire echoed through the corridors, proof positive that the other platoons had met the enemy.

Tran glanced back at Decker, who gave him thumbs up.

"Go. Head straight for their command post. With any luck, Nik and Sal will keep them guessing in the rabbit warren below."

He nodded and then spat out a few quick orders, sending his lead squad down the corridor to the nearest intersection, where they took covering positions in case anyone tried to take them from the side. Then, the next team leapfrogged past them to do the same at the second intersection. It wasn't until the third squad ran past the remainder that shooting broke out on their level.

Zack, biting back his desire to join in the fight, stayed well out of it, letting Kidder's sergeants to their thing. He knew they were good: he'd trained them. Then it seemed like it was all over. Those Kalin who weren't lying half-charred in a pool of their own blood were surrendering in droves.

They burst into the improvised control center, cuffing the few technicians who didn't want to fight.

"That was a little too easy," the platoon leader commented, flipping up his visor to show a sweat-streaked face. "I don't understand why the security goons couldn't handle it. I've got a few singed troops, a couple of bruised ones, but nothing that a few days rest won't cure."

Decker grinned.

"Surprise, my son. One of the principles of war. We caught them with their pants around their ankles. They figured we couldn't get in the lower entrances without making a big noise that would give the game away. And the local rent-a-cops? They simply aren't trained to do what we do. Sometimes size isn't everything."

"Major," Nik Vulin called out from the far corridor, "there's a ship docked at this end."

"Really?" He leaned over one of the consoles and quickly scanned the readout. "It's locked on. Can't go anywhere without our permission, at least not without tearing off the outside of their airlock. Shall we go say hi and see if they shouldn't be paying some docking fees to the proper management of Tortuga?"

Then, something tugged at his memory, and he looked at the readout again, staring long and hard at the ship's image. His face tightened as the vision of a wrecked freighter and a dying woman danced before his eyes. Rage blossomed so suddenly and with such force that a red veil descended over him.

"Oh, we're definitely going to say hi," he said between clenched teeth as he fought to retain his self-control. "Just in case they decide to play dumb, call *Dragonfly* and have someone send a rocket launcher and a few rounds. That ship isn't going anywhere ever again under that crew."

He tapped a communications screen.

"Vessel docked to the Kalin syndicate's airlock, this is Tortuga station security. Your captain is ordered to step ashore and join us in the control room. We have administrative matters to discuss, now that the Kalin have joined with the station management. Do not try to leave – you'll just damage yourself."

When he didn't get a reply, he repeated his message.

"You'd think they've at least seen Nik's guys on their security sensor." Aran glanced down the corridor leading to the dock.

"Just as long as they haven't seen me yet," he replied through clenched teeth.

The heavy platoon leader eyed him curiously.

"Would I be right to think you have a grudge against that ship?"

"Not the ship, Sal, but its crew. I'll know it's the right one when I see its captain."

"Airlock's opening, major. Someone's coming out."

Decker turned to the security monitor and watched intently as a human female of indeterminate age with close-cropped hair appeared. He had no difficulties recognizing the hard, black eyes set deeply in a seamed face turned almost leathery by decades of exposure to deep space radiation.

She could still pass for any number of humanoid aliens whose reptilian ancestry left them with a rough hide, but she was clearly of his own species. A smile promising deadly violence spread across his face, alarming the nearest troopers.

When she stepped into the control room, she suddenly stopped, eyes on Zack's face

"You..." she whispered, fear replacing the look of annoyance she'd worn seconds earlier.

"Glad you recognize me." He started walking towards her, tossing his carbine at a nearby soldier. "We have some unfinished business."

She tried to back away, but Vulin's platoon sergeant pushed her towards Zack.

"It was just a contract, Decker, you know how it is," she gibbered, terror turning her worn features into a gargoyle mask. "No hard feelings."

"You owe me a life," he roared, wrapping his massive hand around her throat, lifting her off the floor.

"Zack, no!" Cyone's shout momentarily stopped him from tossing the pirate captain headfirst into the wall.

"This is none of your business, Lora. I've told you that I had a debt to collect, and her life is the first installment."

"She's the one whose crew captured you and killed your wife."

"Right on target."

The soldiers stared at their infuriated commanding officer and his captive with sick interest. Most of them had nurtured their own revenge fantasies since the day they fell into slaver hands. Watching Zack's vengeance unfold right before their eyes was as close to a private heaven as they could come. None would object if he executed pirate captain right there and then.

"She didn't hold the trigger, but she took the money," he said.

"Then get the guys behind the trigger out of her ship and kill them too."

Surprised at Lora's calm suggestion, he walked his prisoner over to the console and roughly dropped her to the ground.

"Tell your crew to disembark."

"So you can kill them?"

"They're dead already, but you're not - yet."

"You're seriously going to spare my life?" She cackled. "Why don't you go get them yourself?"

Decker smacked the woman hard behind the head, sending her nose on a direct collision with the smooth metal of the panel. In the silence, they heard a sickening crack, and then a flow of blood erupted.

"Tell your crew to get off the ship."

"Go fuck yourself."

This time, he slammed her midriff hard with a gauntleted fist, sending her into a paroxysm of dry heaves as she struggled to breathe beneath a badly bruised sternum.

"Tell your crew to get off the ship or I'm going to shoot it open with my rocket launcher, and you'll be my aiming point for the first round."

"Spare my life and I'll do it," she finally said, between tortured puffs of breath.

"Sure." Decker's evil grin didn't fool Lora, but it seemed not to register with the agonizing pirate.

"Nik," he called out in Danjori, sure that his prisoner didn't understand a word of it, "get some men by the airlock, the moment it opens, seize the ship. I don't trust the bitch. She'll manage to warn her crew somehow."

"Got it, balukbashi."

When he was sure Vulin and his men had taken up their positions, he tapped the communications panel and jabbed the pirate hard in the kidney.

"Talk to them. One word out of place, and I'll rip off your right ear. After that, I might just get nasty."

She tried to staunch the flow of blood from her nose but gave up under Decker's glare.

"Do it now."

Leaning over the communications panel, she said, "Garek, it's the captain. Have the crew join me here."

A raspy voice responded a few moments later.

"Are you all right? You sound funny and not ha-ha funny either."

"Just have the crew come out here." She tried not to think about the blaster stuck in her ear. "We've got some explaining to do."

There was a second or two of silence. Then, "Wilco, captain."

"That was foolish of you." Decker cut the communication and screwed the barrel of his gun deeper into the side of her head. "Not that it matters."

Shouts suddenly rang out in the corridor to the docking bay, punctuated by the cough of plasma weapons. Sal Aran gestured at his senior sergeant to get ready, but Vulin's men didn't need the support.

A steady stream of beaten, bleeding and shot pirates began to emerge into the control center, hands firmly placed on the top of their heads. Each was roughly taken in charge by Kidder's troops, had his hands tied behind his back with plastic restraints and was forced down on his knees. Decker watched in silence until he saw the faces that had leered at him as he was captured and beaten, and the woman he loved more than anything in the universe lying on the deck of *Demetria*, gut shot.

Finally, the fighting died down. Vulin showed up shortly after that and gave Zack a thumbs-up.

"There are a couple of fatalities and severely injured pirates we left in place. They got one of mine, but the bastard who did for him died a second later. Other than that, I've got a few singed and bruised troops."

"Shoot the pirates you left on the ship."

Vulin looked surprised but nodded.

"I'll do it myself."

"Good man."

"Now," Zack turned on the row of kneeling pirates, to whose number the captain had been added, and removed his helmet. "I sincerely hope that you fuckers recognize me because I sure as hell remember who you are. You ever heard the saying that payback's a bitch?"

They stared at him uncomprehendingly, until a light went on in the eyes of the crewman he'd sucker-punched before leaving their ship.

"Yeah," he pointed at the grey-skinned humanoid, "you remember, don't you."

"Captain Cyone, form the troops in a hollow square. I'm about to hold a summary court-martial."

She gave him a sad look but obeyed without demur. When they were done, Decker walked up and down the line of kneeling pirates, staring each one in the eyes – at least those who were brave enough to meet his.

"You are hereby accused of piracy, kidnapping, murder, and slavery. As a victim of said piracy, kidnapping, and slavery, and eyewitness of the charge of murder, I find you guilty on all counts. Under the laws of all civilized sentient species, the punishment for those crimes is death."

Decker looked around the room at his soldiers and found nothing but approval in their expressions, although some seemed a little squeamish. Lora gave him a slight nod, knowing honest folks in the badlands wouldn't question summary execution for piracy. She also understood that the soldiers of Decker's Demons wouldn't refuse the chance to get their own back on the likes of those who'd captured them.

Stopping in front of the captain, Zack raised his blaster in a fluid motion and pulled the trigger. It coughed, leaving a smoking hole between her eyes and she slumped down, instantly dead. In the stunned silence that followed, he quickly shot the pirates who'd boarded *Demetria*.

The stench of burned flesh and voided bowels filled the compartment until it became almost unbearable. He looked within himself for a reaction, a feeling of liberation if not of triumph and felt nothing.

The deaths had given him neither pleasure nor guilt. Perhaps he'd lost his ability to feel when they took away the one person he'd cared for the most. If that was the case, then all that remained was the implacable mathematics of frontier justice. It was time to end this and move on.

"Platoon leaders," he called out, voice harsh, "one volunteer from each squad to execute the remainder."

Sorting that out took longer than expected. Almost every single former slave soldier raised his hand, but in the end, the entire crew of the ship was sprawled on the deck, in various poses of death.

Lora walked up to him after dismissing the company.

"You don't look like someone who's happy at having handed out retribution."

"It wasn't supposed to make me happy," he replied, eyes still on the row of bodies. "It was meant to get scum out of the star lanes permanently. Nothing will ever bring her back, and nothing will ever give me back what they've taken. I will however, keep taking from those responsible. This was only the first step, and I'm damned lucky I got to them so quickly. Now I won't have to scour the badlands."

"Perhaps the Fates had something to do with it." Her voice was soft, almost philosophical. Decker would do what he wanted, and she could no more hold him back than she could strap hyperdrives to her legs and sail home solo.

He shrugged.

"It's time to get our payment and leave this rotting hunk of stone before I give in to my urge to sterilize the entire place."

He reached for the comms panel.

"Manager Tragg, this is Major Decker."

After almost a minute, the man's voice came on.

"I gather you're about to report that you've completed the mission. I've just been watching your soldiers exit the galleries in good order."

"The Kalin are all either dead or have been captured. The area is yours again. I expect our payment to be delivered to *Dragonfly* within the hour."

"Now, now, major, let's not be hasty. The job appears to have been much easier than expected and payment was contingent on the level of difficulty. I fear I must insist we review the terms of our contract."

Decker's face twisted in anger.

"The only review that's going to happen is a clean-up of the station's management, Demon-style. You think the Kalin gave you trouble? Wait until a company of pissed-off professional infantry comes down on your fat ass. I'll have my payment delivered to the ship now, Tragg, or you'll be chatting with the Kalin and their pirate friends in whatever hell scum like you get sent to."

There was a moment of silence.

"Pirate friends?"

"Didn't I tell you? You're getting a bonus, sunshine. They had a marauder docked. It's now minus a crew and therefore all yours. Consider it my gift to you for the prompt delivery of our payment. In case your scruples keep you from enjoying my present, I know from first-hand experience that they were slave takers. They made the mistake of taking me. Don't make that kind of error, Mister Tragg."

"All right, all right." He sounded more irritated that frightened. "I'll have everything at the docking port in an hour. You're welcome to run a full scan and satisfy yourself that I'm not trying to screw you over. The quicker you get off my station, the happier I'll be."

Decker's evil smile returned.

"Pleasure doing business with you."

He cut the link and glanced at Lora.

"Time to make tracks. I don't think we'll need to worry about rowdy troops on shore leave after all."

**

Tragg had been honest, probably frightened by a free mercenary unit that could solve his long-standing problem in a matter of hours and take on a pirate crew as well. The parts were new, in working condition and the food fresh. They undocked minutes after the last case of ale had been stowed, Berand wanting to get away from Tortuga as fast as he could before the business manager changed his mind.

That night, after holding a brief memorial service for the dead trooper, the men and women of Decker's Demons, less the more severely wounded still in the freighter's small sickbay, hoisted their first ale in a long, long time. For some, the first time in their lives. Because of that, Zack had restricted them to one bulb apiece. The remainder was under lock and key in the captain's private hold. They'd gone to bed rather quickly after that, the ship already in hyperspace and leaving the Coalsack far behind.

Decker, lying on his bunk in a darkened cabin, ran his hand over Cyone's lean limbs, feeling the warmth of her perspiration and the hardness of her muscles. When his fingers danced up her neck and over the back of her head, he chuckled.

"I'll be damned. You're growing peach fuzz on your noggin. The suppressant must be wearing off. It'll be interesting to see how you look with hair."

Lora snorted.

"It'll be gray and stringy, so I won't be any closer to winning a beauty prize. You on the other hand," she said, reaching up to touch his skull, "are still as slick and shiny as a newborn."

"Could a newborn do this," he asked, guiding her hand down.

"Considering its size, I'd say no."

"No meaning you're not interested?"

She grabbed a hold of him and latched her lips onto his. There was no need for conversation after that.

— TWENTY-ONE —

"Yotai?" Decker raised his eyebrows in surprise. "That's a change in plans."

He carefully filled his coffee mug, all too aware that the captain's stock of roasted beans was dwindling fast.

"Sure," Dirk Berand nodded at the navigation plot shimmering on the cabin's screen, "but we can make it in two jumps. Right now, I want to get us as far away as possible from our previously planned course, so your little hunting friends lose the scent. If I could do it in one, I would, but we need to get a clean fix and retune the drives. I doubt they'll track us down that far from the nebula and dare go that close to the Commonwealth. Plus, seeing as how it's the biggest shipping hub in the sector these days, I wouldn't be surprised to find a Navy ship patrolling the system."

"Hey, whatever gets us home the fastest. As much as I like a good pleasure cruise with amusing shore excursions, I have unfinished business to take care of."

Berand nodded, understanding the sentiment. His only reaction upon hearing about the summary execution of an entire pirate ship's crew was 'good riddance.'

"At least we have enough fresh food to last us until then. No need to go back on those awful rations you folks carry."

"It does keep the risk of mutiny down to a controllable level. So what happens after Yotai?" He dropped into the compartment's only other chair.

"Depends on your Navy, doesn't it. I expect we'll be carrying you into the Commonwealth proper, but when it comes to where we set you loose, I'm sure we'll get very precise instructions. Somehow, I can't see anyone wanting an unlicensed mercenary outfit running around without adult supervision."

Zack chuckled at the mental image.

"More so once they find out I'm in charge."

**

It ended up taking over a week, but the Atabek's hunters would be returning home empty handed, no doubt to the slave master's fury, for *Dragonfly* emerged at the Yotai hyperlimit without any more doubtful encounters.

"Captain," Markus reported after a lengthy scan, "I make out a Navy ship in orbit. IFF has her as the *Rodrigo Diaz*, frigate."

"The good old El Cid. Excellent." Decker grinned broadly, rubbing his hands. "When we're close enough for a radio link without time lag, I'd like to speak to them."

"El Cid?"

"Didn't you study your medieval history, Dirk? El Cid was the nickname of Rodrigo Diaz de Vivar, supposedly a fierce military leader back in the day."

Berand shrugged languidly.

"I'm sure it's a fascinating story, but I have more important things to memorize, like the private subspace address of someone who can help me sell off all that lovely military gear you're giving me as payment for your passage."

"Just make sure the Fleet doesn't get wind of it. They might not be too happy about the sale of unapproved, alien technology, even if it's a few generations behind ours."

"And that's why, when we land or dock somewhere, you and your people are going run off *Dragonfly* as fast as your little legs will allow so I can leave quickly." He shrugged, nodding at the Yotai system schematic the second officer had called up. "You might as well go take a nap or something. We won't be in range for a few hours."

"I'll give 'or something' a try." He waved his fingers at Berand and returned to his cabin, hoping that Cyone wasn't otherwise occupied.

**

When Decker stepped back on the bridge, a lean, hard face was staring out from the main screen, the face of a naval officer with three stripes on each shoulder.

"I'm Commander Nayaf, Captain Berand. What can the Navy do for you today?"

"I've got a passenger who wants to speak with you, commander." He nodded at Zack to step into video pick up range.

Nayaf's eyes widened in surprise at Decker's outlandish head decorations and his unfamiliar uniform.

"Sir, my name is Zachary T. Decker, late of the 9th Marine Regiment. Might I ask you to please look up the code 'rookie trooper sigma one seven three alpha' in your classified data banks?"

Both captains stared at him for a few moments, Berand without understanding, Nayaf with a knowing look. He turned his head to the side and nodded at someone.

"It'll just take a moment, Mister Decker." He glanced down at his command chair's console. "Or should I say Warrant Officer Decker."

"Sir?" Zack frowned. "I'm not sure I understand."

"You are Warrant Officer Decker, Commonwealth Marine Corps, Reserve, detailed to intelligence, are you not?"

"I suppose so, sir, but last time I checked, I was a command sergeant."

"Congratulations for your promotion are in order then." Nayaf's quick smile verged on the sardonic. "It says that you vanished without a trace almost a year ago. And now that you're back, I'm to send a specially coded message to your former superiors."

"If you would please, sir."

"I actually don't have a choice in the matter, Mister Decker. The recognition code you just gave me means I'm bound to assist you in your travels. Is there anything you need in the immediate, while we wait for a reply from headquarters?"

"Sir, I've drafted an after action report of sorts that should go with the message. You see, I brought a company group's worth of former slave soldiers back with me from the trans-Coalsack sector, and the Fleet is going to have to make arrangements concerning repatriation. Well, at least repatriation of those who were born in the Commonwealth. Sorry to be cryptic but it gets complicated fast. My report has the details."

"My, my," Nayaf's eyebrows shot up in surprise. "You're quite the dark horse, aren't you? I shall be reading your communiqué with keen interest. Do you need food, medical supplies, or sundries?"

"No sir, but thank you for offering. We took on enough at our last stop to get us to the nearest Fleet installation, with some to spare." Berand caught his eye, and he nodded. "We did, for a while, have a pair of ships on our tail, though, commissioned by our former owner to bring us back in chains and and hand us over for summary execution. They were last on our sensors when we transited through the nebula, but there's a chance they might come this far. The consequences for failing to recapture us are likely to be brutal so they'll be persistent."

"Understood. I'll have Yotai control assign an orbit that allows us to protect you from any interlopers. I suspect my orders will be to escort you back anyway, so we might as well get better acquainted. Perhaps you could shuttle over when you've arrived. I confess myself curious with Warrant Officer Decker's story and willing to spring for a quiet meal to hear it in person."

"Much appreciated, captain. We accept." Berand dipped his head briefly.

"If that's all for now, I'll expect your report shortly, Mister Decker, and then we'll see each other over a meal. *Rodrigo Diaz*, out."

"Well isn't that a kick in the pants." The master of *Dragonfly* looked at Zack suspiciously.

"What is, Dirk?"

"You being a Fleet intelligence spook and all. That's quite the mission you just pulled off."

Zack laughed bitterly.

"As you might have heard Nayaf mention, I'm reserve and more to the point, inactive reserve, like every trained Marine who's honorably discharged. I did do some small stuff for intelligence at one point, and I suppose they've kept tabs on me. What happened from the moment those damn pirates showed up to kidnap me was exactly as I told you. I was nothing more than a simple trader, doing my stuff shifting cargo from planet to planet."

"And yet you have a code that gets us protection from a Navy frigate, no questions asked." Heavy sarcasm mixed with skepticism in Berand's tone.

Decker shrugged.

"They told me it was to prove my identity if I ever needed to duck and hide under the Fleet's skirts. Some people out there with a grudge against me might want to take it a step too far. I had no idea they'd reported me missing and made sure that if ever I showed up, the Navy would carry me home."

"Well," Berand rose and stretched, "I suppose it'll simplify things for us. Jenny can handle the approach, and I find myself thirsty all of a sudden. How about you, Zack?"

**

The shuttle from *Rodrigo Diaz* docked on *Dragonfly*'s port airlock, and after it had cycled through, a young ensign stepped into the freighter, saluting Dirk Berand the moment she saw him.

"Tress Kennig, sir. I'm your pilot." She turned to Zack and held out a pad. "Mister Decker, Captain Nayaf has asked that I take a scan. If you could put your hand on the reader."

Decker gave her an amused smile.

"Nothing lost on your skipper is there. I suppose I'd do the same if some outlandish brute looking like me showed up, claiming to be a warrant officer and gentleman."

He touched the smooth surface and waited patiently. When the pad beeped, he removed his hand and looked at her expectantly.

"Thank you, warrant. Your biomarkers match those attached to the rookie trooper identification code. If you two gentlemen would like to follow me, please..."

"By the way, Zack, why rookie trooper?" Dirk asked as they strapped themselves in.

"It's an old joke, taken from a Pathfinder song that goes back to the days of pre-spaceflight Earth. The first line is, *He was just a rookie trooper, and he surely shook with fright.*"

"I can't picture you shaking with anything other than alcohol deprivation."

"Like I said, it's a joke."

"If you say so."

The flight over to the frigate didn't take long, and when Zack saw her through the thick porthole, he thought he'd feel the longing for his old career, much of which was spent as a pathfinder sailing into trouble spots aboard a frigate not too different from this one. But all he felt was a certain admiration for the ship's clean, powerful lines, a symbol of the Commonwealth's naval might. The expected homesickness failed to materialize.

A very polite petty officer met them on the hangar deck and led them to the wardroom, where the captain of the frigate was waiting. Walking down the familiar passageways, Decker breathed in the comforting aura of a taut, well-run warship and he felt his first pang of longing. Perhaps he should have taken the offer to return to active duty when it was made. A lot of unpleasantness might have been avoided, and she would likely still be alive. On the other hand, he reminded himself, the men and women he'd brought back from the trans-Coalsack would probably be dead. Karma.

He got some very pointed stares from crewmembers they met along the way, thanks to his outlandish appearance, and for the first time in a long time, he felt uneasy in his own skin. Going back to the old Zack Decker's appearance suddenly took on a lot of importance.

Even Captain Nayaf examined him critically as they shook hands.

"I guess the markings on your skull are as a result of your captivity, Mister Decker?"

"Yes sir, a sign of both being owned and a member of the slave soldier caste on Danjori, the planet where I was sold. You get them once you pass their version of basic training."

"If you'd like, I can have my surgeon take a look and see if she can remove the things."

"I appreciate the offer, sir, but until I've handed my people over to the proper authorities for repatriation, I'm still their CO, and that means I get to keep looking like them."

Amused respect glimmered in Nayaf's eyes.

"I understand."

He gestured towards a cloth-covered table that held a number of bottles, mostly alcoholic.

"Can I offer you a pre-dinner drink?"

"Do you have any Shrehari Ale, captain?"

Nayaf smiled.

"But of course. I would never invite a Marine aboard without making sure we have some on hand. It'll be in the cabinet beside the drinks."

Zack opened the refrigerator and reverently pulled out a dark green bottle with an alien label on its side. He stared at it for a few moments before reaching for the cap and twisting it open. The expression on his face as he took the first swig must have been something to behold since both Nayaf and Berand burst out laughing.

"I gather the life of a slave soldier is alcohol-free."

"It is sir and mores' the pity. I haven't tasted one of these in over a year, and the stuff we picked up at our last stop before coming here is horse piss in comparison."

"Glad we could provide you with your favorite libation as a way of welcoming you back. Your health, gentlemen."

After the toast, he invited them to sit, staring speculatively at Decker.

"Although I didn't want to make you pay for your supper by regaling me with your adventures, after reading your report, I confess that I'm vastly intrigued."

Zack shrugged off the half-hearted apology. He could understand the man's interest. If he hadn't lived through the events himself, he'd have been equally fascinated.

"Well, sir, I guess it all started a long time before we were attacked by the pirates, but unfortunately that part is classified – it was an operation that occurred while I was working more or less informally for intelligence after I retired from the Corps. But because of my part in it, relatives of the folks we put away permanently came looking for revenge and arranged to have my ship attacked, my wife killed, and me sold off to trans-Coalsack slavers. It pretty much went downhill from there..."

All through the meal, between bites, he told the tale, encouraged by Nayaf's obvious interest. He finally came to the end at just about the same time coffee was served.

"That's pretty much all there is to know, sir."

"And now what?"

"Now? I bring the folks with me home, hand them over to the Fleet, and then go off to find the people who ordered the pirate attack. They still owe me a life, and I intend to collect."

The matter-of-fact tone in Decker's voice struck Nayaf by its contrast with the violent intent of his words. It was clear that no one would be able to dissuade him from his goal and woe betides anyone who tried.

The door to the wardroom opened, revealing a fresh-faced ensign.

"Sorry, sir. You asked to be notified when the answer came back from HQ." She held out a pad. "We've received our orders and the message also contains orders for Warrant Officer Decker."

Nayaf glanced at Zack.

"It looks like you may have been recalled to active service if someone is presuming to order you around."

"Provided they get me where I need to go, it doesn't really matter, captain."

"Perhaps." He studied the screen and nodded. "I was right in that I'll be escorting *Dragonfly* to Parth. Once there, Captain Berand, you'll be landing on the military side of the Frederica spaceport to disembark Mister Decker's troops. You'll be met by a naval official to discuss compensation. As you might be aware, there's a bounty for every kidnapped Commonwealth citizen returned home."

"I do, and it'll be welcome compensation for my expenses."

"Your turn." Nayaf shoved the pad across the table.

Decker picked it up and began reading, his face impassive.

"Is everything good?" Berand asked after a while.

The Marine held up his hand, palm down, and wiggled it from side to side.

"The Corps is going to take charge of my troops. Those who want to serve will be given the chance to do so; the ones wanting a discharge will be given a ticket to the planet of their choice and a stipend. Until then, we're all to consider ourselves bound by the Rules of War and the Code of Military Discipline — me in particular, since I have indeed been recalled to active duty."

"Isn't that good news?"

"The part about my people is, captain. The rest on the other hand..." He grimaced. "Once I've handed the unit over to the senior Marine officer on Parth, I get to report to a Commander Hera Talyn of naval intelligence, who I know from previous operations. I'll bet she's to blame for my promotion while I was on the inactive list. I know for sure she has to be the one who got the brass to reactive my warrant, and that means intelligence wants me for some crap mission or other. I don't have time for spook games. Like I said, I have a debt to collect."

Nayaf nodded.

"I guess the old saying is true: once you turn spy, they own your ass forever."

Zack grunted in agreement, eyes staring through the pad and into a distance only he could see.

Turning to Berand, the Navy officer asked, "How soon would you be ready to break orbit?"

"Any time you call it."

"Good. Once you're back on your ship, I'll have my sailing master link up with your navigator to synchronize us. We'll be right behind you for the entire distance to Parth. If the bounty hunters working for that Atabek fellow decide to do any funny stuff, they'll get a lesson they'll likely not survive."

"That's reassuring," Dirk nudged Decker, "isn't it, Zack?"

"Huh?" Decker looked up, seemingly lost. "Oh, yeah." He suddenly felt impatient to leave.

"Sir, thank you for inviting us to supper. It's been a long time since I had a good meal and even longer since I had Shrehari Ale of that vintage."

Nayaf smiled, sensing Zack's sudden desire to be on his way.

"My pleasure, warrant. Welcoming home a man captured by slavers is an exceedingly rare occurrence and one to be celebrated. I'll wish you a safe return, though we'll no doubt speak again before leaving you at Parth."

As if summoned by telepathy, their pilot appeared to collect them and take them back to *Dragonfly*. Four hours later, they broke orbit and twelve hours after that, Zack felt the universe shift when they went FTL.

He intended to spend what time he could with Lora Cyone, for once they reached Parth, their paths would diverge, and they might never see each other again. But he could at least take comfort in the fact that unlike his previous lovers, she would make it out of a relationship with Zack Decker alive.

**

"It's not exactly small," the stocky Marine officer commented, watching *Dragonfly* land on the military side of the spaceport. "Though spending weeks cooped up in a cargo hold for the transit from the other end of the Coalsack would probably make it seem the size of a bathtub."

"I'm pretty sure that after years of captivity, the inmates don't really need much luxury," his companion, a tall, thin, long-limbed Navy commander replied. Her black hair, cut just below the ears and swept back, showed strands of gray at the temples. The lines around her mouth and crows' feet in the corners of her dark, deep-set eyes marked her as mature, if not middle-aged.

"Knowing Zack Decker, he'll have figured out two dozen ways to keep them busy and tired enough to not care."

"I've never served with him," the Marine said, "but the scuttlebutt in the Corps concerning Decker is pretty mixed, Commander Talyn. He's supposed to have retired as an alternative to a court martial."

"Correct, colonel, though letting him go was one of the more stupid things I've seen the Marine brass do. Fortunately, I'll be correcting that mistake. A man who can escape from captivity with two hundred slave soldiers in tow belongs in the Fleet, not roaming the stars on a tramp freighter."

"I won't argue that point with you, commander," he replied, smiling, "though I suspect your plans don't involve sending him back to a Pathfinder squadron."

"That would be a waste of talent indeed." She returned the smile, but there was a predatory edge to it.

The freighter finally touched the ground, thick legs absorbing its weight and its thrusters fell silent. Even at a distance, the two officers could hear the ticking of heated metal and tarmac contracting as it cooled. For several minutes, nothing happened, and then a section of the lower hull broke open to form a ramp.

"Do I hear singing?" Hera Talyn asked.

Colonel Faran frowned in concentration as he listened.

"Yes, that's what it is alright. It sounds just like a French marching song that was old even before the first FTL ships left Earth. Rather appropriate under the circumstances, I'd say."

A column of troops appeared at the head of the ramp, marching slowly to the rhythm of the song, arms swinging, weapons slung across the chest, and helmet visors raised.

"Definitely not any kind of uniform I've ever seen. Nor the weapons either. Is that Decker out in front?"

Talyn nodded.

"Can't see who else it would be."

They watched with fascination as the former slave soldiers paraded by in orderly ranks, still singing the ancient marching song until a command barked out in an alien tongue brought them to a crashing halt. Another order and the column turned into three ranks facing the two officers. To Colonel Faran's eyes, it looked exactly like a regular Marine parade, other than the unfamiliar commands, and he said so to Talyn.

"I'm not surprised. If he's had a hand in their training, he's giving the Corps two hundred professional quality troops; that's if they all decide to accept enlistment."

"If they do, we might just raise a sixth battalion for the Marine Light Infantry Regiment, which would be apt since a fair number of them are, for all intents and purposes, foreigners even if they are human."

"You'll have to do it without Decker, even though I have no doubt staying with his soldiers would be his first choice."

The big man at the front of the formation marched towards the officers with precise movements. As he got close, his eyes met Talyn's. She saw from his reaction that he wasn't exactly pleased to see her. He'd likely be even less delighted once she told him the news.

Decker stopped three paces in front of them and saluted crisply. Colonel Faran, as the senior officer, returned the gesture.

"Warrant Officer Zachary T. Decker, Commonwealth Marine Corps Reserve, reporting with one hundred and ninety-eight escaped slave soldiers."

"Welcome home, Mister Decker," Faran smiled warmly and stretched out his hand.

"Good to be back, sir." They shook vigorously. "Would the colonel care to inspect the troops?"

Sensing that it was important to the returnees, he replied, "I'd be delighted," and stepped off beside Zack, the two of them trailed by Talyn.

"They look like hardened veterans," the colonel commented after they'd walked through the formation. "Those who choose to enlist in the Corps will be welcome additions, and we'll make sure they get the right rank for their experience and ability."

"Good to hear it, sir. They're dependable soldiers, as capable as any in the Corps or the Army, and you'll find them loyal too. What happens now?"

"Now, Mister Decker," Talyn said, "you'll hand your outfit over to your second-in-command who'll be getting his orders from Colonel Faran. They'll be processed by the local garrison before shipping out on naval transports."

"Don't worry," the Marine officer said, "the Corps will take good care of them."

"And me?" Though he'd expected the order, Zack sounded surprisingly mulish, even to his own ears.

"You and I are going to climb into that skimmer over there and go somewhere we can have a long, quiet talk." Talyn pointed at the sleek vehicle.

"I suppose I have no choice?"

"None whatsoever. You're back on active duty, Marine, and you've been detailed to my unit."

Decker stopped and faced Faran.

"Sir, I place my troops under your care. Since it doesn't look like Commander Talyn will allow me to speak with them one last time, let 'em know I'm proud of them. And just so you understand, the Nelvans in the ranks will likely suffer some culture shock, so I suggest you keep them together as a unit until they adapt, though I think most of them will jump at the chance to enlist. Soldiering is all they've known."

"Understood, Mister Decker. I'm sure they'll make superb additions to the Corps. Good luck." They exchanged salutes and then Faran turned back to the formation, making a beeline for Jase Resson, now in Zack's place at the front.

"You want to put your gear in the skimmer, Zack?" Talyn pointed at the rear seats.

"Whatever you say, sir." He tossed his carbine in, followed by his pack. When he removed his helmet, he had the pleasure of seeing the intelligence officer's eyes widen in shock.

"The mark of the silahdar, commander. All of us have these tattoos and the shaved scalp that goes with them."

"Alright," she shook her head, "one more item on the to-do list. We can't have a Marine Corps chief warrant officer looking like a gang member. I'm sure the garrison hospital can remove the markings."

"Chief Warrant Officer?"

It was his turn to look incredulous.

"Not only a chief, Mister Decker, but a chief first class. You've just spent how long in command of a company group?" She slipped behind the controls. "I got them to promote you to warrant officer effective the day of the attack on the Amali compound, so you've got the minimum time and experience for a jump to chief's bars. If you're coming back into the Service to work for me, you might as well do it at a proper rank."

"And what if I don't want to?"

"You'd do what? Crawl back into a bottle? Ship out with half-pirates like the crew of the *Shokoten*? At least coming back into the Corps will give you a life and a purpose."

"Are you trying to tell me that she's really dead?"

Talyn gunned the skimmer's fans, and it took off at a steep angle, headed towards the military base.

"I'm sorry, Zack. We found your ship, or what was left of it, a few months ago. She was probably dead within minutes of being shot. There would have been nothing you could have done."

A sudden spasm of grief twisted his entrails, and he felt tears gather in the corners of his eyes. Until this moment, somewhere deep inside, he'd held out the insane hope that she might somehow have survived. That hope had just been irredeemably smashed. The rage returned just as suddenly, and he gripped the edge of the control panel until his knuckles turned white.

"I have private business to take care of, commander," he replied through clenched teeth, "so I'll have to decline the offer of a chief's warrant and a return to active duty."

"I was afraid you'd say that, Zack, which is why your recall was made under the involuntary provisions. You can still turn down the promotion and remain a warrant officer second class, though it would be stupid, but you're back in and have no say in the matter."

"Bitch," he muttered.

"Maybe I am that," by the tone of her voice it was evident she not only hadn't taken offense but also seemed amused. "However, if you'll bear with me, perhaps we can discuss how to take down the Amali clan properly as opposed to a one-man rogue operation."

Zack stared at her uncomprehendingly.

"Did you think," she continued, "that the Fleet would tolerate anyone conspiring to enslave a citizen of the Commonwealth, let alone a member of the Armed Services? There has to be a reckoning, especially with the Coalition, so they understand that some things just aren't done."

"You sure are full of surprises this morning," he finally admitted, shaking his head ruefully, his temper once more under control. "Okay, commander. I'll take the chief's bars and the pay that goes with it, and I'll take the job with intelligence, but I will collect the debt I'm owed, either with sanction or without."

"Since you've already started by executing the pirates who took you and killed Avril, it would be foolish of me to try and stop you."

"Glad we understand each other, commander."

His patented grin had returned, but with a hard edge that made it look almost manic.

**

Decker stared at himself in the mirror, feeling an unexpected sense of dislocation. When he'd woken up that morning, he'd been an escaped slave soldier, with the outward markings to prove the Atabek of Danjor once owned him. Now, with the tattoos gone and wearing a black Marine uniform, complete with the jump wings, Master Gunner insignia, and ribbons he'd earned over a twenty year career, he was an entirely different person.

The four shiny silver bars of a chief warrant officer first class on each shoulder strap merely added to the surrealism of the moment. Tossed out on his ear as a command sergeant for decking a captain, he was now back and wearing the most senior warrant rank, drawing the same pay as a major. They'd even given him the collar insignia of the 9th Marines rather than those of the intelligence branch.

He placed the sky blue beret of the Commonwealth Armed Services on his head and, in a moment of whimsy, saluted himself. If only the folks back at the regiment could see him now. He knew some officers who'd have a fit. Then he remembered that he'd likely be back on the books of the 9th as detached on extra-regimental duty, which meant the Corps' gossip network would go into overdrive soon enough.

"Ready?" Hera Talyn's reflection joined his in the silvery sheen of the mirror, nodding with approval at the well-fitted uniform.

"Looks good on you, Zack."

"What now?"

"We take a shuttle to the orbital station and hop on the sloop *Sparrow,* which has been diverted to take us to Fleet HQ."

"Caledonia, eh? Been a long time since I set foot there. I wonder if they still make that god-awful thick oatmeal stout. It felt like drinking sludge."

She gave him an affectionate punch on the shoulder, laughing.

"Glad to see some things haven't changed. Grab your duffel and follow me."

They stepped out of the transient officers' quarters and into the thick atmosphere of a humid, equatorial late afternoon. On the far side of the base's central square, Zack saw Decker's Demons drawn up in ranks, ready to head for the mess hall and their first Marine Corps supper.

He felt a stab of sadness at leaving them, but nothing was forever, especially not unit command. At least he could console himself with the idea that the Corps was a small enough place that he'd probably meet a lot of them again at some point. As for Lora Cyone...

"Did you leave something in your room?" Talyn asked impatiently, standing beside the skimmer.

"Sorry." He shook his head and trotted down the stairs. The intelligence officer turned to look at what had attracted Zack's absent gaze and when she saw the former slaves, she nodded knowingly.

"It's never easy to say goodbye." She smiled sadly at him. "Not that I want to pry, but I'm going to guess you had a lover."

Decker snorted.

"Is that what you think I do all day and night: drink beer and shag any woman who'll have me?"

"Hey, I just go by the evidence I find."

"If that's the quality of your intelligence gathering, I can see why you need me."

"Screw you, Decker." Talyn laughed.

"Sure. We can get on to that as soon as we're aboard *Sparrow*."

"See! I did get my analysis right."

— TWENTY-TWO —

"Mister Amali, sir," a tentative voice called out from the open doorway.

The narrow-faced aristocrat seated at a wide intricately carved desk looked up from his pad, irritated by the interruption. Ever since Fleet operatives had killed his cousin and the family compound destroyed, the full weight of affairs had fallen on his shoulders, especially those involving the Coalition.

Restoring the old rights and powers of the Home World leaders over the Commonwealth, and especially over the Fleet, was never going to be as quick and painless as Walker had wanted, but since his spectacular failure, things had become tough indeed. Naval intelligence now knew in which dark corners to look and that made things more perilous.

"What is it, Lyle?" Harmon Amali asked his aide.

"We've just received a message from our man in Fleet HQ. It seems that Zack Decker came back from the dead some time ago." The younger man seemed stunned and not a little scared as he delivered the unwanted news.

Amali blanched.

"How is that possible?" His voice was a mere whisper. "We had proof that he was sold to trans-Coalsack slavers."

"Apparently he managed to escape captivity and brought back almost two hundred others with him."

"No." Amali shook his head convulsively. "It must be a mistake."

"Our man's positive that it's Decker. He's back in the Corps as a chief warrant officer as well, assigned to naval intelligence."

The aide handed him a pad, and he stared at the screen, speechless, then he nodded.

"That's him alright, the man who dared touch our family. I can't understand how he got away but since he did, that makes him a very, very dangerous man indeed."

"He'll be out for revenge then, sir?"

"Count on it, Lyle."

The head of the Amali clan, now over his initial fright, began to think furiously. They'd not rebuilt the family island compound, preferring to let it revert to nature. After what had happened there, it was best they kept their distance and even if they had, the raid by the Marine pathfinders had proven for all time that it wasn't a secure haven from the Fleet.

He also knew from experience that a determined assassin would almost always get his target if he found it. After using enough of them on his own enemies, he appreciated the swiftness of unexpected death.

If Decker had the full weight of naval intelligence behind him, then he wouldn't be safe anywhere on Pacifica. He had to start moving and keep moving until he could figure out a way to have the man killed, which is what he should have ordered in the first place, instead of an elaborate scheme to sell him into alien slavery.

"Have the yacht prepared and have our man at Fleet HQ notify us the moment Decker leaves Caledonia."

"Of course, sir."

The aide bowed and left his master to stew over the slavers' failure to contain Decker. Not for the first time, Amali knew he'd have to do a job himself if he wanted it done properly.

******

None of the former silahdar would have recognized Zack Decker as he walked up the gangway to board the tramp freighter *Xenophon*, a few months after Harmon Amali heard the dreadful news of his survival. A layer of sandy hair covered a tanned scalp above a face artfully transformed into someone else's, while a short, scruffy beard ran along his square jaw line from ear to ear.

He wore faded, vaguely military trousers tucked into calf-high boots and a dark leather jacket over a white collarless shirt. An Imperial Armaments 15mm blaster, liberated from the intelligence storeroom to replace the one lost to the pirates, was tucked under his armpit.

He'd had to make a side trip to the Pathfinder School at Fort Arnhem to buy a replacement dagger, now strapped to his left forearm, hidden by his clothing. The school sergeant major hadn't hidden his incredulity and delight at seeing him back in uniform, and a chief warrant officer to boot. If he hadn't been able to beg off for reasons of security, he'd have been dragged out into the field for an impromptu inspection of the latest class of advanced pathfinder candidates.

It wasn't so much because Decker was an inspiration to all who jumped out of perfectly good shuttles from low orbit, but because he was one of the more notorious Corps legends who'd finally done well for himself.

He caught sight of his reflection in a window and smiled crookedly. Chief warrant officers first class were supposed to look like models for a recruiting poster. Zack's appearance was more like the precise opposite, which was the point of his disguise after all.

No one could have identified the middle-aged woman, similarly dressed as a spacer between paying jobs, who followed him through the ship's airlock. Where Decker's size made him stand out in any crowd, Hera Talyn could easily blend into the background.

They handed their identification wafers to the purser standing at the head of the brow. He tapped them against his pad and looked up, matching their faces to the pictures.

"Welcome aboard. You've got cabin twenty-four, one deck up." He jerked a thumb over his shoulder at the open staircase behind him, then turned his attention to the next in line, ignoring Decker's nod of thanks.

******

"Oh the joys of traveling steerage class," Talyn sighed as she looked around their cabin a short while later.

"That's what happens when you blow your budget on new office furniture. If you'd stayed with the old stuff, we might have had enough to take a liner and live in style."

"Screw you, Zack."

"What? Again?" He aimed a punch at her upper arm. "Remember that we only have to look like we're an innocuous pair-bond to outsiders."

"Doesn't seem to be working too well," she replied. "Did you notice the unassuming little guy in the unfashionable business suit who seems stuck to our butts ever since we got up here?"

"Yeah. What of it?" He dropped into the lower bunk and stretched out. "Maybe he wants to know how much you charge."

"Funny." She made as if to swat him on the chest. "Remember the time when Amali's hired guns nailed you on an orbital station?"

"Sure. It ended with the bastard becoming bug food. But that was a tag team, and they didn't look like seedy, out of work professors. If you're thinking hired assassin or Coalition operative, or better yet, Sécurité Spéciale, if they're not all the same by now, he'd blend in better, no?"

"The slightly creepy but harmless look is still good camouflage. We just happen to have better bullshit detectors than most people, Zack."

"As long as we don't see him on this tub, who cares."

"I guess I need to cut off both the booze and the sex, buddy. You're not thinking this through."

"Cruel woman."

He sat up and tried to grab her around the waist, but she escaped his hands.

"If we were being tailed by the creepy professor, chances are he'll have handed off to someone already aboard *Xenophon*. Someone we can't easily spot as being way too interested in a pair of vaguely disreputable, worn-out spacers."

"Paranoia's an ugly thing."

"Even paranoids have real enemies." She sat down across from him on a chair bolted to the bulkhead. "I just hope that the sighting of Amali's yacht at Nabhka was accurate. I don't know how long the boss is going to let us keep roaming before he hauls us home for a new mission."

"If he does, I'll just go AWOL," Zack responded philosophically. "Once I've killed Amali, I really don't care if they send me to a penal battalion for my thirty days penance."

"You know, for all that you had officer-level command responsibilities in a desperate situation, you still sometimes think like an irresponsible private."

He leered at her.

"Speaking of which, wanna see my privates, little girl?"

"You can be a major pain in the ass when you put your mind to it, Zack."

"Does that mean I get myself a direct commission? I've always wanted to introduce myself as Major Pain."

She groaned loudly.

"That's it. I'm going to go speak to the purser about getting my own cabin."

"And miss out on all of this? Enjoy it while you can. If you've never been to Nabhka, you have no idea what a planet without fun feels like."

"But it must be good for something if Amali's gone to ground there."

"Not necessarily. Anyone coming after him is going to stick out like a sore thumb in all but the largest cities. After what the Shrehari did to the place seventy years ago, during their occupation, the natives aren't keen on outsiders in the more traditional towns and villages. All he needs is a little out of the way fortress that's not on anyone's map and on Nabhka, pretty much everything is out of the way."

"I wish I knew how he was tipped off." She got up again and started pacing the small cabin.

"He probably wasn't, at least not to our little operation." Decker slumped back and stared at the underside of the upper bunk. "What I think happened is that he got news of my return to civilization. It doesn't take a genius to figure out Zack Decker, hothead, killer, and all-around charming guy would be out for revenge. He ordered the pirates to tell me he was behind my kidnapping and sale into slavery, and that little mistake sealed the deal. I'm sure he has people on the lookout for me, but I'm not at all convinced he knows that intelligence has sanctioned a hit on him. In fact, I pretty much doubt it. He's probably got me down as a rogue agent."

"Makes sense. She glanced at her timepiece. "Another two hours before we sail and they open the dining room."

"I've got a couple of ideas about things we could do in the meantime."

"Like I said, beer and sex: a Marine's biggest motivators," she smirked at him, "and since there's no beer to be had until the dining room opens..."

**

Hera Talyn was wrong. The slight, seedy-looking man from the station was sitting forlornly in a corner of the lounge, nursing a glass of purplish wine. He looked up as the two operatives entered and a faint smile played on his thin lips before he returned his gaze to the scarred tabletop.

"Should we go introduce ourselves?" Decker asked in a low voice as they made their way to the bar.

"And tip our hand? No."

They looked at the drinks selection offered by the automat.

"No Shrehari Ale. Bastards," Decker groused. "All they have is Pacifican horse piss."

"You're too picky." She touched the screen to order a gin and tonic. "Have a nice whiskey-soda."

"Can't," he replied after scanning the list. "No decent whiskey either. Just some so-so rotgut, but I suppose that's still better than what passes for beer on this tub."

He took a sip after the machine spat out an amber-colored bulb and grimaced.

"I think I just insulted rotgut."

"Cry-baby. Let's go grab a table. They should be ringing the chow bell any time now, and we don't know how full this place will get."

"Could the professor be a decoy?" Zack asked as they sat. "You know, just a bit too obvious so we notice and don't see the guy with the shiv behind us?"

"Possible." She nodded slowly. "With that kind of paranoid thinking, we'll make an agent out of you yet."

"And if my grandmother had wheels, she'd be a chariot. When this is over, I want to go back to a line regiment, Hera."

She made an exasperated face.

"I'm tired of repeating it, but your ass belongs to us, for now, and forever."

"I guess it's true love then."

"More like borderline toleration, but whatever you might do in a pathfinder unit won't be as important as working in the special duties section."

"So you keep saying. By the way, that creepy little fuck is still glancing at us." He took a long sip of his down-market whiskey. "Are you sure it wouldn't clear the air if I went over there for a chat?"

She considered the question, thinking Decker might have the right idea after all, but a chime rang out, notifying the passengers that the buffet line was open.

"Shall we?" She asked.

"Give it a moment."

Other passengers began to stream into the dining compartment, responding to the bell like cattle in the field.

"Let's see if our professor makes eye contact with anyone," Zack suggested, taking another sip of his drink.

"Tall woman in the lavender suit, with slicked back pink hair," she murmured.

"Too flashy. If the prof's a distraction, his partner will be more like the chubby blonde who's determined not to look at him."

"The one with the convoluted necklace?"

"Right. That thing around her neck would make an excellent short range bolo."

"Looks too soft for an assassin."

"And I look too stupid for an intelligence operative," Zack pointed out with a small grin.

"Touché"

"You didn't have to agree with me."

"No, but you'd have been disappointed if I hadn't. Time to get some food. I think everyone that's going to show up for supper is in line, including our seedy sod." She stood up in a fluid movement that hinted at a lithe and well-honed musculature. Feeling his admiring eyes on her, she winked.

"Mind out of the gutter, lover boy."

******

"I've had better in worse places."

He belched as if to underline his critique of the food. They were alone in the passageway, walking back to their quarters, the other passengers having either drifted off before them or still in the dining lounge, shoving creds into the drinks machine.

"And you've had worse in better places, so I'll save my sympathy for someone who deserves it," she replied.

Something suddenly tugged at his subconscious.

"When was the last time you saw the prof?"

"About ten minutes ago. Why?"

"You ever watch that really silly kid's show where everyone keeps saying they had a bad feeling about something?"

"Who didn't? It was all the rage a few decades ago."

"Well, I've got a bad feeling about this."

He motioned her to take up position on the other side of their cabin door before pulling out his blaster. Then, he touched the lock panel.

The seedy-looking little man was sitting on the lower bunk, legs crossed. Eyes devoid of emotion belied his ingratiating smile.

"Please come in and put your undersized cannon away."

"Who the heck are you, buddy?" Decker growled, stepping in and to the side so that Hera could join him. "And what are you doing in our compartment?"

"Close the door and, as I just asked, put your gun away. I'm not about to try anything stupid with two obviously well-trained operatives in a confined space."

Talyn nodded at Zack, who touched the controls. The door slid back into place with a sigh, cutting them off from any passers-by.

"I'll holster his," Decker waggled the blaster, "once you tell me who you are."

"May I pull my ID from my pocket?" He raised his right hand and pointed at his left breast.

Decker nodded. "Yes, but if anything else comes out, you're going to need an artificial hand."

The man dipped his thumb and forefinger into the narrow opening and made a great show of pulling out a gray wafer, which he held up, shiny side facing the intelligence officers.

Zack snorted after reading the display.

"Inspector Grint, Commonwealth Constabulary. Why does a cop think he can just bust into someone else's cabin? Even you guys have to follow the law."

"On board a commercial starship? Please. I can do whatever I believe is covered by the doctrine of reasonable suspicion." The smile didn't waver. "I just want to have a quiet conversation with the two of you. If I'm happy, you won't have to talk to me for the rest of the voyage. Now about your gun?"

Decker looked down at the weapon and shrugged.

"Sure. I'll stow it. If you get uppity, I can just reach out and break your scrawny neck."

"Thank you. I won't insult your intelligence by asking you for ID or names. It's a given that you're traveling under aliases." When neither of them reacted, he continued. "I'll get straight to the point, then. I've been following a known team of private contractors, guns for hire, if you like, who, for the longest time, seemed to be waiting for someone. They appeared to take keen interest in you two the moment you appeared on the station, though I could sense a certain hesitancy, as if they weren't entirely convinced you were their intended targets. It makes sense that if you're traveling under assumed identities, you probably don't look like yourselves either. It could also be that they expected only one of you and when two showed up, they had to re-arrange their plans. So I asked myself why the folks I was watching were fascinated by a pair of rather rough-looking, middle-aged spacers. You know what I deduced?"

He glanced at each of them in turn, as if expecting an answer when the question was obviously meant to be rhetorical.

"I'm sure you're about to enlighten us, inspector," Talyn said, not bothering to hide the sarcasm in her tone. He seemed momentarily annoyed at the interruption.

"I told myself that perhaps these lovely people were operatives of some government agency other than the one I represent. You two, especially you, buddy, carry the military aroma that long-service veterans can never quite wash away. That, of course, made me wonder why hired guns were on your scent."

"Why wouldn't we be private sector types?" Decker shrugged dismissively. "Think about outfits like the Avalon Corporation."

Grint chuckled softly.

"I've yet to see private sector operatives warrant the attention of high priced contractors and I've been in this game for thirty years."

They stared at him impassively.

"You have no idea then, why someone might wish to make you vanish?"

"Nope. We're just ordinary spacers between jobs and haven't annoyed anyone lately." He glanced at his companion. "Did you piss someone off that I don't know about, honey?"

"Other than that idiot on Dordogne who got miffed when I flirted with his wife? No."

"Huh. Well, she was kind of cute, and he was a bit of a dork so I can understand where he saw you as serious competition."

"Funny." Grint tilted his head to the side, seemingly unimpressed by the banter. "You don't seem especially concerned about the information I've just imparted."

"We can handle ourselves, inspector," Talyn replied nonchalantly. "And I really don't believe someone would send pros after nobodies like us. You're on the wrong scent."

The policeman rose to his feet.

"Alright. Have it your way. I just thought you might be willing to help me catch some dangerous people and perhaps save your own skins. If you change your minds, just let me know."

As he passed between them to leave the cabin, Decker held up his hand.

"Are these supposed assassins on board?"

Grint's broad grin was as counterfeit as their identities.

"But of course. If they weren't here, I wouldn't be either. Have an excellent night."

When the door was shut once again, Decker grimaced.

"Do you believe him?"

"What reason would he have to wind up a pair of perfect strangers?"

"That can only mean Amali's put out a contract on me. His last attempt went sideways, so now he's called in the best his dirty money can buy, while he's hiding on one of the most miserable colonies in human space."

"I suppose you should feel flattered if you scared him that much, Zack." She began to undress for bed, tossing her sidearm on the upper bunk. "Make sure the door's properly locked from the inside. If a Constabulary flatfoot got in, there's no telling who else might try."

— TWENTY-THREE —

"Ser Wenn." An unwanted hand tapped on Zack's shoulder. "Ser Wenn."

He looked up from his meal into the face of a solemn man wearing the three stripes of a merchant first officer.

"What is it?" He sounded irritable, mostly because he'd momentarily forgotten his cover name.

"Might I have a word with you and your companion?"

"What is this about?" Hera asked, dark eyes examining the man with undisguised suspicion.

"It would be better if we moved to a more private space." He gestured towards a door leading from the passenger lounge to a compartment closed to all but the crew.

Decker glanced at Talyn, who gave him a slight nod.

"As you wish." He rose to his full height. "Lead on."

Once they were in the otherwise unoccupied room, the first officer asked them to sit and took a facing chair.

"I'm investigating the disappearance of a passenger who was last seen leaving your cabin almost two standard days ago."

"And who might that be?" Talyn asked

"Regar Grint. A short man, somewhat disheveled looking by all accounts. A witness places him in the corridor by your compartment shortly after one bell in the evening watch. He's not been in his quarters since that time, and no one aboard can remember seeing him."

"Nothing to do with us, first officer."

"Perhaps, Ser Wenn, but would you be kind enough to tell me about your relationship with the passenger?"

"He thought my partner here," Zack nodded towards Hera, "looked familiar and wanted to renew his acquaintance."

"And were you an acquaintance, Sera Venzi?"

"No." She shook her head. "I've never met the gentleman. Told him as much and after that, he left. We went to bed and did what pair-bonds usually do when they're bored."

Decker fought hard to restrain his amusement at the first officer's almost prudish reaction to Talyn's quip. Some cultures preferred not to think about where babies came from.

"Well," he said, hiding his momentary confusion, "do let me know if you remember anything. Losing a passenger while the ship's in hyperspace is quite an unusual thing and as you can appreciate, we'd rather resolve it before touching port."

"Understood." Zack dipped his head. "Was there anything else?"

"Not at this time, Ser Wenn, Sera Venzi. Thank you for your cooperation."

"Glad to be of service," Talyn murmured as the merchant officer guided them back to the main lounge.

They grabbed a drink from the dispenser, neither willing to speak within earshot of another living being, so instead of staying in the common compartment, they headed back to their cabin, eyes, and ears on full alert. If Grint was the real deal and hadn't been spinning tales, his disappearance was worrisome.

"Why do I figure they won't find our friendly neighborhood copper until they drain the environmental sludge vats during the next major maintenance cycle?"

Decker dropped into his bunk and took a long sip of rotgut and soda.

Talyn didn't answer, preferring to pace like a caged lioness, drinking from her bulb every so often.

"Let's say Grint really was a Constabulary Inspector, and let's also say he was on the tail of a hit squad that just happened to have a contract for our demise, why kill him?"

"So we'd be easier to take? He did seem to know who they might be."

"Seriously, Zack? In what universe does that scan? Whether the inspector was alive or not, the work of assassinating us on board a ship in hyperspace would be equally difficult. Now, they've more or less tipped their hand."

"So maybe they've got a ninja hidden in the closet, just waiting for you to start snoring."

"I do not snore."

"Suit yourself. Next thing you're going to say is that you don't moan during sex."

"Try and take this seriously, Zack."

"Why? Grint's probably dead, for whatever reasons his murderer or murderers had. We're alive and a lot harder to take down, if only because there are two of us. We can cover each other's back."

"You're saying that if we'd gone along with Grint, he might still be alive, us keeping an eye on him and all."

"Yeah." Decker nodded, altogether unhappy at the turn of events. "He might have come across as a pain in the ass that had all the fashion sense of a cactus, but he was still a Service cousin, as the bloody gray legs go."

"Sleep in shifts?"

"No question. I'll take the first watch until eight bells."

"We get off at the next port," Talyn climbed into her bunk fully dressed, blaster close at hand, "and find alternate transportation to Nabhka."

"Or we find whoever's behind Grint's disappearance and do unto them."

"Don't you think several passengers vanishing while the ship's in hyperspace will attract some attention from law enforcement when we dock? The first officer seems to believe that we're potential suspects already, and he will radio ahead when we drop out of FTL."

"We make him disappear as well?" Decker asked facetiously.

"Grow up, Zack." With that, she wrapped herself in a blanket and turned her face to towards the bulkhead.

Whistling under his breath, he quickly stripped his blaster, checked every part, and then put it back together again. Anyone coming through the cabin door uninvited would sport a charred, smoking hole in the middle of the chest before he could take more than a step.

******

"He fell down an access shaft?" Decker didn't bother hiding his incredulity. "That's the oldest trick in the book, older even than stashing a body in a Townson tube."

The rumors of Inspector Grint's demise were bouncing around the lounge two days later. The crew hadn't bothered to confirm anything beyond regretfully informing the passengers that an unfortunate accident had occurred.

"Considering non-crew aren't allowed anywhere near the mechanical areas, you'd think they'd have had a camera or two detecting our detective leaving these hallowed decks." Talyn took a bite of her bland breakfast sandwich and grimaced.

"Or someone carrying his dead body to the head of the shaft."

"Whatever." She shook her head. "Let's not get any ideas about snooping around, okay Ser Wenn. Otherwise, people will be wondering why two spacers with, as Grint said, a military aroma to them, are playing investigator."

"Sure. We'll just let whoever killed him come after us at their leisure, Sera Venzi."

"At this point, if they haven't made a move yet, I'm pretty sure they'll wait until we're off the ship. Killing Grint was probably a way to stampede us onto the next station instead of staying until Nabhka."

"So why not keep riding *Xenophon*?"

"Because we'll never make down to the planet's surface alive. They'll have buddies ready to greet us on the orbital and flush us into the station's garbage compactor."

"I wish Grint had told us who he suspected," he grumbled.

"We would have had to collaborate with him, you know that. Plus there's the little matter that telling a Constabulary Inspector we're merrily on our way to excise a cancerous pustule called Harmon Amali would have caused him to arrest us on the spot."

"Or help us on our way."

"No. The one thing the Constabulary has going for it is scrupulous honesty. While the Fleet might think it a splendid idea to turn Amali into an example for the rest of the Coalition and thereby teach them that you don't sell naval personnel into slavery, Grint and his people would call it first-degree murder, not justice."

"You know, Hera," he said after a moment's silence, "I think we haven't been touched yet because Grint's unknown killers are waiting for confirmation. I look different enough as Ser Wenn, and you're not even supposed to be traveling with me."

"That would mean they're top drawer pros, the kind that makes completely sure they have the right target before pulling the trigger."

"And it also means that the moment we dock at Merseaux, confirmation will likely be waiting for them. My altered appearance and cover identity will only go so far with that level of scrutiny. Unless, by a fluke, they make you, you're likely to be either knocked around enough to make it look like a robbery or simply become collateral damage."

"You're so cheerful in the morning, Ser Wenn."

"Hey," his face took on a wounded expression, "I've explained how you can put a smile on my face. If you don't want to do it, then it's no longer my problem."

**

"To all passengers, this is the bridge. We have docked at Merseaux Station, and the gangway is now open to those wishing to disembark. For passengers continuing on *Xenophon* until Cimmeria please be back aboard ship by sixteen-hundred hours, station time. If Merseaux is your final destination, thank you for sailing with us. We hope to see you again someday."

Decker made a rude gesture at the loudspeaker as he dropped his duffle bag on the table to compact its contents. He tightened the straps to the point where it took no more space than a small day pack.

"Primed and loaded, Zack?" Hera Talyn shouldered her bag easily, making sure she had unimpeded access to her shoulder holster.

"Let's get off this tub and find a place that understands the difference between whiskey and battery acid."

"You sound a tad miffed."

"It's probably related to the fact that the cousin of the morally bankrupt idiot I killed is trying to kill me and paying big money to hire prime shooters. I suppose it beats getting eaten by two-meter tall bugs but whatever, if you've never lived it, you can't quite get how deeply I feel the nuances of suckage inherent in our current situation."

"You'd be surprised. I didn't get to become a commander in the intelligence branch without living through some major suckage myself."

"I guess." He slung his pack over his left shoulder. "Time to keep our eyes and ears open because someone will be watching us leave *Xenophon* ahead of schedule."

**

It seemed like everyone who'd booked passage on the tramp was trying to go ashore at the same time. Zack and Hera found themselves hemmed in by the crowd that flowed through the airlock and down the gangway tube.

Merseaux Station was no different from any other civilian orbital with its scuffed decks, harsh lighting, and the metallic tang flavoring the air. Prominent signs in several languages pointed visitors towards the commercial levels, transit lounges and the shuttle service to the surface.

They went with the crowd down to the promenade where their nostrils were attacked by the competing aromas of a dozen different eateries offering food from two dozen different cultures. Though they tried to see if anyone had anything other than a passing interest in them, it was to no avail.

Talyn walked over to a public computer console and, while Decker stood guard, eyes roving over the crowd, she looked for a berthed ship about to leave in the general direction of Nabhka.

"Nothing doing on the station," she said after a few minutes of fruitless searching. "I'll try and see if I can get data on ships sitting dirtside."

"Don't look up," he murmured in response. "Pink hair and bolo necklace have come ashore, and while they're pretending not to notice each other, I can see them signaling."

"How's that?" She kept moving her hand over the screen, surfing the local data net.

"Sideways glances that always seem to involve twitching fingers. Either they both have the shakes from that rotgut I was drinking or they're talking in code."

"They seem interested in us?"

"In everything but us, yet they're slowly moving around to make sure we can't get off the promenade without being seen. Very slick, very professional."

"So they got confirmation that Ser Wenn is really Zack Decker?"

"Could be. As long as we're in a crowd like this, we ought to be okay. If they can cut us out of the herd, though, it'll get ugly."

"Want to try a turn-around?"

"What if I'm just paranoid, and they're perfectly harmless people?"

"Then we'll have two first degree murders on our hands."

"Now who's being the cheerful one?" He smirked at her reflection in the screen. "Any luck?"

"One ship headed in the right direction is sitting on the ground at Mishka spaceport. She's not due to leave for another sixty hours." Hera tapped the screen a few times. "We're lucky: she's advertising available cabin space. There – I've booked us. Now we just have to get to the surface. How are the supposed pros doing?"

"They stopped signaling. I figure they've got us covered no matter where we go."

"We've got to get to the shuttle service dock, two decks down. The next run dirtside is in an hour, but it heads to Ushan, which is pretty much at the opposite end of the main continent from Mishka. The next direct to Mishka is in twelve hours, but I don't think we can afford to wait that long."

"Can we charter or rent one?"

"Probably, but it wouldn't do our covers much good if we flashed that kind of money around." She turned, eyes scanning the crowded promenade, passing lightly over pink hair and bolo necklace. "How about we split up? You take the stairs on the left — the ones past the food court — and I'll go right. If they both go after you, we'll know for sure. If they split up and follow each of us, then we'll have to think some more."

He glanced down at her, face expressionless.

"I'll do you one better. I'll head for the stairs while you go grab a coffee over there. If they both follow me, come on down. If one of them stays to keep an eye on you, maybe I'll see if I can get some answers from the other."

Without waiting for a reply, he stepped into the flow of people, merging with the midday crowd as if he didn't have a care in the universe. Talyn cut her way across the promenade to the nearest restaurant the moment she spied bolo necklace abandoning her window-shopping to head in the same direction as Zack. When she slowly scanned the crowd to see what pink hair was up to, her heart nearly stopped. The tall, plain-faced woman was gone.

Talyn quickly made her way to the encased stairs Zack had taken moments earlier. Designed as emergency airlocks in case a particular deck suffered decompression, the shafts were isolated by heavy doors that could be locked and sealed in an instant. They slid aside at her approach and shut behind her just as smoothly, cutting off the noise from the promenade. She heard voices below and cautiously made her way down, keeping to the outside wall, weapon drawn and ready.

To her surprise, Decker was discussing something with bolo necklace, who now looked nothing like the soft business traveler she'd seemed aboard *Xenophon*. They stopped talking and looked up at her approach.

"This is Superintendent Rowan of the Constabulary's Professional Compliance Bureau." Decker's eyes met

Talyn's. "The person with the pink hair is Inspector Crava."

"What happened?"

"Mister Wenn ambushed me as I came down the stairs," the woman replied in a deep alto, "and demanded to know why my partner and I were following you. I assume that you work for one of the Services?"

"She's genuine?" Talyn asked Decker, jerking her head towards Rowan.

"As genuine as our friend Inspector Grint used to be before someone broke his neck. Superintendent Rowan was about to explain to me why she was interested in speaking with us."

"Do you know what the Professional Compliance Bureau is?" The constabulary officer's eyes darted from one to the other.

"Cops who investigate other cops."

"Right, Sera Venzi. Hence, our motto *quis custodiet ipsos custodies* – who will guard the guards themselves. As I was just explaining to Ser Wenn, after I convinced him not to fillet me with that sweet Pathfinder dagger, we were trailing Inspector Grint. We found his interest in you both unusual and after his death, worthy of further scrutiny."

"What did Grint do to attract the attention of the firing squad?"

Rowan chuckled grimly.

"You've heard of our nickname, Ser Wenn. Grint was suspected of acting on the orders of a secretive government organization answerable to the SecGen directly."

"The Sécurité Spéciale." Decker's tone was flat, devoid of emotion, though his eyes spoke of a deep, abiding hatred. "We've met them before. They're not friendly people."

"Just so." Rowan nodded, taken aback at Zack's intensity.

"Did you and your partner kill him?"

"No, Sera Venzi. We wanted to uncover his reason for traveling on *Xenophon* and possibly find out more about his handlers. His death is a setback for us since I'm sure others within the Constabulary have been turned. I would ask you the same question."

"No. We had no reason to. After the brief conversation in our cabin, we didn't see him again."

"It's not beyond the realm of possibility that the Sécurité Spéciale had an operative on board who figured out that Inspector Crava and I were from the PCB. Killing Grint would be the most efficient way of ending our investigation."

The door to the lower level opened, admitting the pink haired woman.

"Everything okay, Ange?" She asked.

"Yes. I've explained to Ser Wenn and Sera Venzi that we only wanted to have a quiet chat where no one else would notice, such as whoever did Grint."

"Well, we're all here and about as isolated as we'll get on this station," the inspector replied. "Folks seem to prefer the lift to a little exercise."

She pulled out a small device.

"This will distort our sound waves. So tell us, what did Grint want with you?"

"He claimed that we'd been followed by a professional hit team and wanted to know why a pair of ordinary spacers attracted that kind of attention." Talyn related the entire conversation almost verbatim.

"Grint was sure the supposed pros if they existed, were after you two?" Rowan sounded skeptical.

"Seemed that way. Are you now trying to tell us the Sécurité Spéciale is in play?"

"Probably."

Decker and Talyn glanced briefly at each other, sharing a single thought. Grint had been the one on their tail, either alone or with an as yet unknown partner. His ploy in their cabin had been to gain some certainty about Zack's identity and to find out who she was. Of course, they couldn't tell the PCB officers because then the inevitable questions would start. Cops sent to investigate other cops tended to be extraordinarily good at it.

"I'm guessing you know more than you're willing to tell." Crava's tone was matter-of-fact. "Just as I guess that you're from our black-legged cousins. You made us too quickly."

Decker locked eyes with her.

"You may well think so, but we certainly couldn't comment."

"So you're not going to tell us why naval intelligence operatives have the Sécurité Spéciale on their ass?" Rowan was gratified to see a flicker of emotion in the big man's eyes.

"Can't tell you something I don't know about, seeing as I don't know any naval intelligence spooks."

"But you are ex-Fleet?" Crava wasn't about to let it go.

"Sure. Staff Sergeant Tom Wenn, Commonwealth Marine Corps, retired. I was in the infantry."

"And you?" She turned to Talyn.

"I'm just a sucker for uniforms." She smiled. "And what's underneath them. I used to be a Guild-certified merchant spacer, inspector."

The cop didn't bother hiding her disbelief.

"I suppose you've got all the necessary proof too. Maybe we should run them in, Ange."

"On what grounds?" Decker cocked his head to the side and looked at her with undisguised amusement. "We've told you all we know. The only other thing I'd say is don't sneak up on people like that – you almost got pig stuck for your troubles. Sera Venzi, I suggest we get going. The milk run won't wait for our sweet little fannies."

Just then the lower door opened and from the corner of his eyes, Decker saw the barrel of a scattergun poke through.

"DOWN!"

His shout echoed through the shaft, followed moments later by a dull cough and the clatter of pellets on metal walls.

Talyn, her reactions as finely honed as Zack's had followed him to the deck with split-second timing. The two PCB investigators weren't so lucky. Decker, operating purely on instinct, had pulled out his blaster as he dropped down and was returning fire. He thought he heard a scream, but with Crava howling in pain at her half-shredded arm, he couldn't be certain.

Talyn scuttled over to the cops and began applying first aid.

"What the fuck was that?" She snarled. "Pros doing the old spray and pray?"

"No," Decker shook his head, adrenaline surging through his veins as he rose to his feet. "They're still trying to stampede us. Getting our friends here was just a bonus. How are they?"

"Losing a lot of blood. We'll need medevac for Crava pretty soon."

Zack nodded, went to a public comm panel by the door, and touched the red emergency circle.

"Put a tourniquet on her arm and leave them. We're about to have company of the lawful kind and can't afford to stay on the station at this rate. Security will want to question us at length, and that'll do no one any good."

She worked quickly and then they hurried down one more level, escaping the shaft just as the first responders showed up. Stepping into an almost empty corridor, he came face to face with a blandly dressed but muscular man who stuck a gun into his midriff. Without breaking stride, Decker grabbed the man's wrist and twisted him around in a smooth movement, causing intense pain to shoot through the would-be assassin's arm.

Another man, similarly clad in dull gray, stepped out of an alcove and aimed a scattergun. Zack turned to place his captive between them and the second man just as he pulled the trigger. The shot tore a deep hole into the first man's chest. Before the assassin could recover from his mistake, Decker threw his partner's body at him. In the ensuing confusion, he tore the scattergun from the killer's hands, flipped it end for end then stuck the barrel into the man's face and fired.

"If those were pros," he commented, tossing the weapon aside, "then their technique needs some work. Like I said, they're trying to stampede us."

"Why?"

She led the way down the deserted passage to the next stair shaft.

"That's the question, isn't it? Where are we going?"

"Back to the ship. Hopefully by the time they've sorted out this mess, she'll have sailed. If we stay at Merseaux, they'll eventually track us down, even dirtside."

They took the stairs two by two, senses alert, but no other killers popped out of the shadows. Back on the promenade deck, Decker and Talyn caught their breaths and tried to look completely normal as they joined the flow of people moving through the commercial ring.

"Crap," Zack swore under his breath. "Security goons heading for the docks. Either our two PCB buddies squealed or they picked up enough of a visual to link us to *Xenophon*."

"Or our unknown enemies are still trying to stampede us."

"That would mean the two idiots just now weren't alone."

"Local talent maybe, disposable muscle hired for a one-shot deal. It's time to burn the Wenn and Venzi identities. There won't be a record of our new covers coming onto the station, but sometimes people do slip through the checks by accident or laziness. The washrooms are over there."

Ten minutes later, Ren Tally and Noree Pruw came out of the stalls, looking different enough to fool facial recognition software, if not every single human eye. Naval intelligence had provided them with the means to quickly alter their appearance and identities, but only once. The parts of them that were pure Wenn and Venzi, along with their credentials, were now nothing more than ash at the bottom of a garbage disposal.

"What's next, Sera Pruw?" He grinned at her new, more sensual look. "I could suggest we take a room on the station until things die down. There's a lot we could do without being seen."

She snorted, shaking her blonde head.

"Still a one-track mind, I see, Ser Tally. Some things never change. No. I suggest we stick to the original plan and get a shuttle to the surface, make our way to Mishka and get on that ship."

"But you made reservations in the name of Wenn and Venzi."

"When they don't show, I'm sure the captain will be glad to give us their cabin. Try and hunch down a little while we're still on the station. Your size isn't quite a dead giveaway, but why take chances?"

"You've never complained about my size before."

She groaned while elbowing him in the ribs with all the force she could muster.

The ticketing computer at the shuttle dock sputtered a little when it discovered their IDs hadn't been registered upon arrival on the station, but since their intent was to leave it within the next ten minutes on the Ushan shuttle, the human supervisor overrode the machine.

He smiled warmly at Hera.

"Have a nice trip, Sera Pruw."

"Thank you." She inclined her head graciously.

"No nice trip wishes for Ser Tally," Zack grumbled once they were out of earshot. "Some things never change: attractive, slightly vulgar looks do get you more than an honest face."

"Don't hate me for my beauty." She laughed. "It has its uses."

They were the last to board the shuttle and took seats at the rear. None of the other hundred or so passengers seemed to pay them the slightest attention, nor did any look even a bit familiar.

"So," he tilted his body to the side until their heads touched, "how long before Pruw and Tally get the Constabulary and the Sécurité Spéciale back on their pink butts?"

"Hopefully never," she whispered back, "but at least now we know what we're up against."

"And if the pros Grint talked about are Sécurité Spéciale and not private contractors, we should be good. I've killed a few of them in my time and for a spook organization, they're sadly lacking in some areas."

"That still doesn't answer the question as to why they're gunning for an active duty Marine officer and his charming, also active duty naval companion. They know nothing good comes from annoying the Armed Services."

"Unless Harmon Amali's the one pulling the strings. His cousin sure was the last time they sicced the bastards on me."

He fell silent as the shuttle, dangling from a gantry frame, was lifted off the deck and out the hangar door. There was a brief moment when the butterflies in his stomach threatened to erupt from his nostrils before the pilot lit his thrusters and re-established a semblance of gravity in the small craft.

An hour later, they walked out of the shuttle's controlled environment and into a gray, damp afternoon that seemed to wish them an apathetic welcome to Ushan. They entered the terminal and passed by the security console without stopping. Though neither Decker nor Talyn got any greater scrutiny than the other passengers did, they noticed a pair of gray-uniformed Constabulary officers staring at the console's inset screen.

"I think our buddies roused their kin down here," Decker murmured, eyes searching the cavernous hall. "Let's hope they don't have anything that's better grade than the usual."

"If their machine had given them a hint, we'd have been pulled aside by now." She led him to the far end, out of sight of the cops.

"We need to find a ride for Mishka that won't take two days to get there." They scanned the departures screen but got no satisfaction. "The daily flight left thirty minutes ago."

"Taking tomorrow's will still get us there in a timely manner," Decker pointed out.

"Sure, but I'd rather not stay here any longer than I have to. Remember, the gray legs and the other lot can follow thread just as well as you or I. Breaking it cleanly at Ushan would be nice."

"Rent an aircar? I'm sure our Tally and Pruw creds will cover it."

She grimaced.

"Not ideal and it'll be a longer run than the suborbital."

"You want out of this place quickly, that's the best solution other than ground transportation." He looked over his shoulder. "The rental counter is back by the arrivals, but we could kill some time until things have quieted down. I'd rather not have a cop overhear us negotiating a one-way fee."

"Let's sample the food while we wait." She pointed at a restaurant halfway between the two ends of the terminal. "It'll be overpriced, probably overcooked, but the panoramic windows will let us see the continuing parade of humanity, gray-legged or not. I suggest you skip the ale. If we're flying ourselves, you'll be taking a turn at the controls."

"Yes, mother." He made a face at her.

— TWENTY-FOUR —

Decker swore as he read the advisory that overrode the movie he was watching on the aircar's entertainment system. Talyn's head turned away from the controls, and she looked at him with a raised eyebrow.

"Someone's put out a bulletin on us," he said. "The local authorities want to speak to a male, early to mid-forties, around 190 centimeters tall, muscular build, traveling with a female, mid to late forties, around 175 centimeters tall, slender. They're suspected to have landed in Ushan, coming from the Merseaux station and possibly headed overland to one of the other spaceports."

"I'm going to guess Superintendent Rowan finally got her thumbs out. Good thing I used the disposable credit card for the rental, so our current cover identities are probably still relatively safe."

"You hope." Zack snorted. "The gray legs aren't stupid. They'll eventually figure out Ser Tally and Sera Pruw used to be the Wenn and Venzi comedy act."

"Hopefully, we'll have lifted from Mishka by then." She bit her lower lip and thought. "It'll probably be prudent to land somewhere in the outback and just abandon the car. I think once we're slotted into the Mishka traffic control system, they'll bring us down for a little chat. Heck, make that any traffic control system along the way. These rentals can be remotely flown by the cops, and there's nothing we'd be able to do but sit tight."

He nodded and called up a map of the area. After a few moments of intense study, he looked out the clear cockpit bubble at a rapidly growing dark mass on the starlit horizon.

"If we're going dump this thing, it'll have to be soon. After that mountain range, it's flat, open terrain and nowhere to hide."

"Oh, joy. A night landing in the bush." Talyn flexed her fingers a few times and took hold of the control yoke, shutting off the autopilot. She took the aircar down until they were level with the top of the crests and throttled back their speed.

A few minutes later, with more and more of the sky blotted out by brooding peaks, they slipped between two ridges and dropped into a valley, virtually vanishing off any ground-based air traffic control screen. Zack brought up a schematic of the proposed landing area.

"Another fifty kilometers should do it. We'll be within a few hours' walk from the closest town. From there we can find alternate transportation."

Talyn nodded and gradually slowed the craft down, even more, flying mere meters above the valley floor. Suddenly, the navigation system screamed at them, and a new schematic came up on the screen. She had just enough time to correct their trajectory so they could pass over a low saddle and slip into the next valley without reappearing on sensors.

After taking a few deep breaths to calm herself, she said, "A bit more warning next time, Zack. If you're going to play navigator, don't let surprises creep up on your beloved pilot."

"Hey, I'm usually in the back, waiting to be kicked out by the jumpmaster, not sitting in the left-hand seat. Anyway, we're almost there so it won't happen again — on this trip."

Soon, the aircar flew only on grav repulsers as it crept into a small box canyon. Talyn flicked on the headlights, figuring that unless someone were right overhead, the canyon's steep walls would contain the burst of illumination.

Flying almost at a walking pace, she gingerly guided the craft deeper into the crevice until she spied an overhang that seemed just high enough. But it wasn't quite good enough. They heard an unearthly screech of metal against stone and Talyn cut the engines. The short drop shook them momentarily, and then all was still.

"I don't think we're getting our deposit back."

"They'd have to find the thing first." She unfastened her seat restraints and stretched. "I just hope we're in deep enough to make that a bit of a challenge. Show me where we are."

She studied the map and sighed.

"It's going to be a bitch getting to the town. Take a look outside now that the sun's coming up."

In the gray light of dawn, they began to appreciate just how desolate and barren the mountain range really was. What little vegetation they saw was no better than a mossy fungal growth while the air, rushing into the compartment now that she'd opened the door, was dry and flinty, which meant little, if any surface water. They'd have to make their meager reserves last.

"Let's saddle up," he replied, grabbing his duffel and stuffing the contents of the aircar's emergency compartment into it. "The sooner we get to civilization, the faster we can get our fannies to Mishka."

They made it out of the box canyon within the first hour, though not without discovering that the sere landscape hid life a bit more dangerous than moss. A little less life now, after Decker holstered his weapon. Whatever the animal had been, it was ugly and had big teeth. Really big teeth. And claws. And it stank to high heaven.

After that encounter, they slowed their pace and paid better attention to the surroundings. The critter had pounced too soon, and that was the only reason Decker had been able to nail it before he became minced meat.

As a result, the half-day walk to the nearest town turned into a full day hike, and the sun was setting by the time they crossed the ridge overlooking a cluster of dusty, dilapidated buildings surrounding an obscenely huge mining operation. It was surface extraction at its finest: an immense hole in the ground with a constant stream of anti-gravity propelled buckets coming out of the depths, each the size of a small house.

By the time they reached the first of the cheap plastic and sheet metal huts, full darkness had fallen. Decker listened for a few moments and sniffed the air. Then he grinned at Talyn as he homed in on the small town's watering hole. If they couldn't find transport tonight, they could at least find a drink and a meal.

The local honky-tonk was in full swing, with noise and beer fumes spilling out onto the dusty street. Decker stopped in the shadows by the door and took one last look around. If it weren't for the bar, the town would have seemed deserted, even though the mine operated around the clock.

An unholy stench of fried food, stale booze, and unwashed bodies hit them as soon as they stepped in, accompanied by the kind of loud music and flashing lights that made the two operatives feel nostalgic for the relative quiet of ship-to-ship combat.

Even though Decker was a big man, he didn't look much out of place in this crowd. His leather jacket and dark pants were dusty enough to look like work clothes. Most of the men wore their hair long and faces unshaven, just like Ser Tally, though the tough looking women tended to have buzz cuts. Fortunately, none of the ladies looked like they needed a shave. It did mean that Talyn, still looking sultrier than was decent under the coating of dust, stood out enough to attract more than a few admiring leers from both sexes.

They headed for the bar, a long, scarred thing covered in beaten metal sheeting that might have come off a starship, based on the pitting and blackening. It fit in well with the rest of the furnishings and decoration. They looked suspiciously like they'd been scavenged from the wreck of a tramp freighter some time before the last Shrehari war.

Since Merseaux had been a pirate hideout in the previous century, before the Fleet had cleaned house, this bar could be a relic of those days. And why not? Out on the frontier, they lived the motto 'waste not, want not.'

Talyn put her mouth against his ear.

"Over to the side, sucking on a beer bulb. Cop or mine security?"

He shrugged, too busy with a bit of good-natured elbow play to get space at the bar and catch the bartender's eye.

The man, a hulking, bald giant with a barrel-shaped paunch, waddled up to Zack and stared at him curiously before taking a good long look at his companion.

"You new in town?" He shouted over the noise of the live band playing behind a shimmering force screen. "Never seen your faces in here before."

"Just passing through. We spent some time rambling in the mountains, and we're looking for a ride to the nearest place from which we can get to the coast."

The bartender straightened up and frowned. Then, without another word, he walked down the bar and spoke to someone, pointing back at them. Decker tried to see who it was, but failed thanks to the crush of bodies, though based on the man's reaction, he'd have bet on the security guy.

That suspicion was confirmed before Decker could do anything more than turn around and pick up his pack. A muscular, mean looking guy with a thin carpet of hair covering his angular skull parted the crowd and grabbed Decker's upper arm. When he felt something hard and round poke at his side, he glanced at Talyn, but she shook her head. Hemmed in as they were by the crowd, it wasn't the place or the time to resist.

With a toss of his chin, the security man pointed towards the back of the room, where the bartender was waiting with a scattergun loosely held in his hands. The band kept playing, but patrons around Decker, Talyn, and the guard fell silent, moving out of the way with commendable speed. The guard pushed them through an open door and into a dingy backroom.

"Okay, Mister and Miz Just-Passing-Through," he said with a gravelly voice. "You can turn around and face me. Josh, over there's got his gun aimed right at your heads, so try and stay cooperative."

Decker nodded and felt the officer release his arm. He and Talyn moved slowly, holding their hands well away from their bodies in a sign of submission.

"So," Zack tried a sardonic grin, "is this how visitors usually get treated or are you having a special sale on nasty today?"

"Josh said you're coming from over the mountains and are looking for transport to the coast. We've got a bit of a problem with that, chum. No one goes into the hills, not even prospecting. The whole area belongs to the Company and is off limits. Seeing as how the next bit of civilization north of here is almost a thousand klicks away, I think you're not telling the truth. You didn't walk all that way with just a small pack. Not without being armed to the teeth. Some nasty critters out there."

"We met one of 'em. He didn't like me much. He's not liking much of anything now."

"Funny guy, eh? Okay, friend. Your story is bullshit, I know it, you know it, and Josh smelled it on you. Now if it were up to me, I'd send you on your way on the next bus to Carvalla, the nearest town. The problem I have is that this mine's a restricted area. Only people vetted by the Company are allowed, and you my friends aren't. Not if you just walked out of the mountains. So now I have to figure out what to do with you."

"You could let us have a cold beer while you think about it," Decker smiled.

"Sorry, pal. You don't get to go back in there. The only one in this place you're talking to is me. That way, when the Company finds out we had intruders, I can show them I did everything by the book."

"Tough employer?" Zack cocked an eyebrow.

"None of your business," Josh growled from the corner. His aim remained steady as a rock, ready to take Decker's head off on command.

The guard thought for a moment, gnawing on his lower lip.

"Okay. Let's take it to my office. I got to think this through some." He glared at Decker. "Tell you what, funny guy; we can do this the hard way or the easy way. You walk in front of me and do everything I tell you, and I won't have to cuff you. Josh here will be covering your missus."

Zack nodded.

"Whatever you say, man. We're not looking for trouble, just for a ride."

Josh chortled. It was not a pleasant sound.

"We can give you a ride, mister."

"Turn around and head for the door back there," the guard said. "Don't go through until I say so."

Decker obeyed, glad that they hadn't noticed his pack for some reason. That was a mistake. He was carrying what was in effect a twenty-kilogram mace on the end of a few straps that lengthened his reach by half an arm.

Josh, scattergun still pointed at them, slipped around, unlocked the door, and shoved it open. Then he stepped out, looking left and right to make sure no one could see them. He nodded at the guard, who gestured with his gun.

"Start walking straight down the alley. I'll tell you when to stop."

Zack and Hera stepped into the dusty night air, eyes briefly looking up at the stars, to get their orientation. Within a few minutes, they'd covered half the distance to the mine pit and were ordered to enter a non-descript container-style building marked 'Security.' They didn't meet another soul along the way, and Decker was starting to feel twitchy. Two guns on them, no witnesses, in the dark and now in an otherwise empty office. That kind of scenario never ended well for someone.

"In the corner over there." The guard pointed towards an open space between two desks. Then he glanced at Josh.

"I gotta figure out what to do. The Company won't be happy we got folks coming from where no one should be and walking right in here. They're gonna want to know what they've been doing and what they've seen."

Decker's eyes darted from one to the other. This was beginning to sound bad.

"Triple S, Reg," the fat bartender replied. "Shoot, shovel, shut-up. Even if they've seen something, they won't have told anyone else yet. The company doesn't need to find out about it."

"What if one of them has a radio and called something in?" Reg, the guard, finally noticed their packs and frowned.

"What if they did?" An evil smile spread across Josh's bloated face. "Company won't find out if the radio vanishes with them."

Time to find our own transportation, Zack old boy, Decker thought as he quickly measured the distance between him and his captors, mentally adding the additional reach from his pack. Josh, with his scattergun, was the most dangerous of the two. Though neither of them looked like crack shots, the bartender could just go in spray and pray mode. At this range, they were toast. Of course, it was likely they'd want to keep the security office from being covered in gore.

He subvocalized a soft warning only Talyn, standing next to him, could hear before tensing up and shifting his balance slightly. Then, in a sudden burst of movement, he spun to the right, pack swinging up and out, catching Josh across the face. The bartender was thrown backward, his head hitting the wall with a hollow thud. He dropped his gun and fell over.

Reg seemed frozen to the spot by the unexpected violence and Decker, using the momentum from his attack on Josh, closed the distance between them, ducked down low and aimed his pack at the man's knees. A sharp sound cracked in the small room, and Zack felt the warmth of a plasma round singe the hair on the side of his head. If he hadn't gone into a crouch, that shot would have punched through his heart. Then Reg crashed to the floor.

Decker jumped on him, pinning both arms with his knees and repeatedly punched him in the face until he slumped into unconsciousness. He heard a soft groan behind him and turned to see Josh slowly reaching for his gun. Talyn bent down to grab the guard's blaster and aimed it at the bartender.

"I think we'll all be happy if you just calm down and sit back, hands on your head."

Josh gave her a vicious stare but obeyed.

"Shoot, shovel and shut-up, eh?" Decker snarled as he looked around for something to tie both men up. "Is that the usual hospitality around here? Or are we special for some reason? You guys sound like you've done this before."

The bartender didn't answer. He kept his hate-filled eyes on Zack while Talyn quickly searched the battered old desk. She found some disposable plastic cuffs in a bottom drawer.

Tossing a pair at Josh, she said, "Lucky for you I don't go around killing strangers just because I don't like paperwork. Take the restraints, and stick your right hand into one loop. Just like that. Pull it nice and tight. Now stick your left hand into the other loop and tighten that with your teeth."

Once Josh had cuffed himself, she motioned with the captured blaster.

"Now you're going to stretch out on the floor, on your stomach. Don't worry; I'm not going to shoot you in the back of the head."

Decker picked up the ugly scattergun and butt-stroked the man. He then quickly tied Reg up before the latter could wake. After a few moments' thought, he pulled out his knife, cut Josh's apron into strips and then used the grimy material to muzzle both men.

"There. Nice and neat." He stood up. "Now what?"

"Now we get out of here. Those bozos were going to kill us simply for walking into town without permission. Whatever this mining company is up to, they really like to keep it in the family. It's probably something as dumb as prospecting and extracting in the backcountry without paying royalties to the local government. When we get back to HQ, I'll have our Constabulary liaison drop a word in the right ear. Let's see if we can liberate some transport."

She very carefully opened the inner door. In the darkness, they could see a hallway with three further closed doors, one on the far end, and one on each side. The furthest one probably led back to the outside. Talyn silently tried the one on the right, finding an empty guard room, the desks abandoned for the night, computer terminals shut down.

"If this Company is so concerned with security, it sure as hell isn't running a twenty-four-hour watch," she commented acidly.

"Or there could be patrols roaming all over the place right now. This security guy seemed to be a boss of sorts." Decker opened the third door. "And here is his car."

"What are we waiting for?" She tossed her pack in the back before taking the passenger seat.

Moments later, Decker was carefully threading his way through the camp, hoping he hadn't lost his orientation. According to the map, the single road out went due south. Mercifully, it didn't pass too close to the mine pit and whatever passed for a grinding mill. If there was security walking around, that's where they'd be.

Zack whistled with relief when they emerged on stabilized earth ribbon disappearing into the darkness. He poured on the power, and they quickly left the mining operation behind.

"If things stay quiet for a few hours, we'll make it to the main road where we can ditch this thing."

"We can only hope. Once someone finds our buddies Reg and Josh, the hunt will be on unless they really want to keep it quiet. Letting themselves get snookered and then having a company car stolen isn't exactly good for the reputation, or job security."

Almost exactly two hours later, they saw the lights of Carvalla over the next rise. Decker pulled the car off the road and behind a cluster of boulders. A few hard slashes with his knife and the exposed back end of the car was covered by some dirty brush. It wouldn't stand much scrutiny, but at least it would keep the sun from reflecting off the rear window come morning. That way, it wouldn't be seen from a distance.

"I've sabotaged the system," Hera announced, backing out of the driver's seat. "It'll take a while to get it running again."

"Good. C'mon."

Decker pointed to a set of distant lights on the highway running parallel to the mountain range.

"That might just be our transport out of here."

The massive road train slowed down just enough as it passed through the sleepy hamlet for the two of them to jump on the last trailer, a flatbed with industrial machinery tied down by heavy cables. One after the other, they crawled into a narrow opening between two covered, yet massive, pieces, out of the slipstream but not out of the dust. Not by a long shot. Decker lifted up a corner of the tarp on the largest one and grinned at Talyn.

"This is perfect."

They slipped under the stiff plastic material and found themselves between the wheels of a heavy loader.

"I'll take the first watch," she said, settling down on her pack. "You grab some shut eye."

**

Hours later, they felt the road train slow down, and Decker peeked out. They were approaching a large urban area. Since the sun was already past its zenith, they had to be almost a thousand kilometers away. He pulled out his pad, called up the map, and studied it intently.

"This has to be Undine. It's got a spaceport, but unless things have changed, it won't have a ship going in our direction."

Hera glanced at her timepiece.

"We can still make Mishka if we find some way of covering the final few hundred kilometers quickly, but right now the trick will be to get off before anyone sees us. I doubt they look kindly on stowaways in these parts."

"Too late for a drop and roll," he replied. "We entered the town."

"So we wait until this rig gets to its destination, which might well be the spaceport."

A short time later, after the road train had slowed to a walking pace, they crawled out from under the tarp and found themselves in a narrow canyon between two rows of windowless concrete warehouses. A sudden rumble echoed overhead, heralding the passage of a small spacecraft that streaked upwards, quickly disappearing against the bright blue sky.

Nodding at Talyn, he jumped off the end of the trailer, landing on his feet with the balance of a natural athlete. She followed with an equally graceful recovery.

After briefly glancing at their former ride, Zack looked at the way they'd come and swore: a gated fence gleamed dully across the narrow horizon. He really didn't want another run-in with a company rent-a-cop. Leaving a trail of tied-up security guards wouldn't help their cover.

Packs slung over their shoulders they walked along one side of the cracked pavement, trying to look as nonchalant as possible as if they worked in the warehouse district. When they got near the gate, Decker examined it.

"Fully automated and not a guard hut in sight. That's both good and bad. There's no one to see us in person, but there's also no way to get out unless it's over the fence."

She grimaced. "It doesn't look electrified, but it probably has some kind of sensor network tied to it.

"I think this fence is more to keep people from wandering onto the runway than anything else. That means we can probably climb over and be away before security can send someone to see what's going on."

Then, they heard a loud roar behind them as a large cargo carrier loaded with a dozen dented containers came around the corner. Decker touched her arm briefly, and they just kept walking towards the gate, trying to look for all the world like spaceport workers coming off a long shift.

Talyn waved at the puzzled driver as the truck passed, and then they accelerated the pace to keep up with it. As Decker had hoped, the gate slid open automatically at the vehicle's approach, and they were able to slip through without a hitch. Someone might have seen them on the video feed, but they didn't intend to hang around and find out.

**

The spacetown dive they found just off the main drag was typical. Run-down, noisy and aromatic. Very aromatic. But they needed a quick, cheap meal and a cold beer. It was just as well that they weren't going to be too picky. The food was filling, and that was pretty much it. At least the beer didn't taste like horse piss and no one paid them any attention. After a few days living rough, even Hera had lost her luster and didn't look out of place.

Decker dropped a couple of creds on the bar and motioned to the bartender. When the man saw the healthy tip included in the sum, he smiled.

"Where can a guy get some quiet network access?" Zack asked.

The bartender looked at him searchingly. Then, "I can rent you net time, so long as it won't be for anything illegal, but it'll cost you." The man worked his jaw muscles for a few moments. "What outfit were you in?"

Zack raised an eyebrow. "Ninth."

The bartender nodded.

"Had you figured for a Marine. Too squared away to be a spacetown rat. I was in the Twenty-Third's pathfinder company before I retired."

Decker grinned.

"I should have pegged you for one of those idiots who jump out of perfectly functioning shuttles. Did some time in the Pathfinders too, before they let me go."

The man stuck out his hand, and they shook.

"Holger Dansk is the name. What's an ex-pathfinder doing on a shit hole like Merseaux?"

Decker's grin vanished.

"Trying to get to Mishka and off this shit hole, or if there's a ship going our way sitting at the Undine spaceport, we'll see if it has a cabin."

"That's what you want the net for." He grimaced knowingly. "I can save you the trouble. Ain't no ship lifting for two days, and you don't look like you got that long. Train to Mishka's leaving in two hours. It'll do you better. Station's a klick to the left when you get out on the street."

"Thanks, buddy."

The bartender shrugged.

"Us old jumpers need to watch out for each other, eh?"

"For sure. Thanks again."

As Decker and Talyn left the bar, he chuckled.

"What is it about Marines and the dream of opening this kind of joint when they retire? Just like my buddy on Aramis."

"Like I said before, you jarheads live for two things: sex and booze. A bar takes care of the latter, and enough of it might get you the other."

It didn't occur to Zack until much later that he hadn't given Dansk his name, nor had the other ex-Marine asked. Another member of the loose network of retirees with one foot still in the Corps, perhaps?

**

The train ran on steel rails, and it was massive, the engine powered by its own fusion plant and pulling a dozen two-story passenger cars at speeds of more than three-hundred kilometers an hour.

The ticketing machine had accepted the Tally credit card without triggering any alarms, and they boarded along with the remainder of the anonymous throng destined to enjoy the dubious comforts of third class benches that reeked of cattle class filth.

The tough looking Marine and his equally dusty, road-worn companion were given plenty of space by the other passengers, and they were able to talk quietly.

When they got to Mishka, the crowd was thick enough that they slipped past police patrols without a hitch and hopped on a public transport platform advertising the spaceport among its destinations.

"Do you think we've shed any tails?" Decker glanced around at the grimy street as they neared the terminal building.

"Almost certainly." She laughed humorlessly. "I defy even the best operatives to have kept up with us. We couldn't have planned it to be so convoluted. The question is how fast they can piece things together from the various clues we left along the way. For example, if that idiot at the mine reported us and added a good enough description, someone sifting through the net might stumble across that part of our little cross-country excursion. The same could happen as a result of the security cameras at the Undine spaceport, but with any luck, we'll have lifted on *Aranjuez* before they can figure it out."

"I wouldn't be too sure about that." He pointed at the entrance, where a pair of grey-clad constables and a pair of blue-clad local cops were scrutinizing anyone entering or exiting the building.

"Probably not for us and if it is, it'll just be them covering all the possible places we might show up."

"At what berth is *Aranjuez* docked?"

"Twenty-two alpha."

"Then we stay on this thing until it goes past the terminal and around the far corner. That way when we do get off, the guys at the door won't see us. We'll just go in through the freight end."

"We'd still have to get past the security barrier."

"One thing at a time."

As Zack expected, when they left the transport platform, it was along with a small crowd of merchant spacers returning to their ships. The bored security guard simply waved them through as a group rather than take the time to check them one by one. Since they looked the part, no one questioned their right to be there.

"Let me use that public terminal." Hera put her hand on his arm to stop him from heading down the line of berths. "Showing up unannounced at the gangway, asking to take the cabin from previously registered passengers might get us sent away with a flea in our ear."

"We're in luck," she said after a short surf to *Aranjuez* business site. "They have a cabin for two available. No need to cancel the Wenn and Venzi reservations, and possibly raise suspicion that we're a mere substitution. There, it's been booked and," she tapped her Pruw credit card against the reader, "been paid for."

Their reception at *Aranjuez*'s gangway was matter-of-fact. The tramps sailing between frontier worlds were used to planet-hopping passengers showing up at the last minute.

Like most of its kind, it was primarily a freighter with extra cabin space to pad the bottom line when cargo got scarce. The quarters they were given likely weren't very different from those of the small crew.

Decker dropped his massive frame on the bottom bunk and stretched out.

"Should we check each passenger, this time, to make sure there are no Sécurité Spéciale or Constabulary operatives on board?"

"You do what you want," Hera replied. "Me, I'm taking a shower. It's been a fun few days and I know I smell like it. So do you for that matter."

"Go ahead. I'll wait until we've broken orbit. Wet and sudsy's no way to be found when the inertial dampeners hiccup."

"Live a little. There's no such thing as safe space. It only exists in the imagination of small minds and timid souls."

"I could join you."

"Have you seen the size of the shower stall? You and me in there at the same time, no one's going to play pick up the soap."

He leered at her as she dropped the last piece of clothing on the deck, not bothering to hide his interest. In return, she blew him a kiss and raised the one finger salute before vanishing into the small washroom.

— TWENTY-FIVE —

The pinkish-beige glare of the Great Erg, a sea of sand dunes that stretched to the horizon in frozen waves under a relentless sun, held Harmon Amali in a quasi-meditative trance.

Here and there, surrounding his private oasis, he could see rocky crags that broke through the surface, like forlorn islands standing silent sentry duty over an army of dust devils swirling along the sharp ridges, animated by the relentless wind. It seemed like nothing could live in the dry heat, yet Amali knew the desert was teeming with hidden life, most of it predatory, from the sand sharks lurking in the dunes, to the two-legged, nomadic kind moving from oasis to oasis on native pack animals adapted to the harsh environment.

Were it not for the different luminosity of Nabhka's sun and the occasional glimpse of strange animals, his remote, fortified compound could well have been the updated version of an old Foreign Legion outpost lost in the immensity of Earth's Sahara desert.

The door behind him slid open, but Amali kept his eyes on the horizon, knowing that it would be his aide.

"Do you ever wonder why we experience thirst simply by looking at it?" He gestured towards the window with a hand holding a half-full glass of water. "A curious quirk of the human mind, I suppose. You have news?"

"Yes, sir." Lyle came to stand beside his employer. "We've lost track of Decker and his unknown companion. As you may recall, it took some effort to confirm his cover identity and track him down, which was finally accomplished once their ship docked at Merseaux station. There, however, he managed to kill two of the operatives charged with his discreet elimination before escaping to the surface under a new name and appearance. Even though our Sécurité Spéciale friends helped us, tracking his movements after that became tricky, not least because the Constabulary chose to show an interest in his movements. He was last spotted in Mishka, the second largest city on the planet. After that, nothing."

"This is not pleasing news, Lyle." Amali's voice was almost hypnotically soft. "I paid good money to have Decker removed once and for all."

The fact that his employer chose to use euphemisms for the word 'murdered' didn't escape Lyle's attention. Though powerful and ruthless, Amali had all his dirty work done at several removes and his choice of language reflected that detachment.

"I'm sure he'll be found again, sir."

"He'd better be. I would be chagrined to hear that he's reached Nabhka, not only because it means we have a leak somewhere and he found out about my little retreat, but because the best hired operatives in the Commonwealth couldn't track down one dumb non-com."

The statement didn't call for a reply and Lyle, staring out at the midday glare, let it pass in silence, though he thought his employer's low opinion of Decker to be a mistake. Any man who escaped slavery the way he had was far from stupid and if he was operating with the sanction and help of naval intelligence...

"Just a reminder, sir," he finally said, "Shayk Hysan will be arriving at four to present his business proposal. The kitchen has been ordered to prepare a traditional meal."

Amali took a sip of his rose-flavored water and nodded absently. Though he could run his vast business empire from this remote place, he enjoyed nothing more than making deals face-to-face, even the small ones found on Nabhka. Frontier planets, especially those who remained in the Commonwealth grudgingly, always presented interesting opportunities in what he liked to call the gray zone. The Shrehari occupation, some seventy years earlier, had left its mark on a planet and a population that had felt set apart from the rest of humanity long before the war, mostly by choice.

"Indeed. Thank you, Lyle. You may carry on with your duties."

"Thank you, sir."

The aide briefly bowed before leaving Amali to his silent contemplation of the Great Erg.

**

"Hmm," Talyn sounded puzzled as she stared at the screen. "According to the passenger manifest, it seems that a Wenn and a Venzi did take the reserved berth."

"What?" Decker sat up so fast that he bumped the top of his skull against the upper bunk. "Who'd be playing a joke like that?"

"Perhaps people who tracked us down on Merseaux? Since we seem to have vanished, they may have thought we might still take the same outbound ship under different names."

"Not good." He stood and looked over her shoulder. "Either someone is way too smart, or they've got enough people to seed all outbound ships on spec. The only reason we're on this one instead of another is that we need to make Nabhka sooner rather than later. If Amali decides to leave and hide elsewhere, we lose months of work tracking him down."

"And there's your answer, Zack." She turned around and looked up at him. "*Aranjuez* is the most obvious ship for someone in a hurry to reach Nabhka. If these iterations of Wenn and Venzi are half-way able, they'll make us pretty quickly in confined quarters."

"It might already be done. We did enjoy the passenger lounge for supper and a drink after we broke orbit and weren't particularly paying attention to folks who might be tailing us. Still, pretty ballsy to take those names. It's almost as if they want to get a reaction."

"So we find out who they are and deal with them."

"Kill them, you mean? What if they're gray legs and not Amali's henchmen?"

"Why does the word 'deal' always seem to mean 'kill' for you?"

"Professional deformation." He shrugged. "Why don't we ask the purser to point them out to us at lunch? Then, we go sit at their table and have a nice conversation."

She considered his off-hand suggestion and nodded.

"Sounds crazy, but sure, let's do it. A little chutzpah can't hurt, and if they're Constabulary, we can fast-talk our way into a deal by showing some of our cards."

Aranjuez lacked even *Xenophon*'s primitive frills, and the passenger lounge wasn't much more luxurious than the chow hall in a forward operating base. The drinks dispenser, however, met with Zack's grudging approval, though he figured the only reason it held decent booze was so that passengers would get plastered enough to ignore the shitty surroundings.

When they entered, it was already mostly full and noisy. Spotting one of the purser's mates by the food line, they went over for a quick chat. The woman pointed at a table in the far corner, commenting that they'd come aboard literally as they were about to retract the gangplank in preparation for take-off.

The little interplay didn't go unnoticed by the pair who had taken on the Wenn and Venzi identities, and they looked at Zack and Hera expectantly as the two intelligence officers made their way across the compartment.

"Mind if we join you?" Zack pulled out a chair and sat down without waiting for an answer. The woman stared at him with an amused smile, merriment dancing in her eyes. Talyn, who'd taken the other seat, looked from one to the other with a growing sense of suspicion. There was nothing remarkable about the middle-aged, bland looking couple, though, to a trained observer, their unfashionable clothing clearly hid strong, muscular limbs and possibly any number of deadly weapons.

"I doubt they'll mind," she said to her partner. "If I'm not mistaken, Ser Wenn and Sera Venzi are related to Uncle Josiah. It makes a lot more sense than any of the alternatives."

"Indeed, Sera Pruw." The male half of the duo inclined his head. "Word of your unpleasant experiences on Merseaux Station made it to our uncle's ears via the subspace net, and as we were already on the planet, wrapping up another piece of business, he asked us to take on those identities and offer our assistance. HQ's understanding is that the cousin has several teams trying to find you and remove you from the game."

While he was talking, his fingers were dancing on the tabletop, signaling in the secret battle language known only to naval intelligence operatives. Talyn replied in kind, acknowledging proof of their identity. Uncle Josiah was the current nickname for the head of their particular section.

"So what now?" Venzi, who resembled a washed-out version of Hera Talyn, looked at Decker expectantly.

"Now? We eat." Decker stood up and without waiting for the others, made his way to the food line.

**

The cabin was crowded with all four of them. Wenn might not have been as big as Decker, but he still took up a fair amount of space on the lower bunk.

"Let me say up front that we don't know anything about the mission," Venzi said, "or who the cousin and the game are. If we're not to ask questions but only obey orders, we'll understand. This doesn't feel like a standard sort of outing."

Zack took a sip of his whiskey-soda, eyes on Talyn who, as the senior officer present, would have to make that call even though it was his personal mission.

"This is about as black as it gets," she started, "and if it goes pear-shaped 'Uncle Josiah' will disavow us. He'll have no choice."

"Understood." Wenn nodded gravely. "The Service wouldn't have authorized it without an excellent reason."

"The very best. We're on our way to Nabhka, where we believe Harmon Amali has holed up after finding out Chief Warrant Officer Decker, whom he had sold into slavery, came back from the dead."

Venzi let out a low whistle.

"That's nasty. I assume your orders are to terminate Mister Amali so no one else gets the idea that selling Armed Forces members is a fine thing to do?"

"Terminate with extreme prejudice." She nodded at Zack. "As a matter of fact, that's his job — a kind of personal crusade, if you like. Mine, and now yours, is to get him where he can do it."

"Understood." Venzi nodded, examining Zack in light of Talyn's revelations.

Between them, Decker and Talyn gave an edited account of their adventures, beginning with Inspector Grint.

"I'm not surprised at the crooked cop," Wenn said when they finished speaking. "The Sécurité Spéciale has infiltrated most government agencies, though hopefully intelligence remains clean. What I am surprised about is that they used him as a control for an assassination team in the first place. It's probably what attracted the Professional Compliance Bureau's attention and ended up with those two cops following him on *Xenophon*."

"And that earned him a broken neck. The folks we're dealing with play for keeps." Zack took another thoughtful sip.

"Amali's scared. Rich, powerful men like him, when they're scared they lash out hard," Venzi replied.

"So do Marines who get sold as slaves — lash out hard, I mean."

"You guys have a plan, or is this on the fly?" Venzi asked.

Decker shrugged.

"The latest from your 'uncle' has Amali's yacht in the Nabhka system, and we believe he has a gracious country home somewhere in the desert, which doesn't exactly narrow it down since most of the bloody planet is a desert. What makes this double fun is the fact that the Nabhkans don't really like outsiders, even those of their own faith, so finding help is going to be down to my picking up the contacts I made when I did a tour on Nabhka."

At the curious looks from the others, he explained.

"The Corps rotates a regiment through there every nine months instead of posting a permanent garrison because it's considered a hardship assignment, so that should tell you a lot. The Shrehari managed to suborn a splinter group of Nabhkan separatists at the onset of the last war, arm them and when the invasion fleet arrived got them to rise up against the Commonwealth garrison. Many of our folks didn't make the evacuation ships. Hard feelings die slowly on a planet like that."

"But they've let Amali set up house?"

"Money talks when you're dealing with their shayks. The majority of the population might be zealously pious, culturally narrow, and technologically retarded, but their upper crust has no problems exchanging filthy lucre for luxuries." Decker smirked. "Nabhka has nothing to offer except a lovely clearing house for smugglers and other assorted interstellar scum, and fat commissions tend to stick to rich fingers."

"How do you intend to find his place, let alone get there?"

"Track down someone who's got fat rich fingers, dislikes Amali, and wave some credits in his face. I can still remember how things work."

"Easier said than done, though." Wenn didn't sound enthusiastic.

"Hey, I'm making this up as I'm going along," Decker said, shrugging. "Intelligence work is new to me, so give me some slack."

"From what I've heard, you're a natural," the man replied with a friendly smile.

"He's a natural something alright," Talyn muttered. Then in a louder voice, "Did anyone else aboard strike you as being not quite what they purport to be?"

Venzi shook her head.

"No, but that doesn't mean much. The kind of money Amali's got, he can pay for the best."

Zack snorted derisively.

"The ones we came across on Merseaux station weren't exactly the greatest."

"In a straight-on fight with you? Probably not," Wenn agreed. "There aren't too many assassins who can go toe-to-toe with an experienced pathfinder. But I'm speaking of hiding in plain sight."

"We'll just have to keep our eyes open and our backs against the bulkhead until we get to Nabhka." Talyn rose from the sole chair. "After that, it'll be wild frontier territory where everything goes, including the Wenn and Venzi identities. You can revert back to whatever you were using on Merseaux the moment we step off because it's a given your current names will raise big red flags."

"And yours won't?"

"It's a chance we'll have to take," Talyn replied.

"We just have to get through customs on the orbital," Decker said. "Once on the surface, no one will be asking for credentials, only for creds."

**

Nabhka station looked suitably dilapidated for something that passed as the primary orbital of a planet still trying hard to turn its back on the rest of human civilization. When they walked off the ship and down the gangway, a faint odor of garbage mixed with badly maintained environmental scrubbers hit their nostrils.

"Do they do it on purpose to discourage visitors or are they just lousy engineers?" Venzi asked, not particularly expecting an answer.

"Both," Zack grunted. "Wait until you've visited the main souk dirtside."

The customs officer, a dark, unpleasant man with suspicious eyes, took his own sweet time to process each new arrival, making it clear that he wasn't in any particular hurry.

Many of the people ahead of them were ordered to the side for a detailed inspection of their luggage and persons by none too gentle underlings. When Decker stepped up to the raised podium, he handed over his ID wafer, to which he had stuck a fifty-cred chip.

"A good day to you, honorable officer." He nodded politely. The man, feeling the little disc as he took Zack's papers, looked at him with sudden interest.

"Your purpose on Nabhka?"

"Business, honorable officer."

After deftly removing the money, he gave the wafer back and nodded.

"Welcome. Next."

"As I said," Decker grinned at the others after they'd walked onto the station's promenade, "leaving something on sticky fingers makes life easier and since it's not coming out of our own pockets..."

"Just how much of the discretionary money do you intend to pay out as bribes?"

"As much as I have to, darling." He blew Talyn a kiss. "And now to find a shuttle for Kish. Are you coming Ser Croyle and Sera Vasser?" The other agents had slowed their pace and were examining their surroundings intently.

"No surveillance we could see," the agent now known as Croyle whispered, "and no one paying us more attention than normal."

"First, they were looking for one man. A man and a woman threw them off," Vasser said, "now that we're a group of four, they'll be even more confused until they figure it out, that is."

"Hopefully, we'll have lost ourselves among the teeming multitudes dirt, or shall I say sandside."

The ticket price for the shuttle ride was extortionate, the bribes even more so, but they got first class seats on the next run to Kish, Nabhka's capital and largest oasis. After seeing what second class looked like, they were happy to have paid extra.

As Zack had said, it wasn't coming out of their pockets, and the black ops fund didn't exactly go for precise expense accounting.

**

"Very stylish," Croyle said as he looked at his reflection in the mirror. "Desert chic."

"It'll provide camouflage, and it really helps keep you cool in the midday heat." Decker tossed the lower end of his kufiya around his face leaving only the eyes visible.

They'd bought traditional robes and head covers the moment they landed in Kish, the two women going so far as to wear the veil favored by the most conservative members of Nabhkan society, which meant nearly everyone outside the wealthy classes.

"Locals won't talk to you if you're an obvious off-worlder. If you respect their social rules and don't stand out, they may decide the ancient laws of hospitality do apply just a little bit even for those, not of the faith." Zack examined Talyn and Vasser critically, to make sure they would appear modest in the eyes of the locals.

"It may be backward to make women cover up, but in this case, it's pretty convenient. If the bad guys haven't found us yet, now that we're under a layer of Nabhka fashion, they don't stand much of a chance."

"So far your 'on the fly' planning seems to be working out," Croyle said, dropping on one of the sagging beds. "Any thoughts as to what we'll do next?"

"Find something to eat that won't give us the runs," Decker replied. "The locals are used to the bugs that have adapted to Nabhka. Us, not so much."

"We got our full spectrum inoculations within the last year." The agent sounded dismissive.

"Some of what can make the rounds here will laugh at your inoculations while it makes you camp out in the toilet." Decker grimaced. "Saw a few of my troopers lose twenty percent of their body weight in less than two weeks when we were stationed here. Rule number one: never eat the street food and rule number two: never drink at any public fountain."

"Cheerful place." Vasser snorted.

"Rule number three: no cheerfulness allowed."

"Are you intending to contact the local Marine garrison?" Talyn moved her veil aside.

"No. Not unless it's the last alternative. Pathfinder squadrons can keep their mouths shut but this is a line regiment, and they tend to live off gossip. Intelligence agents looking for Harmon Amali's desert compound is pretty juicy. We'll go to a restaurant I remember from my tour. It had been around for decades back then so chances are it's still operating. They don't mind off-worlders, the food is safe, and maybe, just maybe the old one-eyed bugger who makes the coffee will remember me and answer some questions."

"So that's why you removed most of your disguise. I was beginning to wonder. Did Amali know you were an old Nabhka hand when he decided to hole up here?" Croyle asked.

"If he'd bothered to check my service record, he'd have known, though I doubt his hideout is a recent thing. It may even have already been here when I came through a few years ago." Decker paused, struck by an idea. "Is there any way we can contact 'Uncle Josiah' and not burn our cover?"

Talyn thought about it for a few moments, and then slowly nodded.

"There might be a way although if someone does intercept it, they'll be on to us eventually. Nothing remains untraceable. What are you thinking?"

"When the 9th did its tour here, I'm pretty sure the S-2 section updated the maps of all oases and inhabited spots. I remember we went out to some of the harder to find ones by skimmer, so it makes sense that they were using the information for something. If we can get a copy of what they did, we might get a leg up on our search."

"That explains the sudden 'I'm an idiot' look on your face," she smiled at him. "It might take a few days, though."

"So might going through all the information merchants in the souk."

"True, but keep in mind," Croyle warned, "that some bright spark on the opposite team will eventually put all the clues together and figure out we're in Kish already, meaning we'll need to get out of town and on our way sooner rather than later."

"Things move at their own speed on Nabhka." Zack shrugged. "Ladies, time to pull the veil in front of your delicate features. I'm getting hungry, and the pseudo-lamb at the Ghurab won't eat itself."

"Pseudo-lamb?" Vasser stared at him as if he'd just propositioned her. "Don't tell me that it's made from native life-forms."

"Okay, I won't."

With that, he led the way out of the dingy hotel and into the bright sun. The sudden slap of heat momentarily stunned them, but then with Decker as point man, they headed down a narrow, winding alley into the heart of the souk.

Since he spoke some of the local dialect and the others didn't, they stayed silent, contenting themselves by taking in the sights, sounds, and unfortunate smells. Talyn was glad that all but her eyes were hidden so no one could see her grimace at the less than salubrious surroundings.

After what seemed like an epic hike through a torturous labyrinth, they emerged in a large plaza filled with brightly colored awnings covering hundreds of stalls hawking just about everything imaginable.

Keeping to one side rather than wading through the throng, Decker led them towards an increasingly tantalizing aroma of grilled meat until they stood on the threshold of a large two-story building with a flat roof and arched windows through which they could see finely detailed wood screens designed to tame the harsh sun's rays.

Inside, dozens of glow globes encased in fixtures made from beaten copper provided soft lighting that seemed strangely inadequate after the brightness of the late afternoon. Their eyes soon adapted however and took in a large communal space filled with low tables and cushions, its walls covered with geometric designs in many complementary colors.

A wizened old man appeared from behind a bead curtain and smiled broadly at them. He spoke in a rapid-fire guttural tongue, revealing large, yellowed teeth. Decker's reply, in the same language, was slower and more hesitant as he worked to remember the appropriate words.

When he fell silent, the man nodded and motioned them to follow him to the back of the building. There, a large corridor opened onto a number of small rooms furnished just like their larger brother. They took the first one to the right, overlooking the souk, and settled on thick, comfortable cushions.

"I asked for a private room so the ladies can eat without having to flap their veils about. It's quite acceptable to show your face in private if the only males are family. Just remember to cover your faces when a waiter comes in."

"You know," Vasser muttered, "the disguise part is useful, but I'd hate to be a woman living full-time in this society."

"That's why the ones who don't want a traditional lifestyle emigrate," Decker replied. "As someone once said, if you can't handle the customs, don't stick around."

The old man returned before the other agent could launch what would likely have been a very tart reply. He dropped off four glasses and a large pitcher of water with sliced fruit floating in it and looked at Zack expectantly. Decker nodded his thanks and placed their food order.

"That pseudo-lamb better be good," Vasser warned him, "otherwise I'll have to practice my more arcane interrogation techniques on you."

"I told him to get us a sampler of all the grilled meats they had going, with the usual rice, beans, and figs. If it's still the same cook, you'll love it. The only thing missing is a cold beer, but you won't find alcohol in the regular establishments around here. It's some sort of taboo for the lower classes. The rich folks on the other hand, drink themselves silly on a regular basis. They used to flock to the regimental mess in droves whenever they could."

"So where's your coffee guy?" Croyle asked.

"Ahmat will show up at the end of the meal if he's still working here, so there's no point in worrying about it now. Keep in mind that patience is considered a great virtue on Nabhka."

The food was as simple as it was tasty and even Vasser gave the pseudo-lamb two greasy thumbs up. After bringing the overloaded platters, the waiter had left them alone so the women could unveil and eat in comfort. Throughout the meal, he would knock delicately on the wooden doorframe as a warning when he came to retrieve empty plates, giving the two female agents time to make themselves decent again.

Once the table was cleared, a one-eyed man with a withered face, wearing an impossibly ornate robe, entered the room carrying a stack of tiny cups and a tall metal coffee pot exuding a rich aroma. He bowed and then poured the thick black liquid with the artistry of a great showman before serving them with a practiced flourish. When he was done, Decker smiled at him engagingly.

"Do you perchance remember me, Sidi Ahmat?"

The server's single eye narrowed as he contemplated the Marine's muscular bulk and square face, startled by an off-worlder addressing him with the traditional title of respect.

"You are vaguely familiar to my tired sight, honored guest. Were you a soldier of the Commonwealth once?"

"I was. When my unit was stationed on Nabhka, I used to come here whenever I could, to sample the meats and the most excellent coffee. You and I used to exchange gossip and jokes. It's doubtful that any other Marine would have done this, much less learned to tell tales of the deep desert."

"Decker?" The man looked startled and then delighted, as he reached down to touch the Marine. "You've changed, my friend."

"Life does that."

"So it does. What brings you here, to Nabhka, I mean, not the Ghurab."

"Business of sorts, my friend. Why don't you pour yourself a coffee and join us."

Ahmat dropped down beside Zack and pulled another cup from the folds of his robe, filling it with one quick pour. He took a sip and sighed.

"You enjoyed your meal, good sir?" He looked at Croyle, avoiding the women's eyes so as not to offend their modesty.

"My associates don't understand your language."

"Then you must teach them, Decker, so they can praise the Ghurab's kitchen to all comers."

For nearly half an hour and through several refills, they spoke of this and that, catching up, talking about the weather, the upcoming race week, all the while watched by envious eyes belonging to intelligence agents unable to decipher a single word.

Ahmat finished his coffee and made his cup disappear again.

"So you're here on business, you said. Is it to be profitable?"

"Only if profit is to be measured by a man's expiation for his crimes. He owes me a life."

"Oho! A feud then." His seamed face lit up with sudden interest. "An off-worlder who comes to hide here or one of my people?"

"An off-worlder. I believe that he is hiding in an oasis in the deep desert, one that he owns and lets no one else visit."

Ahmat stroked his short beard and nodded sagely.

"There might be such a man if the rumors about Shayk Hysan are true."

"What might those rumors be, my friend?" Zack pulled a hundred cred chip from his pocket and played idly with it. No one mistook the gleam of avarice in Ahmat's eye for anything else.

"Profit, Decker, to be gleaned in a project financed by the man Shayk Hysan has been courting. It is said he lives like an emir in a castle to the south of here, on the edge of the Great Erg or even in the Great Erg itself. Perhaps this is the man against whom you hold that debt, but if he is, you'll not find it easy. He is rumored to be well defended. Even the Shayk can only go if he's expressly invited."

Zack flicked the cred chip in the air, watching as Ahmat snatched and pocketed it in one fluid gesture.

"It is also said that this off-worlder is evil." The coffee man rose and stacked the four empty cups before lifting his large serving pot. "The desert nomads speak of a clan that had used the oasis for generations but was barred the moment he bought it, and they died in the Great Erg for lack of water on their subsequent migration to the Ferouz."

"He's an evil bugger all right. Take care, my friend."

"No, Decker, you must take care. Evil can be powerful, especially out in the desert."

"Then I'll make sure I'm the most powerful one."

"In that case, God guard you." Ahmat pushed the curtain aside and vanished.

"Judging by the expression on your face, you've got something useful from that strange man," Talyn remarked in an idle tone.

"Indeed, Hera." Decker's face was split by a mad grin. "Here's what Ahmat told me..."

"Harmon Amali sounds like he's a hell of a snake alright." Croyle grimaced after the Marine finished relating his conversation with Ahmat

"A snake or some kind of slimy, poisonous lizard." Decker shrugged. "Mind you, the whole Amali clan suffers from a reptile dysfunction, so it isn't all that surprising."

Ignoring Talyn's groan at the bad pun, Vasser asked, "Do you believe him? For a hundred creds, anyone would spin a good tale."

"Maybe, maybe not. Before I pulled out the hundred-cred chip, he was speaking of possibilities. Once he saw the money, he became very particular. Denying anyone access to an oasis is considered lower than engaging in bestiality with a camelot, so it's not an accusation to make lightly. Knowing what a sweetheart Amali is, I'm not surprised that he didn't give a damn about a nomad clan. Human beings are simply tools where he's concerned, to be used and then discarded."

"What the heck is a camelot, other than the mythical place?"

"That's what some people call a native beast used as transport on Nabhka. The things look like a camel designed by a madman with a fetish for six limbs: camel, with lots of legs — camelot. The natives have another name for it, of course."

"Cute." Croyle shook his head. "Why do I get the feeling that we'll be seeing these critters up close soon?"

"Because the best way to travel in the Great Erg without attracting notice is by riding them, just like any other backcountry dweller. Skimmers are for the wealthy and townies.”

“Have you given some thought about using this shayk fellow to find and infiltrate Amali’s compound?”

Decker nodded.

“It had occurred to me, but there are too many variables outside my control for it to be a good idea, not least because whatever the shayk is riding when he goes for a visit will be checked over carefully. Remember, the bugger knows I’m coming for him and, with luck, he knows that his hired guns have lost my trail so his paranoia will be playing in overtime.”

He stood, shaking out his colorful robes.

“Come on, time to return to our room and figure out the best way to contact Uncle Josiah. Now that Ahmat has given us a smaller area to work with, all I need are the charts for the near edge of the Great Erg. We can be pretty sure he wouldn’t be sitting on the far side, where there’s just about no civilization for thousands of kilometers and where the weather can be thoroughly brutal, even for the nomads, let alone a pink-skinned aristo.”

— TWENTY-SIX —

"There." Zack pointed at a spot south of Assur, the last sizeable town before the deep desert. They'd received the charts earlier that morning via an anonymous subspace transmission that had cost a small fortune to arrange. The previous three days had been spent laying low, with Decker occasionally visiting other possible sources of information he could remember from his tour of duty on Nabhka to little effect. He didn't want to push his luck to the point where rumors of a big Marine, disguised as a local and asking too many questions, got back to someone who wished to put a target on his back.

"Take a look." He enlarged the picture. "That's not Fort Zinderneuf, children, even though it seems like the Foreign Legion set up a factory outlet on top of the Nippur oasis. No local shayk would bother with a country house on the edge of the deep dunes. They like the comfort of civilization too much. And it's pretty much in the area Ahmat described."

"Fort what?" Vasser gave Zack a quizzical look.

"Don't mind my partner." Talyn waved away the question. "He's got a treasure trove of useless historical information in that thick skull of his. Please don't get him started."

She examined the map. "How do we get there? I'm presuming you don't intend to set out in a camelot caravan from Kish."

"No. There has to be regular service, either overland or by air to Assur. That's where we'll get ourselves a half dozen of the six-legged critters and make like desert people, maybe even join a regular caravan for a spell."

"And when we get there?" Vasser again, sounding unconvinced.

"We make it up on the fly. There are a few rocky outcrops around the oasis that'll make excellent observation posts and give us places to hide. Apart from the sun, there are critters in the sand who like the taste of human and camelot flesh, so you want to have solid stone under your ass if you're not moving. The nomads go from rock to rock when they cross the Erg, sometimes staying on the move for a day and a half if they have to, even sleeping in the saddle."

"Charming." Croyle made a face. "Any other little surprises we need to know about?"

"Plenty, and I'll tell you about them when I remember." Talyn looked up from the room's antiquated computer console.

"There's a regular skimmer run between Kish and Assur twice a week. The next one leaves this afternoon."

"Then we'd better pack up and get ourselves to whatever passes for a station around here." Decker shut off the pad he'd been using to project the chart and slid it into a pocket beneath his robes. "We need to buy water and food. It'll be six hours at least, and if they do have a catering service on board, it likely won't be one I want to touch."

"Why don't Vasser and I go out and hunt for supplies," Croyle suggested, "that way the two of you can finish planning. After all, we're supposed to be the support team."

Decker nodded absently, his mind already thinking about what he'd need to do once they got to Assur.

**

The gentle rap of knuckles on the doorframe startled Harmon Amali out of his intense contemplation of Shayk Hysan's proposal. He looked up at Lyle, irritated.

"What is it?"

"Our contractors have reported to their superiors, sir. Decker is on Nabhka. I've been assured that he and his companion will be dealt with shortly."

"That's good news, though I'd have preferred they take him before he set foot on the planet."

Lyle nodded.

"So would I, sir, but apparently the contractors chose to wait until they could be made to vanish unobtrusively. Decker and his partner gave them enough of a run-around that killing them before arriving on Nabhka would have raised too many questions."

Amali considered the explanation while he took a sip of his scented water.

"I suppose it makes sense from their point of view. However, the next time we need to use their services, let's make sure the contract is more specific, such as carrying out the work much further away from me. In this case, a few light years would have been preferable, but seeing as they missed at Merseaux..."

"Agreed, sir, and when I so informed the liaison, she did point out that the terms included a clause giving wide latitude to the operatives in the field. Before I go, might I remind you that you still haven't set a date for the shayk's return visit? His personal assistant has been contacting me several times a day."

"Let him learn the virtues of patience, Lyle. No response until I say so."

"As you wish." The aide bowed his head briefly before vanishing back into the bowels of the fortified mansion.

Amali swiveled his chair around so he could stare out at the desert. Its stark beauty, with an ever-changing dunescape punctuated by dramatic crags, never ceased to please him. The only thing that fascinated him more in this desolate place were the occasional sandstorms. His retreat could be sealed up tightly and weather anything nature could throw at it, and watching a tempest through the thick, port-like windows took on the aura of a front-row seat to Armageddon.

Decker had landed on Nabhka. Interesting that the news provoked a mild frisson of fear rather than the abject terror he'd felt upon hearing the Marine had escaped slavery in the trans-Coalsack sector. Getting into the compound without permission would be next to impossible, and he knew the contractors would finally put an end to this game.

Decker and the woman accompanying him had reached the end of their road. It was only fitting that this end would happen at the far terminus of the frontier star lanes, on a planet that seemed to have been rejected by God.

**

The skimmer had started life as a bulk transport and was large, noisy, smelly, and poorly maintained. Livestock of all sorts mixed with loud passengers and created a bedlam that only a master of the absurd could appreciate. The four intelligence officers tried to find a corner where they would suffer the assault on their senses the least, but the rumble of de-tuned engines and a driver who seemed to have graduated from camelot jockey school the day before made the trip a miserable experience.

After about three hours travel over rocky terrain dotted here and there with patches of low-lying vegetation, the skimmer crested a rise and rushed down a steep slope towards a small cluster of houses surrounded by a dense tree plantation.

"Girsu," Decker informed his companions.

"Are we going to stop?" Talyn's voice sounded muffled behind the veil.

He grinned. "Wait for it."

The transport ground to a noisy halt in front of what had likely been a caravanserai in the distant past and the driver got up, turned to the unruly mass of passengers, and shouted something that seemed to both amuse him and provide him with some satisfaction.

"He said he needs to take a long piss and then have a lot of coffee," Decker translated, "so we'll be staying here an hour or so. My guess is that he gets kickbacks from the owners of that inn."

"Maybe if he cut back on the coffee he wouldn't need to take a long piss," Croyle commented acidly, getting to his feet. "I won't say no to a nice leg stretch, though. Let's go see what those trees are good for."

"Why not? Sampling anything that place serves would be a dangerous idea," Zack said nodding towards the inn's entrance. "The hygiene standards around here are probably so low you could trip over them. Just keep your eyes open. We wouldn't want to stumble across anyone looking for us."

They strolled idly towards the date trees, pointedly ignoring the stench of livestock and bad plumbing, their eyes darting around the oasis, looking for anything out of place or anyone overly interested in the little group. As they went deeper into the grove, Zack didn't notice right away that Croyle and Vasser had dropped behind them, but soon enough, his instincts began to wave a big red flag. The sound of a pebble rolling on the hard ground somewhere to his right caught him up short and suddenly he knew.

"We've been had. Get ready," he murmured to Talyn, keeping his voice so low only she could hear it.

He drew his blaster out from under his robes and pivoted as he dropped down to reduce his silhouette. It was almost too late. Croyle fired, but the shot passed millimeters above his head. Had he been a fraction of a second slower...

Talyn had been almost as fast as Decker, following his lead, but Vasser's shot came close enough to singe her veil and left cheek.

Decker's gun coughed twice and, without checking that his target was down, he turned left just in time to see a man in desert robes take aim at him from behind a date tree. Dropping to the ground for a roll into a more protected position, he shot at the newcomer, burning furrows into the smooth trunk that hid his body. A piercing scream behind him briefly drew his attention, and he looked back to see Vasser lying on the ground with most of her right arm blown off.

The gunman took that occasion to step out and shoot three times in rapid succession, the last round clipping the side of Zack's kufiya. Before he could hide again, the Marine's Imperial Armaments blaster coughed once more, burning a hole through the man's left shoulder. He crumpled to the ground.

"There's a fourth one somewhere," he called out, looking around desperately. "They always work in pairs."

A blaster sounded to their left and Talyn gasped. Decker turned towards the sound fast enough to see a silhouette move between the trees. He fired twice, without success and then looked at his partner. She was holding her arm, blood seeping between her fingers. A quick shake of the head told him that she didn't need immediate aid. Vasser was still gasping, but he wasn't about to waste time on a woman who'd just tried to kill them.

The fourth man was good, almost as good as Zack. He erupted from behind a larger tree and tried to close the remaining distance, gun aimed at the Marine's head. Just as his finger began to squeeze the trigger, Decker fired. The first shot spun the man around; the second took him down, and the third blew away most of his face. It was all over in a matter of seconds.

A dead silence fell over the grove, punctuated only by Vasser's pain-induced gasps and Decker's heavy breathing.

"What the fuck?" He finally spat out, staring at the carnage around them. "Are you okay, Hera?"

"He just winged me. No major blood vessels hit, but it hurts like stink." There were tears of pain in the corners of her eyes. "I don't get it – Croyle and Vasser were ours."

"Maybe they decided to change employers or were moonlighting as assassins." He got up slowly and shook debris from his clothes, then walked over to Talyn and examined her arm. "A simple bandage should do until we find some first aid material, though around here, it might be pretty basic. I hope your inoculations are up to date."

Tearing a strip from the hem of his robe, he quickly dressed the wound, trying not to worsen her pain. Then he went to examine Vasser. The woman was barely conscious, face twisted in agony, but she looked up at him and grimaced.

"We underestimated you," she wheezed.

"A lot of people make that mistake. What's this about?"

"It was just business, you understand." She closed her eyes and bit back a surge of pain. "Croyle and I sometimes contract out to pad our Navy pay when we're on detached duty. It just happened that HQ got to us at the same time as the folks we sometimes work for. Since we were already on Merseaux, there was no way to refuse Uncle Josiah and the bounty for your head was the biggest we'd ever been offered. We just had to make sure the Service couldn't trace it back to us."

She stopped to catch her breath.

"Considering your reputation and what you did to the team on the station, we arranged for backup to shadow us until we could bring you to an isolated spot for the hit. They could then take the blame, and we could come out of it hurt but still alive."

"You talked to your other employer when you and Croyle went out to buy water and food."

"Our liaison, yes."

"Does Amali know I'm on Nabhka?"

"Yes. When we called to arrange for backup, we reported our position."

"Damn. He'll be harder to get now."

"Not if he thinks the hit succeeded," Talyn suggested. "As long as we don't get back on that wreck over there, whoever might be watching the Assur station would think we didn't make it."

"Then we have to find another mode of transport."

"Our backup," Vasser gasped, clearly going into shock, "must have their own vehicle hidden somewhere around here."

"Feeling remorse?" Decker asked in a cruel tone. "Is that why you're so helpful?"

"Like I said, it was just business, and I'm realistic enough to know that you can't afford to leave me alive, so why not? I'll never get to collect the bounty. The bastard who posted it shouldn't get to keep the money either." She wheezed again, her face turning ashen. "Anytime you want, Decker. I'm not going to make it anyway so it'll be a mercy shot."

He glanced at Talyn. She gave him a quick nod, her face looking grim. Blaster pointed at Vasser's heart, he pulled the trigger once. She had a brief spasm and then her muscles relaxed in death as the stench of voided bowels mixed with that of charred flesh.

"What a mess." Decker shook his head. "How many more of ours are working the other side of the street? You have to be a frigging sociopath to do that."

Talyn staggered to her feet.

"I've got bad news for you, lover-boy. The best intelligence agents I've known all have a more or less dark streak of sociopathy. We have to lie, deceive, and kill to do our jobs."

"And you?" He took her gently by the unwounded arm and led the way deeper into the plantation, trying to find a trail that would take them to wherever the other two killers had hidden their car.

"I'm not fit for conventional society either, Zack, which is why I'm in this line of work and not a desk analyst or even a deck officer on a starship."

"And what does that make me?" He stopped and looked her in the eyes.

"Someone who built a hard shell around his humanity so he could survive, I think. You have a sense of honor and morality that most of us in the black ops branch have either lost or never had in the first place. For example, I don't think that I or most of the others would have bothered to bring back the surviving members of your slave regiment. We'd have seen them as a hindrance to our own survival."

"That's reassuring to know," he grumbled. "After this is over, we need to talk about my getting back to honest Marine work. I don't think I want to be in an outfit where people screw each other like this."

"We'll see." She stopped and pointed at a bush with broken branches. "There — someone's been through and was in a hurry."

They soon found a small four-place skimmer with no identifying marks parked out of sight at the far end of the grove. The craft looked like it had seen some hard service in its day.

"Seems pretty beat-up," Talyn said. "I'm not sure I'd trust that thing in the open desert."

Decker opened the driver's side hatch and stuck his head inside.

"Looks to be in decent shape." Reaching behind the passenger seat, he pulled out a red box. "And it's got a first aid kit. Let's hope someone thought of filling it since the Shrehari were kicked off Nabhka."

Someone had. With a topical painkiller and clean bandages in place, Talyn was able to settle into the skimmer without too much discomfort.

"And now we head for Amali's little fort? Should we do anything about the bodies?"

"No. The locals will make them disappear. They don't want the police to come snooping, I think. A place like this is likely to be doing more business under the table than in full view of the taxman. As for Amali," he started the drives, happy to hear that they were better tuned than the cattle transport they'd just left, "a skimmer, they can see coming from a long, long way in this kind of terrain. If I were the bastard, I wouldn't let anyone come unannounced, so showing up on their sensors with this thing will get us shot at, if not shot down."

"We'll go to Assur as planned," he continued, gingerly extracting them from the tree line and looking for a way to get within sight of the old trail that the transport had been following. "Once there, we get some camelots and make like a small caravan heading for the Great Erg."

"In the meantime, Amali will be waiting for a report that confirms our deaths and the liaison Vasser talked about won't have heard anything from either hit team. If I were him, I'd assume you were still on the loose somewhere."

"Can't be helped. He's not climbing out of his hole except to take a shuttle upstairs, so we have to go to him whether he suspects we're alive or not." Decker gunned the drives, and their skimmer shot forward at a speed that would have left the fat, ungainly one still sitting by the caravanserai in the dust.

**

They made Assur just as the last light of day was fading on the purplish horizon. Decker parked by the central square, near other vehicles in various states of disrepair and they got out into the rapidly chilling night air. This close to the barren desert, it got surprisingly cold after sunset.

Talyn's veil was back in place, though she looked like the survivor of a house fire. Zack had already decided that she would be trading it for a kufiya tomorrow morning, as soon as the shops opened.

They took their packs and headed for the dingy inn looming over the plaza with leprous walls and deep, dark window slits. To their relief, it was almost empty and a quick meal later, they were in a small, surprisingly clean room on the second floor, pleased to use the facilities to scrub off the dust of the road and the death stench of their would-be assassins.

"I'm still having a hard time understanding why Croyle and Vasser would so casually turn on one of their own."

"Not me," Talyn replied wearily. "They didn't see you as one of them, Zack. You were an accidental agent when we maneuvered you into *Shokoten,* and right now, you're a hired gun whose target just happens to be a convenient one for the sociopaths running our dear Navy's covert apparatus. To Croyle and Vasser, you'd always be an outsider."

"You're one of them, and they were about to kill you as well."

"I was going to be collateral damage. The opposition didn't know who I was when the contract was posted. Croyle and Vasser only found out when we met on *Aranjuez,* but by then it was too late."

"You're not exactly selling a career in naval intelligence, Hera. I'm just a simple Marine with no known deviant tendencies."

"Maybe we need a bit of fresh blood that'll put a check on the Croyles and Vassers of the branch. You can't tell me that you don't enjoy the work."

"I don't enjoy the consequences of the work." He gave her a hard stare.

"Point taken." She held out her bandaged arm. "I think this consequence will need a refresh before we go visit Mister Amali."

"I guess there's no play time tonight, then?" He leered at her.

"After a day like today, you've still got your mind in the gutter. Unbelievable."

"There's no beer to be had, so that's all that I've got left to live for."

**

A pink dawn painted their room's walls with delicate shades of pastel. Outside, the town was slowly coming to life, its reawakening punctuated by the insistent crowing of what sounded like an entire regiment of roosters.

Decker gently pulled his arm out from under Talyn's narrow shoulders and got up, stretching. The bed had been reasonably comfortable but a little small for someone his size to share with another. Thankfully Hera wasn't anywhere near as wide has he was.

He padded over to the window and let his eyes wander over Assur's main square, where the brightly hued peddlers' tents and awnings were already sprouting from the hard ground, like magical plants, giving the dun-colored surroundings an intense splash of life.

Watching as they unpacked their wares, he spotted one who had exactly what they needed. He quickly got dressed, tucking his blaster in its place under the now dirty and torn robes, and pulled his kufiya over his head.

"Leaving me, Zack?" A half-asleep, dreamy voice asked. "I didn't think you were a pump-and-dump kind of guy."

"We, and specifically you, need new clothes. The local bazaar is setting up, and I saw a guy peddling just the right stuff for where we're going. Stay here and don't let anyone in; a naked off-world woman could cause a massive riot in a backwater place like this."

"No worries." She looked down at herself. "I don't have the body that launched a thousand camelots."

He snapped his fingers and pointed at her.

"That's the other thing I need to find."

"And breakfast."

"Demanding one, aren't you."

Decker sketched an ironic salute and slipped out the door, a fold of the kufiya covering the lower part of his face. If Amali had watchdogs in town, there was no point in making their lives any easier than they had to be.

He came back twenty minutes later, carrying a bundle under his arm.

"Success?" Hera had put on some underclothes and strapped her gun holster in place.

Dumping the bundle on the rumpled bed he nodded.

"Genuine desert nomad togs, targi-style."

At her questioning look, he added, "Targi are what the folks call themselves. Pretty convenient for us in that they traditionally keep their faces covered a lot of the time, letting only the eyes show. It helps keep the blowing sand out of various orifices."

They swapped their city robes for the dark indigo ones of the desert dwellers, fumbling somewhat with the turban-like head covering.

"There," Zack finally said, sounding satisfied. "Now, no one can tell if you're a man or a woman, and only the pale skin around your eyes proves that you don't spend your spare time cavorting around the Great Erg. I hope you're packed. The guy who sold me this stuff says a caravan is heading out as soon as the sun sets and he reckons it's headed in the general direction of Amali's hideout, seeing as how the bastard built it over a traditional waypoint."

"Just like that — we jump on a couple of camelots, join a caravan, and hope we get to Amali unseen?"

"Yeah. Just like that. Simple plans usually have the best chance of working."

"That's no plan, Zack, and as they teach at the Naval War College, hope isn't a valid course of action."

"Okay. We disguise the skimmer to make it look like a mutated critter, go screaming into his compound, and jump out guns blazing, pretending we're members of a Targi rebel group."

She smacked him on the arm with her open palm.

“You’re an ass, Decker.”

“And you’ve got a very nice one.”

“Thanks – I think.” She shook her head. “It’s a good thing I know behind that leering grin sits a decent tactical mind. Otherwise, I’d despair.”

“Decent?” He put on a mock-wounded look. “There’s absolutely nothing decent about me.”

“Finally,” she snorted with suppressed laughter, “something we agree on. How about your indecent tactical mind finds us breakfast?”

— TWENTY-SEVEN —

Hera Talyn's first glimpse of a camelot nearly had her in stitches. As advertised, it had six legs which seemed to move independently of each other and of the rest of the body, which was long, thick, and covered in purplish fur. A flat head dominated by oversized nostrils sat atop a muscular neck, bulging eyes staring out on each side of a huge, rubbery-lipped mouth. And it stank.

"Doesn't look much like an Earth camel, does it?" She almost gagged on her food as the animal swayed by, a blue-clad Targi sitting on its back in a strange, saddle-like contraption that looked extremely uncomfortable.

"No, but it does just about the same job." Decker, still chewing his meat-filled bread pocket with gusto, seemed unaffected by the smell. "Apparently the buggers can go for weeks without water. There have been stories of caravans coming out of the deep desert with desiccated corpses in the saddles, but the critters still able to walk to the next oasis."

"Charming. I'm glad we don't have to cross the entire Great Erg." She suddenly stopped talking and quickly wrapped the bottom of her turban around her lower face, hissing at Decker. "Cover yourself."

A skimmer, much newer and in better condition than the one they'd abandoned the previous evening, was slowly making its way through the growing crowd. The two men sitting in the open compartment didn't much look like Nabhkans. Clad in some sort of sand-colored battledress, wearing wide, polarized eye protectors and carrying a small arsenal on their persons, they could have passed for mercenaries anywhere.

The two spies bowed their heads over their plates, to avoid attracting attention, but they watched the new arrivals from the corners of their eyes. The skimmer passed them and the food stand where they sat, stopping about fifty meters further down the side of the town square. Both occupants jumped out and scanned the crowd.

"Amali's men, do you think?"

"Probably." Zack watched them as they began to move about. "Trained in any case, and by professionals, so unless there's a war going on that we haven't heard about or a shayk living in these hinterlands who likes to pay a premium for off-world guards, I'd say there's a good chance they're looking for us. Or at least, doing due diligence by patrolling the town closest to the Nippur oasis."

"The hit squad liaison would have figured out by now that we got away. Someone might have reported the bodies we left at Girsu."

"Not necessarily. As I said, many folks try to avoid dealing with the police in these parts. The motto 'serve and protect' doesn't exactly translate into the local lingo."

"Still, with no contact for a day, someone's bound to get worried, especially since yesterday was intended to mark our demise."

The two men slowly made their way across the square, examining people, looking into tents, storefronts and under awnings. When they got to the cluster of parked ground vehicles, they stopped and examined the abandoned skimmer. One of them pulled out a pad and glanced at its screen, then back at the skimmer. Then, both turned and scanned the square with what seemed to be a greater sense of urgency.

"They've made the damn clunker," Decker swore under his breath. "We should have dumped it outside of town."

"Where it would have stuck out even more. What's done is done. The real question is what do we do now?"

"Stay right here, like good little Targi having a bit of a laugh before we head back into the desert."

"Your eyes will be a dead giveaway, Zack."

He chuckled.

"You'd be surprised how many Targi have eyes like mine. No, the biggest giveaway is around them."

Talyn, head cocked to the side, stared at the little bit of his skin that remained visible, then bent over to grab a handful of the sandy dust that had accumulated at the base of the wall. With quick movements, her head turned away from the two men, she scrubbed her face beneath the veil. When she looked at Zack again, there was now nothing to identify her as an off-worlder. Decker nodded and quickly followed suit.

"I have to say, the dirt around your eyes really brings out the blue."

"Simmer down, sweetie," Decker growled. "Now's not the time to get frisky."

"Nor the place."

Secure in their disguise, they watched the mercenaries take a greater interest than before in anyone who looked even the slightest bit out of place in the town of Assur on a hot and dusty morning.

There were Targi going about their business and for a moment, Decker thought the men were going to force them to show their faces, but apart from a good hard look at the eyes and bit of skin open to the world, they didn't bother the nomads.

"Time to go," he whispered. "We don't want to be sitting down if they find us more fascinating than the rest."

They rose without haste, as if unconcerned with the world around them, and Zack led the way out of the square, heading towards the edge of town where the Targi caravan was forming.

The Marine's size must have triggered something because he heard a shout in a much-mangled version of the Nabhka patois ordering him to stop, just as they were about to slip down a narrow alley.

"Crap." He pulled Talyn deeper into the shadows. "The bastards aren't going to let up, and Assur isn't so big that we can vanish without a trace."

They ran around a corner and into a dead end strewn with broken crates, rusty parts from long dead machinery and other assorted debris. The moment

Decker realized his mistake, he heard the pounding of booted feet echoing in the lane.

"Let's make like we're digging through this garbage," he whispered at Talyn, "but be ready for a quick draw."

They dropped into a crouch, sideways to where the dead-end joined the alley and began handling the parts strewn about. The men appeared, skidding to a halt when they saw two shapes in blue desert robes.

"You there," one of them snarled, in that same execrable pidgin he'd used to order them to stop. "Look at me."

Decker slowly turned his head and stared at the mercenary.

"What do you want with a son of the Targi?" He demanded in a much better but by no means perfect rendition of Nabhkan. "We are free people and don't like being ordered around by filthy ghareeb."

Zack met the man's eyes and held them, displaying neither fear nor anger but, to the mercenary's evident surprise, undisguised contempt.

"Go back to your fornicating ghareeb shayk and leave the desert people alone."

The second man made as if to step forward and take Decker to task for his arrogant tone, but his companion restrained him. He'd seen danger in the Targi's dark blue eyes and knew enough about the nomads to realize that pushing things any further would spark a fight that they might not win, especially if there were others of his clan nearby.

"It's not Decker," he said in Anglic, eyes still on the big native. When he didn't see a flicker of recognition at the name, he shrugged. "Our mistake."

The men made as if to turn and Zack began to relax, prematurely as it turned out. In a move almost too fast for the eye to register, the one who'd done all the talking whirled towards Zack, grabbed the end of his turban and yanked it away, his eyes widening in triumph as he saw that he had indeed cornered the right prey.

Decker pulled his dagger from its forearm sheath and thrust upwards to bury it in the mercenary's throat, just above his adam's apple. The blade went deep into the brain, killing him instantly. Stunned, the second man didn't react quickly enough when Talyn whipped out her blaster and drilled a small, smoking hole into his forehead.

The entire fight had lasted mere seconds, not long enough or even noisy enough to attract the attention of passersby.

"Let's hide these morons behind the crates. They'll start stinking in a few hours, but hopefully, we'll be long gone by then. Strip off their weapons. I'd rather not be responsible for neighborhood toughs getting their hands on modern guns."

One passing local briefly stared at them as they dragged the second body behind the garbage pile but a hard look from the big, menacing tribesman sent him scurrying away.

"I think that gent will be back soon enough with some pals to strip the bodies. Let's get out of here."

"Should we take their skimmer? If they work for Amali, it'll be keyed to whatever defensive system the compound's got."

Decker thought about the suggestion for a moment, then shook his head.

"Also too risky. We don't know about passwords or recognition signs. A good security set-up doesn't just rely on IFF signals. The plan to go with the Targi caravan is still the best alternative."

"At this point, with the trail of bodies we've left in our wake, a kinetic strike from orbit would have been the best alternative," she replied, sounding uncharacteristically weary.

"It wouldn't quite have had the same effect on Amali's buddies and the rest of his rotten clan. You want to send a message, you have to get up close and personal. Me, I don't give a damn about messaging. I just need to collect a debt. But your boss at HQ seemed pretty insistent about it."

"He's your boss too, Zack."

"For now." With a last glance back at the dead-end alley, they walked away, hoping to shake Assur's filth from their boots before the day was out.

**

The stench of a camelot herd was something no amount of experience could prepare one to expect. The Targi milling about the cantankerous beasts seemed to have become so used to the smell that they didn't notice it anymore. Talyn hoped that she would be able to imitate them quickly; otherwise eating might become a problem.

Decker spent almost two hours in negotiations with a white-bearded nomad who didn't seem put off by his obviously ghareeb face when he removed the veil. Between straining to understand the old man's accent and drinking gallons of overly sweet tea, he had a pounding headache by the time he handed over a stack of cred chips.

"We're now the proud owners of two riding and one pack camelot, complete with saddles and tack. Since I gave Idriss – that's his name - a satisfactory haggle and still left him with a good price, he's more than happy to have us join his caravan until we pass near the evil ghareeb shayk's fortress. He'll even shift his route enough so that we can drop out at one of the rocky outcrops without being obvious about it."

"Mighty nice of him." She looked at Zack strangely. "If I didn't know you were a rock-hard and overly stoic fighter, I'd say you're on the verge of doing the pee dance."

"Tea will do that to a body."

He glanced at the old man and motioned that he had to go. A dry, stick-like finger pointed towards a wall enclosing a manure pile.

"Alfresco facilities, eh." Zack shrugged. "When in Assur..."

"That's going to be so much fun for someone with my kind of plumbing," Talyn muttered unenthusiastically.

"Get used to it. It's a day and a half to the Nippur oasis, and then however much time it takes me to figure out how to get inside."

"And then the trip back."

"I seem to recall you know how to pilot a shuttle. Did you really think that I'd planned to walk back once Amali had joined his cousin in the afterlife?"

"A bit visible, no? The point of the operation is to get in, do it, and get out without being spotted."

As Zack's grin widened, she shook her head.

"No. No way. Not on my watch, Chief Warrant Officer Decker. We're not doing that. I'm still your commanding officer, even if you've got the lead for the mission."

"You don't mind killing, but you balk at theft and piracy? I guess you really are nuts. We'll have that conversation in a few days, commander, sir, and then we'll see how you feel about it. There's nothing like quality time in the back of beyond to make you appreciate convenience."

"Next, you'll be telling me that we'll hijack Amali's yacht as well."

"Sure. No point in stealing his shuttle if we're not going all the way. I'm surprised I have to spell this out for an agent of your advanced years and experience."

"I'll get you for that one, Decker."

"Not until the mission's done."

The sun vanished with the abruptness so common in the lower latitudes, though a soft purplish light still lingered on the far horizon when the long line of loaded beasts set out, Decker and Talyn among the last of the riders.

They'd seen another skimmer appear from the general direction of Nippur late in the afternoon, but no one came to the Targi encampment looking for a big man with deep blue eyes who'd last been seen dragging a mercenary's body behind a garbage pile in the souk.

By the time full night had fallen and a sky filled with stars watched over Assur, quiet now that the day's work was done, the caravan had vanished into the rocky landscape that bordered the vast desert.

**

"Any news, Lyle?" Harmon Amali looked up from his antipasto plate as the aide sat down.

"Some. The liaison had promised an update, but she's been strangely silent. It's only been two days, but still. The relief team I sent to Assur found the skimmer, but they haven't found the men yet. The local police are as useless as ever, and no one wants to talk much. Our guys were last seen chasing a pair of Targi nomads."

"Disquieting, don't you think?" He took a sip of wine, hiding his sudden fear behind a calm expression while savoring the delicious taste. It had come from his family's own vineyards, light years away from this dismal hole of a planet.

"Not only is there no 'mission accomplished' from our very expensive contractors, but the regular patrol seems to have vanished. If I were to lay odds, I'd say our Mister Decker is behind both events."

The aide paled under his fresh Nabhka tan.

"Do you mean he's in Assur, sir?"

"Possibly. Have surveillance of the area increased, Lyle. If that damned Marine is coming near, I want him intercepted and killed."

It was a measure of the man's dread that he'd dropped his usual euphemisms in favor of an uncharacteristic directness.

"Perhaps we should consider leaving."

"Why? Decker will never give up, and Nippur is the most inaccessible and most secure residence I own. Were I to ask asylum from anyone with better facilities, the inevitable questions would arise, and I can't afford to be known publically as the man who'd arranged to sell a Marine into slavery. I'd be torn limb from limb by anyone in uniform. No. We stay here and let him come to us. He'll be easier to exterminate if he's close."

The little surge of bravado did raise Amali's spirits, and he contemplated, as he popped another delicacy in his mouth, the possibility of shooting Decker himself in a desert hunt, an idea which sounded delicious. The smile that twisted his lips was of such cruelty that even Lyle, used to his master's ways, felt an unaccustomed chill.

He nodded politely at Amali and left the room, anxious to go outside and clear his head. Stepping through the airlock-like door opening onto an inner courtyard, he was struck again by the speed with which the desert cooled after sunset. A short flight of stairs led him up to the roof of the connected outbuildings that formed a sort of hollow wall around the mansion, giving Amali's retreat the appearance of a small citadel.

Here, standing alone above the oasis, he felt disconnected, almost lost in a dark world punctuated only by the occasional whisper of the wind over the dunes. His eyes scanned the black, menacing fingers of the rocky outcrops surrounding Nippur, knowing that beyond the compound's walls, they wouldn't find a single sign of life, let alone civilization. Even Assur, somewhere to the north, didn't leave the hint of a glow in the night air. It was too distant and too small.

Lyle slowly paced the rooftop walk, stopping over an archway big enough to allow even sizeable skimmers through, and let his eyes drift up the barely discernable road.

Beneath his feet, a thick door barred the entrance, watched over and controlled by a guard on duty in the neighboring security room. Made up entirely of off-worlders, Amali's security detail had some of the finest hired muscle money could buy.

Even if Decker were still alive and gunning for his employer, he'd have to get through not only the fortifications but also a wall of men paid handsomely to protect Amali, even sacrifice themselves for him if needed. The damned Marine might be good, but he wasn't invincible.

He stared up at the stars, as if looking for reassurance, but they gave him no answers. After a final glance at the still desert, he went back to the mansion, to make one more check of the communications log and see if someone had finally reported in.

**

"It's pretty ironic, isn't it?"

"What is?" Zack shifted his eyes from the camelot dung fire to Talyn, who was squatting next to him.

"We've traveled hundreds of light years on FTL capable starships to get at Amali and yet we're making the final little bit of the trip on the back of a pack animal in what is probably the most primitive environment in human space. Look around: we're in a nomad encampment in the lee of a sand dune, using a fire fueled by animal droppings, eating food that's been cooked over that same fire in a simple iron pot. The contrast doesn't get much starker than this."

He shrugged.

"It is what it is. We could have used a modern skimmer, but in this case, primitive will work better. Besides, these are good folk who believe in their chosen lifestyle. We could do worse than hang out with them for a while. It makes a nice change from the scum we've dealt with recently."

"You really are the last romantic, Decker." She shook her head in disbelief.

"At least I didn't lose my supper after only ten minutes riding a critter."

"Don't remind me." Talyn grimaced. "Damn thing sways more than a sloop caught in an ionic storm. It must be those six legs moving without any sort of coordination."

The pink of sunrise was starting to paint the far horizon and Decker got up, shaking the sand from his robes.

"Time to crawl into the tent. It'll start getting hot soon, and we're no camelots, able to sit there and bake."

She pulled herself up wearily, thighs and buttocks sore from the ten hours they'd spent in the saddle.

"I could use a good massage just about now."

"Sorry, toots, the Zack Decker Pleasure Palace and Spa isn't open right now."

"Then I'm faced with a miracle: you not interested in sex and not even complaining about the lack of cold beer."

"Take a whiff of yourself, princess. A day of sweating while riding on a camelot sort of takes the appeal out of naked time."

Talyn grunted, then dropped to her knees and crawled into the low Targi tent, just about big enough for the two of them, and likely the most high tech item the nomads carried. Not bothering to strip, they sprawled out and quickly fell asleep to the soft song of the wind and the less appealing snorts of over two dozen six-legged beasts dozing away.

Their tent shook as a voice called out, and Decker's eyes snapped open. Daylight was fading, which meant he'd slept for a long time, more than any night in recent months. The ride had tired him out and, lying here in the great desert where few dared go, he'd felt incongruously safe. He nudged Hera until she reluctantly stirred.

"Time to get up, eat, pack this thing, and start moving again."

"Can't I just walk? The thought of climbing back on a camelot gives me the dry heaves."

"Cry baby." He opened the tent flap and crawled out. "I should have figured Navy pukes can't handle ground operations."

She made an obscene gesture in response.

"Not until you've had a shower," Zack replied, laughing.

The old man came to sit by their fire while they ate a frugal meal of boiled grains and dried meat.

"Have you thought of my proposal, Decker? It is not only you that has a feud with the off-worlder shayk who stole Nippur oasis from the desert people."

"I have, and my mind remains as it was, Idriss. I don't wish to see your family destroyed, which it will if you attempt to storm Amali's compound. Your jezails are no match for the modern weapons carried by the guards."

"And yet you intend to attack alone."

He spat into the fire, to show his disapproval.

"I intend to use stealth, not open combat."

"Then perhaps you can use stealth to open his doors so we can enter like djinns of legend and cut every throat in the accursed fortress."

When Zack had translated for Talyn's benefit, she laid a hand on his arm.

"It might be useful to have a backup and even more helpful to blur the trail of evidence through the involvement of Targi tribesmen with a known grudge against Amali."

Her eyes challenged him to deny the truth of her words, and so he just nodded.

"Very well."

Turning to the chieftain, he bowed his head.

"So it shall be done. We will take Nippur together, but under my orders, that is not negotiable."

"Agreed." Idriss rose to his feet in a motion that belied his advanced age. "We will arrive at the oasis tomorrow and hide in the Cave of Winds while you make your plan of attack. If any of the off-world shayk's men try to dislodge us, they will die."

As she watched him return to his pack animal, Talyn remarked, "They do hold a grudge around here, don't they."

"Yep." Decker kicked sand over the flaming dung to douse the fire in preparation for departure. "Apparently some feuds in the Nabhka backcountry date to when their ancestors still lived on Earth, so it's not a good idea to get on their bad side."

The following dawn saw them come up to a large stone outcrop a short distance from Nippur and Amali's fortress. The dunes and the moonless night had mostly covered their approach, though as they filed through a crack in the granite and entered the cold darkness of the Cave of Winds, the customary pink light on the horizon turned to gray. Sniffing the air, the old man hurried them out of the open and into confined quarters where the stench of the camelots came to dominate within moments.

"Sandstorm," he announced when Decker looked at him questioningly. "It was the will of God that we accompanied you here. A sandstorm in the open Erg is a dangerous thing. The caves will protect us and our beasts."

"Will it last long?"

Idriss shrugged with the fatalism of all nomads.

"Only God knows, and he'll tell us when it ends."

They soon discovered why their refuge had been so named when the tempest was directly overhead. A deep thrumming resonance, coming from the gale passing through the rocky spires, filled the air. Though it sounded menacing, they were well protected from the blinding wall of sand.

Zack went back to the opening, to get a glimpse of nature's fury and when he returned, Talyn looked up from her dismantled weapons.

"So?"

"I couldn't see a damn thing. Put a piece of starship hull out there and it'll be stripped down to the bare metal in seconds. I'm glad we got here when we did, but we're stuck until it stops."

"It is kind of cozy once you get used to the smell."

— TWENTY-EIGHT —

Amali stared out at his compound, unable to see anything beyond the swirling sand and dust driven by a howling gale. No one would be able to get in or out while it lasted, giving him a few hours or even days of peace before the deadly game resumed.

The relief patrol had returned from Assur the previous evening, confirming the worst. Apart from the skimmer, nothing remained of the vanished men and no one in town was willing to talk. If it weren't for the abandoned vehicle, the two mercenaries might never have existed. While the desert nomads and indeed the townspeople themselves resented him and his men, they had so far taken no concrete action which meant someone else could be in play.

"Are you out there, Mister Decker?" He murmured. "Or am I just being overly paranoid?"

The storm made him feel as if he was no longer in control of his destiny, an uncomfortable thought for a man used to being obeyed by all, if not exactly liked by many. His compound was secure, of course. Even Decker wasn't crazy enough to try anything while nature raged outside and perhaps if he was very, very lucky, the damned Marine would have been caught far from shelter and was even now being flayed alive. That is if he was anywhere near the desert.

There was still a small chance the contractors had killed him and preferred to be far away before reporting in, lest anyone in authority intercept a message that might hint at murder. But there was still the matter of the missing guards in Assur, though bandits might be responsible, or the men themselves might have violated a taboo or other in their dealings with the locals and paid for it with their lives.

A few hours earlier, during the darkest part of the night when spirits were at their lowest ebb and fears took up free residence in his soul, he had almost ordered his shuttle made ready for departure. Being on the move seemed infinitely preferable to waiting for his pursuer, even though it would only prolong the inevitable. With the appearance of daylight, such as it was, logic had retaken its rightful place, especially with the display of raw power descending on the Great Erg.

"Sir," Lyle stuck his head through the doorway, "breakfast is ready."

A dull flash of light tried to fight its way through the dust-laden air, followed by a loud thunderclap that managed to drown out the wind's howl. Amali sighed, both awed and annoyed by the majesty of nature's fury, then followed his aide to the dining room where his meal awaited.

"You may inform Shayk Hysan that I'm ready to see him about the proposal. He may come once the storm has lifted."

At least he still had control over his business dealings.

******

"That was fun," Talyn commented after the rolling thunder had finished shaking their subterranean refuge.

"What would really be fun," Decker replied, pacing the cavern as he fought with his impatience, "would be a company's worth of armored troops. Heck, just a full suit for you and I, and we could infiltrate the place while everyone's hunkering down. Their sensor net is probably useless right now."

Idriss asked Zack to translate what he'd just said and when the Marine had done so, he scratched his white beard, eyes narrowed as he contemplated the wailing of the wind and the hissing sound of tiny grains rubbing against stone.

"When the worst of the storm has lifted, we can put on our sand masks and venture out while there's still enough dust in the air to hide us from their magic eyes."

"Sand mask?"

Reaching into the large pouch at his waist, the chieftain pulled out a canvas hood with glass ports for the eyes and a filter for the nose and mouth. He put it on, transforming his wizened appearance into a nightmarish apparition that, if seen coming out of the tempest, would frighten even the bravest of men.

"It is what we wear when we cannot find shelter." His voice sounded muffled. "I'm surprised a man of your learning didn't know about them."

Decker acknowledged the comment with a quick tilt of the head.

"We all have our failings."

Face uncovered once more, the old man handed his mask to Zack, who put it on with a certain amount of trepidation, but it smelled no worse than anything else in the cavern did.

"You have spares?"

"Certainly."

He shouted a few words at the knot of Targi chatting quietly in the far corner and was quickly handed two more masks taken from the caravan's common holdings.

A shiver of excitement began to radiate from the base of Zack's spine as he thought about the possibilities offered by this simple, primitive implement. If they could move into the oasis under cover of the storm's tail end...

******

A wrinkled hand shook Decker out of a light slumber and as his eyes snapped open, he saw that the ghostly glow of the muted sun had gone, leaving the mouth of the cave in darkness.

"The storm has weakened enough that it will be safe for us to venture out. Come. I will take you to the off-world shayk's castle."

Idriss pulled on his sand mask and, jezail in hand, waved towards the outside.

The Targi chieftain moved like a ghost in the dusty gloom, stopping every few steps to make sure Decker and Talyn were still behind him. They, carrying the weapons stolen from Amali's patrol in Assur, struggled to keep up even as Zack consulted his small hand-held sensor frequently, trying to pinpoint the surveillance gear he knew had to be planted around the perimeter.

The dust particles appeared to be highly charged, distorting his readings and presumably those of the enemy as well. If there ever was a right moment to attack, this was it, provided they could find a way inside a compound that would be tightly battened down against the storm.

Suddenly the dark mass of the walls appeared out of the gloom, and he could just about see the main entrance to his left, recessed into an alcove rapidly filling with sand. He briefly thought of the poor bastard who was going to be on clean-up duty when this was over. Amali should have invested the extra money to dome the place, but it was probably cheaper to get a couple of shovels and send out the hired help for the few times a year they got hit this bad. Then, an idea struck him. He tugged on Idriss' sleeve and put his mask-covered mouth against the side of the chieftain's hood.

"I think that once the storm is over, they'll open up to do some cleaning. That might be our chance, provided we can hide right near the gate and rush in."

Instead of answering, the Targi chief wiggled around vigorously and in the space of less than a minute, had vanished, hidden by the sand. Sensors would spot them, but if Amali's security had no reason to scan the ground immediately by the main gate, it might just work. He looked at Talyn, her face hidden behind the hideous mask. She nodded before making the signal to turn around and head back to the caves.

"How long do you reckon until the storm peters out?" Zack asked Idriss once they were back under shelter and had removed their hoods.

The old man shrugged.

"A few hours. Perhaps at dawn. Best we go soon. Once daylight comes, they'll see us even through the dust."

"You sure you want to do this?" He put his hand on the Targi's shoulder and looked him in the eye. "It could get nasty very quickly."

"Life is hard, Decker, and the off-world shayk made it harder by denying us the waters of Nippur. If we don't fight now, then off-worlders will take all the oases. Perhaps God brought you to us for this purpose. We are warriors and can fight, but you are a soldier who knows how to lead warriors to victory. We go."

With those words, Idriss went off to collect the fighting men of his clan, each armed with his jezail and wearing a hideous mask. An hour later, Decker, Talyn, and twenty-five Targi tribesmen were hidden in the sand at the base of Amali's compound, ready to storm the gate.

As the last to dig in, Decker examined the area in the growing orange glow of dawn and saw no trace of the fighters. He placed one of their two sensors beneath a flat rock, leaving just enough room to allow it visual contact with the gate and linked it to the other, which he would hold in front of his mask's glass ports once he dug in.

No more than an hour had passed by the time the storm weakened and finally died away, revealing a brilliant sun that twinkled off the piles of sand wedged everywhere in and around the small fort. Decker's limbs felt almost painfully stiff, and he worried that they wouldn't be able to move quickly enough to seize the open gate, giving the defenders just enough time to shut it in their faces. They'd get one chance and one only. After that, Amali would likely bugger off in his shuttle.

After what seemed like an eternity since the last wisps of dust had settled, the sensor's small screen flickered and he tensed. The gate was grinding open to reveal the clean-up crew. He was about to rise and give the signal to attack when he caught a small dot speeding towards them on the edge of the screen. It quickly resolved into a fancy skimmer throwing up clouds of freshly settled grit with its antigrav repulsers.

Even better. Decker smiled to himself.

The moment the skimmer passed through the gate, he pushed himself up and bellowed a Targi battle cry Idriss had taught him. Within a fraction of a second, the smooth desert sand on either side of the archway sprouted nightmarish creatures in flowing desert robes, with huge glassy eyes and thick muzzles, brandishing long, homemade plasma rifles.

The startled guards froze, staring in disbelief at the apparitions until weapons coughed. They fell to the ground almost in unison, smoking holes punched into battledress tunics.

Like silent ghosts, the attack force streamed through the gate with Idriss leading the charge. He found the security station and before the men inside could react, burst through the door, shooting from the hip.

Decker and Talyn, with a half-dozen Targi on their heels, broke off from the main group and followed the skimmer through an open door into a well-lit hangar.

"Secure the shuttle," he shouted at Hera, pointing to the far end of the expansive space where a sleek extra-orbital craft sat in apparent readiness to lift.

Ignoring the well-dressed Nabhkan climbing out of the vehicle, Decker rushed towards the obvious off-worlder standing by the inner door, evidently there to greet the new arrival.

He recognized Amali's aide, Lyle, from the intelligence report and stuck his blaster in the man's face. The aide crumpled to the ground in a dead faint at the sight of the ghastly, enormous *thing* coming to kill him.

It had been less than thirty seconds since Decker had given the signal to attack and as of yet, no alarm sounded, but it wouldn't last. Even now, he heard the cough of plasma fire from the inner courtyard, punctuated by shouts in Nabhkan as the tribesmen systematically eliminated any guards foolish enough to challenge them.

The inner door opened at his touch and, followed by three of the Targi, he walked into a world of cool, clean air that spoke of wealth and luxury here on the edge of one of the deadliest deserts in human space.

He pointed at two of the tribesmen and then down the right-hand corridor, sending them to clear the mansion from that direction.   Taking the other one as his wingman, he went left, cautiously checking every room until he found a door that opened onto a large, tastefully appointed space with a row of outward-facing windows.

A man stood by one of them, holding a blaster while anxiously peering outside. At the sound of the intruders, he whirled around, ready to fire. Upon seeing the masked men, his face turned ashen with fright and his first shot went wide. Before he could try again, the sight of a jezail and a large bore blaster pointed at his head made him drop his gun and fall to his knees.

Decker tore off his hood and walked up to the man until he stood a bare meter away, towering over the quivering creature.

"Harmon Amali, I presume. I'm Chief Warrant Officer Zachary T. Decker, Commonwealth Marine Corps, at your service."

The wretch looked up into his hard face and, like his aide, he fainted.

**

"Now what?" Talyn asked jutting her chin towards their bound and gagged prisoner. "You're like the dog that caught the skimmer and doesn't know what to do with it. Simply executing Amali isn't your style, Zack, no matter how much you think you want blood for blood."

He nodded wearily, feeling the full weight of the past year push down on him, now that the adrenaline of the raid had worn off.

"You're probably right. Killing him isn't like killing the pirates on Tortuga station. Their lives were forfeit in any decent civilization." He sat on the edge of the desk and stared at his prisoner. "You know, it took me a long time to stop getting nightmares from the way his cousin died."

"I'm glad to hear you say that," she replied in a soft tone. "Like I said a few days ago, you're no sociopath, and this proves it."

Idriss cleared his throat, and when Decker turned towards him, he asked for a translation. Upon hearing it, the chieftain nodded knowingly.

"It speaks to your honor, Zachary Decker. This man," he pointed at Amali, "deserves to die, but it has to be in a way that will not displease God. Shooting him in the heat of battle would have been fine, but now that he is a prisoner, he must be judged by the laws of the tribe. If you wish to take him to be judged by your laws, I will recognize your claim on him."

"That, I can't do, Idriss. My law will be perverted to save his life. He's rich and has powerful friends who'll make sure that I die while he lives."

"So be it then. He shall be judged by the tribe for taking the waters of Nippur away from the nomadic clans, thereby causing the death of several of my kin until we could change our caravan routes."

"I'd like to witness that."

"You shall, Decker, but you and your companion must come with us to our destination, where my entire tribe is meeting for the lunar feast. There, you too will give testimony against this evil shayk before the elders. If found guilty, we will execute him in accordance with desert customs."

"If found guilty?"

Decker immediately regretted the sarcastic edge to his tone.

"All men are innocent before God until proven guilty under His laws, though, with the evidence against this one, I have no doubt he will not live to see the new moon." There was no hint of reproach in his voice.

Zack glanced at Talyn, giving her a quick translation back into Anglic and she smiled wanly.

"A good solution, I think. You get to collect the debt Amali owes, the Targi get to collect theirs and regain the Nippur oasis, and we have clean hands in his upcoming death, something that will please our superiors to no end."

Decker nodded, understanding the additional, unspoken reason for her approval of the plan: the fact that he would not go further down the path of darkness by killing a man in cold blood to avenge himself.

"We're in agreement, Idriss. If I may make a proposal: the Nippur oasis is now yours again, and if you have the means to contact the other caravans of your people, you can hold the lunar feast here, within these walls."

The Targi tilted his head to the side as he studied Zack's face, considering the proposal.

"It can be done. Each caravan has an emergency radio." He looked around the room. "If we can find a powerful transmitter, I should be able to call them to Nippur."

"You obviously have something else in that fertile tactical mind of yours, Zack," Talyn said when they were alone in the office after they'd found the communications room and let Idriss call his kin.

"There is that small matter of making sure we keep the other survivors under guard until the trial is over. It wouldn't do to have anyone contacting the authorities and hunting us down before the bastard meets his maker, and none of them deserve to die. I also want to stay close to that shuttle."

A slow grin spread across his face as he saw her eyes harden.

"You're still thinking of taking Amali's yacht, aren't you? I thought I said no."

"We need a quick way home. Word of what happened here is bound to spread the moment we leave. Once that happens, the Coalition might just decide to shake off their cloak of secrecy and remove the major irritant we've become before we can report back to HQ. Think about it. Even taking a skimmer from this place, it'll be a long time before we make Kish, and there's no guarantee we can get off planet fast, let alone find a ship headed in the right direction."

"And how do you propose to get the yacht's crew to let us come aboard."

"Simple. We spoof the comms. Once the shuttle's in the hangar bay, there's no reason why two superbly trained officers like you and me can't seize it."

"Sailing it back to Caledonia might be another story." She shook her head, still unconvinced.

"You're a Navy puke, Hera. I'm sure you can remember enough about astrogation to get us away from this system. After that, we call Uncle Josiah for help. No one will see a black ops ship pick us off the yacht in interstellar space. Heck, the service might even want to keep Amali's toy. Once he's gone to Targi hell, no one will be around to claim it."

"Always the optimist, aren't you? Okay. We'll try it your way."

"Excellent." He rubbed his hands together. "Now that we've got the next steps settled, how about you and me find a couple-sized shower and scrub each other's back."

She nodded.

"At this point, I'll be glad enough to get the camelot stench off me that I won't make any cracks about playing hide the soap. I'll even help you find some beer, Mister Marine with two obsessions."

Later, as they lay on Amali's opulent bed, Decker staring at the ceiling and Hera Talyn half draped over his naked body, she absently ran her fingers through his chest hair as she studied his square profile.

"Zack, if you really don't want to stay in intelligence after this is over, I'll see what I can do to get you sent to a regular Marine posting. The chief warrant officer's bars are permanent, and I'm sure there are plenty of billets, even in a regiment, where someone will be glad to have you. But you could probably do a lot more for the Fleet by staying with us, with me.   Naval intelligence operations are a hell of a force multiplier. One or two agents can put more bad guys away than several pathfinder squadrons."

He grunted wordlessly. After a moment, he turned towards her, their faces millimeters apart and leaned forward, cutting off any further attempt at conversation.

— TWENTY-NINE —

The slow beat of camelot-skin drums echoed through the small fort, bouncing off stone walls again and again. Torches flickered all around the perimeter, casting an uncertain light over a solemn crowd sitting patiently along three sides of an open square.

Beyond the dancing flames, out in the desert night, herds of the six-legged beasts snorted and brayed as they settled down for the evening, watched over by the unblooded boys of the tribe.

Talyn and Decker, wearing their old clothes again in preparation for departure, watched from the doorway to the mansion as six chieftains, Idriss among them, marched in through the open gate to the sound of a soft chant that had begun the moment the eldest appeared.

They slowly strolled around the u-shaped formation of their fellow clansmen and women, meeting the eyes of each and every one in a centuries-old ceremony that cemented the bond between them. Once the ritual completed, they sat down on thick pillows that had been laid on the ground facing the assembly. The drumming and chanting stopped.

Prodded by jezail-wielding warriors, Amali was taken from the guardhouse and brought before the clan leaders, where they forced him to kneel. In the days it had taken to gather the tribe, his appearance had deteriorated alarmingly. Unshaven, unkempt, and hollow-eyed, he bore little resemblance to the arrogant Coalition leader who'd condemned Decker to slavery and his wife to an early death.

When he heard the tribal elder begin reciting the charges against Amali, Zack nudged Talyn.

"It's time for me to join them. They'll want my testimony soon enough."

He walked up to the edge of the hollow square and waited politely, adopting the parade-rest position.

"I summon the off-worlder Zachary Decker to tell his story," Idriss called out soon after that.

Zack came to attention and briskly marched into the square, wheeling with precision until he stood in front of the elders. He figured that this was the Targi version of a court-martial so going through the proper drill wouldn't come amiss.

At the tribe leader's nod, he relaxed his stance and began speaking in his halting Nabhkan about how the accused had rightly held him responsible for his cousin's death, but that the cousin had been an evil man bent on enslaving humanity. He then told of his life as a trader, his love for his wife and the awful moment pirates attacked them, kill her, and enslaved him.

The audience was deathly still as his words rang out over the compound, the elders listening with fascination of a life and events beyond their experience. Zack must have spoken for a long time because when he fell silent, his mouth and throat were parched.

"Thank you, Zachary Decker." Idriss nodded. "You may go."

He snapped to attention again, did a quick right turn, and marched off to the side, brushing by Talyn and into the darkness of the mansion door. Alarmed by the look on his face, she followed him while the Targi continued with their trial, calling on the survivors of the caravan denied water by Amali to testify.

"Are you okay?" She asked softly, touching his shoulder.

When he turned to face her, she could see the tears rolling down his grizzled cheeks and instinctively put her arms around him.

"Let it go, Zack," Talyn murmured. "You've held it in for so long that it had to come out eventually and tonight's the night."

He was wracked with sobs for what seemed like a long time, but when he'd finally emptied his soul, the trial was still in full swing. Brushing away the last tears with a rough swipe, he gave her a weak grin.

"Thanks, Hera. But let's not speak of this again, shall we?"

She shook her head.

"Men! You never want to admit you have emotions." After a long kiss, she let him go and stepped back. "Don't worry. This'll stay between us."

The beating of the drums suddenly resumed behind them.

"I think we're about to get a verdict," he said. "Let's go back out there."

They took up position on the flank of the open square, just in time to see the tribal eldest rise from his cushion and raise both gnarled hands in the air.

"In the sight of God and the tribe, you, Harmon Amali, have been accused of causing the deaths of many, of stealing an oasis and denying water, of selling a man into slavery and when that failed, of attempting to have him murdered. The words spoken tonight were true testimony and prove your guilt beyond any doubt. This council, therefore, condemns you to death in the traditional manner reserved for the worst criminals. Seize him and bring him to the execution grounds."

"Any idea how they're going to do it?" Talyn's whisper was loud enough to cut through the rhythmic ululating of the crowd at the verdict.

"Not a clue. Idriss wouldn't tell me in advance."

The clan chieftain, now standing along with his fellow elders and the entire tribe, made a come-hither motion at the intelligence officers.

"I guess we're about to find out."

Half-carried and half-dragged by his guards, Amali was taken through the gate and out into the open desert, the procession swollen by torch-carrying Targi. At a safe distance from the fort, they staked him out spread-eagle and cut his clothes from his body. The tribe eldest pulled a curved dagger from the sheath at his hip and slashed each of Amali's limbs, his torso, and his scalp so that blood dripped heavily and soaked the sand beneath him.

Then, he stepped back, leaving the condemned man alone in the center of a wide, bare circle.

Within moments, the sand stirred and a collective gasp escaped from the audience. Then, a grayish *thing* erupted between Amali's legs and latched onto his thigh, drawing a scream of agony that reverberated against the rocky outcrops dotting the dunes.

When it vanished seconds later, there was a large, reddish gap where the flesh had been. As if the first strike were a long awaited signal, many more of the creatures came to the surface and began feeding off the writhing body, slowly reducing one of the richest and most powerful men in the Commonwealth to a bloody skeleton. Decker and Talyn watched the native Nabhkan desert predators strike time after time, encouraged by the continuous shouts of the tribesmen.

When it was finished, Zack shook his head.

"I don't think I could have inflicted that much pain on him if I'd been his executioner," he murmured, voice harsh to the point of sounding raw. "If it weren't for losing face in front of the Targi, I'd probably puke right now."

"You and me both, lover-boy." She gripped his arm as if to steady herself. "When can we bugger off and not seem rude? The bastard's dead and that's all we were waiting for. We can think about the rest of his rotten kin later."

Decker glanced over at Idriss. The old man's face softened with compassion.

"Revenge is one of the most difficult dishes to eat, whether hot or cold, Decker. It leaves no one untouched, but justice has been done tonight." He lifted his hand to his brow and bowed. "God be with both of you in your travels. The tribe will be forever in your debt for returning the oasis to us."

Decker and Talyn imitated the gesture.

"And we will forever be in yours. God watch over your people, Idriss."

They left the circle of torchlight and headed back to the compound in silence.

"I can't wait to see how you're going to report this," he finally said. "Target became sand shark food on Nabhka; operatives were not involved in the death."

"You're the junior officer on this team, buddy. Doing your first mission write-up is going to be a good learning experience."

"Screw you, commander, sir."

"Not again, Zack. Aren't you ever satisfied?"

"Nope. Never. Now show me how well you can fly that shuttle."

**

"Yacht *Syrah*, this is shuttle *Amarone*." Decker shook his head. "The man had a drinking problem if he named everything after fancy wines."

"*Amarone*, this is *Syrah*. Is Mister Amali aboard?" A sharp female voice asked.

"He is indeed."

"What happened to the usual warning?"

They exchanged alarmed looks. If there was a verbal recognition signal, they were about to get burned.

"The compound suffered a native incursion. We had to evacuate quickly for Mister Amali's safety."

"May I speak with him?"

Decker activated the computer routine that would transform his voice into Amali's, something he'd prepared while waiting for the Targi clans to assemble.

"This is Amali, captain. We were fortunate to get out in time. The contractors who warned me of the impending attack also helped me escape."

"Glad to hear you're okay, sir. The hangar doors are open, and you're cleared to land at your leisure. Let us know when you're in a position to be tractored."

"Shuttle *Amarone* is on final approach," Decker announced a few minutes later, staring at the compact starship ahead of them. It looked like a small sloop, with a full-sized sloop's hyperdrive nacelles. Gun blisters dotted the pure white hull at regular intervals and, apart from the name and registration number, no other markings appeared, not even a corporate logo.

Talyn was too busy to admire the ship. She had to make sure they matched *Syrah*'s velocity and were lined up perfectly with the bright square delineating the open hangar deck.

"We're in position, *Syrah*."

"We've got you," a male voice replied. Slowly the shuttle was pulled up to and then through the opening. The tractor beam operator gently deposited them on the deck while a red light began to flash as the space doors slid shut. Then, the flashing changed rhythm, indicating that the hangar was being pressurized. It was the signal for Decker and Talyn to climb out of the cockpit and get ready. They'd have a few seconds at most to seize control of the situation. The yacht had a crew of ten, and even though they were better trained than any of them was likely to be, the odds were still a bit steep.

"The captain's there to greet Amali personally." Hera pointed out the viewport at a short woman wearing a formal uniform with four gold stripes on the sleeves.

"I figured she would. This will make it easier." He touched the controls, and the starboard door broke its airtight seal, swinging aside. Decker jumped out and smiled broadly at the yacht's commander.

"Pleasure to be aboard, captain."

"Do I know you?" She looked at him suspiciously. Talyn stepped out at that moment, diverting her attention just long enough for Zack to pull his blaster and stick it in the woman's stomach.

"You don't, captain, but your former employer did. I suggest that you cooperate if you don't want to join him."

"Former?" Her eyes widened in shock. "You mean Mister Amali is dead? But I spoke to him on the radio not five minutes ago."

"That was me." Decker let a cruel smile play on his lips. "Amali died at the hands of natives he'd pissed off some time ago. We helped them take their revenge, and now we'll be taking his ship, seeing as how he owes us a ride home."

"How's that?" She'd quickly recovered her composure, and her eyes met the Marine's with calm calculation.

"He tried to have me assassinated. I figure for all the trouble he's caused, I deserve compensation."

"You're Decker," she hissed, the fear coming back.

"At your service. If you want to live, you're going to do as you're told. My problem was with your ex-boss, not you. All we need is transport away from this system, and you have no reason to hang around here anymore. We can help each other."

"What if I refuse?"

"My colleague and I can sail an FTL starship. Besides, *Syrah* probably has the finest in automation. Tell you what, the way I see it, we have three options. One, we put the lot of you on this shuttle and drop you off far enough away from Nabhka that by the time you reach the orbital, we'll have jumped out. Two, we lock you in a few compartments for the trip and shoot anyone trying to escape; or three, you can treat us as passengers, take us where we want to go and once we're out of your hair, you're free to go roaming the galaxy. Oh, before I forget, option three also comes with the caveat that we'll shoot anyone buggering us about."

"There's also option four," Talyn said. "We kill you all now and space your bodies. Like my friend here said, between the two of us, we can sail this little toy, no problems."

"Who the hell are you people?" *Syrah*'s captain sounded plaintive.

"Would you believe Sécurité Spéciale?"

Her eyes widened to the point of almost bugging out. "No."

"Yes," Zack grinned. "Your ex-boss tried to have an intelligence officer assassinated, not just some washed-out ex-Marine. Well, two if you count my colleague here who'd have been collateral damage."

"Your cooperation would go far in removing any suspicion that you were in on it." Hera Talyn toyed with her blaster, looking significantly at the captain. "In fact, your crew never needs to know anything other than Amali ordered you to transport us while he remained on the planet. I'm sure our service will show appropriate gratitude."

"Do you have any proof of what you're claiming?" The suspicious disbelief was back.

Decker pushed the barrel of his blaster harder into her midriff.

"This."

"Or perhaps this." Talyn held up her sensor so that the woman could see the screen. "I recorded his execution by the nomads."

Images began to move, and the blood drained from the captain's face. When the moment of the feeding frenzy came, Zack had just enough time to step away before she vomited on the deck, alternating between heaves and sobs.

"Opt now, captain." The intelligence officer returned the sensor to her pocket. "Our patience is finite, and we wasted most of it on your late owner."

"Put us ashore, you maniac."

"Why?"

"You two are bad news. I certainly don't want to spend time aboard a small ship with crazy people who say they're with the Sécurité Spéciale and let that – that horror happen. I'm not stupid, and since none of us have jobs anymore, the sooner we get away, the better."

"Fair enough." Talyn pointed at the intercom panel by the inner door. "Call them together here. We know how many there are, so no cute tricks. I don't mind scrubbing blood off the deck."

"What about our personal items?"

"Once everyone's here, captain, we'll figure something out. We don't intend to steal from you, just from the Amali family."

Syrah's captain gave her a look of pure loathing but did as they ordered.

**

"You know we're now pirates in all but some details," Talyn remarked as they watched the shuttle receded on the screen.

"How many pirates set their victims free unharmed and with all their possessions?"

"Like I said, some details. How long until they wake up?"

"Twelve hours or so. Then they'll be at least another four to six hours getting through the locks I put on the computer. We should be well away by then."

"Let's hope so." She called up the astrogation program. "I'm going to take us near the Talkin subspace array. We get in close and set up an optical link, that way we lessen the risk of interception."

"It's just going to let you do that?"

"If you know the code," she smiled angelically at Zack, "you can unlock anything."

Decker, sitting at the engineering console, looked around the small bridge and at Hera Talyn seated in the pilot's chair. Without warning, he had an unexpected and painful flashback to another ship and another woman, both gone now. The sting of tears in the corners of his eyes was as startling as it was brief and he quickly clamped down on his emotions.

The past was long gone, the future yet to come. In the present, they still had to get clean away from the Nabhka system and vanish before anyone could track them down. By now the tribesmen would have released Amali's aide, his surviving staff, and the visiting shayk. Word of Decker and Talyn's involvement would be filtering across the stars soon enough and whoever owed the late magnate allegiance in death as well as life would come after them.

"Are you alright, Zack?"

He nodded.

"Yeah. Just some memories intruding."

Talyn compressed her lips, knowing full well what he meant. The only relief she could offer was work.

"Status, Mister Decker?"

"All systems up and running. FTL's spooled up and ready as soon as we reach the hyperlimit."

"That won't be long. A ship this size can jump relatively close to a star."

"Then —" he broke off and touched a screen. "Nabhka traffic control is hailing us. They want us to return to orbit and wait for inspection."

"I guess someone got wise to the change in ownership. No reply."

"I wasn't going to." Decker snorted. "Just pour it on, dear captain and get our hairy asses out of here."

— THIRTY —

"How's that for astrogation?"

Talyn sounded smug. They'd emerged less than five million kilometers from the Talkin subspace array after a one-parsec jump during which they'd sampled the luxuries of the yacht, a distraction that had restored Zack's good mood.

"Not bad, commander. I've seen better, but for someone who's out of practice, it'll do."

She made an obscene gesture, but the smile remained.

"Let's see how well you can aim the laser, Marine-boy. We'll save time if we don't have to decelerate and maneuver closer."

"That's master gunner-boy to you, swabbie." He blew her a wet kiss before getting busy at the communications station.

"There," he said a good fifteen minutes later. "I've got a pingback from the array. It wants to know who the hell we are and why we're talking to it."

Talyn got up and leaned over Decker, her head so close to his that he could smell Amali's expensive shampoo. He was going to miss all of this once they were picked up. She entered a code.

"There. When you get the acknowledgment, you can send the report."

Decker nodded, prepared to show as much patience as necessary. The identification code would likely have to make its way back to headquarters, and that could take a long time. He needn't have worried. The invitation to send flashed on the screen in the time it took for light to reach the array and return to the ship.

"The report's sent."

"And now we wait." She locked the systems on automatic. "We might as well take another few hours of rest and recreation. Until headquarters sends instructions, we're not jumping out."

"Good idea. I could always use more recreation."

"I thought you'd say that."

They were dozing when the proximity alarms went off. *Syrah* was running with systems on minimal power consumption, to reduce her electronic signature, while they waited for instructions. It had been almost a day since the report made its way across the light years to Caledonia and it could still be a few more until they received a response.

Decker was up first, pulling on his clothes as he got the screen in the stateroom to show whatever it was that had woken them. When he read the data scrolling by, he cursed.

"What?"

Talyn rolled off the bed and began to get dressed as well.

"Sloop-sized vessel just popped out of hyperspace ten million kilometers away, or rather it popped out of hyperspace half a minute ago. The IFF shows it as being the *Mordred*, belonging to the Avalon Group."

This time, Hera cursed with a vocabulary strong enough to make a longshoreman blush.

"Avalon belongs to Amali through a chain of holding companies. They're a private military corporation, which means that sloop is well-armed."

"You think they're after us?"

Decker shrugged on his jacket and checked his blaster.

"It'd be too much of a coincidence if they've just popped out in interstellar space near our general vicinity."

"The array is a known navigation point," she replied.

"True."

They headed for the bridge at a run.

"If they're on our ass and not just tacking, how would they have found us?" Decker slipped into his chair and ran a systems check, including the weapons this time.

"Either a traitor at headquarters..."

“More of them? What kind of clown show is intelligence running?”

“…or more likely there’s a transponder on this ship we haven’t found, something that damned captain activated before we kicked the crew off.”

“We can’t out-shoot the buggers, you know that, right?”

“And we can’t outrun them either until we determine whether or not we’re leaving a breadcrumb trail.”

Talyn frantically scanned through the available frequencies, looking for something that could pass as a beacon.

“I would suggest we start accelerating before they’re in range.”

“Already laid in and engaged.”

Decker looked at his sensor readout again.

“So it is. They’re accelerating as well, and hailing us. They’d like us to start braking, drop all shields, and down weapons in preparation for boarding, seeing that we’ve stolen this ship from its rightful owners. I’m going to guess we’re not sticking around to wait for the reply from HQ.”

“Can’t hide anything from you, can I?”

“Not anymore.” His quick grin vanished. “They’ve launched missiles.”

“I guess they’re not as interested in recovering the ship as they are in getting us.”

“Gee, I wonder why that would be.” He studied the sensor readout again. “How long before we jump?”

“I need to find out what we’re transmitting that led them here. Otherwise, we’re in for a long stern chase with no chance of getting away.”

“Yeah, we may have to go anyway. Two more birds just appeared on my screen, for a total of four. That’ll be enough to overwhelm the popguns on this tub.”

“Let me correct course so we can at least jump to the next subspace array.”

“Do it quick because another ship just joined the party.”

“Avalon?”

“Nope,” he replied with a resigned tone after a few moments. “The frigate *Garibaldi*. We’ve just both been told to stand down and await orders. The mercenaries have been told to blow their missile warheads immediately."

Four bright points appeared on the screen.

"Thank God for that," Talyn said.

"What now?"

"We cooperate fully. However this plays out, we're about to end up in Navy hands, and that'll protect us from the Avalonians."

"Would the two of you," a deep voice erupted from the speaker, "please tell me what you were playing at? Civilian ships lobbing missiles at each other isn't considered acceptable under any of our laws."

"This is Captain Meeks of the Avalon Corporation ship *Mordred*, we're a registered private military corporation vessel, fully bonded, and accredited by the Adjudicating Authority. The ship we're pursuing is the yacht *Syrah*, stolen from our parent company by pirates in the Nabhka system. If you consult your copy of the Lloyd's Register, you'll find that I'm telling the truth."

"How about you, *Syrah*, anything to say?"

Talyn quickly shook her head, signaling that Decker was to remain silent.

"Very well," the Navy voice continued, "what's going to happen is as follows: I am arresting *Syrah* and her crew on suspicion of piracy. Since this is now a Navy matter, *Mordred* is ordered to withdraw to a minimum distance of one light hour and let us handle things."

"And what about our property?" Meeks asked with more than a touch of indignation. "You're just trying to get yourself prize money by interfering."

"Compliance is expected and will be enforced," the man from *Garibaldi* replied, "any attempt to prevent my ship from going about its business will be dealt with by force. Do you understand *Mordred*?"

"Yes," was the truculent reply after a stretch of silence.

"How about you, *Syrah*?"

Talyn shrugged.

"We'll cooperate fully, Navy."

"Good. Now get out of here, *Mordred*, and make sure we don't see you again. Your company will be contacted by the Navy to recover their ship in due course. Right now it's evidence in a piracy investigation. As for you, *Syrah* shut down all offensive and defensive systems, remain at your current heading and speed, and prepare to receive a boarding party that will take control of the yacht. You'll be transferred to my ship."

"As I said, we'll cooperate fully," Talyn repeated, sounding bored by the whole affair.

"Good. Although my missile gunners could use the exercise, I don't exactly feel like filling in the paperwork that HQ will demand if I have to open fire on either of you. I will, however, let them hone their targeting skills. If you look at your sensors, you'll see we have the both of you locked in."

Decker nodded.

"We're being painted good and hard."

Mordred's sublight nozzles glowed bright, and she accelerated away before vanishing when her hyperdrives came online.

"*Syrah*, my shuttle will be leaving in a few minutes. Have your hangar deck open and ready. Don't try any stupid crap. General Order Eighty-Eight is in force, so you'll not survive."

"I'll say this again, *Garibaldi*, we intend to fully cooperate." This time, she sounded more exasperated than bored.

**

The shuttle pilot was skilled. He'd declined the offer of a tractor beam and landed the craft on his own. As soon as the deck was pressurized, a dozen spacers in combat armor poured down the rear ramp, weapons at the ready. Decker and Talyn stepped through the inner door, hands on their heads and waited.

"You're the only crew?" A lieutenant with a youthful but hard face examined them suspiciously.

"We are. Your sensors should be able to confirm that," Talyn replied.

"Put your hands out in front of you, wrists together." When they'd obeyed, a petty officer slapped on restraints, then frisked them. "Any weapons I didn't find that you'd like to declare?"

"You'll find all of ours piled out in the corridor," Decker said, "though I wouldn't mind if you set the dagger aside so I can recover it once we've sorted out this little matter. I'd rather not keep replacing the damn things."

The officer shook his head in disgust.

"Freaking pirates. Take them aboard the shuttle and shackle them to the deck. Once we've cleared the ship they can go back to *Garibaldi* and enjoy the hospitality of our brig."

Talyn and Decker glanced at each other. She made a small grimace.

"Standard procedure, Zack. Try to be polite. We might need friends someday."

******

"You look right at home," Hera commented, watching her companion stretch out on the bunk, hands beneath his head, a smile of contentment on his face.

"I've spent quality time in a frigate's brig before."

She chuckled.

"Yes, you have. I almost forgot about your less than glorious exit from the Corps."

"Then take a piece of advice from an old pro. Lie down and enjoy the enforced rest. There's bugger-all you can do until they decide to have a chat with us, or serve up some food for that matter."

"He's right, you know," an amused voice said behind her.

She turned around to see a tall, thin officer wearing three stripes on each shoulder board.

"I'm Bezan, *Garibaldi*'s captain. Welcome aboard. I'm glad we got here just in time. The idea of a three ship stern chase doesn't really appeal to me."

"You know who we are?" She walked to the transparent cell wall while Decker sat up.

"I was instructed to head for the Talkin subspace array and pick up two agents traveling on the yacht *Syrah*, one male, one female, corresponding to your general descriptions, and impound the ship itself. We didn't expect to see Avalon mercenaries on your tail."

"*Syrah* has some kind of transponder we haven't been able to find. My guess is that they've been combing the sector since before we jumped out of the Nabhka system."

"Then I shall congratulate myself on my good timing," Bezan smiled. "I seem to have met your companion over a video link some time ago, but I doubt any of my crew will make the connection. How would you like to play this out? My people are unaware of my orders and believe you're pirates, or at the very least, ship thieves of the darkest sort."

Talyn turned to look at Decker. He shook his head.

"We'll keep up the pretense, captain, and remain in the brig until you hand us over to whoever is tasked with taking us off the playing field and back to HQ."

"I thought as much. My crew will treat you with all due courtesy, have no fear. We should be four days in FTL to Cimmeria, where I've been ordered to head next. Presumably, your ride to Caledonia will be waiting when we arrive. Now if you'll excuse me, I've got to get us on our way."

"Life is funny," Zack mused, once they were alone. "And I don't mean running across *Garibaldi* for a rescue again."

"When you were on *Shokoten*, right?"

"Yeah, inward bound with Amali's special cargo, but what I meant was that we've gone from living like desert nomads to extreme luxury and then down the ladder into jail."

"Welcome to the intelligence service, sweetheart. This is all in a day's work for our kind. I hope you enjoyed your time on *Syrah* as much as I did."

"Hey, nothing says we can't enjoy our time some more."

"Right." She giggled. "You're going to add exhibitionism to your many vices now? You know brigs are under constant surveillance."

"Yeah. I guess it wouldn't be fair to show off." He paused, as if in thought. "I wonder if we could get them to serve us beer. Doing without either of my main preoccupations does come under cruel and unusual punishment."

— THIRTY-ONE —

Captain Ulrich, head of the naval intelligence special operations section and sometimes known as 'Uncle Josiah,' smiled grimly at Decker and Talyn.

"Needless to say, Harmon Amali's fellow Coalition members are scurrying around like cockroaches high on reactor fuel, so I'd say message received and understood where they're concerned. I'd be very surprised if anyone ever again tried something like what they did to you, Mister Decker, so well done."

"I needed to collect my debt in full. Mission accomplished." Zack shrugged dismissively.

"It was quite a stroke of genius having the Targi carry out his judgment and execution. It puts us at a decent remove, what we in the service like to call plausible deniability."

"There wasn't any genius involved, sir. It was sheer luck that the bastard had his hideout on a planet I knew from having been stationed there, sir."

"I'm sure you would have figured something else if you'd been on another world," Ulrich replied smoothly. "You have all the makings of a good operative."

Decker recognized the old soft soap treatment when he heard it and figured it was time to choose. As much as he wanted to go back to a regiment, Talyn had been right. He was good at undercover black ops and enjoyed the work. There were still a lot of people like Harmon Amali out there who needed looking after.

"Seeing as I don't have much on my social calendar for the next year or so, captain," he said, "I might consider playing spook with this fine officer to my right, just to see if I like it, you understand."

"You seem to like me," she replied in an arch tone.

Ulrich, sensing there was more to it, chose to keep a neutral expression on his face.

"Glad to hear you say so, Mister Decker. I'd welcome you aboard, but you've been one of us for a while, especially since your effective posting to my department has been backdated to the day you left the 9th Marines. Take a few weeks off, both of you, but stay on the planet, just in case something comes up."

"Thank you, sir."

They rose and saluted.

"Enjoy your holidays."

"We will, captain," Zack winked at him, "we will."

**

That same night they found themselves sitting on a darkened patio half a continent away from the HQ offices, admiring the stars and listening to the gentle sound of the surf while sipping on cold drinks.

"Do you still think of her a lot?"

"Every day, Hera, but doesn't hurt quite as much as before. Seeing the bastard die took some of the fire out of the pain."

"And who said revenge can't be cathartic." She smiled sadly at him, reaching out to touch his hand.

"So can a regular romp in the hay with a good partner."

"Aaaaand," she laughed, "we're back on track, Marine-boy. Ever done it on a beach?"

"Nope. Wouldn't want to get sand in sensitive places."

"That's why you bring a towel, you dunderhead."

"Oh."

"I just happen to have one handy."

"Oh!"

Then her hand unexpectedly tightened on his wrist in a decidedly non-amorous way. She tapped him with her thumb, and he nodded, reaching down for his blaster.

The little critters who'd been singing the praises of the tropical night around their beach bungalow had fallen still as if an unwanted intruder had invaded their territory. Hera released his arm and slowly shifted forward in her seat, ready to jump up, her other hand searching for her gun.

All senses alert, they probed the darkness for a threat they knew was encroaching on their solitude. A faint scuffing sound reached Zack's ears from the small footpath that led around the dense copse encircling the building.

He very slowly and quietly got up, keeping his back hunched to present a smaller target and stepped off the veranda. Hera followed him down, keeping watch in the other direction, to cover his back.

The faint red glow of a blaster battery suddenly appeared over the dark mass of a flowering bush and Decker yanked Talyn down. A plasma round lit up the night, passing through the spot he'd occupied a fraction of a second earlier.

Instinctively, he'd shut one eye to preserve some of his night vision and quickly found the shooter when he raised his head again. The Imperial Armaments blaster spoke twice, his would-be killer screamed once and a clattering sound confirmed that he'd scored a clean hit.

They heard the bungalow door open behind them, and Talyn whirled around, still in a crouch, bringing up her gun. She double-tapped the shadow that filled the opening. This one didn't even have time to scream.

"That's two. What are the odds of more?" Decker whispered.

"Negligible. They tried to take us from two sides, with my dead friend there climbing through a rear window. If they had a backup, we'd be seeing fireworks right now."

"More contractors?"

"Probably. Either the hit on us is still out because someone didn't cancel it, or these idiots just didn't get the word."

"Or it's a new one. How did they know who we were?"

"Because Croyle and Vasser weren't the only ones moonlighting. Let's get the word to Ulrich. We need our own team to handle the forensics here, then we need to vanish someplace more secure."

"I guess a romp on the beach is out."

"Be glad they gave themselves away before we stripped down to our essentials and made the beast with two backs. That might have been a somewhat less than dignified way to go."

"Meh, I've always said I wanted to die in the arms of a young lady because I was having too much fun. But I guess I meant when I was a hundred years old."

"And I'm not a young lady."

"You're not a lady at all, darling."

"Bastard." Her communicator beeped. She held it up to her ear and listened. After a moment, she started to laugh.

"Too little, too late again, Frank. They tried and died. Send in the cleaners. What? Okay, I think I can live with that idea."

She smirked.

"That was the duty officer warning us they'd got wind of a hit team on our tail. We'll stick around until someone shows up, then we're going to be taken to the safe house on Uluru Island a few hundred klicks to the south of here. It's a bit more isolated than this place, but a lot safer. We'll just have to make sure they turn off all the surveillance devices before we try the towel on the beach trick."

"If you say so." He took her chin between his thumb and forefinger and leaned over to kiss her. "Though I don't mind making the guys in the control center jealous."

"And what about the women?"

"I don't mind making them envious either."

About the Author

Eric Thomson is the pen name of a retired Canadian soldier with thirty-one years of service, both in the Regular Army and the Army Reserve. He spent his Regular Army career in the Infantry and his Reserve service in the Armoured Corps. He currently works as an Information Technology specialist.

Eric has been a voracious reader of science-fiction, military fiction and history all his life. Several years ago, he put fingers to keyboard and started writing his own military sci-fi, with a definite space opera slant, using many of his own experiences as a soldier for inspiration.

When he's not writing fiction, Eric indulges in his other passions: photography, hiking and scuba diving, all of which he shares with his wife.

Join Eric Thomson at:

http://www.thomsonfiction.ca/

where you'll find news about upcoming books and more information about the universe in which his heroes fight for humanity's survival.

Read his blog at:

https://ericthomsonblog.wordpress.com

If you enjoyed this book, consider leaving a review on Goodreads or with your favorite retailer to help others discover it.

Also by Eric Thomson

Siobhan Dunmoore

No Honor in Death (Siobhan Dunmoore Book 1)
The Path of Duty (Siobhan Dunmoore Book 2)
Like Stars in Heaven (Siobhan Dunmoore Book 3)
Victory's Bright Dawn (Siobhan Dunmoore Book 4)
Without Mercy (Siobhan Dunmoore Book 5)

Decker's War

Death Comes But Once (Decker's War Book 1)
Cold Comfort (Decker's War Book 2)
Fatal Blade (Decker's War Book 3)
Howling Stars (Decker's War Book 4)
Black Sword (Decker's War Book 5)
No Remorse (Decker's War Book 6)
Hard Strike (Decker's War Book 7)

Quis Custodiet

The Warrior's Knife (Quis Custodiet No 1)

Ashes of Empire

Imperial Sunset (Ashes of Empire #1)